Joy Martin was born in Limerick. She trained as a journalist and worked on Dublin's *Evening Press*, then moved to writing news for the Zambia Broadcasting Corporation and the BBC Home and External Services. She has broadcast in Ireland, Zambia, South Africa and Britain.

Grafton
An Imprint of HarperCollins*Publishers*
77–85 Fulham Palace Road,
Hammersmith, London W6 8JB

Published by Grafton 1992
9 8 7 6 5 4 3 2 1

First published in Great Britain by
HarperCollins*Publishers* 1991

ISBN 0 586 21024 5

Set in Linotron Palatino

Printed in Great Britain by
HarperCollinsManufacturing Glasgow

JOY MARTIN

A Heritage of Wrong

Grafton
An Imprint of HarperCollins*Publishers*

To the memory of Dragoslav Petrovic

ACKNOWLEDGEMENTS

I am particularly grateful to Gearóid O Maidín, Cathaoirleach (Chairman) of the East Clare Heritage Group, for the advice he has given me in researching this book; to Jude James for his descriptions of Dorset life in the first two decades of this century; to the Abbey Theatre, the Slade School of Art, the Royal Academy of Dramatic Art and Trinity College Dublin; and to the following writers: Ulick O'Connor, E.H. Mikhail, Sheridan Morley, Tim Pat Coogan, John Buchan, Padraic Farrell, Nathan Silver, Timothy Hilton, Vincent Cronin, Marion Sichel, Ian Clarke, Denis Bablet, Michael R. Booth, Ronald Bergan, Dacre Balsdon, Stuart Cloete, Anthony Glyn, D. Newman Johnson, Richard Gale and C. R. M. F. Crutwell.

A LAMPSHADE, thought Aoibheal when she came across the photograph years later – I looked *exactly* like a lampshade.

Her pale pink Liberty frock had a low round neckline, three-quarter-length loose sleeves gathered on to a cuff and a puffy bodice which terminated at the hips in a narrow band. Beneath this was a brief skirt which stuck out stiffly just above her knees. By contrast to all the swathing, her feet in their white socks and matching strapped shoes looked much too small for her body – more like doll's feet than those of a nine-year-old girl.

And as if that wasn't enough there was the hat. A real horror of a hat, made from matching lace, frilled and ruffled and trimmed with silk braid and tied rather too tightly under her chin so her head had been inadvertently tilted back.

'You look lovely,' Rosaleen O'Mahoney, Aoibheal's mother, said. 'Doesn't she look lovely, Cathal?'

'She does indeed,' agreed her father, but he brought his hand up to his face and put his chin into the palm of it and ran his index finger along his cheek the way he did when he was trying to evaluate something.

The hat maybe? Even then Aoibheal was not sure about the hat.

'Maybe I'll leave it off,' she suggested tentatively, but Rosaleen wouldn't hear of it.

'The hat is the best part,' she said, and she checked the too-taut bow to make certain it hadn't become undone and peeked in the mirror to verify that she

1

looked as smart as her daughter.

Although Rosaleen O'Mahoney was a very small woman, her hat was even larger than her daughter's – a frothy feathered edifice, more like a tropical palm tree than a hat, resting somewhat precariously on an island of dark brown hair draped Pompadour style and held hopefully in place by three tortoise-shell combs and a plethora of hairpins.

The hat, like Rosaleen's bolero suit and pouched high-necked blouse, was violet-blue, as were Rosaleen's eyes. That fact, of course, had not been recorded by the photographer, forced to work in black and white, but Aoibheal's memory had not been so restricted. In colour the image of her mother that day was sweet instead of ostentatious. The photographer had also failed to capture the discomfort Rosaleen surely must have been suffering, viciously strapped in by the special straight-fronted corset the fashionable 'S' shape of the time demanded, her bosom thrust forward and her posterior (the word 'bottom' was strictly forbidden) pushed out at the back.

Suspended from Rosaleen's arm was the large leather handbag which went everywhere with her. The bag was made on a metal frame which had a snap closure and it had a matching leather handle so it could be suspended from Rosaleen's arm. It, too, was incongruous, being much too big for a small person to carry, something that had not occurred to Cathal when he bought it for his wife, or to Rosaleen herself, who simply thought it was smart.

'Am I all right?' Rosaleen asked Cathal, turning her pale, oval-shaped face towards his long, angular one.

Cathal joined the fingertips of both his hands into a church steeple. He was tall and thin and serious looking but he didn't seem grave that day.

2

Nor should he be, considering where they were going . . .

'You're always all right.'

Rosaleen sighed and turned her attention back to her daughter.

'Aren't you the lucky one!'

'I am!'

And she was. Other children did not go round with their parents the way Aoibheal did, especially at night. But then Cathal and Rosaleen (she thought of them by their Christian names instead of as Father and Mother) were not like other parents. They were Intellectuals, like the academics at Columbia University on Harlem Heights.

Aoibheal had been to see the campus and her attention had been drawn to its neo-classical buildings. Cathal and Rosaleen had also shown her the granite and marble tomb which contained the remains of President S. Grant and the newly-erected St Paul's Cathedral which was modelled after the Santa Croce Cathedral in Florence, Italy, where they were all going to go one day.

The campus and the tomb and the cathedral were within walking distance of their own home which was near Lenox Avenue on West 133rd Street. It was a three-storey house with a brown sandstone façade. There were three houses in the row and each of them had eight identical windows which looked across the street at another such row positioned directly opposite.

Most of New York was red and brown. Even the old brick buildings had been painted red with white joints so they could become part of this stylish supremacy. But to Aoibheal the city was multi-coloured and this evening they were going to the brightest and most exciting part of it.

3

It would be her fourth visit to Coney Island. On the previous ones she had marvelled at the noble spectacles of Luna Park and gaped open-mouthed at the huge resort built in the shape of an elephant that straddled West Brighton Beach. And at The Steeplechase, called The Funny Place, she had perched bravely on the back of a wooden horse which had zoomed up and down and around the vast pavilion, looping in and out of its walls.

The pleasure-parks had not been designed for young children but for adults. Fun was for them, not for her age group. Children were not welcome in the Tunnels of Love, only courting couples.

But Cathal and Rosaleen took her with them into all their worlds, and tonight they were going to Dreamland where electric bulbs illuminated the brilliant wings of dragons.

She would have danced with joy at the thought of it, only if she did her hat would fall off.

'I'm the lucky one all right,' she said to Cathal and Rosaleen, and to her relief Cathal got up from his chair and reached for his bowler hat.

She had been named Aoibheal after the Irish fairy queen, the one who had foreknowledge of the outcome of battles and the names of the ill-fated soldiers. Aoibheal was the heroine of two vision poems, called *Aislings*, which Cathal used to read to Rosaleen in their own courting days.

It was a controversial name – one to which Father Scanlon had objected vehemently on the day of her baptism.

'A pagan name!' he had said. 'Doesn't it sound it – *Ee-vul*! It's a saint's name we want, Mr O'Mahoney – a saint's name, not one that has the Devil's ring to it.'

But Cathal hadn't climbed down. In the end a

compromise had been reached and Hilde, the name of a saintly Irish abbess who was venerated on 18 November, had been added on at the font.

At school they called her 'Evil'.

'Don't mind them,' Rosaleen had said when this had been reported to her. 'And don't let them think you mind.'

But Aoibheal didn't mind. Father Scanlon might not have approved of any of it, but from her own point of view there was cachet, a satisfactory element of menace, in 'Evil' which added spice to her reputation in the schoolyard and sent bullies looking elsewhere for victims. The nickname provided a cover for her against the intrusion of her classmates. Only with Cathal and Rosaleen did she dare to be herself, to express her innermost thoughts.

She walked between the two of them, a thin, small-boned child with her mother's oval-shaped face, *retroussé* nose and soft, full mouth, and her father's deep-set blue eyes, hoping that the three of them were not going to be waylaid and diverted by any of Cathal's friends.

These people – a cross-section of Irishmen, some of whom had made good and others who plainly never would – came to the house at all hours to discuss the situation in their country of birth.

There was Mr O'Donovan Rossa and Mr Thomas Clarke and others who were members of Clann na Gael, the American branch of the movement that hoped one day to bring freedom to Ireland.

Having been reared to believe that Home Rule was an issue of supreme importance, one only surpassed by the need to gain entry to Heaven, Aoibheal would not have dreamt of questioning its validity; she merely hoped that the men who talked about it with Cathal could be avoided tonight.

Constant in their aspirations for Ireland, some of these visitors were disparaging about each other, the rich ones calling the poor 'Shanty Irish' and the less affluent proclaiming that they had no time for 'Lace Curtain Irish' trying to imitate Protestant airs and graces.

There were other Irish, scholars, who went further still and renounced their Catholic faith. They were the most talkative of the whole lot, being anxious to justify their actions, and one of them, Brian O'Leary, lived on the top floor of a house they were just about to pass.

Holding her breath but unable to hang on to her thumbs since she was gripping her parents' hands, Aoibheal approached Brian O'Leary's residence, waiting for the man to come out and accost them.

He did not. Sure now that this was her lucky day, she hurried along to Dreamland.

It was indeed the material out of which dreams were made, but by nine o'clock Aoibheal had come to the disappointing conclusion that she didn't really like it. It wasn't sophisticated and elegant like Luna Park or thrilling like The Steeplechase or stunning to look at like The Elephant. It was, well, *too* fantastical, too overdone with stucco ornamentation. She had come for the excitement, the thrill of semi-conviction, the sensation of having one foot in fantasy and one on the ground; but the Dionysian failed to deceive her, and she found herself gazing unimpressed at its strangely Sullivanian forms.

Her disenchantment showed itself many years later when she looked at the photographs taken that night.

And then her attention was well and truly diverted from Dreamland. The three of them went to the refreshment room where Cathal ordered ice-cream.

When it came, Rosaleen said they had something important to tell her.

'What is it?' asked Aoibheal. 'Are we going on vacation?'

Cathal and Rosaleen looked at each other.

'Not on vacation,' Cathal said. 'We're going back.'

'Going back where?' Aoibheal demanded, bewildered.

'Going back home,' they said in unison. 'Back to Ireland.'

She stared at them nonplussed, temporarily deprived of the power of speech.

Going? Leaving New York? She forgot that, in the last few hours, it had failed to live up to her expectations. This was her city, her birthplace. *She* – unlike Cathal and Rosaleen – would not be going back. What reason did she have?

Blinking, she stared down at her ice-cream, and she could not for a minute remember any of the things her parents had told her about Ireland except that it was green.

A cold colour. The coldest – much colder than blue. A colour she did not like.

A small wave of rebellion washed through her. How could they – the people she loved and trusted – do this to her, propose to take her away from her multi-coloured, multifaceted city, and plonk her down on a small green island because *they* wanted to go back?

And then, as her small, unrecognized rebellion ebbed away and she was left on the shore of familial love, she remembered the real reason Cathal and Rosaleen would have for going back.

The Boys. Rosaleen's sons by her first marriage, Daniel and Eugene.

Her half-brothers whom she had never met, whom she only knew from their letters. Whom she had been dying to meet for years, for as long as she could remember.

The tears that had been threatening to well up in her eyes were never shed. When she looked at her parents they were shining with excitement.

'We'll be seeing The Twins!' she said.

O N that July day in 1905, thousands of miles away in County Clare, Kate Keegan was also looking forward to a reunion with the O'Brien twins.

Four miles – the distance from her home in Killaloe to theirs in O'Brien's Bridge – separated them. Still, you never knew what might happen on the way. Kate was never certain that things might turn out for the best, even a simple social arrangement. When – as was most often the case – they did, she, who had so great a capacity for ecstasy, did not yet relax. There was always the possibility that Heaven might extract retribution for favours granted in a fit of divine impetuosity.

With a fervour more characteristic of a Catholic than an Anglican, Kate silently implored Heaven not to intervene with her plans for the day. Daniel and Eugene were her special friends, she pleaded, her childhood comrades, the same age as herself, of more worth to her any day than her two older sisters.

As it was she saw all too little of them. Most of the year they were over in England at school.

But not any more. This summer, the twins, like herself, had finished school. They were back in Crag Liath House for a long break before going their separate ways: Daniel to study medicine in Dublin and Eugene to art school in London.

She wondered how they would react to the separation. They had never been apart for long, not since they were three years old and Eugene had scarlet fever, and Milliora O'Brien – owner of Crag Liath, guardian to the twins, their bossy, stuck-up Aunt Milly – had first taken Daniel into her home for a prolonged visit.

Thinking of Daniel, Kate began to feel more positive about life. Daniel had that kind of effect on her, having the ability to see the lighter, funnier and yet more realistic side of the whole human condition; gently mocking, able to laugh at himself as well as at others, he could do so without being cruel.

Auburn-haired Daniel with his healthy, rounded face and amazing violet-blue eyes. Daniel the would-be doctor who was so different from his brother you were hard put to it to accept that they could be twins.

Her mind switched to Eugene, conjuring up his pale, fine-boned, aesthetic face, his black curly head of hair, his deep blue eyes.

In spite of his modest manner, Daniel radiated optimism like the sun on an April day, but Eugene was brooding and dark by nature, sad and sensitive and introverted and fascinating.

Their interests, too, were dissimilar. Daniel loved being out of doors. He was a grand horseman with kind hands and massive courage, while Eugene was artistic – brilliantly artistic, if you were to believe Milliora O'Brien.

In all matters relating to the twins Milliora was absurdly prejudiced, seeing the boys as young gods rather than very attractive mortals, the children she had brought up as her own when their mother had gone to live in America. And a possessive mother she was, too, thought Kate – not that pleased to see them making friends with girls of their own age.

Girls like Kate Keegan . . .

Soon, however, the twins would be off on their own, away from Milliora's influence: Eugene at the

10

Slade School of Art and Daniel at Trinity College Dublin.

Dublin! Remembering her own plans, Kate's heart lurched. Wait till the twins heard. Oh, she was dying to tell them. And it would be just terrible if anything got in the way of her doing so this hot day.

So far the only obstacle in her path appeared to be that of the relationship between her father and his bicycle.

Jamie's bicycle was six months old, the same age as Kate's, both of them purchased from Mulligan Brothers and Todd in Ennis at a cost of £6 0s 0d each. They both had pneumatic rubber tyres and two wheels which ran in perfect alignment. But while Kate saw hers as a miracle of modern invention, a remarkable piece of engineering which was capable of carrying up to ten times its own weight without the need to tame or water or feed it, Jamie regarded his as a dangerous contraption, more of a bull than a bicycle, a taurine monster with a mind of its own and a sinister wish to annihilate its owner. You'd think, being a vet, he would be used to bulls . . .

Left with the fact that one light vehicle, mounted in a frame of steel tubes, might well be a lion the way it terrified Jamie, his daughter went downstairs and resumed her case for the bicycle versus the horse. Her father groaned loudly.

'Will you get up on to it, Pa. Nothing can happen to you – I promise,' she urged, and the tall, thin, grey-haired man with her own slender face and her grey eyes, took a deep breath and prepared to meet his fate.

After a while he got more into the hang of it. When they had swung away from the thirteen-arched bridge and gone past St Flannan's Cathedral with its magnificent ornamental Romanesque doorway, past the tombstone of Murchad O'Brien, great-grandson of Brian Boru, the last high king of Ireland, from whom the O'Brien twins were descended, past the stone with its bilingual inscription in Irish ogham and Scandinavian runes, Jamie Keegan came to the conclusion that, after all, cycling wasn't so bad.

Beside him his daughter, to judge from her chatter (he dared not look at her lest he fall off), was elated by the experience of riding a steel steed across the flat Clare countryside.

Her exceptionally long legs made it that much easier for her to maintain her balance. In his mind's eye he saw her as others did, in her sunray pleated skirt and her embroidered blouse, her curly fair hair plaited and tied with a large black bow. Kate's hair had no need of permanent waving or curling tongs – wavy wisps of it were already struggling to break free of the plait and coil around her hairline.

Tall, slim, elegant, the beauty of the family, Kate nevertheless was the one who worried her father the most, aroused in him a constant sense of guilt, reminding him that, as a baby, a toddler, she had been neglected.

It had been inevitable, he tried to persuade himself; her mother dying at her birth, leaving the infant to be dragged up in a distracted kind of a way by her two older sisters, not much more than babies themselves.

Fran and Finola had responded to Kate's screams on a when-it-suited-them basis, pouring cold milk into her agitated stomach and wrapping too-tight napkins round her spotty red bottom. If they weren't ignoring her they were terrorizing her, wheeling her pram too fast and laughing when she yelled.

In between these acts of sadism they had crushed the baby with love, allowing her either to get away with too much or nothing at all.

Small wonder that, to this day, Kate did not altogether know where she was. The boundaries of truth and reality were blurred for her. Having fought to get notice she was now exhibitionistic, a girl of emotional extremes with no shading in her feelings. When Kate was down she was deeply, intensely miserable, those around her were seen as enemies and traitors, and she could not envisage ever being happy again.

Then, often for reasons right outside his own comprehension, she would perk up, zoom into delight, and the friends of whom she had been so suspicious would be viewed as dear and loyal.

In spite of these vacillations she got on well with most people and was surprisingly popular.

Only one person did not like her, though why he could not work out. And the dislike was mutual. Milliora O'Brien quite obviously did not think much of Kate, and Kate had said in his own hearing that the owner of Crag Liath was no more than a cranky, bad-tempered old hen.

Kate had no business talking like that, for Milly O'Brien was in fact a lovely woman. So far from being old she was only in her early forties and not a sign of grey in her wonderful red-gold head.

Kate, he thought, how could you?

Kate, if only you'd keep your head!

If you did you would one day come to the conclusion that young Daniel O'Brien is the right man for you – the perfect balancing agent for your intensity. A compassionate fellow with a good sense of humour who would take your woes seriously and then laugh you out of them.

But would Kate, with her predisposition for suffering, her inclination to fling herself whole-heartedly into life before working out the consequences of doing so; Kate, who was never neutral; would she ever have the common sense to set her cap at Daniel?

She would have to convert, of course, Daniel being a Catholic, but it would be worth even that in order to have her settled.

'Use your head, woman!' Jamie exhorted his daughter silently. 'Keep Daniel O'Brien in mind!'

'Pa!' shouted Kate beside him. 'Pa – *look*!'

'Look at what?'

'At that beautiful kingfisher!' marvelled Kate. 'Don't you see him there, in front of you!'

Briefly Jamie did see the vivid blue bird with its brilliant orange markings, there for a minute, then gone. But a minute was enough to undo him.

'Watch out, Pa!' cautioned Kate.

It was too late. Jamie's attention having been diverted from the vagaries of his hostile steed, the pesky thing hit a stone, veered into the grass verge and shook its rider off.

'It's gone four,' Daniel O'Brien said when afternoon tea was laid out. 'What would you say was keeping Kate?'

'She'll be here in a minute,' his brother Eugene said. 'Listen, to get back again to the letter –'

Daniel groaned. 'Do we have to? You've gone on about it enough already!'

'Then why don't you tell me *your* views?'

'You mean you'll keep quiet for a couple of minutes? I'm delighted they're coming home. I'm dying to see Mother again – to meet Aoibheal –'

I sound as if I am, anyway, thought Daniel, uneasy himself about the forthcoming arrival. What will they be like, he wondered, and are we going to get on? With more truth he added: 'I'm not so sure about him.'

'Why would you be, he having taken her away from us? Not that it seems to have worried her. She didn't care about us. She never cared about us.'

'That's not true,' said Daniel, determined to be positive.

'As she demonstrated by going off to America and leaving us behind. Two eight-year-old boys.'

'Who were already at boarding school in England. We were settled at Downside by then. She didn't anticipate being away for so long. She's said so in her letters.'

'Her letters!' mocked Eugene in the same sour tone. 'The weekly mail from our correspondent in New York! Reporting on her life there with Cathal O'Mahoney and The Brat.'

'It would be stranger still if she didn't mention them,' Daniel said, sympathetic nevertheless towards Eugene's anger. 'Have a piece of Mary Markham's Madeira cake – it's recommended!'

But Eugene, after scowling at the cake as if it, too, was culpable, got up from his chair and walked to the window to glower out at the garden.

Beyond it again, beyond the fields running adjacent to it, was the river – the Shannon river, named after the Lady Sinann, granddaughter of the sea-king Lir, she who had defied the law which debarred women from wisdom and learning and had lost her life when the waters of St Connla's Well rose up to engulf her.

In that same silver river Aunt Milly had lost her young husband Tom, and there were times when she also stood by the window with sadness on her face.

On the other side of the river the blue-black Clare hills leant back against the rich blue sky. The landscape, normally muted but on this warm day cheerfully florid, was at odds with Eugene's anger. With his back still turned to Daniel he said brusquely, 'Have

15

you ever worked out how long Cathal O'Mahoney and Mother were married before The Brat was born? Six months! No wonder they got out of Ireland in a hurry! Father died that same month, just before they left. They were lovers during his lifetime.'

Daniel did not answer at once. Eyeing the cake he reached out for the knife and cut himself a second enormous slice.

'Doesn't that bother you?' persisted Eugene.

'Sometimes,' Daniel said reluctantly. 'Only when it does, I remind myself that Father was not normal. He didn't know her and he didn't know us either. Don't you remember the way he used to go about the house with his eyes glazed over? And Mother trying to hide it from us? But she didn't leave him. She didn't go off with Cathal until after he was dead.'

'And then she left *us*.'

Daniel lapsed into temporary silence, munching his cake, brushing away the stray crumbs that landed on his trousers. Without offering any to Eugene he poured himself a third cup of tea, added three spoons of sugar and a dollop of milk and settled back in his chair.

After a long pause the voice from the window resumed its tirade. 'If it hadn't been for Aunt Milly we'd have had no one . . .'

Daniel frowned. He said, 'Aunt Milly had gone to Limerick already before the post came. What do you think *she* will say when she hears the latest news?'

Sitting bolt upright in her carriage, Milliora O'Brien surreptitiously eased off one of her bronze suede shoes and thought how extraordinary it was in this day and age – when there were motor-cars on the roads of Ireland and telephones in the homes of the well-to-do – that footwear still inflicted pain on the feet of middle-aged women.

And what pain! Cutting into her instep with such ferocity she might have been caught in a snare. She reached down and massaged the sore spot with the tips of her long, graceful fingers.

Still, it was all her own undeniable fault, racing from one end of Limerick to the other, starting with Cannock's sale, proceeding on to Catherine Street to have her sunshade relined, and then to McCarthy's, the wholesale grocer's and wine merchant's in William Street, after which she had kept her dentist's appointment as planned.

Remembering her visit to the dentist she became aware again of the secondary pain in her gum as the effects of the cocaine wore off.

'No wonder I forgot the raising powder!' she said to the back of her coachman's head. Being deaf this lament went unheard by Liam Lenihan.

To divert herself from her irritations, Milliora began to tick off the rest of her duties for the week ahead. The County Clare Agricultural Show Meeting – as a member she had to attend. The sale of lambs on the lands of Rindifin, Viscount Gough's estate, at which forty fat sheep were also to be auctioned. One of these days – the way tenants were now able to buy land on so-called favourable terms – there would be no estates at all left in Ireland, only fields in peasant hands; and where would the twins and herself be then in terms of Crag Liath?

At that point she turned her mind to the twins and the pleasure of their being home. Thank God there had been no problem getting a dispensation from Rome for Daniel to attend Trinity College. What if he had been forced to wait until the Catholic university of which the nationalists dreamed was finally opened up? Years maybe – and then a lengthy course at the end of them.

And thank God, too, that Eugene was fixed up with the Slade, although she had reservations about his attending an art school at all. Was it really right to permit a young man to observe and depict the naked female form? She wondered what the Reverend John Hannon, or Father Glynn or Father Garry, all of whom were on the show committee with her, would say about such a thing.

The fear of Eugene being corrupted by this experi- ence was still with her when the carriage reached the turn-off to Crag Liath and she saw a man and a woman walking in front of her pushing two bikes.

More accurately, the woman was walking and the man was limping along. Another fellow sufferer having problems with his feet! As this thought struck her she recognized the Keegans.

Leaning forward she rapped Liam sharply on the shoulder with the point of her blue umbrella. At the same moment the Keegans stopped and half-turned.

'Milly!' said Jamie, pleased.

She was almost as glad to see him. He had not always been her friend. In the early days of her brief marriage she had been jealous of his relationship with Tom, had hated him for keeping her young husband out all night drinking.

But that rancour was all in the past. Jamie had been a godsend to her over the years since then, always ready to attend to her sick animals and to give moral support to herself. She knew he was in love with her and that he would, if encouraged, propose.

But she had no intention of marrying him, or any other man either. The two men who had loved her had both died tragic deaths. She was done with love for good.

18

Acknowledging Jamie's greeting with her warmest smile, she looked down her thin, pointed nose at his daughter.

'Are you coming up to the house?'

'We are,' Jamie told her. 'It's time I took a look at your new widar.'

There was no need for a vet to inspect the castrated ram, as they both knew, but Milly did not say so.

'Come and sit with me,' she commanded him. 'Liam here will wheel your bicycle to the house and I will take the reins.'

Kate might not have been present for all the notice that Milly took of her. As a relieved Jamie got into the carriage, his daughter stuck out the tip of her red tongue at that oh-so-rigid back.

'That's her coming so,' observed Mrs Cash the washerwoman as Milly's carriage came round the back of the house. 'What will she make of the news?'

' 'Tisn't for the likes of us to be cogitating about such things,' the housekeeper, Mary Markham, said tartly. 'Will you take your eyes off of that table before she comes in the door?'

On the crude deal table was a letter in Rosaleen O'Mahoney's writing addressed to Milliora O'Brien, announcing, thought Mary, what Daniel had told her this morning – that his mother was coming home.

'She'll take them away from us,' predicted Mrs Cash, not one to be easily silenced. 'Herself will be distracted surely. The Divil's own children have the Divil's own luck and Mrs O'Brien isn't one of them. If 'twas raining soup she's the kind that would have a fork in her hand.'

'And you're the kind that would open your grave with your mouth!' Mary had time to retort before the mistress of Crag Liath strode in the back door followed by Mr Keegan.

Mary returned his smile with a big one of her own. Then, thankful that he was there to take the edge off the tidings, she made some fresh tea.

By the time Kate got to Crag Liath the news had already been broken and Milly O'Brien was wearing a brave face.

'Where will the three of them live?' asked Kate, trying to assimilate the facts herself. 'At Mr O'Mahoney's farm?'

'It's passed out of his hands,' Milly said absently. 'No, they'll have to stay here. There's plenty of room. Part of the year I'm away from Crag Liath myself and they can have the place to themselves.'

As well as Crag Liath Milly owned a large estate in Wimborne in Dorset which had been left to her by Harry Fielding, to whom she had been engaged.

'Will Mr O'Mahoney want to stay here?'

'Why wouldn't he?'

'Daniel says that he's against the concept of land-lordism,' Kate said, finding it hard to forgive the way Milly had virtually snubbed her on the road. 'Maybe he won't feel at home in Crag Liath.'

'Since he's been gone the tenants in this country have been allowed to purchase their holdings,' said Milly angrily. 'The Wyndham Act saw to that, arranging for the sale of entire estates to the tenantry, advancing money to them on ridiculously low terms, offering bonuses to landlords to sell. He should have nothing to complain about. Mr Arthur Balfour and his Conservative Party have done great things to remove the causes of Irish discontent. Those who criticize them for opposing Home Rule forget what they have given to Ireland already.'

The spotlight was on Milly. Upstaged, Kate had no

chance to announce her own good news.

Seven months earlier the Keegans had spent Christmas in Dublin with Jamie's sister and Kate had been taken to the opening night of the new Abbey Theatre.

The city was throbbing with the excitement of it. Thanks to the money put up by an Englishwoman called Miss Anne Horniman, the old Mechanics' Hall had been turned into a full proscenium stage, pit and balcony capable of holding nearly 600 people who could appreciate Irish nationalistic theatre.

Miss Horniman, a friend of Mr William Butler Yeats whose play *Cathleen ni Houlihan* was to be performed that evening, was known to be eccentric. She had an inordinate affection for cats, liked to be known as 'Tabby', and when she got angry she held out her hands like two claws and emitted low hisses. It was rumoured that she would walk unannounced on stage and interrupt the play by telling stories about her favourite pets.

Miss Horniman wore heavy tapestry gowns and a piece of silver jewellery carved in the shape of a dragon, but Kate had to content herself with wearing one of her sister Fran's evening dresses, a very pale blue chiffon creation, extravagantly décolleté, which cascaded lace over the bodice and elbows and train. She had her mother's engagement ring on the third finger of her right hand and Finola's pearls twisted about her neck.

'Will you leave my things alone!' Finola said when they had gone through the glass doors that led into the theatre from Marlborough Street.

The best thing was to pretend not to hear, to be engrossed in looking around the theatre. On the walls were copper-framed mirrors and embroidered tapestries and on two sides stained-glass windows of a tree in leaf. There were paintings hanging up too: portraits of Lady Gregory and Mr George Russell, the playwrights; of Miss Horniman; of the actress Maire nic Shiubhlaigh and of the producer brothers, Mr Frank and Mr Willie Fay.

Off to the left – between herself and the distinguished-looking visitors standing in little knots discussing the history of the Irish National Theatre Society – was the Green Room, the actors' own place. Until then Kate had not thought about the actors, but all of a sudden she realized that live people must, at this moment, be preparing to come on stage in order to entertain the likes of herself. What would they be doing at this moment: having a whiskey to steady their nerves, reading through the play again to ensure that their lines would be safe in their heads?

'There's Mr Yeats,' Aunt Iseult whispered, and a man in evening dress made his way through the lobby. 'He has a proud defiant eye and a strong chin, but his hair should be trimmed back.'

There were other celebrities present, too, according to Aunt Iseult, including John Dillon the MP who had been second-in-command to Mr Parnell and a co-founder of the Land League.

Ushered into her seat, Kate surveyed the drawn hessian curtain without any perception that her life was about to change.

The entertainment started off with a curtain raiser, Lady Gregory's comedy *Spreading the News*, and the dignified evening turned into a right laugh. The audience, Kate amongst them, shrieked at the way rumour could give currency to things that hadn't occurred. The best part was undoubtedly that of the deaf apple-woman, thought Kate, she being on stage all the time.

The hessian curtain closed. When it whooshed back again the story of *Cathleen ni Houlihan* unfolded and the mood of the night changed.

This was the hoped-for theatre – one that cried out for Ireland's freedom; Ireland symbolized by the figure of the *Sean Bhean Bhoct*, the Poor Old Woman, immortal, spiritual, divine, bowed down by sorrow.

And yet unbeaten. In a blend of poetry and peasant speech, Maire nic Shiubhlaigh spoke of her hope of putting the stranger out of her house; of regaining her beautiful fields.

Transported, Kate heard the chant of the old woman:

> They shall be remembered forever
> They shall be alive forever
> They shall be speaking forever
> The people shall hear them forever

and she knew that the young men called to sacrifice would make Ireland free, for wasn't the joy of that on the face of the actress on stage?

The audience got to their feet and cheered. Kate stood with them, tears streaming down her cheeks.

But her thoughts were less with Ireland's freedom than with her own exigencies. Even as she applauded the performance of the great actress taking her bow on stage she was thinking: That's what I want – that outlet; above all, that applause.

The minute the Keegans were out into Marlborough Street again, Aunt Iseult accused Mr Yeats of using the Abbey to put on a political play of a propagandist nature. Jamie said he didn't see it like that. To him, it was a passionate drama about the feelings and hopes of men. The altercation continued all the way home to Blackrock. Kate paid no heed to it. She had no interest in Mr Yeats's motives. The play itself did

23

enthral her. But if the truth be told the interaction between Maire nic Shiubhlaigh and the audience was even more thrilling to Kate.

Jamie took his daughters back to Killaloe without any idea one of them was already making up her mind to become an actress.

Kate did not make any announcements over the next few weeks. But in that time she summoned up the courage to write to Lady Gregory at the Abbey, asking how she could go about joining the company after leaving school.

Lady Gregory wrote back, cautiously explaining that Kate's was not the only application she had received lately from a young lady who wished to embark upon a stage career. The acting profession was hard, overcrowded and underpaid, wrote Lady Gregory, as she did to several other stage-struck girls that same month. And the Abbey Players were particularly gifted artistes. Still, added Lady Gregory, promising nothing more than hospitality, if Kate happened to be in Dublin in the near future, she would be welcome to visit the Green Room.

Kate, who had not expected such a quick response to her letter, was reassured rather than discouraged by the guarded invitation. How soon could she get back to Dublin? The Keegans seldom visited the capital. Aunt Iseult was not normally that forthcoming, and staying alone at a hotel was something none of the girls had done.

But at the end of June Aunt Iseult's youngest daughter got married, and the three Keegan sisters went to Dublin to attend the wedding. The day afterwards, Kate was able to slip into town on her own. She was not keen to let anyone in the family know precisely where she was going. Fran and Finola would be bound to deride her ambitions, and Aunt Iseult, who was even worse than Milly O'Brien in many ways, would only write to her father, warning Jamie of the dangers of letting his daughter act. But she had been in contact with Lady Gregory and a meeting had been arranged.

Kate had prepared for it by familiarizing herself not only with the plays she had seen but also with the new Yeats–George Moore *Diarmuid and Grania*. She particularly liked the thought of reading Grania's part, acting out for Lady Gregory the role of a woman doomed to bring death and destruction in her wake. As it turned out, she did not get the chance to do so. This was all to the good. She woke that morning in a blaze of euphoria and remained in that state all day. She would not have been convincing as a harbinger of doom.

She sped to the Abbey like a meteor and arrived radiant in Lady Gregory's presence. The luminance of her mood, combined with the pale hues of her eyes and hair, was startling, and Lady Gregory, who had been expecting a spotty schoolgirl, was astonished by her beauty and captivated by her enthusiasm.

She sat Kate down and plied her with tea and a slice of her homemade barmbrack.

'Did you travel to Dublin alone?'

'I came with my sisters,' said Kate, observing that Lady Gregory, a small woman with beautiful brown eyes, spoke with a trace of a lisp. 'We are staying with my aunt.'

Lady Gregory, having established that she was not dealing with a runaway, asked if the relations were also theatre-goers.

'We were all together at the Abbey on your opening night,' Kate said. 'My father and aunt are still talking about *Cathleen ni Houlihan*.'

Lady Gregory, who idolized Mr Yeats, beamed.

25

'Why wouldn't they be? I will tell Mr Yeats of their compliments.'

Kate, thinking of Aunt Iseult's condemnation of the playwright, blenched. Such sadness all of a sudden, thought Lady Gregory, but what an expressive face. The child has presence, no doubt about that. But whether she was Abbey material was another matter.

She asked Kate to read from a poem by the Irish poet Rafferty, which celebrated the beauty of a Galway girl called Mary Hynes. The poem had been translated from Irish. Did Kate speak the language fluently?

She did not.

'But would you be prepared to learn it?' asked Lady Gregory. 'It is essential to our work that you do.'

'Yes,' said Kate, glowing with fervour. '*Of course.*'

Such passion could surely be put to good use at the Abbey, where the prime feature of its acting was freedom from artifice, reasoned Lady Gregory. She was seeing Kate at her best but she did not know that.

Kate could join the group in September. An arrangement could be made for her to stay with one of the other players.

She told Kate this, and any misgivings she had were dulled by the girl's rapture.

'I *can*?'

'But I must write to your father about it,' said Lady Gregory. 'I must make sure he approves.'

And she had written and Jamie, although surprised, had not raised any objections beyond saying that he would have Iseult on his trail for encouraging Kate to go into politics.

Even Fran and Finola were impressed.

All this Kate had been longing to announce to Daniel and Eugene so that they, too, could pay homage to what she had achieved. And now they were distracted. Still, it was not every day that your mother wrote from America to say she was coming home.

Two weeks before the twins and Kate went to Dublin and London, the ship bearing the O'Mahoneys and their possessions docked at Queen's Town and Aoibheal caught her first glimpse of Ireland.

Her initial impression was bad. From her parents, whose descriptions of their birthplace had been rhapsodic and romanticized by the passing of the years, she had imagined Irish rain to be nothing but a light mist which, tinged with the pale colours of fairyland, would only add to the beauty of the landscape.

Instead she was confronted with a vulgar and apparently incessant downpour and a howling wind to boot. The harbour was barely visible. The first people she saw were two fat fellows with scowls on their faces, as put out as herself by the unexpected gale.

Her stomach, which had not forgiven her for embarking on a sea journey, reacted adversely to a greasy hotel meal. By the time she and the food had precipitously parted company, she was in no frame of mind to return the smiles of the maid who showed them to their rooms.

The next morning, unreconciled to Ireland, she was dragged too early from bed by her eager parents, both of whom could not wait to get to Limerick, and on to a slow-moving train. When she put down the window to get a breath of fresh air, black smoke spat at her as if to say: 'Get back to New York where you came from – you're not wanted here.'

After a couple of hours she dozed off. The next thing she knew they had pulled in to Limerick station, and Rosaleen, ticking with excitement like a newly wound clock, was tucking the travel rug around her

27

shoulders and propelling her out of the carriage door and on to the platform where Cathal was waiting already.

And then a husky Irish voice called out: 'Rosaleen – Cathal! *There* you are at last!' and a slim lady with red-gold hair and hazel eyes was standing in front of them holding her arms out.

Behind her were two young men, one with dark hair and one with auburn, and a tall, fair-haired girl.

Aunt Milly. And the twins, Daniel and Eugene. But who was the fair-haired girl?

Under normal circumstances Milly would not have encouraged Kate to accompany the twins and herself to Limerick station, or anywhere else for that matter.

But Milly's plans to meet the O'Mahoneys along with only Daniel and Eugene (she had no intention of allowing them to meet their mother without her being there) were frustrated by the problem of the home-comers' luggage. Two carriages, not one, she realized, would be required to take them to Crag Liath.

She enlisted Jamie's help. In theory he was only too pleased to drive into Limerick on the arrival day and provide alternative transport. But when the time came, Jamie was called out to attend to a sick horse and Kate was sent in his place.

Milly was forced to put a good face on it. Only the rigidity of her back conveyed her inner disapproval of the way things had worked out.

Sandwiched between Daniel and Eugene, Kate told herself that she didn't mind the message spelt out by the back. Why should she? Milly O'Brien's opinion of herself was neither here nor there.

And still she cared – still she wanted Milly's approval, in spite of not liking Milly herself.

The train pulled in to the station and Kate's attention was diverted. What would They look like? What would They be wearing? How would They react to what must turn out an emotional reunion?

Amongst the passengers piling on to the platform was a small, dark-haired woman. Milly called out and the woman rushed forward to embrace her.

Rosaleen, mother to the twins. Kate turned instinctively to gauge the boys' reaction, looking at Daniel first. He was grinning. Good.

Then a hand, Eugene's hand, gripped her right arm, clutching it so tight she winced in pain.

'Oof – that *hurts*!'

She glared up at him – and her vexation changed into fear. On Eugene's face was an expression she had never seen on any person, a terrible combination of acrimony and bitterness.

She heard herself whisper, 'Eugene . . . ?'

'Hmm?' he said – and his grip on her arm relaxed. 'What is it?'

He might well ask, she thought, because the hate was gone out of his face. Had it ever been there at all?

'What are you on about?' he said, his eyes going to the small woman who had got out of the train and was still in Milly O'Brien's embrace.

The woman broke loose, laughing, and turned towards the twins.

'Daniel!' she exclaimed. 'Eugene! Oh, my babies – but you've grown so big!'

At this sentimental but accurate observation they all began to laugh, Eugene as well.

What was I thinking of? wondered Kate, seeing the twins go forward together, jostling each other good-humouredly in their rush to cuddle their mother and to join in her exclamations. Eugene isn't angry and bitter. Fran and Finola say I see drama in everything, and I suppose they're right. The sooner I join the

Abbey Players the better for us all!

The hugging and the marvelling were going on at a grand rate with the tall man who must be Cathal O'Mahoney being pulled in to be part of it.

Kate stood apart, watching until the small, dark-haired girl who had been lost amongst the adults disentangled herself from between their limbs and came over.

'I'm Aoibheal O'Mahoney,' she said. 'You belong with us, too?'

'I hope I do,' said Kate, and turned her mind to the matter of transportation.

How were they going to divide themselves into the two carriages? Should the twins travel with their mother and stepfather and Aoibheal with Milly O'Brien and herself?

That seemed the best scheme, but Kate did not get the chance to implement it.

'Rosaleen, you and I will go with Daniel and Eugene,' said Milly. 'And Cathal and Aoibheal can follow behind with Kate.'

Maintaining her position in the twins' lives, thought Kate. Showing their mother her power.

Rosaleen O'Mahoney did not seem to resent being bossed around. In the manner proscribed by Milly they headed for Crag Liath.

Although she would have enjoyed the status of travelling with her brothers, Aoibheal was quite content to share the carriage with Cathal and Kate. Her father – in spite of the advent of the handsome twins – was still the important man in her life. She also, like most children, rated beauty highly, so Kate was certainly someone to be admired. Added to which Kate was friendly, and asked her questions about her life in New York. Driving past the Georgian doorways of

Limerick, Aoibheal felt more positive about Ireland than she had been in Cork. Obligingly, the weather had cleared up. When they reached St Mary's Cathedral the sun peeked out, and was still looking down at them when they crossed from Limerick to Clare.

The deeper they went into the countryside, the more attention they got from people on the road and in the fields and at cottage doors, most of whom raised their hands in greeting. Aoibheal waved back. Animals stared at them, too: squat, short-legged cows, shaggy donkeys, and now and again a pig. Dogs barked at the carriage and hens ran out of its way, clucking. Once, to her amazement, a billy-goat leaped a big height over a stone wall and left in his wake a stench repellent to city-bred nostrils.

Eventually the other carriage turned in at an open gateway and theirs followed suit. They went along an avenue flanked by trees and stopped in front of a house.

From the outside Crag Liath was a solemn owl of a house, grey-stoned, flat-faced and ponderous. Although it had a fine oak front door with a smart Italian bronze knocker in the shape of a man's head, and wide, low steps running up to it, the house, at this stage, gave the impression of being displeased by the arrival of guests.

Aoibheal glared at the house and Crag Liath's solid plate-glass windows of eyes scrutinized her in turn, before the place changed its mind altogether and welcomed the newcomers in. The oak door opened wide like a smile and a white-haired woman came out.

'Mrs Markham, how are you?' Rosaleen said, and Milly O'Brien ushered everyone up the steps and into a warm and cordial hall.

* * *

Someone with imagination had painted the walls a soft orange and hung rich paintings on them. And above the staircase, impressively sweeping, was a picture of a hunt, with men in gaudy coats.

Aoibheal cheered up again.

'Come in, come in. You must be exhausted from travelling,' said Milly O'Brien. 'Don't worry about your trunks. Liam Lenihan will look after them,' and she conducted them into a drawing-room where the walls were rose pink and the mantel, representing Baby Jesus and His Angels, was fashioned out of marble.

'Tea, tea, Mary Markham. We're all famished,' Milly O'Brien said in her husky voice. But this state of affairs would obviously soon be remedied, for a feast of an afternoon tea was spread out on a table. Scones and thick cream and four different cakes, and bread and butter sliced so thin it could have been paper.

Where to start?

'Between you and me, Mary Markham is the best baker in Clare!' said a voice in her ear, and Daniel sat down beside her. 'Shall I butter a scone for you?' he said.

'Yes, please!' said Aoibheal.

Her appetite was back. Sitting proudly next to her new-found brother she thought that, coaxed in this way, she might grow to like Ireland.

The grown-ups were, they said, only beginning to talk when Aoibheal went to bed. She slept well and woke comparatively early – too early, at any event, for the loquacious ones to be up. Cathal and Rosaleen's and Milly's bedroom doors were all firmly shut.

Aoibheal made her way tentatively down the sweeping stairs. In the hall she hesitated, wondering whether or not to go down another flight. In the

32

kitchen Mrs Markham, who had baked those memorable scones and cakes, might be making more.

But it was very dark on the lower flight of stairs. She peered down and then, to her relief, she heard a door there open and Eugene appeared in the gloom.

She had not talked much to Eugene the night before. It was Daniel who had sat next to her for most of the time – Daniel and Kate, whom she now thought of as a couple, boyfriend and girlfriend, although no one had said as much.

Daniel and Kate had become her allies last evening, and she was now looking forward to forming a similar relationship with Eugene, whom she thought was amazingly handsome.

Seeing him at the bottom of the stairs, she thought it was a pity that he had not visited New York during her sojourn there. It would have been very pleasant to show off such a noteworthy brother to the other girls at school.

'Good morning!' she called out to him.

Eugene paused with one foot on the lowest step.

'Oh,' he said. 'It's Aoibheal. You're coming down, are you? Hurry then.'

Obeying, she passed a door in the wall and remembered Rosaleen's story of Crag Liath's secret passage, long since walled up, which ran from a cupboard in the stairs to the river's edge so less scrupulous O'Briens could smuggle in their French wines without paying excise duty. This must be the spot.

'Is that where the secret passage is?' she asked Eugene when she was down. 'Didn't Daniel fall in there once?'

This was another favourite story, and she expected Eugene to laugh at the recollection and tell her again how, on their third birthday, he had given his twin a push.

33

But Eugene did not laugh. He said, 'He did. And where you're standing now – just there – a fellow was stabbed to death.'

Aoibheal swallowed nervously. 'He was?'

It was very shadowy at the bottom of the stairs but she saw Eugene nod. 'Oh yes. And his ghost is in the house. A huge black angry fellow who's out to seek revenge.'

Taught tolerance towards people of all races, Aoibheal had always thought well of black people whose main neighbourhood, Harlem, was not far from her old house. But Eugene's black ghost sounded large and vicious and scary. She shivered and held her breath.

'You're not frightened, are you?' Eugene asked.

There was something in his voice, a taunting note, that angered and challenged her. Aoibheal was a self-sufficient, confident, logical child whose powers of observation had been sharpened from an early age. She was good at seeing through people. Her own brother was trying to intimidate her.

She tried to control her fear.

'No,' she said, as casually as possible. 'Why would a ghost frighten me?'

'Why indeed!' said Eugene. 'I'm glad you're not easily scared, because now I can show you the cellars. We have wonderful cellars at Crag Liath. Look, they're over here.'

She was more used to the shadows now, and she saw that there was another door between themselves and the kitchen.

'What's in there?'

'Have a look,' Eugene said, and he pushed the door open and made way for her to go through.

She did not want to do so. She did not care what was in the cellars, but she also wanted to show her big brother that she was not at heart a coward – that she was big enough to stand up to his teasing.

She went in. And as soon as she did, Eugene shut the door.

It was as if she had been simultaneously struck dumb as well as blind: the horror of being alone in the dark rendered her temporarily mute.

But not for long. Common sense told her that without visibility she should not immediately attempt to find the door in case she only succeeded in penetrating deeper into the cellars.

She stood perfectly still and screamed. After what seemed like ages but was in fact less than a minute, the cellar door was miraculously thrown open.

On the other side, standing in a blessed puddle of light, was Daniel.

'You poor little pet!' he said. 'Did you think it was the kitchen door? Come on out and we'll get some breakfast. Hold on to my hand. Yours is cold! You must have got a terrible fright in there.'

'I did,' Aoibheal said.

It was all she was to say on the subject.

'You need breakfast!' said Daniel again. 'Porridge and bacon and eggs and Mary Markham's soda bread. Doctor Daniel's prescription! Did I tell you I was going to study medicine in Dublin?'

'You did.'

And it helped to hold his hand.

At breakfast another minor drama began to develop.

'I've lost my leather handbag,' revealed Rosaleen. 'Does anyone know where it is?'

The others shook their heads.

'Are you sure you didn't leave it on the train?' Cathal said to her.

'I don't *think* so.'

'Or even on the boat?'

'No. I'm sure I had it last night . . .'

'Never mind,' said Cathal in a comforting voice. 'I'll get you another just like it if this one doesn't turn up.'

'I don't know what I could have done with it,' Rosaleen said ruefully. 'I must be getting old,' and everyone round her laughed.

'At least I can rest assured that Daniel will be on the train with you,' Jamie said at the end of the following week.

Kate, having packed her trunk, was ready to go to Dublin.

'Make sure you write,' Finola said in her older sister voice, and – 'Don't be doing anything stupid,' said Fran, as if, of course, she would.

At Crag Liath, too, when they stopped off to collect Daniel, Kate was rebuffed again.

Milly had been outraged by Kate's decision to choose a stage career. To her, actresses were creatures beyond The Pale – women of the ilk of Lillie Langtry, an associate of the dreadful Mr Wilde, who had flaunted herself as the King's mistress in the presence of his poor, long-suffering wife, and Sarah Bernhardt, whose eyes were said to be outlined in kohl and her hair to have been dyed.

That the Abbey was a nationalistic theatre cut no ice with her. Milly O'Brien wanted the poor people of Ireland to remain in their place. The efforts of the Irish Literary Movement to bring their poetic speech into the heart of theatreland went right over her head.

'The Abbey will never last!' Milly said as a more or less Parthian shot when Daniel's bags had also been hoisted into the carriage.

Her hand rested on Daniel's arm as if she would stop him from going. Daniel's mother, by contrast, was not clinging on to her son, although she did look wistful.

'Why won't it last?' Kate asked, ready for a fight. 'Lady Gregory and Mr Yeats and the rest have been planning for it for years. It isn't just a passing fancy on any of their parts.'

'Oh, the public will get tired of it soon,' said Milly in her infuriatingly know-all way. 'Theatre-goers in this country want *real* plays, not these old bardic tales!'

Kate could have strangled her. Fortunately, the combined efforts of Daniel and Jamie to concentrate the attention of the women on whether or not all the bags were loaded, passed the whole thing off.

'It will be your turn next to say goodbye,' Kate called out to Eugene as they were setting out. 'I hope you'll enjoy London.'

'I'm bound to,' he called back, but he looked sad, at parting with Daniel no doubt.

Then the train began to hiss and puff and the great adventure began.

The train pulled out from Limerick station and Kate and Daniel were alone. It occurred to Kate that this was a novel experience. She had never before been on her own with just one of the twins.

It prompted her to say, 'You're going to miss Eugene a lot,' expecting Daniel to agree.

Instead he paused, then surprised her.

'Yes and no,' he said. 'Maybe it's always like that with twins, wanting to be together but wishing you were free at the same time. You see, people don't think of you as two different human beings. Not really. They lump you together whether you like it or not. They want you to act in unison. The truth is Eugene and I are very different people and we don't always agree.'

'You've never said that before.'

'I've never been alone with you before. Anyway, having a yearning for peace, there are lots of things I prefer to keep to myself. The fact is that people don't like twins to be different and they get cross if you show that you are!'

Digesting this, Kate said, 'Does Eugene feel the way you do?'

'It would be odder still if he didn't!' said Daniel. 'It's a contrary business. Because as well as wanting to be free of each other, you have this strange pull back. I have this funny sense of responsibility towards Eugene. My brother and I might have different opinions, but I understand him well enough. I know he needs my support.'

'And you his?'

Daniel hesitated again.

'Eugene's maybe more sensitive than I am,' he said finally. 'He was more cut up than I was when our mother went away.'

It was odd to consider Eugene, whom Kate had hitherto seen as dashing and slightly mysterious, in this vulnerable light. Even though the train was taking her further and further away from his physical self, she felt closer to him than she had ever been. Underneath his well-developed poise, she thought, he was really a bit like herself, just as easily hurt.

'Has he talked to you about the time your mother went off?'

'Innumerable times!' said Daniel, grinning, yet not sounding malicious. 'That's the other drawback to being a twin – you have to listen a lot!'

Shortly afterwards the train stopped. A woman with two children came into their compartment, and the conversation moved from the personal on to the more general. After a while Daniel dozed off, and

Kate looked out of the carriage window at the green fields sliding back to Limerick. A light mist was falling which made her look up on the rack to check that she had her umbrella with her.

The world which was about to open up for her seemed rather like an umbrella, too, on the inside of which beautiful things were painted. She was going to become a great Abbey actress whose talent would invoke laughter or tears from her audience according to her will.

She closed her eyes. Instead of the growl of wheels she could hear the sound of hands clapping: nearly 600 pairs of hands, it went without saying that any production with Kate Keegan in it would have the Abbey packed.

She thought again of Maire nic Shiubhlaigh in the part of the *Sean Bhean Bhoct*, recalled the cheers of the elated audience, and imagined herself in the part. Maire nic Shiubhlaigh, it was to be hoped, would not envy her big success!

'You were wonderful, Kate – just wonderful!' she could hear her father saying appreciatively, gazing at her in admiration; and there was a nice moment in her fantasy when Milliora O'Brien, who had also been present to witness her moment of glory, was forced to agree with Jamie's words.

She came out of her reverie to find Daniel gazing at her with his amazing violet-blue eyes – tenderly, she thought, as if he too was amongst her admirers.

Adulation of any kind always went to her head. She felt dizzy with excitement about the delights that were in store for her in Dublin, and dazzled by the brilliance of her new world.

'Daniel,' she wanted to shout, 'look up above you! Reach up and pull down all the wonders you see, and give them to me now!'

Daniel *must* be having exactly the same reaction . . .

Yet he did not speak about chromatics, either. His eyes sent signals of approbation, to be sure, but his next words were to do with the stomach rather than the heart.

'I'm starving!'

Although they had both consumed hearty breakfasts, he reached up for the picnic basket which Fiona had thoughtfully prepared and prised open its lid.

'Ham sandwiches! Just what I feel like!'

Trust a man!

'Don't tell me *you're* not hungry.'

'Well – maybe.'

'Good girl yourself.'

Munching and talking of this and that, they sped on their way to Dublin.

Lady Gregory – who had been having various thoughts about Kate Keegan – had arranged to accommodate her, not with one of the other Abbey Players, but with a distant relation of her own who lived in Leeson Park. Daniel saw her to these lodgings and then took himself off to his own rooms in Trinity College.

It was a week before they met again, and in that time Kate had encountered a bewildering number of playwrights, actors and actresses, producers, men of letters, directors, stage carpenters and house electricians.

Amongst them was Mr Synge, a sad-eyed man with a sallow face and a little beard who had written a tragedy about the battle of men with the sea which Lady Gregory described as supreme art. *Riders to the Sea* had been presented by the Irish National Theatre Society at the beginning of the present year, but Kate was already hoping that it would be revived at the Abbey with herself in a prominent role.

Maybe even that of the mother of the family? She could make herself look old quite easily, she thought. She would wear a grey wig, whiten her eyebrows and her eyelashes and give herself the requisite number of wrinkles with the aid of an eyebrow pencil.

'That's serious theatre,' said Daniel. 'I suppose it's no use my asking you to the Gaiety to have a laugh at *Charley's Aunt*!'

'Can a Trinity student afford to take me out?'

This was a joke. There were sixpenny seats at the Gaiety and Daniel, as Kate knew, received a more than generous allowance from his doting Aunt Milly.

'How else can I get away from dissections?'

'That's what you do all day?'

'Ten A.M. to five P.M.!' Daniel said lugubriously, and then relented, grinning. 'Slight exaggeration. I've had time to join the Boat Club, I've bought a bicycle, and I've had a letter from Eugene.'

'Is he liking the Slade?'

'He says so. He's found somewhere to stay.'

'One of these days I'll go to London,' said Kate, 'to play a lead role –'

'Of course.'

'– and I'll look Eugene up.'

'What else would you do?' said Daniel.

He paused, then added, 'I wish he was nearer. He needs to go home more often now that Mother's there again.'

'Did he say that in his letter?'

'No. But he wouldn't want to admit needing to see her. We both do. And Mother needs to see us. The separation was as bad for her as it was for us, I realize that now. I used to be angry with her for going away from us, but she and I have been able to talk this last

41

while and it's helped me a lot. Eugene and Mother haven't talked. He's been polite, friendly even, but he's kept his distance. I watched him. He didn't give Mother the chance for them to be alone.'

'Maybe they talked after you left for Dublin.'

'I doubt it. If they had – if anything worthwhile had gone on between them – Eugene would have written to me about it. As it is, I think he took his anger with him to London.'

They turned into South King Street. Ahead of them a queue was forming outside the Gaiety Theatre.

'We'll never get tickets,' moaned Kate, casting Eugene and his problems with Rosaleen out of her mind for the time being. 'The whole of Dublin is here.'

'And the whole of the country as well,' said Daniel. 'We don't have to worry about queues. I've got our tickets here.'

And he pulled them out of his pocket and held them triumphantly out.

That was the marvellous thing about Daniel – his dependable nature. And his good humour. And the flattering way he tended to look at a girl.

Eugene, meanwhile, was looking at another girl, very different from Kate.

This girl was pale and slender and quite naked, standing motionless on a dais at one end of the Slade life-room.

In front of her a long crescent of donkey-stools was stretched out. Eugene had been warned that the middle places in this room were sacred to the older students. Newcomers were required to find seats at the side, or risk what his informant had intimated were truly heinous consequences.

This he had done and, like the others, he was alternately sketching and glancing up in order to refresh his newly acquired impression of the unclothed female form.

After a while a very tall, very grim-faced figure came into the room and began to inspect the work. This was Professor Tonks, who had started life as a surgeon and who saw drawing as a scientific process of intense thought, conveyed by the truest poetry.

Eugene had been warned that the professor's criticisms were amongst the most scathing in art history. Almost to a man the students' shoulders tensed.

When the tall man stopped to inspect the drawing of a slight, fair-haired student, twenty-two different faces mirrored the same apprehensive look.

'What *is* it?' demanded Professor Tonks in a slow, horrified voice, holding the drawing up. '*What is it*? Is it an insect? Horrible! *Horrible!*'

A quiver ran through the class. Only the girl on the dais stood perfectly still.

Tonks said, 'Artists – painters – can be distinctly divided into those who are intensely anxious to express something, and those who are more anxious about the manner than the matter. It is out of the ranks of the first that the great ones come. Below the level of the second group are the common people, who possess no artistic talent whatsoever. It is amongst that amorphous subdivision that this young man belongs.'

Expecting the young man in question to leave the room, head bent in defeat, Eugene was surprised to see him remain where he was.

Professor Tonks moved on.

'*Disgusting!*' he exclaimed, inspecting the next man's work. '*Look at the woman*! What do you see – a twig!'

Eugene's neighbour sighed resignedly, awaiting his own turn.

The tour continued in the same vein, with occasional variations. The class, although wary and nervous, was obviously used to scathing attacks.

Eventually the tall figure loomed over Eugene.

'Let me see!' it said.

The onslaught did not follow. Men glanced over their shoulders to ascertain the cause of the unusual delay.

'Your name?' demanded Professor Tonks. 'What is your name, young man?'

'O'Brien.'

'O'Brien, *Professor Tonks*! Irish, I imagine. No, don't tell me. It's irrelevant where you come from, only where you are. *You may* – I emphasize *may* – learn from being here. The essence of the Slade is its tradition, founded on the study and admiration of the Old Masters – but not in a slavish spirit. Do you understand?'

Mutely, Eugene nodded his head.

The Professor said, 'The basis of that tradition is the intense study of constructive drawing. *That* cannot change with time. Here!'

He returned the drawing to Eugene with a nervous jerk of his hand.

Then –

'*Rest!*' the Professor barked.

The girl on the dais came to life, reached out for a gown which had been lying on the back of a chair, pulled it round her thin, white, cold body.

Without speaking again, the grim figure walked out of the room. A sigh went round the class.

Close to, the girl who had sat for the life class was not as young as she had looked from afar. Her name was Charlotte – Lottie for short – and she lived with six members of her family in two rooms in Ethelm Street where her father had a stall.

44

She was twenty-four and she was pretty enough in a hard, all-knowing way, with her thin, pert, sharp-featured little face and her strong, wiry body.

So Eugene thought, catching up with her as she was about to turn left out of the Slade grounds and head for Tottenham Court Road.

'Are you going home?'

Lottie pursed her lips. The Slade did not like its models to fraternize with students. Young men who attended life classes were warned to look at the girls objectively – as inanimate objects where emotions were concerned, rather than as real women.

These directions did not prevent some of the bolder ones trying and proving advantageous to Lottie.

Tired now – no one at home understood how weary she got, just standing up – she summoned up enough energy to say, 'What's that got to do with you?' the answer that always intrigued them. As part of her routine she began to walk more quickly towards where the trams stopped.

The young man with the dark curly hair and blue eyes increased his own pace in order to keep up with her.

'I'm Eugene O'Brien,' he said.

'The one what Professor Tonks praised.'

'You thought that was praise?'

'For him,' Lottie said, sounding cool and uninterested.

'He's always so bad-tempered?'

'Last term when he came in he looked at a student's drawing of me. "Can you sew?" he said – and he marched straight out of the room.'

Eugene O'Brien did not react with amusement to her story. *Artists*, thought Lottie disparagingly. Taking themselves so seriously. Striking more poses than I do in a day's work. What is it all about, drawing naked women and throwing paint around? How many of them ever think of the likes of me, what *I'm* feeling.

But what was really on her mind was the need to eat, which she hadn't done all day. There was no sign of the tram, and other than her fare she had no money on her. Hunger, she thought, was something Mr Eugene O'Brien had never known in the whole of his privileged life, not if you were to judge from the cut of his clothes. He had a new Chesterfield overcoat on him, and a watch on his left wrist. The coat had a black collar and concealed buttons and four pockets, one over the left breast and the others at midriff, and it epitomized at that moment all that was different between them, between people like him with money and those like herself who saw no hope of ever being able to buy a coat at all.

The likes of him wouldn't be seen dead in Ethelm Street – Kill 'Em and Eat 'Em Street, as the people who lived there said. What would he know about her kind of life, she thought, the family living on £1 0s 0d a week and the whole street knowing your business, people talking in doorways and hallways, on the stairs and the balconies, taking note of who was in receipt of parish relief and who had nits in their hair.

Or about the way her stomach was groaning for food?

'I am going to eat in that restaurant,' said Eugene, as if he had been reading Lottie's mind. 'If you come with me, I will buy you dinner.'

Eyeing the restaurant, Lottie was only worried that it was so near the Slade. What if Professor Tonks – or Professor Brown or Professor Steer, for that matter, all three of whom were friends of each other as well as colleagues – should happen to come along and see her there with one of the young men whom they had so vociferously warned off such encounters?

Their dictates had not curtailed her activities in the past, but she wanted no trouble. It was difficult enough making a bit extra to supplement her official earnings, most art students not being that wealthy and most of them convinced that immortalizing her on canvas was adequate payment for services rendered.

Eugene O'Brien, without waiting for her answer, was striding towards the restaurant, so she took a risk and followed him.

The restaurateur frowned on seeing her shabby clothes, but Eugene overrode any objections he might have had by nodding coolly to him and making his way to the nearest vacant table.

Seated, their orders placed, Eugene began to make enquiries.

'You work on a full-time basis at the Slade – or is there other work you do?'

'In the mornings I clean for Mrs Hicks – Miss Ellaline Terriss, her stage name is, who's married to Mr Hicks the actor. They live in Bedford Square so I can come on to the Slade when I'm done.'

'Seymour Hicks? I saw them both in *Quality Street* at the Vaudeville when Daniel and I were on our way home from school.'

'That's right,' said Lottie. 'She's beautiful, isn't she, Miss Terriss? Her father was murdered, you know.'

'Oh?'

'Stabbed to death by another actor when he was walking through the stage door to go on in *Secret Service*! The motive was revenge! Could you understand that – hating someone so much you'd stick a knife in his chest?'

'Hating, yes – stabbing, no!' Eugene exclaimed drily. 'There are other less messy ways of getting your own back without spilling blood.'

47

'You mean strangling?' Lottie asked with interest.

This was a subject after her own heart. She had been reared on her father's stories of the gruesome murders carried out by Jack the Ripper during her early childhood. Eugene, as a boy, had listened wide-eyed to the Germanic folk tales of the Brothers Grimm, but Lottie and her siblings had been regaled with the news that half a human kidney, removed from the body of one of the Ripper's victims, had been tauntingly mailed to the police.

So involved with the prostitutes' murders, so captured was his imagination by their unknown assailant's attacks, that Lottie sometimes wondered if her father had not carried them out himself. That would be a right turn-about for the books – your own father a bloodthirsty killer.

Sometimes, still, as she held a pose – cold and bored and tired – she amused herself by envisaging her father cutting throats.

To her disappointment, Eugene did not take up this grisly theme, or any at all for a while.

Their meal arrived and she attacked it like the hungry animal she was. Her mouth was full when Eugene asked her if she would be prepared to pose for him on a freelance basis outside the Slade hours.

She nodded, unable to speak, delighted that on the first day of the new term she should have netted a student who not only had money in his pocket but a handsome face. Sooner or later, as she well knew, they would end up in his bed.

To Kate, Dublin was a city quivering with literary renaissance on the one hand and social excitement on the other: a beautiful city with glorious Georgian squares and wide streets and houses with pretty fanlights.

For the first few months of her stay there she marvelled at everything, constantly elated, so that the
charladies with their buckets, the children carrying
the fish they had caught in jam jars, the flower stands
in the streets, the motor-cars which were raced in the
Phoenix Park, were all bright fragments of the mental
picture she retained of the capital city.

Daniel, on the other hand, saw Dublin in different
terms. He thought it was artificial, that it tried to
imitate England. Once, travelling with him on the top
of an open tram, looking down at the goings-on in the
city, she was shocked when he pointed out a sight
she had altogether missed – armed soldiers manning
a checkpoint.

'What's going on?'

'Nothing much – now,' he said soberly. 'But I think
there'll be trouble here yet. This town is full up with
migrants from the provinces hungry for jobs and food.
Life for people in the back streets isn't pretty. You'd
be surprised what I see when I go around on my
bike.'

'What?' said Kate sharply.

Why was Daniel drawing her attention to these
gloomy matters? Why couldn't he see life in its vivid
shades instead of these drab tones?

'The other day I saw two women having a fight,
leathering each other! "I'd tear the heart out of yez
and sell it for offal," one of them shouted. "Only the
pigs wouldn't dare ate it!" '

This, of course, made Kate laugh. Daniel, she
decided, would appreciate Dublin all the more if he
was to come into the Abbey Green Room and meet
some of the personalities. There were so many stimulating characters. Mr Yeats holding forth about the
philosopher Nietzsche. Miss Horniman working ener-
getically on costumes. Miss Maire nic Shiubhlaigh,

spiritual and beautiful, just being her dazzling and imaginative self.

And marvellous Lady Gregory. Here was a woman who, herself a playwright, did all in her power to assist others of a creative bent to fulfil their ambitions, regardless of how humble or outrageous those people might be.

Mr James Joyce had got five pounds from Lady Gregory when he asked friends for a loan to cover his fare out to Switzerland where he had been promised work. The fare was actually only three pounds and fifteen shillings but Mr Joyce – so it was later discovered – had been in need of twice that sum, having persuaded Miss Nora Barnacle, a chambermaid from Finn's Hotel on Leinster Street, to run off with him as an unwed bride. Their elopement was still causing scandal in Dublin. The couple, so it was whispered, had since had a child.

Lady Gregory was very charitable about Mr Joyce, whom she described as a genius. She even forgave him for having printed and distributed a farewell poem about the Literary Movement which he dismissed as 'a mumming company'. She reminded members of whom he had made public fun of the times he had joined them in impromptu concerts, impressing all of them with his delightful tenor voice.

At one such concert Kate, too, was invited to sing. She had a sweet, light soprano voice, expressive and with the ability to float up to the high notes with consummate ease, while retaining a warmth in the middle register which gave a hint of drama and intensity of emotion.

Because she was happy, her performance that evening in the Abbey Green Room was, as Lady Gregory said, just delightful.

'My dear child, you have an enchanting voice.'

50

Kate shrugged. Singing was completely natural to her. It required no physical effort. What, she wondered, as other players began to express their appreciation, was all the fuss about? Fran and Finola had never praised her voice. So how could it be so good?

As Kate saw it, being able to sing was a minor skill in comparison to acting. Natural – the word Maire nic Shiubhlaigh had used about her performance a minute ago – was something she associated with such Abbey Players rather than with herself.

The hold the Abbey Players had on their craft seemed elemental. They knew instinctively how to save their voices and their gestures for the important and poignant passages; how to stand still when they sensed that no truly artistic effect could be achieved by moving; how to fade away altogether so the attention of the audience could be concentrated on another important player.

These characteristics of the new Irish theatre were being noted with approval by critics in London and even in New York. The *Globe* newspaper had likened the Abbey Players to Russian actors who, even when they had no lines to deliver, could sit or stand, facing each other on stage in – there was that word again – *natural* attitudes.

That's talent, thought Kate.

But when she tried to emulate this method of acting, her spontaneity ebbed away and her whole body tensed.

'It's only nerves,' said Sara Allgood, who had played the part of Cathleen, the daughter, in the original production of *Riders to the Sea*. 'You'll get over them in no time, I promise.'

'You see,' said Lady Gregory, 'most of the other players are either the children of peasants or have that blood in their veins. They move and act as peasants do

51

because they are absolutely familiar with their habits. Whereas you are not – '

Her voice trailed away and she looked slightly worried.

'But I'm a country girl!' exclaimed Kate. 'I grew up in County Clare. My father is a vet. All my life I have lived amongst peasant people.'

'But not *as* one of them. You have been brought up to imitate English accent and manner. It isn't natural to you to speak with what Mr Frank Fay always calls Biblical frankness.'

Natural – oh, that word!

'I suppose the more I mix with the players the more I will learn to be like them,' said Kate hopefully.

'I suppose so,' said Lady Gregory. 'You do have talent, my dear. And that marvellous voice . . .'

'The voice is a joy,' pronounced Mr Willie Fay, brother to Mr Frank.

Mr Willie Fay was said to be the black sheep of his family, having once run away to join a circus and travel with an Uncle Tom show, whereas Mr Frank, a little man whose black coat reached down almost to his heels, was much more serious by nature.

They were great talkers, like most of those Kate met in the Green Room. Mixing with the players was no trouble to her. Socializing was no problem either, as 1905 fizzled out and the New Year came in.

Plays for possible production were read regularly at general meetings in the Green Room. Lady Gregory's *The Workhouse Ward*, which she had written as a scenario after a visit to Gort workhouse, was being considered for March.

The play was set around the snipings of two old men, Miskell and McInerney, and Kate had been asked to read the part of the sister of one of them.

She sat with the script in her hands, listening to the men.

'And you were no grabber yourself, I suppose, till your land and all you had grabbed wore away from you,' said one, and – 'If I lost itself, it was through the crosses I met and I going through the world,' riposted the other crossly. 'I never was a rambler and card-player like yourself, Mike McInerney, that ran through all and lavished it unknown to your mother!'

They were not actors at all, but two cranky old men in their beds speaking to an imaginary audience of workhouse inmates.

Sighing, Kate reminded herself that she was a woman who had been left a legacy and that she wanted to take her brother home to her farmhouse – but not his quarrelsome friend.

She began to read. But when she listened to her own voice she knew it was that of Kate. She faltered, tried again and plunged into despair. There was a lump in her throat at her failure. All she could produce third time round was an inaudible whisper.

'A sore throat – you poor child. No, don't try to force yourself,' said Lady Gregory, saving Kate's face.

While Brigid Fay took up the lines instead, Lady Gregory whispered in Kate's ear.

'We must have a talk. Stay behind when the others have gone.'

This was like being back at school. Kate descended even further into the depths of gloom.

What a tragedienne! thought Lady Gregory. But can she fit in here?

'Don't look so unhappy,' she said to Kate. 'This is not the end of the world. You are much too young, in any case, to have that part.'

'It's not that part,' wailed Kate. 'It's any part! I'm useless.'

53

'You're not useless,' said Lady Gregory firmly. 'Dry your eyes. You have in you the makings of a fine actress. Whether you and the Abbey Theatre are right for each other is another matter. We'll have to think about that.'

'So, you see, I have failed,' said Kate to Daniel. 'Ireland is too clever for me, too poetic and too tragic. I wanted to give something of myself to our country, but I don't have the ability.'

'You have ability all right,' said Daniel, sympathetic but not stricken. 'Listen to yourself and you'll break down and weep! Didn't Lady Gregory say you have talent?'

'She was just trying to make me feel better.'

'I don't think she was at all. She was straightforward about the rest of it, so why should she butter you up? And maybe you and the Abbey *aren't* right for each other. Maybe you should forget about it and concentrate on a style of acting that's closer to your upbringing.'

'How could I do that?' Kate sighed deeply.

'Stop feeling sorry for yourself,' Daniel commanded. 'It won't solve anything and it's a waste of good energy that could go into plotting instead.'

'Plotting what?'

'Wait. Something's coming back to me. That's right – there was a fellow with us at Downside who wanted to go on the stage. I remember hearing afterwards that he had been accepted at the Academy of Dramatic Art in London. He must be there now. Would you like me to write to him and ask if they take women as well as men?'

'They must do,' Kate said. 'But Daniel, you don't really understand. The Abbey Theatre – '

' – is the whole world. That's what you were going

to say, isn't it? But it's not for *you*, Kate. Why don't you accept that fact and go on from there?'

'But Mr Yeats says that Irish artists should keep their talent for the glory of their own nation,' said Kate earnestly. 'Even if I was any good – which I don't think I am any more – wouldn't that be abusing a wonderful principle?'

Daniel raised his eyes to Heaven. 'The Lord save us!' he said. 'Have you ever heard the like? What is in your head, girl? Never mind about Mr Yeats and his philosophies and start thinking about yourself. Do you want me to write to this fellow or not?'

To her surprise, Kate was feeling better about life. Daniel had that effect on her.

'I suppose you might as well.'

'Not enthusiastic enough! Put a bit more effort into it!'

'All right then!' said Kate. 'Do.'

'But you appreciate my heroic gesture in encouraging you to move away from Dublin – and myself?'

'I'm not rushing. I've made no decisions to leave the Abbey . . .'

'Soon enough you'll go. And when you're famous I will visit you in your dressing-room, along with all your other admirers, and ask humbly if you'd be free any night for dinner.'

'Oh, but I will be!' said Kate. 'For you I'd always be free for dinner!'

She was seized by an onrush of fondness for him. His eyes were full of tenderness and she wanted to thank him for what he had done to light up her darkness.

They had been strolling along Leeson Street, and now, as if by mutual consent, they both stopped under a street light.

Pleased with themselves and with each other they

smiled and for the first time kissed. It was a hasty kiss, there being other people further along the street.

'Ah, Kate, what will I do when you're gone?' Daniel said when they drew apart.

And what will you do without me, he might well have added.

Instead he caught her hand and held tightly on to it.

They walked slowly on towards Kate's lodgings. At the gate they kissed once more.

'Kate Keegan,' he said. 'It won't be long before I'll be fighting off those other admirers outside your dressing-room door.'

Aoibheal, left behind at Crag Liath, wondered if the adults intended to reside there forever. But other plans were afoot. Cathal and Rosaleen, it transpired, intended to buy a house.

'You know you're welcome to stay here,' Milly said to them. 'It isn't as if I'm always in Ireland myself.'

Nor would she be for very much longer, but off to England to stay at her other estate. The original owner of this estate, Mr Harry Fielding, had been trampled to death by a rogue horse, or so it was said.

'That's very kind of you,' Cathal said. 'And we're very grateful for what you have done. But ultimately we have to set up a home of our own.'

Cathal was always very courteous to Milly, although even Aoibheal could see that there were times when she tried him sorely. Their political views were so polarized that it was surprising that they tolerated each other at all: Milly was opposed to sudden change of any kind and thus suspicious of calls for Home Rule, and Cathal was growing more and more impatient with the slow progress of the Parliamentary struggles in order to bring it about.

Yet tolerate each other they did.

'Milly is a wonderful woman when you get to know her well,' said Cathal to Aoibheal when they were on their own one November day.

That was at the end of an afternoon during which views on politics had – most unwisely – been aired, and tempers had threatened to flare; and although Cathal was directing his words at his daughter, she had a suspicion that he was also addressing them to himself, in case he needed reminding of Milly's true worth.

Yes, it made sense to look for a house. Rosaleen said she had beautiful memories of boating on Lough Derg and that she wanted to live somewhere on the shores of the lake, and Cathal talked to auctioneers in Killaloe to see what properties were coming up on the New Year market. Something had to be done and quickly, everyone agreed, because there was the problem of Aoibheal's schooling.

That in itself almost provoked a row between her parents and Milly. Cathal and Rosaleen said they wanted Aoibheal to attend a national school.

'A *national* school?' said Milly, and she made it sound as if 'national' was a distinctly dirty word. 'Why not send her to Laurel Hill?'

'To board?'

That was Rosaleen, and 'board', the way she said it, sounded insalubrious, too.

'Why not? You and I did.'

'But I was so *lonely* –' said Rosaleen and –

'I don't want my daughter to go to a private school,' said Cathal at the same time. 'She should be with all our people.'

But then Rosaleen said, 'Except, of course, I had you, Milly. You were my saving grace.'

And she smiled lovingly at Milly, and Cathal,

watching the two of them, relaxed his censorious face.

After that boarding school was not mentioned again, to Aoibheal's immense relief, and Milly went off to England to spend Christmas there with Eugene. He was not coming back for the holiday, but Daniel was and stayed at Crag Liath.

In January they found the new house. It was, said Cathal, in the parish of Whitegate in a place called Nutgrove Bay, and he was going to drive them there in his newly-acquired motor-car.

The car had a steering wheel stuck at the end of a long rod, and high, upright seats. Being serious travellers, Cathal had goggles over his eyes, and on his head a peaked cap, and Rosaleen had a bonnet secured with a veil which tied beneath her chin.

Cathal's mouth pinched in tight as he drove, and Aoibheal noticed that Rosaleen leant forward and that her hands were clenched tight in her lap as if she was scared stiff by the speed with which they were moving. Aoibheal herself was elated, not frightened, by the ride, and all the way to Whitegate men and women stopped in their tracks and marvelled at this newfangled contraption that was traversing the roads of County Clare.

It was a dull pale grey day, and if you were to look at the pallid sky you would think all life on this earth had come to a sudden end instead of wonderful things like cars and new houses coming into it.

The fields were mostly empty, the animals gathered for shelter in the farmyards. The further they drove around the lake the mistier it got. The plump hills swathed themselves in shawls of it. By the time they had driven through Scariff and Mountshannon the lake waters were lost in the pale veils.

But that didn't stop Rosaleen from urging Cathal to call in at Mountshannon harbour. In the thickening mist there was very little to see, only the water lapping on the shore and a pair of swans who gave the impression of having been incensed by the onset of winter.

'No sign of Holy Island,' said Rosaleen sadly, and she looked at Cathal in a meaningful way that quite excluded Aoibheal. 'Last time we were here you could see the round tower and the ruins and –'

'There won't always be mist,' Cathal replied. 'If we come and live here we can go out there again by boat whenever we want to. Say *Inis Cealtra*, not Holy Island – use Irish!'

'By steamer?' demanded Aoibheal.

There was a lake steamer called *Fairy Queen* which took excursionists out. In September this steamer, returning a party of sixty from the Whitegate Hurling Tournament, had managed to go off course. Two men shooting waterbirds in the vicinity had fired warning shots and Mr Gerald Gleeson had called his servants out of his mansion in order to come to the rescue.

This story, reported in the Nenagh *Guardian* and much talked of at Crag Liath after Aoibheal's arrival, had fired her imagination. The lake did not frighten her. Some of the lady excursionists on board the *Fairy Queen* had apparently grown alarmed. *I* wouldn't have been, thought Aoibheal. *I* would have found it an adventure.

So when Cathal said, 'We'll have our own boat. If we do live here I'll take you to school every day by water. There's another much bigger island called Illaunmore which is just outside Nutgrove Bay and there's a school on it,' she could hardly believe her luck.

They drove back into Mountshannon and lunched at the Derg Hotel, then veered off along the country road towards Whitegate village which had grown up on each side of a rise, with a church dedicated to St Flannan, and a mill, and Burns' store where liquorice could be bought.

So reported Cathal, steering the motor-car away from the village, for it was Fair Day and the place was packed out. With the lake on the right of them now they went past the crenellated harbour and, facing it, the hotel where they were going to spend the night, and on to Nutgrove Bay.

And there at last was the house, an early nineteenth-century white house, hip-roofed, two storeys high, with a central fanlight front door staring out at what it could see of the lake in the mist.

'Cathal, it's perfect!' exclaimed Rosaleen before she attempted even to set foot inside it, quite ignoring the overgrown garden and the fact that one of the many trees had been blown down and was lying across the lawn.

They went in anyway and investigated a drawing-room, study and parlour on one floor, a kitchen and dairy in the basement, and four pleasingly shaped bedrooms at the top of the house as well as a family bathroom.

In a way none of that really mattered. The minute Aoibheal had seen the house from outside she had known it would be their home.

She moved into yet another world. At Crag Liath she had been cloistered in a big house in which its owner dictated the terms, and where, out of deference to the hostess, she had been forced to live the life of an embryo lady. In her new home she lived, according to her parents' wishes, as one of the country people, walking the couple of miles in to Whitegate village when she felt like it; answering, 'Over the road,' to Rosaleen's, 'Where have you been?'

'Over the road' often meant going into people's houses – paying a visit, a *'Cuart'* as the country people said – and, if she was fortunate, being plied with a cup of buttermilk or a mouth-watering cut of recently home-made bread.

And then there was the talk: people asking about her childhood in New York, and whether maybe she had not met a son or a brother or a cousin who was also living there.

'Maybe Cathal did,' she would say, not wanting to disappoint them, and maybe he had, too, since then, as now, he seemed to know an amazing amount of people.

Just as in their New York days, Cathal had friends to the house. Some of these friends came from the Whitegate Hurling Club. Cathal took a keen interest in hurling. Whitegate had a strong team and had won its first championship match the previous year. Much talk was of the bowl-shaped cup, richly chased in Celtic design, which Mr William Redmond, MP for Clare, had presented to the County Board. Or they spoke of what clubs and which players were going to participate during the coming year.

To Cathal's disappointment these friends, content with the achievements of the Land League, were not inclined to be militant about seeking Home Rule.

She did not ponder about these matters for long, because after a week in the new house she finally went to school. Cathal had not yet acquired a boat, so she was sailed out along with other pupils from nearby Gurteeny. The school consisted of one room, and the dozen or so children who attended it were taught by a young woman called Miss Bridget Hogan.

Spring came and calves were delivered and daffodils stuck their heads up and the swallows came home from the foreign places where they had spent the winter months, and in May the bluebells came out.

And somewhere along the line Aoibheal fell in love with Ireland, or at least with County Clare. This turn of events made her feel guilty about New York. In her enchantment with Whitegate, with the lake and the land and the flowers and the birds and, above all, the people who befriended her, surely she was betraying her American origins.

She discussed this seriously with Cathal, who said that it was perfectly possible to love two places at the same time. 'Unlike *people* in love!' he said, straight-faced. 'That wouldn't be right.'

'No,' she said, thinking that he knew best about almost everything.

He was the best father in the world. One day she could go back to New York to reconfirm her affection for it. After that she was able to come to terms with the treacherous feeling.

At the beginning of the Slade's summer term there was an epidemic of influenza and Professor Tonks got sick. In his absence the students relaxed.

Lottie made the most of the more lenient atmosphere by talking to those in whom she thought she had aroused interest, and letting it be known that it could be returned.

Sleeping with Eugene O'Brien twice a week had proved only marginally beneficial, providing her with dinners in smart restaurants and a small bonus in clothes. So that she would at least look like a lady when they went out, Eugene had bought her two blouses with high boned collars from a shop in New Bond Street, spending five pounds and nineteen shillings on the pair. With these she wore a black skirt given to her by Miss Terriss, and a hat which a careless visitor had once left behind in the actress's house and which Lottie had promptly purloined.

But she longed for chiffon and crêpe-de-chine lingerie, for silk stockings with lace fronts and black garters with clusters of fruit on them. Sitting naked on her dais, Lottie fantasized about being dressed.

She looked out at Eugene and the other students frowning over their sketchbooks, and amused herself by assessing them as sources of stay laces, shoe buckles and cashmere hose. She did not think about sex, which she regarded as a necessary but unpleasant chore.

Even with Eugene O'Brien . . . He was the most handsome man she had lain with and sometimes, in his arms, that in itself gave her a thrill, a sensation of triumph for having procured him. But that was as far as it went. Lottie hated men and despised them for, now and again in bed, revealing their vulnerability.

Arriving early at the Slade on a Monday morning, she found only one student in the life-room. Her interest perked up. Robbie Beresford was known to be rich.

'Good morning!' she said, glad she was wearing one of Eugene's blouses. It was stained under the arms by her sweat, but men liked what she had once heard one of them call a *'bouquet de corsage'*. 'You're all alone in here, are you?'

This hardly-riveting beginning to a conversation did as well as anything else. She went over to him on the pretext of looking at his depiction of her from the day before.

'What do you think about when you're sitting up there?' said Robbie Beresford, indicating the dais.

Lottie smiled provocatively. 'That would be telling!' she said.

'About Eugene O'Brien perhaps?'

'What do you know about him?'

'I've seen you together a couple of times. I'm – curious.'

'You want to know what we do?' said Lottie.

Some men liked this kind of detail. In bed with you they asked what their predecessors did.

'What?' asked Robbie.

A wise answer, as she was to conclude, would have been, 'I can't tell you *here!*' so as to lead him on and supply the information in a more intimate place. Instead Lottie gave way to an instinct to betray.

'Not much!' she said untruthfully. 'I'm sorry for him, that's all. He buys me dinners and clothes but he's no good to a woman in bed.'

'Isn't he?'

Robbie Beresford sounded disappointed.

'There are others who are,' said Lottie hastily. 'But he's not one.'

She rubbed her nose and added two sentences which contained an element of truth.

'He's funny. He wants me to pretend to be his mother,' she said. 'He says he wants to be cosseted and cuddled up!'

At this she swivelled her body around as if to prove to Robbie that its contours were not exactly maternal. From this new angle she had a view of the life-room door.

Framed in it was Eugene. Obviously he had heard. If looks could kill . . .

Just my blooming luck, thought Lottie. No more dinners from him.

By the end of the summer, Kate knew for certain that the Abbey was not for her.

Being Kate, she tortured herself, and the information supplied about the Academy of Dramatic Art by Daniel's schoolfriend did not initially cheer her up.

'Apply anyway,' said Daniel. 'You can always change your mind, but at least your application will have gone in.'

'All right,' Kate said reluctantly. 'I suppose you're right.'

'What am I doing with this gloomy woman?' demanded Daniel of the world in general. 'When I could be in the college library reading *The Book of Kells*!'

'Or dissecting bones?'

'Indeed. It's good to see you smile for a change! Have you told Lady Gregory that you've decided to go?'

'I have. I'll leave in November.'

At the end of that month there was to be a first production of Lady Gregory's three-act comedy, *The Canavans*, at the Abbey.

There was a cast of five, the women's parts played by Maire O'Neill and Brigid Dempsey, both of whom had also been picked for roles in Mr Synge's highly controversial *The Playboy of the Western World*, which would run in January 1907.

But by then Kate would be in London . . .

'And in the meantime we'll go home to Clare together for the Christmas holidays,' planned Daniel. 'Don't dare look sad. *I* should be looking that way, at the prospect of being in Dublin without you. And here am I being all pleased instead because you're going to be a success. I'm much too kind!'

Eugene, too, was coming home that Christmas – the first time he would be back in Ireland since enrolling at the Slade.

He and Daniel were going to Crag Liath first to stay

with Milly. Then, with Kate, they were planning a trip to Whitegate.

'Eugene is definitely coming?' enquired Aoibheal in an unenthusiastic tone.

'Eugene too,' repeated her mother in a firm, now-let's-not-have-any-nonsense voice. Aoibheal had not spoken to her parents about her experience in the cellars, but Rosaleen knew without being told that there was no love lost between her daughter and dark-haired son.

Aoibheal sighed audibly.

Ignoring this, Rosaleen resorted to briskness. 'I have a lot to do in the house. Still, come and help me feed the birds,' she said to her grumpy daughter. 'I've soaked breadcrumbs for them. It's very frosty, so put your coat on before you come into the cold.'

One bird, a dumpy, short-legged fellow, was already waiting his chance. While he was pecking, a red-breasted robin interrupted the meal and was duly driven off.

Poor little bird, Aoibheal thought, feeling sorry for the intruder. But he had flown only a few yards away. Soon enough, he shot back in again.

And the beauty of it: the lake hardly stirring, the white sun reflected in its bronze waters, the long thin shadows of trees stretching across the shore.

And tomorrow Eugene was coming, to spoil this magic place!

The next day there was more frost, and it was chilly getting up.

At Daniel's instigation the lunch guests set off for Whitegate at what Kate felt was an unreasonably early hour. She had never been a dawn riser, and through-out her school-days Fran and Finola had forcibly drag-ged her from bed while she kicked and shouted and sulked. Theatrical hours – which encouraged people to stay up talking ages after a show had ended, and linger in bed until late – suited her temperament perfectly.

Now, collected by the twins when her curly hair was still tangled and her temper in much the same state, she failed to comment on the new car bought for Crag Liath use, only really surfacing when they reached the fringes of Mountshannon.

A pink tinge had appeared in the sky over the purple hills, but the rest of the sky was as blue as the lake water. Warty grey trunks of trees had a frizz of branches on top of them, reminding Kate of the present state of her hair. Only the fir trees still looked warm in their all-year-round green coats.

Eugene had driven at the start of the journey, but now Daniel was at the wheel with Kate wrapped in a rug beside him. Then, without any prior warning, the engine spluttered and they came to an abrupt stop.

Daniel muttered darkly and banged his clenched fist on the steering-wheel before getting out and disappearing under the raised bonnet.

'Do you want help?' called Eugene from the back seat.

'I can manage all right,' his brother shouted. 'At least, I *think* I can.'

'Oh, well,' said Eugene resignedly, 'if that's how he feels . . . So, Kate, I hear you're coming to London.'

Turning round the way she could talk to him, Kate found that he had leant forward and that their faces were surprisingly close. How handsome he is, she thought, much more so than Daniel; and she wondered why this had never struck her so forcibly before.

Perhaps because Eugene's face has somehow matured over this last year, become much more adult, more manly, more, well, *knowing* – more experienced.

But that, of course, must be due to living in London.

'Yes, I am,' she said. 'Or, at least, I'm going to audition soon for the Academy of Dramatic Art. If that goes well I'll begin the course at once.'

The course ran for four terms beginning in January, and if she was accepted Jamie would have to pay twelve guineas a term.

'Do you know that we'll be neighbours then?' Eugene said. 'The Academy of Dramatic Art is in Gower Street – a short walk from the Slade.'

'Is that so?' said Kate, still staring at Eugene's handsome face.

'So we'll be able to see a lot of each other, won't we?' Eugene said, and at the thought of that a shiver went through her and she could not bring herself to look away or comment any further.

'That's it, I hope. She should start now,' she heard Daniel proclaim, and his auburn head appeared from under the bonnet and Eugene leant back in his seat.

The car started again. The twins laughed, united in relief. As they travelled the last few miles to Whitegate, only Kate seemed to be aware of the change that had taken place.

'You're leaving the Abbey? *Why*?' demanded Cathal over lunch in a disapproving voice.

Kate tried to explain.

'The poetry isn't in me,' she said finally. 'It's just as simple as that.'

'It sounds to me as if you're giving up too easily,' said Cathal, unconvinced. 'Why don't you rest quietly and try to let the poetry come to you of its own accord. You can't have lived in Ireland all these years without being touched by what it's about.'

'Well –' Kate began and half-turned to Daniel, waiting for him to explain.

But it was Eugene, instead, who spoke.

'Many actors and actresses feel more confident after they have been properly trained,' he said. 'The Academy centres its teaching around voice production and elocution – that will be good for Kate. And she'll have dancing and deportment classes and lessons in stage make-up.'

'That's bound to turn her into an artificial actress,' said Cathal to Kate's indignation. 'The Abbey style of acting is pure rather than artificial.'

'There are those outside the Abbey who believe in a new approach to theatrical style,' riposted Eugene at once. 'Have you heard of Edward Gordon Craig?'

When Cathal shook his head Eugene went on, 'He has been both an actor and a producer. Now he's concentrating on set design, which is how I got to hear about his work. He says, and I quote: "The Art of the Theatre is neither acting nor the play, it is not scene nor dance, but it consists of all the elements of which these things are composed; action, which is the very spirit of acting; words, which are the body of the play; line and colour, which are the very heart of the scene; rhythm, which is the very essence of dance." So you see, Cathal, London too, is reconsidering its attitude to the stage. I don't think it will do Kate much harm to go there and see for herself what is going on. And afterwards she is bound to get herself an engagement either in the West End or touring in the provinces. The students at the Academy invariably manage to get work when their training is complete.'

There was a momentary silence. Then Daniel, holding out his plate to Rosaleen for a second helping of roast mutton, said, 'We'll see you at His Majesty's yet, Kate!'

'More than likely,' said Eugene. 'Mr Herbert

Beerbohm Tree, who founded the Academy, is the manager of His Majesty's.'

It struck Kate that Eugene was both interested in and remarkably well-informed about the English theatre. They were going to have plenty to talk about when she went to London.

'You will be glad to know that I have been accepted. In fact, I started my course today.'

Having got that far in her letter to Daniel, Kate paused for thought.

The gulf that was between them was somehow much further than the Irish Sea. In a very short space of time she had drifted away from Daniel and grown closer to his twin.

Over the Christmas holidays, Eugene and she had talked theatre and art whenever they got the chance, with Eugene expanding on the theory of the theatre standing self-reliant as a creative entity rather than an interpretative craft.

Edward Gordon Craig, said Eugene, was trying to free the theatre from the tyrannous grip of literature. At the same time he was opening the door for artists to work seriously in the theatre, a field to which Eugene was drawn.

Absorbing talk. It was only now, settled in London, that Kate realized Daniel must have felt isolated during the holidays, left out of the threesome for the first time in his life.

She reminded herself that Eugene and she had so much in common. But still she felt mean.

She went on with her letter.

'This term there are fifty students at the Academy, and the women outnumber the men by four to one! Most of them come from artistic and professional backgrounds. There are no so-called working-class pupils – not a bit like the Abbey. Children of actors

71

are half-price. It's a pity Papa is a vet!'

There was much more to tell. The fact that her course included fencing, acrobatics, mime and gesture, as well as the acting of plays. That working actors, amongst them Mr Fred Kerr and Mr J. H. Barnes, were amongst her new teachers. That the students were in constant touch with the professional stage, allowed to take walk-on and small speaking parts in West End productions. That the Academy was heavily influenced both by the American Academy of Dramatic Arts and by the Paris Conservatoire.

And that her course would end in an annual public performance under full professional conditions in a leading West End theatre.

'This year I gather it will be at the St James's, but there is a rumour that when my turn comes I will appear at the Royal Avenue, which is about to be renamed The Playhouse. We will be judged by distinguished actors and the Bancroft Gold Medal will be awarded to the most accomplished. How wonderful if I win!

'And then there is my voice. It's worth having voice lessons, they say. It's strange to be praised for that.'

Her letter ran to four pages and she signed it, 'With love, Kate'.

It was after six. She put Daniel out of her mind and got ready to meet his twin.

'Do you mind if we call at my studio before we go out?' Eugene asked after he had called at Kate's lodgings. 'I've left my money behind.'

They were going to the Apollo Theatre to see a musical adaptation of *Tom Jones*, in which an actress called Cicely Courtneidge was to make her London début.

Eugene's studio, which he was temporarily sharing

with another Slade student, was in Woburn Walk, over a quaint eighteenth-century building.

As they entered, the other student was putting the finishing touches to a study of a pert, sharp-faced girl. The portrait was competent without being inspiring, saying little about the personality of the sitter.

This same face was the subject of a number of other sketches executed by Eugene. In these the sitter had been brilliantly brought to life, revealed as vulgar, grasping and mean.

Any comments Kate might have made were stifled by the sight of Eugene's nude depictions of this girl. Again, the work was superb, but it aroused in Kate a whole series of emotions: anger, jealousy, and desire for Eugene.

That brazen creature had taken her clothes off many a time in *her* man's presence! For that alone Kate could have scratched out her eyes. And on top of that was the worldly-wise expression she had.

Kate blushed. To cover her confusion she sneezed convincingly and buried her nose in her handkerchief, hoping Eugene did not notice her pink face.

As well as being furious with the girl she was angry with herself for being thrown off balance.

Her rage even extended to the other student for sharing the studio with Eugene.

Didn't he know he was intruding – that Eugene and she never got a chance to be alone, really alone, for more than a couple of minutes? Their meetings took place in restaurants and theatres and streets.

Why couldn't the fellow take himself off and leave them on their own?

'Are you all right, Kate?'

'Yes. Thank you,' she managed, feeling as if her heightened colour must be seeping on to her handkerchief, staining it bright red.

She wanted to take to her heels and run, stay away from Eugene until she, too, had turned into a woman of the world.

'Ah, here it is,' said Eugene, triumphantly, retrieving his money. 'Come, we must rush or we'll be late for the show.'

'I'm delighted to hear that things are going so well,' Daniel wrote back.

And they were. The Academy had fulfilled Kate's wildest expectations, drawing her out as the poetic Abbey had not.

This induced mixed feelings in her. The realization that she had failed in her own country, in such an important school, remained a bitter pill to swallow. And succeeding in an alien environment made her feel a traitor to home.

But she *was* succeeding, and with each tiny success her confidence increased. She was making friends in the theatre, good future contacts, which also augured well.

And at the beginning of April she got a small part in a Ben Travers farce at the Aldwych. The main leads were played by Mr Seymour Hicks and his wife Ella-line Terriss.

On the first night the cast went *en masse* to the Hickses' home in Bedford Square for a celebratory party which only ended at dawn.

Eugene was with her, and they were leaving the party together when a thin, sharp-featured girl, a cleaner or maid about to begin early duties, entered the square.

'Lottie!' called Miss Terriss, 'they'll need you downstairs today!'

I've seen you before, Kate thought, surveying the girl. You're Eugene's model.

In the flesh the girl aroused none of the extreme emotions in Kate which her painted form had done.

Without apparently even recognizing Eugene, she took herself off to the servants' quarters.

Nor did Eugene appear to have spotted her. So much for all that anger and jealousy!

'What a coincidence,' began Kate. 'That was –'

She stopped.

On Eugene's face was an expression she had seen there before. Once before, when they had all gone to meet his mother at the station: an angry, bitter expression that had alarmed her then as much as it did now.

'One of the Slade models?' he said. 'I wonder why Miss Terriss allows her into the house. She's a dirty little slut.'

In the cab his anger was gone. He held her hand and talked to her about Paris.

'We must go there together.'

'To Paris!'

'Why not? It is the most stimulating city in the world for people like us: a city of museums and dealers and artists and actors. There are more than forty theatres in Paris. Did you know that? I'll take you to see the best works of Corneille and Racine and Molière and to see Sarah Bernhardt act.'

This programme was irresistible; the only question was, when could they carry it out?

'In May I have another walk-on part,' Kate went on, 'and there's my course and yours. And you'll be away in Ireland during the summer months.'

'We'll go in September,' decreed Eugene. 'I'll come back from Ireland two weeks before I need to go to the Slade. Your term doesn't start until the middle of the month. September and April are the best months for Paris. In August the city is far too hot.'

The cab turned a corner and Eugene pressed her hand. This gentle contact induced in her a powerful response: sexual, anticipatory, presageful. Even before he kissed her she was beginning to shake.

'*Where* did you say, gov'nor?'

Embarrassed by the cabbie's presence, they hastily pulled apart.

If only, for five minutes, they could be on their own!

Although Kate reasoned that she owed nothing to Daniel, that she was a free agent who was perfectly entitled to fall in love with his twin brother, she did not fancy the idea of seeing him that summer. So when Eugene went to Ireland for the summer holidays, she remained in England, fervently reading scripts.

Beginning with Shakespeare and the plays of Oscar Wilde, she moved on to *The Admirable Crichton* and *The Dictator* and, in anticipation of the visit to Paris, she studied Molière.

She thought incessantly of Eugene. He was her soul-mate, an illuminator, a maker of magic, the only man to whom she could ever relate. She was even more in love with him by the end of that summer than she had been at its beginning.

And in eight – five – three days', four hours' time he would return and they'd both be off to France!

On the train, on the ferry, and once more on the train, they were not left alone. And Paris – exquisite Paris with its cobbled, tree-lined streets and stone quais – Paris was riddled with people!

On the boulevards beautiful women in pale dresses and wide-brimmed, flower-decked hats promenaded on the arms of men whose overcoats were lined with black satin and whose trousers had creases down the front.

These men wore gloves and spats and most had canes and their faces were much bushier than Englishmen's for they had all sorts of beards, some known as *à la rivière* which were twelve inches long.

In spite of their whiskers, Kate thought them very gallant and she admired the jaunty way they sported their elegant hats.

'Isn't this fun?'

By contrast the Institut de France which they passed on their way to the hotel was a sober sort of a place.

And no wonder, Eugene said.

'In the fourteenth century three beautiful princesses lived there. At night they made love and in the morning they gave orders to have their lovers thrown into the Seine! So legend maintains, and who am I to deny it?'

Eugene had been in Paris on two previous occasions and knew his way about. More than that, he had friends in the city and intended to look them up.

Their hotel – modest, pretty, pleasingly romantic – was in rue des Prêtres-Saint-Germain l'Auxerrois. Eugene insisted that the musketeers of the King sojourned there in the past, that the cellars were linked to the Louvre by mysterious subterranean passages.

Then, all of a sudden, he laughed.

'I wonder if Aoibheal would like it here,' he said, although why that should amuse him Kate did not know. Distracted by the novel sensation of being in Paris with Eugene, she did not bother to ask.

Unpacking, hanging up her dresses in the strange bedroom, she brushed her hair furiously, muttering at the tangles, grudging every minute that was spent on her own.

Downstairs again, she stepped back into enchantment.

'We'll find a good restaurant and I'll introduce you to the best food in the world,' Eugene promised. 'Then we'll explore.'

'Are you hungry? I'm not. Let's explore *now* in case something terrible happens and we don't get a chance, and eat later on!'

Eugene laughed.

'All right. But you'll get tired, I can assure you. We must at least have coffee so you can sit and appreciate the ambience.'

They set off by foot, past the house in rue des Beaux-Arts where Oscar Wilde had died. Walking along rue Bonaparte across Saint-Germain-des-Prés, away from the river, they stopped to marvel at the sixteenth-century mansions.

In Montparnasse they had coffee.

'Tomorrow we'll go to Montmartre,' said Eugene. 'That's where the artists live. Last time I was here I met an engraver called Ricardo Canals whom I'd like to see again. He goes around with a group of Spanish friends – amusing people, marvellously talented, short of money and food!'

'Montmartre? Sacré-Coeur and the Moulin Rouge?'

'Sacré-Coeur in due course, and the other – we'll see. Maybe!'

'Why not? I am an actress. Why should I not go to a music hall?'

Eugene glanced around, then whispered into her ear.

'*Oh*!' exclaimed Kate. 'Oh – !' once again blushing furiously, asking herself how the can-can dancers could bear to high-kick, having taken their knickers off.

How infuriating to appear gauche and inexperienced in Eugene's eyes, in any way caught off-balance!

The Moulin Rouge was evidently a dangerous subject to pursue. Kate's interest in it came out of her growing interest in light musical shows which theatre managers and writers were speaking about as a potent theatrical form. Owen Hall and Sidney Jones, who had written *A Gaiety Girl*, had begun the fashion, and real-life gaiety girls were flocking into London and from there touring in shows that went to Boston and Philadelphia and Milwaukee. A first-ever black musical comedy, *Dahomey*, had been written and composed and played by coloured people, too.

Reluctantly Kate, who had always taken herself extremely seriously, had to admit that she had a talent for this kind of show, while retaining her ambition to play more artistic roles.

Musical comedy was not a form likely to appeal to someone of Eugene's sensibilities. He had said as much when she had taken him to the Seymour Hickses'.

His milieu, into which she was about to be introduced, was very different. Even now, when she was at her happiest, she was worrying that the two might clash.

At dinner she was more acutely aware of Eugene than ever. With Daniel she had always been relaxed – with his twin she was on edge, challenged to prove herself his equal as an artist, demonstrate her worth as a woman. She felt that she stood on the brink of establishing either of these roles, that she was probably unsuitable for both of them, and that she could quite easily fall into an abyss.

And all this running concurrent to her familiarity with Eugene – for hadn't they known each other for most of their lives? – and the certainty that she loved him.

Sometimes she was sure in her own mind that Eugene loved her. Wasn't that inherent in the intensity of his gaze? When they were together he paid her enough attention.

But sometimes, too, she was conscious that Eugene just wasn't there, or not the Eugene she thought she knew. On these occasions a stranger was looking at her through Eugene's blue eyes – an unfriendly stranger who was summing her up adversely.

A load of nonsense – that's what Daniel would say. For a fleeting moment she wished that Daniel was with her.

But that, too, was nonsense. She was in Paris with Eugene, on their own finally, so who needed Daniel?

'You're very silent,' Eugene said regarding her intently. 'What are you thinking about?'

This was a tricky question. Kate had been thinking about making love with Eugene. She was not ignorant about sex. Fran and Finola had taken it upon themselves to outline the facts of life when Kate was still very young. At ten she had been warned about what men wanted from women and the perils of giving in to their desires. Woe betide the single girl who falls pregnant, they had said over and over again.

What Fran and Finola had failed to mention was the effect of love on the head, that it could over-stimulate the upper as well as the lower regions more lethally than wine – more even than whiskey!

They had not talked about female desires – but maybe, not having fallen in love themselves at the time they had been holding forth about sex, they had not been aware of the existence of these wants.

Nor had they tackled the problem two people had who pined to make love but who – having their respective careers to develop – were not yet ready for marriage.

Instead of replying to Eugene's question, Kate slipped her hand into his. Nor did he speak again for some time. Making their way back to the hotel they were both quiet, lost in separate but similar thoughts.

They stopped at the door. The street was otherwise deserted, the other guests asleep.

They kissed with increasing fervour until Kate broke away.

'Don't be silly,' said Eugene. 'Come here – come up to my room. You're the one who wanted to be alone – this is our chance.'

This was more or less the dialogue for which she had been prepared by her sisters.

'You know I can't.'

'Why not?'

This question would not have surprised Fran and Finola. Men, they said, all knew perfectly well that girls couldn't risk falling pregnant, and yet they continually wanted to know why they wouldn't go to bed.

So Kate, rather than embark on a futile argument, just shook her head.

'You're the one who kept saying how much you wanted us to be alone and now we are! Come on, darling Kate, let's not waste time.'

'No!'

And at that Eugene left and the stranger took his place.

'Just as you like,' he said – and strode ahead of her into the hotel.

Next day the real Eugene took her to Montmartre and told her that once, in the days of Louis XV, two mills – Blute-Fin and le Radet – had been operated there.

81

'When they went out of business, the buildings were turned into cabarets. The King was told that the "worldly" women who frequented them caused considerable damage to the rye and wheat!'

Eugene grinned and Kate blushed again. Wearing what she hoped was her most sophisticated expression, she followed him to the Place Émile-Goudeau from which rue Ravignan ran. On top of a dilapidated building, the most forceful of Eugene's artistic acquaintances, a man in his mid-twenties called Pablo Picasso, was living with a girl.

It was this young man who came to the door and replied to their enquiries for Ricardo Canals by waving them inside. His eyes, black and piercing and bold, looked Kate over. He had a thick lock of black hair that fell over his forehead, and the gestures he made with his oddly feminine hands were awkward rather than graceful. At first encounter his personality gave him more stature than he had. When he turned to lead them into the big untidy studio, she saw he was actually very short.

Within, a group of shabbily dressed young people were talking in Spanish and French. Behind them, others were arriving, piling into the room.

And somehow Eugene and Kate had been separated in the confusion. She searched for him without success, squeezing through the crowd, making her way into a second room, a deserted studio where pictures of a kind Kate had never before seen were propped against the walls.

The women in these paintings had masks instead of faces, their figures were distorted, they stood out from and yet appeared to merge into a background of plains. She thought the work ugly, almost ludicrous.

'Kate, what are you doing in here?'

But Eugene's attention was already not on her but on the strange paintings.

'Aren't they horrible?'

Eugene did not reply. He was standing in front of the most extraordinary canvas, a shrieking depiction of five female nudes, wildly and jaggedly drawn. The picture suggested that one of the women was pulling a curtain back. Another squatted on the side of the canvas.

'My God!' whispered Eugene.

'Are these Pablo Picasso's paintings? You said he was a genius.'

'He is,' murmured Eugene. 'You don't know.'

'He doesn't have your talent.'

Eugene said exasperatedly, 'When you see work of this calibre you know that there is no point in your own. Come on. Picasso never allows anyone to look at his work. He'll be angry if he finds us in here.'

Back in the other room she stayed close to Eugene's side. Occasionally people attempted to converse with her in French, amongst them a girl Eugene introduced as Fernande, Picasso's mistress.

Later Picasso himself exchanged a few words with Eugene, staring at Kate in his disconcerting way.

'What did he say?'

'I told Ricardo about your voice. He wants to know if you will sing.'

Cheered, as always, by recognition, Kate considered her repertoire.

Later that evening, when much wine had been drunk, she sang for them lyrics from 'San Toy', and 'The Runaway Girl' and 'The Belle of New York' and made them laugh by even being able to whistle. Some of the songs were a little out of date, and some had been written not for a woman but for a man, but her Spanish and French audience responded only to her clear, sweet voice and her vivacity, and they responded enthusiastically.

Her success temporarily got rid of the mounting fear that was tormenting her in Paris – that Eugene and she belonged in two very different worlds. Even without being able to understand what was being said that evening amongst this self-consciously advanced group of artists, she understood that they were intellectually far beyond her. Picasso's paintings alone told her that. When they went out into the Place Émile-Goudeau, Eugene observed that Picasso's friends amused themselves by criticizing the naïve painter, Rousseau, with whom they often spent time, on the basis that he had neither anxiety nor pride and was at heart no more than an artisan.

But Kate was elated after her small singing triumph, and Eugene's arm was around her waist and she was in La Butte Montmartre, the pinnacle of Paris. The roofs of the city were at her feet, and if her particular talent was, like the painter Rousseau's, more instinctive than intellectual, why should she think about that? Kate, unlike Rousseau, suffered from both anxiety and pride, but she wasn't in agony then.

Artists, said Eugene, seek out the truth. That was their purpose in life.

And so, obviously, they were as honest about love as about everything else. Women like Fernande – strong, brave women – understood that it was feeling that bound lovers, not wedding rings. They shrugged their shoulders at conventional morality, finding much that was hypocritical in the idea of having to wait to express their passion until a priest, by speaking a few words and making signs in the air, gave them permission to do so.

'Aren't they frightened of becoming pregnant?'

Eugene laughed. 'They make sure that they do not!'

Kate considered. In London an older and more experienced actress had spoken openly of the work of the Malthusian league which spread knowledge of contraception. This, according to Kate's informant, was possible with the aid of mechanical or chemical means, both of which women like Fernande must know all about.

'Is there a branch of the Malthusian league in Paris that they go to?'

'I shouldn't think so!' said Eugene. 'Anyway, making safe love doesn't have to depend on advice from the league, not if a man is skilled.'

'What do you mean?'

'If he has self-control and can withdraw in time. Everyone knows that.'

Not Fran and Finola, thought Kate.

'So you see we can make love.'

How naïve she had been – not like Picasso's Fernande.

'You and I belong together, Kate. Didn't you feel that when we were children even – when we were growing up?'

But in those days Daniel had been her friend, more than Eugene.

Dismissing Daniel from her mind she smiled at his twin, her eyes hazy with love.

He was right, of course – they did belong together. Their union was pre-ordained and Eugene, being so sensitive, had recognized it first.

'It's foolish for us ever to sleep apart.'

If you were in love, truly in love as she was with Eugene, if you had known your lover-to-be for almost all of your life, intended to marry him eventually, you *should* make love.

Apart from which Eugene was now declaring his love for her.

'I love you too,' she said. 'And it is foolish to be apart.'

This statement having been made, Daniel, to her annoyance, crept back into her mind.

He had no business doing that!

In spite of the odd kiss, Daniel was just her friend. She hadn't been in love with him, not one bit. It was only Eugene who could arouse passion in her, ensure that the bright lights of the world without which the artist cannot survive be forever illuminated.

So reasoned Kate, evicting Daniel from her mind for the second time. All her thoughts should be centred on the prospect of making love with his twin.

At first being in bed together was something of an anticlimax rather than a passionate experience. The words 'cosy' and 'friendly' could be used for two people tucked up as they were under the single sheet.

Outside it was still light. The curtains were half-drawn and one of the windows open and in the street outside a man and a woman – lovers also, she thought – were conversing in French.

'You're beautiful,' Eugene said softly.

She actually felt quite sleepy at that stage. How funny if, instead of making love, they should both fall asleep.

Then suddenly everything changed. Eugene freed himself from her embrace and straddled her, touching her mouth very gently with half-open lips. His blue eyes were already dark with want.

He kissed her again, still tentatively, as if he was not convinced that he wanted to do so a third time, and her own desire increased.

When she thought that she would beg him not to

stop, never to stop, and be humiliated by so doing, he put a finger to his own mouth and trailed his spittle in a circular motion round her hardened nipple. When he bent his head to her breast she thought that in itself was enough, all she would ever want of love.

'Hold me,' he said, guiding her hand, 'like this – ' and for a moment she was distracted from pleasure, made aware of her lack of expertise.

She had expected passion to be like a river which carried those who gave themselves to it along in a steady flood; but it wasn't like that. One moment she *was* submerged in its depths, conscious of her tremendous need both to take and to give. The next she was out of it, stranded on passion's shore, detached from the process, thinking, amongst other things, that the object in her hand was grisly and peculiar to the touch.

And yet she was crazily happy. When Eugene slid his hand between her legs, forcing them apart, she gasped.

'I love you,' she whispered, but Eugene did not respond with words.

He looked angry rather than loving, and Kate's reactions changed again.

'I am *lonely*,' she wanted to say to him – but that must be a stupid way to feel in bed with a man.

Desire returned, to be followed by pain. Now she did not speak of love and neither did Eugene.

Weren't men always sad after making love? Someone had told her that.

So there was no need to feel alienated – to imagine that the stranger was in her bed. Only the necessity for them both to sleep – and then to make love again.

And in the morning the impetus to take pictures of Paris – to record their presence there. Eugene had a

Kodak camera, and one of the other guests at the hotel, a short, nervous Jewish accountant who was visiting the city for the first time, was recruited to help.

Herr Bergenhoff was Swiss, and although Eugene said that the Swiss were naturally efficient and he would be bound to take perfect photographs, he was nervous about his assignment.

'*Where* do I look?' he kept saying to Eugene, and '*What* should I press?'

Each time he asked a question, Eugene leapt from Kate's side to give him directions.

Eventually Herr Bergenhoff said he knew what to do, and Eugene and Kate stood side by side with their arms around each other, smiling radiantly.

'Again!' ordered Herr Bergenhoff. 'And again!'

Then he gave the camera back.

It took ten days to process the film, and when it came back only one of the pictures had come out.

That one, although Kate and Eugene were too much to one side and their feet had been cut off, was not too bad. So thought Kate, although Eugene was deprecating.

'I shall treasure it all the same!' she said.

She wrote on the back of it: 'Eugene and Kate – two people in love. Paris, 1907.'

In London, Kate was offered a minor part in a new musical, *The Merry Widow*, with an actress called Lily Elsie playing the leading role.

This news, thrilling at first, later caused her concern. The plot of the new show was considered to be shaky. The composer, Franz Lehár, was reported to have enjoyed considerable success with the operetta in his own country, but Mr George Edwardes, who was putting it on, was including a new act.

Talking to his assistant, Kate learnt that this new act was to be set in Maxim's, the famous French restaurant.

'He is also engaging an American comedian called Joe Coyne as well as several English stock comedians,' the woman went on.

'And my part?' asked Kate.

'Yes – of course. We want you to be one of the can-can girls.'

Mr Edwardes' assistant wondered why the pretty fair-haired actress suddenly went so pink. She looked exceedingly upset. What was the matter with her? She had plagued the life out of Mr Edwardes to give her a part in the new musical but, if you were to judge from her face, you would conclude that she now didn't want it.

A can-can girl, thought Kate, distressed, remembering the Moulin Rouge. Surely Mr Edwardes would not expect –? Not in England –? Wouldn't there be a law?

'What's the matter, dear?' Mr Edwardes' assistant enquired.

I can't possibly put it into words, Kate thought desperately and, out of the blue, she recalled Milliora O'Brien's condemnation of the theatrical life as tantamount to depraved.

On the other hand, if I don't investigate – don't find the courage to do so – I'll simply lose the part.

'One doesn't – I won't have to,' she floundered, gulped, blinked, and finally added, 'take my knickers off?'

Mr Edwardes' assistant looked across the desk at Kate with her mouth half-open, lost herself for words. Surely she had misheard?

Still, there was the girl in front of her very eyes, blushing and concerned.

Actresses! thought Mr Edwardes' assistant. What will they ask me next!

'Certainly not!' she said in an outraged voice. 'Whatever gave you so disgusting an idea? This is *England!*'

The student who had shared Eugene's studio had moved out. Having the place to themselves they were free to make love on a mattress which Eugene had bought and positioned as far away from his painting space as was possible. But the smell of paint and turpentine was pungent.

'I always associate the smell with love!' said Kate, wishing that Eugene would get over his tendency to close in on himself, that he would relax and give the impression that he was happy in her company.

She was not altogether happy herself. The more she and Eugene made love, the more she learnt to enjoy it, the less secure she felt.

The more nervous and frustrated. She could not understand it.

And she was beginning to discover that love could lead not to the concept of freedom epitomized by Picasso and Fernande, but conversely into a trap.

Sometimes she felt as if she was within an enclosure, the fencing of which had been put up without her consent.

Surely not all women who made love had this reaction afterwards? In Paris Fernande had not given the impression of being a prisoner in a cage.

It must be her own fault. Her personality was lacking in some way – was inadequate to conduct a love affair.

Oh to be able to talk about her state of mind with someone sympathetic.

Not Eugene. He must not be allowed to know of

her inadequacies. And not any of her actress friends, either. In the theatre it was best to keep your weaknesses to yourself. Most of the women with whom she mixed would be glad to see her fail, on stage or off.

Backstage at the Gaiety, Kate was making the final adjustments to her stage make-up, pressing powder into the greasepaint she had applied earlier with a firm rolling movement to ensure that it would not patch.

'You need more rouge, darling,' Ruby, one of the other can-can dancers, said.

'But I've set it now with powder,' wailed Kate. 'If I put more rouge on it's going to look terrible on the top.'

'Start again. You've plenty of time.'

'Oh, leave her alone,' another dancer called Liz intervened. 'Who's going to notice her in particular when we're all in a line?'

A lot of petty bitching was going on backstage, even more than was usual for a show. This was partly due to first night nerves, partly to the rumour that Mr Edwardes, who was suffering competition from other managements, was desperately short of money.

What if the show flopped? What if London did not take to an urbane Viennese operetta?

What if I slip, thought Kate, suddenly panic-stricken at the prospect of all the things that – just possibly – might go wrong.

Should she really take off her make-up and start all over again? Eugene was going to be in the audience, a fact that made her even more nervous than she would otherwise have been.

'Mr Edwardes should pay us more,' grumbled Liz. 'Twenty-eight shillings a week is a lot less than the

91

carpenters round here get. I've been told that Miss Bleeding Elsie is getting £100!'

'*No!*' said Ruby, diverted from Kate's make-up. 'He'd never pay her that!'

The curtain was due to go up at 7.30 P.M. Somewhere out there Eugene was sitting, waiting for the overture to start, for 'Rule Britannia' and the English National Anthem.

I shall have to run away, thought Kate wildly. It's no good thinking about anyone else – about the success or otherwise of the show or the difference my absence will make to it. I have to protect myself! If I stay I will make a fool of myself – it's that simple. I – Kate Keegan, all alone – will ruin Mr Edwardes.

This state of jitters, her normal reaction before she went on stage, also had the effect of rooting her to the spot, although in her mind's eye she could see herself quite clearly rising from her chair, walking out of the theatre into the street, to be lost in the heart of London.

Never again to be seen . . .

'Five minutes, ladies!'

Time in which to escape . . .

But for some foolish, inexplicable reason, she had not availed herself of her opportunity, was standing in the wings with the other girls, dressed in her can-can costume, waiting to go on.

And out there was Eugene and the whole of London, getting ready to mock. . . .

Run, Kate, run!

Except that she was on stage, singing and dancing and having the time of her life, giving all of herself to the audience, charged with energy and excitement and wild happiness, and the house was on its feet, the gallery cheering and waving caps and handkerchiefs and although she was one of six dancers she knew with absolute certainty that this response was not for the other five, not for Miss Lily Elsie, who was playing the lead part, but all for the girl who had won their hearts – brilliant Kate Keegan!

'Miss Keegan, there's a young gentleman wants to see you.'

'Ask him to wait for five minutes, please.'

'Your boyfriend?' Ruby wanted to know.

'Mm. His name is Eugene O'Brien,' Kate said blithely.

She could not imagine why she had been nervous earlier on. The show was a fantastic success. Everyone was saying so. The audience had not wanted to let the actors and actresses go – had called them back for encore after encore until they finally had to give up.

'Irish, is he?' said Liz. '*I* wouldn't go out with an Irishman! I think they're very rough!'

'I doubt if you'd ever get asked!' Kate riposted.

Wait till she sees him, she thought. Won't she be jealous then!

She had not seen him herself over the last week, and only once in the previous one. Rehearsals had usurped much of her time, and Eugene had been busy as well on some painting project.

'What's he look like?' demanded Liz. 'What colour is his hair?'

'He has black curly hair and his eyes are a beautiful blue. I'll send for him if you like so you can take a look!'

So when a figure with auburn hair came into the dressing-room all the girls were surprised.

'*Daniel*! What on earth are you doing here?'

'Calling on you like a stage-door Johnny!' said Daniel, smiling at Kate as if nothing had changed between them. 'What else could I do, since you never manage to write!'

'Oh – well . . .' said Kate weakly, her voice petering out.

'And seeing your show,' Daniel continued. 'You were marvellous, Kate. You're a born actress all right.'

This reinforcement of her own opinion was just what she wanted to hear. Even more enjoyable was the fact that Daniel had praised her in front of the other girls.

Liz said archly, 'We thought you had black hair!' drawing attention to herself. So much for her attitudes towards rough Irishmen!

'I have a brother who has,' said Daniel, amused. 'We'll have to introduce you!'

Which raised the subject of Eugene. Where was he in the meantime?

'Were the two of you together out there?' Kate wanted to know.

'No,' said Daniel. 'In fact, that's how I managed to get a ticket for the show. I arrived out of the blue, turned up on Eugene's doorstep and he gave me his. He had something else on apparently – a lecture or work. My good luck.'

Something else, thought Kate, shocked. The happiness with which she had been imbued began to ebb away. A lump came up in her throat. How could Eugene do this to her? Nothing – no lecture or project, no intervention from Heaven – could matter as much as her show!

Her mind began to race, thinking of Eugene during the time *The Merry Widow* had been in rehearsal. Had he perhaps, without her being aware of it, become jealous of her preoccupation with the operetta, more and more disenchanted as the weeks wore on until he decided to reject it altogether? *Was* Eugene like that?

94

Eugene's maybe more sensitive than I am, Daniel once had said. That time he had talked about their mother going away.

I must have been neglecting him a bit, thought Kate, chagrined. I just didn't realize how susceptible and highly sensitive some men can be. I must make it up to him.

At the idea that she could her spirits soared up. And in the meantime there was lovely Daniel who had so appreciated her good performance tonight.

'Are you free to have supper with me?' he asked.

'Yes I am.'

Behind Kate's back, Liz and Ruby, intrigued by this development, mouthed, 'Hmm!'

A nice, chatty evening was just what she needed after all the excitement. Sad as it was to be without Eugene, it was a comfort to be with his twin.

'. . . and at the end of next term the Academy is going to stage *A Midsummer Night's Dream*,' said Kate to Daniel. 'Mr Herbert Beerbohm Tree's original production was poetic and romantic instead of classical, and ours will be like his. That suits me.'

'What part are you going to play?'

'Oberon,' Kate said proudly.

'It's a terrible shame I won't see it,' said Daniel. 'You can think of me learning about the chemistry of animal tissues and organs and blood composition and properties and functions of the kidney and skin while you're up there on stage! I'm immersed in physiology these days. And here are you forging ahead, about to be famous!'

Kate couldn't get over how relaxed they were with each other. I suppose, she thought, that we'll always be great friends. Those kisses we exchanged were affectionate – nothing more. And when Eugene and I marry – as we inevitably will one day – Daniel will become my beloved brother-in-law.

All the same she could not quite bring herself to tell Daniel about her affair. But towards the end of their meal she said, rather too casually, 'What exactly was Eugene doing this evening, did you say?' and Daniel gave her a curious look.

'I didn't,' he said, and it struck her that he had the answer not to her question but to one of his own.

'You had dinner with Daniel, did you?'

Eugene was disgruntled.

'Only because you weren't there.'

'I don't really like Viennese operetta. Besides, I felt like painting.'

Hurt, Kate winced. But *I* was performing, she thought – and then, the next play will be different. He'll be impressed by our production of *A Midsummer Night's Dream*. He couldn't fail to be.

Although she had not seen Mr Beerbohm Tree's version of the play, she felt she could equal the performance of Julia Neilson, his choice for the role. Her costume was to be gold, representing the sun, with pale-green wings and a sun-crown to wear on her head.

The Academy was to emulate Mr Beerbohm Tree's use of light. Electricity would illuminate the heads and wings of the fairies as they slipped between the trees.

Describing the design for the set with Eugene – the secluded glen and mountain ridge which would overlook a moonlit sea – she saw him grimace.

'It sounds sentimental,' he said, unimpressed. 'This approach to theatrical design is changing. I've told you that before. Even Tree realizes that. Apparently he's asked Edward Gordon Craig to design scenes

96

for *Macbeth*. Craig doesn't normally restrict himself to *designing* a production, but he's agreed because it will help him to raise money for a theatre magazine, one that's going to transform play-writing and acting and scenery – even stage architecture, Kate.'

'I've heard about that,' Kate said. 'People say it's only a whim – that Craig's an impossible genius.'

'Well, he's not,' Eugene said, and yawned. 'You have no intellectual understanding of what is happening in the theatre, or anywhere else for that matter. You're purely instinctive, aren't you? That can be very dull. No wonder Craig envisages a theatre in which the actors don't talk!'

He's jealous, thought Kate, desperately reaching out for straws – that's why he's taunting me. But jealousy doesn't explain why he didn't see my show.

'Didn't your boyfriend mind your having dinner with his twin?' asked Liz.

'He did! He's a very jealous man.'

'And you think that's a compliment!' Ruby joined in. 'It isn't. When a man is jealous it's because he's the unfaithful type!'

'Don't be silly!'

'It's true. It's because he thinks you could be as bad as him! Wait and you'll see.'

'You don't know what you're talking about,' said Kate. 'Eugene isn't like that. And I've got more to do than listen to people like you.'

January, February, March – the months of her last term at the Academy slipped away fast. They were worrying months for Kate.

She tried to push her growing concern into the back of her mind and concentrate instead on the forthcoming production. In rehearsals she succeeded.

Her unease off stage was compounded by a letter from Finola reporting that Jamie was ill.

'It's influenza,' Finola wrote. 'It seems to have gone to his chest. He has had severe pains. You should come home now and again!'

'I will,' Kate wrote back, 'as soon as I've finished this term and the play is over.'

After the production the award for the best all-round pupil was to be made.

That year, after a superb performance in *A Midsummer Night's Dream*, the accolade went to Kate.

It should have been a moment of triumph and ecstasy, but the prize meant nothing to Kate.

Her worries were confirmed. She knew beyond any doubt that she was pregnant. Her breasts were sore and swollen and she had never before experienced such fatigue.

These discomforts were nothing compared to her sense of guilt. Papa, she thought, would be disappointed, Fran and Finola contemptuous, and Eugene displeased. He was still a student, only due to finish his course in June. He had not banked on having to marry so soon.

And that was another thing – what would Milly O'Brien have to say about this turn of events?

Not to mention Daniel.

And, she thought, a baby – what am I going to do with a baby? I, Kate, who was going to carve out an illustrious career?

Anticipating the explanations and plans that would have to be made she lay in bed, devoutly wishing that she could pull the blankets over her head and turn the interior into a nice, warm, and impenetrable cave.

It was a particularly wet and miserable day which added to her woes and her excuses for remaining immobile. Eventually she realized that she had to face Eugene. However startled or put out he was they would have to make plans to wed. Being Saturday morning he would be in his studio as he always was then. Far better to talk to him there, in the daylight, rather than wait until the evening when her courage might fail again.

Sure enough Eugene was in, none too pleased at being interrupted, but this was nothing new.

'What made you come this morning?'

'I've got to talk to you.'

Kate blurted it out. She did not want to look at Eugene as she did so, being wary of his reaction, but she peeked nevertheless.

She had expected shock, at worst churlishness, ill humour, complaint. Instead Eugene's face became a mask, as inscrutable as those semblances of faces painted by Picasso.

'That's unfortunate,' he said in the stranger's voice.

'I know,' Kate said. 'I'm sorry.'

Because of course it was all her fault. It was her body that had betrayed them, not his. It never even occurred to her that Eugene was culpable, that his lack of expertise could have let them down.

'When did you find this out?'

'I've suspected for some time.'

'Why didn't you say so?'

More guilt.

'I only suspected. I didn't know. It's bad for me, too. I wanted to be an actress, become famous, not to get married so young.'

'Married?'

Eugene's voice was cold and dispassionate, the stranger's voice; but she said, 'What alternative do we have?'

He stared at her, contemplating her, you would

have thought, as if he was seeing her for the first time – as if she was an unwelcome intruder who had barged her way into his life.

'I don't want to marry you,' said Eugene coldly.

That was when Kate began to feel truly afraid. As if she was playing a part on stage she began to state her case – emphasizing again that they had no alternative, saying that Milliora and Jamie and Fran and Finola and all their relations, while initially surprised and upset, would support them in the end. That after all they loved each other. That they were not the only young couple who had conceived a baby out of marriage.

That they would be happy together.

'There's no question of my marrying you,' Eugene said in the same, pitiless way.

Hating herself, she pleaded with him. Eugene shook his head.

'But we grew up together!' Kate cried, conscious of how trite this argument sounded, even to herself.

It still seemed impossible that Eugene would shrug her off.

'I can't marry you,' he said again. 'It's out of the question.'

'Why not?'

He said, detached and yet hostile, 'I'm in love with someone else.'

'But you said you loved me!'

'Maybe I did at one stage,' said Eugene, 'but not any more.'

'Who is she?'

This was dreadful, horrible, and one of the worst things was hearing her voice go out of control.

'The daughter of an artist I know. I met her at Christmas. I had been going to meet her today for lunch if you hadn't arrived.'

This was like being slapped in the face, and Kate recoiled.

'Then go!' she cried, 'go – don't let me be stopping you!'

Part of her was still wildly hoping that Eugene would not go, that the entire conversation was all a mistake.

But Eugene did. Without another glance in her direction he strode out of the studio, leaving Kate to come to terms with his news.

When the initial shock had worn off she wondered if Eugene could be telling the truth. He was a sensitive man who had demonstrated his jealousy when Daniel had taken her out. Could it be that he was concerned about *her* fidelity, worried that *she* might have another lover – that the baby was not his?

Perhaps he was only hiding his true emotions, was waiting for reassurance behind that horrible mask and was meanwhile making up a story about his love for another girl?

Yes, yes, thought Kate, wanting to believe her own story. It could be the case, and if I wrote him a letter telling him how much I love him, begging him to re-think, all might yet be well.

She found paper and a pen and began to write. Never one to do things by half, she poured out her feelings on the pages, humbling herself in order to reassure Eugene.

She read the letter back, blushing at its contents. Suppose he *was* in love with somebody else? A right fool then she was making of herself.

But maybe it would be worth the risk . . . ?

Then she had another thought. In her handbag was the photograph taken in Paris of Eugene and herself. That should remind him of their love! She wrapped her letter round it and placed the packet on an easel for Eugene to find.

And on the floor she saw another handbag. The property of this other woman that Eugene purported to love?

She did not look closely at the bag itself. It was the identity of its owner that concerned her, not what the bag looked like.

And even if she had taken more notice of it – examined the quality of the leather, observed that it was made on a metal frame which had a snap closure and that it had a matching leather handle – she would probably not have remembered seeing the bag on the arm of Rosaleen O'Mahoney over eighteen months before when they met at Limerick station.

In the hackney going home her fears took over again. There must be another woman in Eugene's life. Wasn't that borne out by the bag?

In which case what on earth was *she* going to do?

Arrive on her sick father's doorstep, pour out her tale of woe to her disgusted sisters, reveal Eugene's name? Stand by while the combined efforts of two families forced Eugene to stand by her and do the decent thing?

I'd rather die, thought Kate. I'd rather throw myself into the Thames this very night than contemplate such a thing.

It might indeed be the only way out.

But Eugene couldn't reject her completely – not Eugene with whom she had grown up. Even if he didn't love her any more – and that possibility must remain in the forefront of her mind – he wouldn't see her disgraced.

Eugene was a gentleman. And he would therefore feel honour-bound to marry a lady in her state, even if he *did* love someone else. An artist's daughter.

I hate her, thought Kate. If she exists, I hate her! Tears welled and fell.

The hackney pulled up outside her lodgings and she climbed sombrely out. As she did so another hackney pulled up. Out of it stepped a familiar figure.

'Kate!' it said. 'What good timing!'

It was the very last person she would have expected to appear at her lodgings' door.

'Mr Keegan is poorly,' Mary Markham had reported to Milliora three weeks before. 'And he that never had a sick day in his life.'

'How do you know about that?'

'Mrs Cash says so,' said Mary.

Mrs Cash had gypsy blood and there were many who thought she had the gift of the supernatural.

'Didn't he see a magpie and he alone on the road the day he went to Cork?' Mary went on.

'Does she say he's going to get better?'

'Well, she thinks he might.'

Or might not . . . The alternative sent Milly over to Killaloe in order to see for herself.

She found Jamie out of bed but coughing his lungs out.

'You mind that chest of yours, Jamie Keegan,' she said to him. 'What's all this nonsense I hear about your seeing a magpie on the road?'

'Not one – four,' corrected Jamie. 'No evil in that!'

'On the contrary,' smiled Milly, reciting the old rhyme:

> 'One for Sorrow,
> Two for Mirth,
> Three for Marriage,
> Four for a Birth.

103

Nothing relevant to you there, I'd say!'

'It's a pity there weren't just three!' he said bravely, thinking to himself – if there had been I might have had more courage, proposed to her on the spot.

He coughed again, lost courage, and raised the subject of Kate.

'I'd been hoping to get to London. Did you hear she won the top award?'

Milly nodded, reluctant, he thought, to heap praise on Kate.

'Anyway, that's off now. Fran and Finola won't hear of my going anywhere for the time being. The two of them have me bullied! But I worry about the girl.'

Since this worry was acutely reflected on his lean, honest face, Milly was drawn in.

'I'm going to London myself in a few weeks,' she said. 'I'll go to see Kate.'

'Would you?'

Jamie cheered up. Milly, however, was not exactly overjoyed by her undertaking.

She had never liked – never would like – Kate Keegan, she thought. A flighty creature who had gone off to London and danced on the West End stage.

She had worries enough of her own without adding Kate to the list. This very week Liam Lenihan, her own coachman, a deaf *omadan* that never did a tap in his life, had approached her about the land.

Her own tenants wanting her to sell at a rate advantageous to themselves! Wanting her to sell at all – break up the estate!

The idea was offensive and unsettling. If Liam was making inroads, who might follow next?

And in England, at her estate in Wimborne, she had heavy responsibilities. This estate was almost as large as the two thousand acres which comprised Crag Liath, but required much more money to run.

A clear income of £100,000 to be precise, as Milly knew only too well. The agricultural depression was still affecting arable farming. More and more land had to be given over to dairying.

That, in turn, meant that farmers were resisting renting arable farms.

On the bright side, dairying was doing well because of the ready markets provided by Poole and Bournemouth and Dorchester.

True she had an excellent estate manager (and so he should be, she thought, since he cost her the princely sum of £400 a year!) and a reasonably efficient bailiff; but these people needed her own watchful eye upon them.

And it was one thing to be thankful that she had invested wisely – in industry, mines and, abroad, in railways – but these investments too had to be sternly watched.

Then there were her own on-going conflicts with the Fieldings, whose family had once owned the estate and manor.

Oh, the Fieldings . . . ! When Harry Fielding and she had been – briefly – engaged, he had made a will leaving his English estate to his fiancée without any suspicion that he would either die so tragically on the hunting field or cause such massive resentment about his bequest. Harry's brothers, Richard and Edward and Anthony, lived in Wimborne too, not far from the Manor, and although they and their families did not come to visit when she was in residence, they somehow made their hostile presence felt.

Of course, they were a very old Wimborne family. Fieldings had lived in the manor for generations. The faces of dead Fieldings scowled down at her from the walls. In the local shops they were spoken of with respect.

It was this very attitude on the part of the shop-keepers – that faint hint, never voiced, that Milliora O'Brien was an adventuress, an outsider – that made her blood boil and her spirit unsettled whenever she went to Wimborne.

But go she must, and often, or the estate would get out of hand.

She looked at Jamie and thought that she wasn't anxious to go a bit. She was an Irishwoman through and through, a countrywoman, she said to herself glibly, although, in fact, she had been born and brought up in the town and her first contact with the harshness of the land had scared her stiff.

'Tell her how much we miss her and how proud we all are of her,' said Jamie, bringing her back to Kate.

The poor deluded man!

Still, she envied him in one sense. It had been a wonderful experience bringing up Daniel and Eugene but – I would have loved a girl too, thought Milly.

'Give her my love, and Fran and Finola's,' said Jamie.

'I'll do all that,' Milly said, and so it was that in due course she turned up at Kate's door.

'You're looking very pale,' she said censoriously when Kate had asked her in.

In the stronger light she took a closer look at Kate and observed red eyes. What's ailing the child? she thought, sympathetic in spite of herself.

'I've been working very hard,' said Kate after a pause.

Milly's compassion increased. There's something terribly wrong, she thought. Look at the way the girl is clenching and opening her hands. What's the matter?

106

And, wise enough in the way of girls, she said to herself, undoubtedly it's a man.

I don't think it's Daniel, even though he was here at Christmas. Kate's never cared for Daniel the way he cares for her. Not the way I loved Tom O'Brien when I was young and mesmerized by love and vulnerable to its pain.

'It's not just overwork, is it?' she said gently to Kate. 'You poor child. Sit down and tell me what's wrong.'

Commiseration from Milly O'Brien, of all people, was too much for Kate. She tried unsuccessfully to fight back her tears.

'Kate,' Milly said reaching out to her, 'my dear – '

'I'm not dear – not worthwhile,' said Kate in a muffled voice. 'You don't like me and you're quite right.'

'What nonsense!' Milly said.

Firm as she sounded she was seriously alarmed. Kate was shaking all over and for one insane moment Milly wondered if she had not murdered the man she loved in a fit of passion and wanted to give herself up.

What else could get her into this state? Only – 'Kate,' she said, 'are you pregnant?'

Silence, which was answer enough in itself. Then they both spoke at once.

Kate said, 'I know, I'm contemptible – you won't want to talk to me ever again'; and Milly said, 'It's just as well I'm here.'

Milly O'Brien was a soft-hearted woman with an adamantine will. She was also an opportunist.

Any woman in Kate's plight would have aroused her compassion. Kate's tears washed away Milly's antipathy for her. She wanted to comfort the girl.

Alongside that, her mind was working fast formulating a solution to the problem that had advantages for

107

herself as well as for Kate. Massive advantages. But that was rushing ahead. There were facts to ascertain.

'Who is the man?' she said.

Kate shook her head.

'You must tell me,' Milly said. 'Does he know what has happened? He does. So I suppose he doesn't want to get married?'

'No!'

'He could be made to change his mind. I could talk to him – '

'*No!*'

'Well, we'll see.'

'No. I couldn't bear it if you talked to him.'

'I see,' Milly said thoughtfully, and stopped.

Eventually she said, 'And have you thought beyond that – about having the baby, bringing it up?'

'There hasn't been much time,' said Kate. 'You see, I've only just told him. I had thought – taken it for granted – that we would marry – '

'I see,' Milly said again. 'Are you going to tell your father? Do you want me to tell him?'

Once more Kate shook her head.

Milly said, 'It's all right. He doesn't have to know. You must come to Wimborne with me, Kate, and stay there until your baby is born. If the father hasn't changed his mind by then I will adopt the child.'

'Milly's done *what*?' Aoibheal was to remember her father exclaiming.

It was Hallow E'en – All Souls' Night, what in America would be November Eve.

Snap-apple night: the time for roasting nuts and drinking punch if you were grown-up, and either way eating apple pie and home-made barmbrack.

Tomorrow – the ancient festival of *Samhain* – was the first day of winter and the end of the farmers' year. Now that there was frost on the grass the cows were brought in from the cold. Aunt Milly had once owned a horse called Samhain after that feast.

'Milly's adopted a child!' said Rosaleen, and Aoibheal forgot about the ancient festival and her ears pricked up. 'Listen, while I read . . .'

In Rosaleen's right hand was a letter which had arrived that morning, bearing an English stamp.

'No, don't read!' insisted Cathal. 'You know I hate people doing that. Read it yourself and tell me about it in one succinct phrase!'

He grinned at Rosaleen and she smiled back. Her eyes dropped to the fat letter she was clutching in her hand. Pages and pages of a letter – seven pages in all. Imagine writing to anyone at that length, thought Aoibheal. How can Rosaleen possibly condense all that into a phrase!

'All right so,' said Cathal, the minute Rosaleen looked up. 'What sex is the child and what is its name?'

'Georgina is her name,' said Rosaleen, in her

amazement answering both questions in one.

'And how old is she?' asked Cathal, interested himself.

'Nearly two months.'

'As young as that? Well, now, there's a turn-about for the books! Why Georgina?'

'George was Milly's father's name. For a man who only wanted one succinct phrase out of me you're asking a lot of questions!'

'I suppose I am,' admitted Cathal, 'but other thoughts crop up. I suppose it's not surprising that Milly's done this. She always wanted a child. But why now – at this stage of her life?'

Rosaleen, mystified, shrugged.

'She doesn't say. Just pages and pages of how wonderful motherhood is! The other strange thing is that she actually seems happy at Wimborne. She never was before. She says here that she's thinking of remaining there for good.'

'In England?' said Cathal. 'Why would she do that when she's mad about Crag Liath?'

'Maybe she sees it as Daniel's and Eugene's place more and more,' Rosaleen said.

They looked at each other, oblivious, it seemed, to the fact that Aoibheal was there, their faces perplexed.

'I suppose this development won't cut Daniel and Eugene out,' said Cathal, after a couple of minutes had passed. 'I mean, she always did say Crag Liath would be theirs.'

'Oh, Milly wouldn't do that,' Rosaleen said confidently. 'She said she'd make it over to them when they were twenty-five. That's four years yet! But nothing *will* change. I'm positive about that.'

'I hope so,' said Cathal seriously. 'They had a lot to put up with, losing you all those years. It would be a nice reward at the end. I wonder how on earth Milly got her hands on the child?'

'She doesn't say. I suppose there are lots of opportunities over in England for a wealthy woman wanting to adopt.'

'I want to see baby Georgina,' Aoibheal interrupted. 'If Aunt Milly isn't going to come home any more, can I go over there for a while?'

'To England?' said Cathal, displeased.

Cathal was becoming more intolerant in his attitude to England as each year went by. Sometimes this caused mild dissent between Rosaleen and himself. Much headway had been made to regain Ireland's pride, she pointed out on these occasions. Apart from the opportunity that now existed for tenants to buy land, the new university projects were scheduled to go ahead in the New Year on a non-sectarian basis. The Sinn Féin movement was succeeding in its efforts to support Irish manufacturers. Home Rule was still within reach. Why hate England at this stage?

But Cathal said the rising generation of young people in Ireland would soon join in his growing impatience with the slow progress of the Parliamentary struggle. Negotiation and the observance of the status quo had left the country where it had been for hundreds of years, under British rule. Rosaleen was an idealist, an academic language enthusiast who believed that Ireland's problems could be solved by simply speaking Gaelic.

Unfair, Rosaleen said. 'I'm all for the Buy-Irish policy that Mr Moran promotes so well in the *Leader*.' There was a copy of the weekly paper in the house on one of these occasions and, to prove her point, she held it up in front of her husband's face.

'*And* I want to see land reform *and* Home Rule.'

'But you're not prepared to fight for your ideals,' said Cathal. 'That's the difference between us. I am.'

111

And Rosaleen would moan.

She didn't moan now, though; merely said that if Aoibheal wanted to go to England to see Milly and the baby one of these days – when she was a little older – Cathal should let her go.

'Soon I'll be *twelve*!' said Aoibheal.

It seemed to her quite old already. And she was mature for her age – everyone said so. Although she was not tall, a number of people, having conversed with her, observed that she couldn't be that young.

'We'll see,' said Cathal, immersing himself in the latest edition of the newspaper, *Sinn Féin*. 'In the meantime, there's enough excitement here in Whitegate for you.'

One of the bits of excitement was whether or not the school in Illaunmore would close. The contention was that the small number of pupils did not justify its existence. There were ninety children going to school on the mainland at Lakyle.

But there, too, another war was being waged. There was no male principal at this school – only Miss Mary Tubridy who had been acting principal for the last seven years.

What good was a woman to supervise the boys under her control? the critics demanded. A request to have her removed had been made, signed by several inhabitants of the district around the school.

Plans were now afoot to build a new school at Lakyle next year, in 1909, at which time, it was rumoured, a good, strict man would be appointed in Miss Tubridy's place.

In the meantime Aoibheal continued to travel to school by boat. The lake often froze over, limiting her movements. Once, in the past, it had been frozen for seventeen whole weeks and a hurling match had been played opposite Slattery's Quay.

But when she did manage to get on to Illaunmore, it was not only education she sought but information about the place, once a monastic settlement. Legends abounded of monks forced to flee from invading armies with precious altar vessels in their arms.

There were three families on the island: the Tiernans, who were eel fishermen, and the O'Mearas and the O'Gradys, farmers. Aoibheal knew them all and explored their fields which had names like the Fern Field, Hickey's, the Drill Field, Tuohy's Acres, Gortnasillia and Uncle Pat's – 250 acres in all. At that time her mind was taken up with important issues like which ewe had calved and how James Tiernan had hooked a fourteen-pounder on the end of his line.

The next year there was even more excitement. Captain Morgan, who had been in the British army, had married Margaret McDermott, a local girl, and the couple had settled in the district. The captain was a keen advocate of hurling, and even Cathal admitted that he was a decent sort of a fellow.

But now Captain Morgan had built a shebeen by the spa at Cregg Cross and followed it with the erection of a hopping ground where on Sunday nights the gentry went to dance.

This development had caused some controversy in the neighbourhood. Father Clune, the parish priest, did not like the goings-on. And when Captain Morgan let it be known that he was thinking of turning the whole thing into a hotel, there were some whose eyes turned green.

Two things followed. The body of a cat was dropped in the well, poisoning the water, and Father Clune got up on the altar and described the scene at Cregg Cross as one of debauchery. The spa fizzled out.

Distracted by all that, Aoibheal did not think much for a while about Milly and Georgina.

But that summer she and Rosaleen went to meet Daniel, who was back at Crag Liath. It was the end of Daniel's third year at Trinity College. He had three more to go before he would qualify as a doctor.

'Three whole years!' exclaimed Rosaleen, hugging him. 'And what then, may I ask? Where will you practise?'

'Here – where else?' said her son. 'I don't want to be anywhere else.'

'You're so different from Eugene,' said Rosaleen.

Eugene, having finished his course at the Slade, had gone to Paris to paint. There he had met the man who had founded the Théâtre des Arts and who also admired Edward Gordon Craig's approach to the theatre.

Eugene's letters were full of Craig's proclamations. Art, he professed, and Eugene repeated, could be created in the theatre without either the use of the written play or of actors, whom he did not see as true artists but only as learners of lines.

'They are slaves of emotions which possess them and prevent them from exercising complete and permanent control over movements, expressions and voice,' Eugene wrote. 'I would concur with that!'

'Our Eugene takes life seriously,' said Daniel.

He was the only one who heard from Eugene.

'He never writes to *me*,' complained Rosaleen. 'And when he was here last summer I hardly saw him. I don't think he's ever forgiven me for leaving him – not like you. *You* understand.'

'I do now. I didn't always in the past.'

'I've tried telling him how it was,' Rosaleen said. 'We had no alternative but to get out of the country. Eugene knows that the authorities were after Cathal for his involvement with rebels. Neither of us wanted to leave Ireland. I *hated* losing my sons, even for a

114

while. But I thought you'd be better off staying in school, coming back to Ireland for the holidays, maintaining the same routine until I came back. I never imagined that would take so *long*. All that I've explained to Eugene, but it makes no difference.'

'Give it time,' said Daniel, trying to inject reassurance into the conversation.

'What else does he say in his letters? Does he have a girlfriend?'

'I think he's had several girlfriends. None of them last very long. He – '

'Yes?'

'I just don't think he *likes* women very much. He's always the one to terminate the romance.'

'That's because of me,' said Rosaleen sadly. 'He doesn't like women because of my leaving him. I suppose he's punishing these poor girls. And it's all my fault!'

'Stop worrying about it,' Daniel said. 'Eugene must work things out for himself. If he's taking out his resentment on his girlfriends he'll only end up hurting himself, and that will make him think. Eugene isn't stupid!'

The conversation was getting too complicated for Aoibheal's liking. Leaving Rosaleen and Daniel to continue their analysis of Eugene, she went down to the kitchen in search of Mary Markham and Mrs Cash.

They, too, were locked in conversation, sitting at the kitchen table.

'Well, if it isn't herself!' said Mrs Cash, and Mary, who had already greeted Rosaleen and Aoibheal at the front door, beamed a second welcome.

It was 29 June, the feast of Saints Peter and Paul, and Mrs Cash had been giving out about who that she knew had got drunk the night before. There was usually feasting about this time. Cathal said it was an excuse, nothing more, for boozing; that the festivities had their roots in pre-Christian Ireland and that people had a nerve adapting the celebrations in honour of Christian saints. He had grinned as he spoke and added that, in the old days, when bonfires were lit, girls, dressed in bibs and brogue boots, would dance all night in the flare.

Mrs Cash and Mary though were not looking merry but, on the contrary, somewhat depressed. Aoibheal thought that the two of them were really getting old.

Old and, as it transpired, missing Milliora and feeling somewhat betrayed by her absence in Wimborne.

'Her and that child!' said Mrs Cash impetuously.

In the past the two women had usually been at loggerheads over what Milly did: Mrs Cash occasionally criticizing and Mary, in high dudgeon at the attack, rushing in immediately to defend her employer.

But today, to Aoibheal's amazement, the two were in accord.

'The house isn't the same without her,' Mary Markham wailed. 'What would make her keep the baby over there?'

'When she could be here,' said Mrs Cash. 'Sure maybe it is there's something wrong with the child?'

They considered this in silence.

'Blind maybe, or crippled?' suggested Mrs Cash in the end.

'Ah!' muttered Mary. 'Why would that bother her, when she has us to help her out?'

There was no answer to it. Their surmise resparked Aoibheal's interest in seeing the baby – finding out for herself what was right or wrong with her – but it threw no light on what was behind Milly's strange carry-on.

* * *

However could I face Jamie with his grandchild in my arms? So thought Milly a few days after baby Georgina was born.

It was not because the baby resembled her mother in any obvious way. Kate was fair – Georgina's hair, even as a tiny baby, was black and thick and curly. Kate's eyes were a lovely grey, Georgina's deep blue. Perhaps when she grew up she would be long and slender like Kate, but it was almost impossible to believe Georgina would ever grow up.

So – Jamie would not know her for his grandchild, not unless Milly did the unthinkable and told him the truth, which she had no intention of doing.

It's the idea of being deceitful, thought Milly to herself. That good man. I can't live a lie in front of him. Not Jamie, who thinks the world of me and would marry me if he could.

And there's something about having a baby which makes you consider being married again. Imagine that for a deception – marrying Jamie and having him act as surrogate father to this child!

And then again, if I were to bring her back to the community, integrate her into Kate's background, I would, in an odd kind of a way, be letting her mother down.

No, it's far better that she and I remain in Wimborne. After all, we're quite content here. Kate can come and go as she wishes and see her own child, so long as she abides by our agreement and does not reveal her identity to Georgina.

Nothing must unsettle my baby's stability as she grows up.

Musing on motherhood and the responsibilities it entailed, Milly's conscience pricked. Her determination to adopt the baby had taken precedence over all else in the months before Georgina's birth.

She had commiserated with Kate – had, indeed, felt desperately sorry for her – when the wretched man who had rejected her had not made contact.

But inside she had been exultant at his desertion, knowing that his re-emergence would weaken her own hopes.

She had never again suggested that she and Kate try to track him down. Each morning she had woken up willing him to stay away, to continue acting the villain.

Did Kate sense her thoughts? If so, she did not let on. Milly winced, remembering Kate's docility. The way she had allowed her saviour to take over her life, as if her own wishes were of no more consequence than debris floating in a river.

When the baby was born Kate had closed her eyes, refusing to look at her. She had kept them shut until Milly had carried the child from the room, glorying in holding her, ecstasy unmarred by the knowledge that Kate was wounded, bleeding emotionally as well as physically.

The birth itself had been straightforward and mercifully quick and, bodily, Kate had recovered with remarkable speed.

Soon – surprisingly soon – she had announced that she was going back to London, returning to the stage. An offer had come up.

Between disclosure and departure Kate had not once looked in on her child.

It isn't as if I forbade her to do so, said Milly to herself. I didn't bar her from contact with Georgina, from picking her up. It was entirely Kate's decision not to visit the nursery, to keep as far as possible from the child. She used to pretend not to mind when she heard a cry . . .

But the situation had changed over this last year.

For a couple of months Kate had stayed away from Wimborne altogether. Then she had written asking if she could come.

On arrival she had greeted Milly with genuine warmth. The two women had hugged. Kate had talked about her work on stage and Milly had thought how matured she was – how likeable.

On that occasion Kate had said simply, 'I'm stronger now. May I look at her?' and Milly had nodded mutely and they had gone together to the nursery where Georgina had been having her after-noon nap.

'She's so beautiful,' Kate had said in a controlled voice. 'And aren't her hands lovely – such long, white fingers!'

Kate's own hands clenched as she spoke and Milly had felt another twinge of guilt.

Which was ridiculous when you thought about it, because, without her help, what would Kate have done? What would have happened to Georgina? mused Milly.

Perhaps, without my intervention, Kate would have tried harder to make the father marry her. She still never speaks of him – has never mentioned his name.

Some actor, I suppose, Milly thought. Really, as I always said, Kate should never have gone on the stage.

Kate had been living life in a trance, operating like someone following directions along a road without caring where it was going. Her senses were numbed. She obeyed such orders and suggestions which made some sort of sense to her, but when good rather than bad results followed she did not react with her old rush of excitement.

She was not conscious of loss of emotion. She just felt nothing at all.

So when a letter came from an unexpected source beckoning her in a new theatrical direction, she did not rejoice, as she would once have done, but followed the lead blindly.

Subtly, the British theatre was changing. It had begun to do so when the Independent Theatre Society started to give performances of plays which had a literary and artistic rather than a commercial value. This theme was taken up at the Stage Society which, in the past, had concentrated most of its efforts on staging foreign drama.

In more recent years the Society had begun to encourage new British playwrights, amongst them Somerset Maugham, St John Hankin, Gilbert Murray, Harley Granville Barker and George Bernard Shaw.

The New Century Theatre was aiming to stage plays of intrinsic interest which found no place on stage in the ordinary way of theatrical business.

Regional companies were being established too, most notably in Manchester and Glasgow, which were designed to promote the new drama.

It was from Glasgow that the hand of opportunity beckoned to Kate. A production of Shaw's *Mrs Warren's Profession* was under consideration. They wanted Kate to read.

She knew about the play. It had first been staged in 1902 causing shock and controversy for, although it was a serious work which examined the exploitation of working-class female labour by the formations of capitalist society, its heroine was a professional prostitute who capitalized on her assets to her own, not others' advantage.

She wondered if the producer had her in mind for

one of the brothel girls. That seemed an appropriate choice for a fallen woman like herself.

Instead she was asked to read the part of Vivie, Mrs Warren's daughter. It was one which required an actress to show the shallow hypocrisy of a girl who, while condemning her mother's 'profession', was nevertheless dependent upon its profits.

Convinced that even the despicable Vivie was superior to herself, Kate began to read. It was a relief to step into fantasy out of her pain.

In front of an empty house she began to laud the virtues of humble respectability and modest sufficiency.

'Everybody has some choice, Mother,' she declared in a prim, clear voice. 'The poorest girl may not be able to choose between being Queen of England or Principal of Newnham; but she can choose between ragpicking and flower-selling, according to her taste. People are always blaming their circumstances for what they are.'

'I was right!' the producer said. 'You're Vivie to perfection.'

In the foreseeable future, while the play was on, she need not be herself.

The play did well. More importantly it helped to establish Kate in the more serious genre.

The following year she auditioned for one of Harley Granville Barker's plays, *The Madras House*, thinking that she might be chosen as one of the six unmarried daughters denied economic activity and independence and atrophying as a result.

Auditions were taking place at the Duke of York's in St Martin's Lane, and she walked with particular care, trying to avoid the mud in the street. The theatre itself was charming and compact. Mr Charles Frohman, who was mounting the production as part of an

121

ambitious repertory season of ten plays, made a point of being gracious.

Mr Frohman, she knew, was an American impresario who had made good money out of the commercial theatre in London and New York. The general opinion was that he was an unlikely supporter of the new drama, although he was very committed.

She waited her turn to read. But when it came its producer turned out to have a different part in mind from that of the sisters.

'We'd like you to try for Marion Yates, the shop assistant,' he said.

This role was a key figure in the play. Kate turned red. Marion Yates was pregnant and unmarried, as Kate had once been; like Kate she, too, refused to reveal the father of her child.

'This bothers you?' asked the producer, frowning at Kate.

The other actresses wanting to get this part promptly cheered up, their expressions becoming hopeful.

Kate's eye fell on Barker's stage directions concerning Marion Yates: 'To the seeing eye she glows in that room like a live coal. She has genius – she has life.'

She heard herself say, 'No – it bothers me not at all,' and the other girls sighed.

She started to read and was once again transformed, released from her real self.

'All right. That's Miss Yates cast,' the producer said decisively. 'Now Miss Chancellor's part. This is a woman who extols her independence from and indifference to men . . .'

'Aren't you sorry you're not playing Emma, the one with a brain?' the girl sitting next to her said. 'That's a much better part, I'd say! There's just as much spirit in that! I mean, this role – well, you'd have to be a bit

122

of a slut to do it, wouldn't you?'

Fed up at losing out, she was ready to provoke a row. Instead, to her amazement, Kate nodded.

'You're probably right,' she said.

As *The Madras House* went into rehearsal, Kate was forced to look more deeply into the character of Marion Yates.

Both the playwright and the producer regarded Marion's behaviour as heroic. This reflected back on Kate's attitude towards herself. The similarities between Marion and Kate were superficial enough, she thought. Marion was braver than she had been, fifty times more courageous.

She had pleaded with Eugene to marry her. Marion refused to consider marriage. She bravely tossed her head at male authority and the need for moral atonement for her immodest behaviour.

But the fact that anyone could take a positive view of an unwed mother gave Kate a necessary jolt.

The play was not a financial success. Mr Frohman's losses over the seventeen weeks at the Duke of York's were very heavy indeed. Audiences had still to come to terms with the concept of such a short theatrical run. In May of that year, 1910, King Edward VII died: his death provided a pretext for terminating the venture.

From it Kate gained two benefits: artistic credit, and a glimpse of herself in a better light.

Milly, if asked, would have confirmed her worth, although she would not have admitted to her fear that perhaps Kate was more commendable than herself.

Kate, of course, did not ask. She believed that Milly saw her as a prodigal child. Her fondness for the older woman did not detract from the continued unease she felt in her presence.

Her sense of guilt kept her away from Ireland until Finola decided to get married and Kate had to go home.

She arrived to find the bride-to-be in a fever of excitement. Finola's fiancé was a newly qualified doctor whose family came from Listowel, but after their honeymoon in Ballyheigue they would be returning to the Killaloe area. Meanwhile they were excitedly making post-wedding plans.

'And Banna – we'll go there too,' Jack, her fiancé, said.

They looked at each other as if to say – anywhere you are I'm all right.

'Jack was at Trinity with Daniel O'Brien,' said Finola after that.

'He was younger than I was, of course,' Jack interjected. 'He'll make a good doctor. He has the temperament for it.'

'We could have had two doctors in the family if Kate had played her cards right,' Finola went on. 'Daniel was always keen on her. You saw a lot of him when you were up in Dublin, didn't you, Kate?'

'A bit.'

'But then off she went to London. Is he interested in anyone else these days?' said Finola to Jack, her eyes on Kate.

Jack laughed.

'I don't know. I wasn't that close to him that he'd be confiding his secrets to me! He's coming to the wedding, isn't he? You can ask him yourself!'

He gave her a little squeeze.

So that was another hurdle Kate had to face.

She was one of Finola's bridesmaids and her first sight of Daniel was out of the corner of her eye as she walked up the aisle holding her sister's train. Kate and Fran's own gowns had been made in imitation of

124

the bride's, but theirs were in a silvery-grey velvet while Finola's was white. All three dresses had fashionable hobble skirts, narrowed towards the hem with a bias band at the base, and they would not go to waste after the wedding, being intended to be worn later as evening gowns.

Thus attired, with her hair worn full and high up, Kate looked straight ahead of her and thought of Daniel.

Now she could truly appreciate his worth, his humour and strength and reliability, the qualities which really mattered in a man and which she had been stupid enough to pass over at the time. Instead of which she had been tricked by passion into loving Eugene.

If you could describe it as love at all. I never actually knew Eugene, she thought bitterly. I still don't – or understand him.

Whereas Daniel . . .

Lucky Finola for marrying a decent man like Jack, and more fool me for seeking an enchanter, getting a devil, and missing out on a fine fellow with whom – in view of the secret there is between us – I can't even be friends.

Daniel gazed at the three girls walking solemnly past in their puffed-sleeve dresses and only noted one.

Kate, he thought, eclipsed all the other women in the church. Aoibheal thought so as well, whispering in his ear, 'Kate looks great!'

'*I* think so,' Daniel whispered back.

Aoibheal and he were confidants in so far as a man of twenty-three can confide in a young girl.

'When I go to England I'll put your case to her,' Aoibheal said cheekily.

'Don't you dare do anything of the kind!' Daniel told her *sotto voce*.

'But you're in love with her. You need my help!'

'I do not!'

Rosaleen, conscious of the seriousness of the occasion, leant sideways and told the pair of them to hush.

Still, all the same, Aoibheal nurtured hopes that romance would bloom, and at the reception she stayed close to Daniel the way she could check.

Kate hardly came near him! And when she did she was – not exactly unfriendly towards Daniel, but unforthcoming.

It was a big disappointment to Aoibheal. Maybe Daniel had no chance, in spite of being in love.

But you never knew. And one day yet she, Aoibheal, might still get the opportunity to present his case to Kate.

PUTTING Daniel's case to Kate was something Aoibheal did not get an opportunity to do until 1913, by which time she was just turning sixteen.

Long before then, Milly – aware that Aoibheal was keen to visit England – had been issuing invitations to Wimborne.

'Let her come,' she wrote, 'it will finish her off nicely. She can't have any sophisticated influences from the school on Islandmore.'

This remark, predictably, infuriated Cathal, and went against Aoibheal's chances, but eventually, under pressure, he was forced to give in.

'I don't want you coming back with any shoneen accent!' he said to his daughter before she went off. 'You be your own Irish self!'

Cathal was half out of the door, about to take off for one of his meetings. Since it was impossible to keep information from Rosaleen and Aoibheal – 'Not a leaf falls,' he frequently remarked, 'but you two don't know' – they were aware that this get-together had political implications.

Rosaleen mentally berated Edward Carson, the Dublin MP and leader of the Protestant Ulster Volunteers. The year before, Carson had stood on the steps of Craigavon and read aloud the Ulster Covenant, a document pledging resistance to Home Rule and signed by 471,414 people, some in their own blood.

It was not long after this that the Unionist lawyers had discovered a loophole in the law allowing for military operations and drilling as long as their object was 'to render citizens efficient in military arts for the defence of the United Kingdom Constitution and protecting their rights and liberties under this Constitution'.

As a result, it had been possible for the Unionists to recruit more than 100,000 men. There was power behind them, and money, a fund of over one million pounds.

The formation of the Ulster Volunteer Force lit a fire, and out of it flared southern rage. And from that anger had been born another, opposing force: the Irish Republican Brotherhood.

Men who had been content to look forward in the course of time to Home Rule were now afraid of being thwarted by the men in Ulster. The constitutionalists at Westminster would surely only dither from now on, wondering what they would dare to give in the way of independence with the Orangemen and the Conservatives hot on their heels.

Why wait any longer? men in the south asked. They, too, could fight – had to fight if they wanted freedom. Rosaleen could have wept for the way it was working out.

Revolutionary emotions were hot springs threatening to spout out of control. Cathal said many a time that it was no longer a question of whether there would be open rebellion, only a matter of when.

So here he was going off to his meetings and once more placing himself in danger, as he had been long ago. Then he had ended up shot, crawling bleeding to the door of Crag Liath, and ultimately fleeing.

When he was out of the house, Rosaleen did not hide her worry from her daughter. What if they had to run away again to America?

Her concern made her tetchy with Cathal. Now she said, half-cross, 'Leave the girl alone! She's only going on a holiday, not for the rest of her life.'

'A long holiday,' Cathal pointed out.

It *was* going to be long, the best part of a year, and it wasn't all going to be holiday, either, because Aoibheal was going to attend a school in Wimborne to keep her studies up.

She felt extremely grown-up, too old for school. Rosaleen had bought her a lace brassière with elastic straps and a little bow in front and there were bows, too, on what she regarded as her very fancy suspenders.

Instead of the dress she usually wore she had a costume with a jacket down to the hips and embroidery on the front and, under it, a blouse with a high neck which was not as comfortable as expected.

'You don't want to be talking to any strangers now, mind,' said Cathal. 'Rosaleen, don't you think she's looking a bit too grown-up?'

'Not at all,' Rosaleen said, more calmly than she felt, for although Cathal and she were travelling up to Dublin with their daughter, and putting her on to the Kingstown boat, after that she was going down to Dorset on her own.

What if she was kidnapped on the way? Such things did happen – happened frequently, out in the big world!

Since Cathal, too, was besieged by these troublesome thoughts, he hid his feelings under a display of irascibility, taking it out on England for enticing his girl.

'You won't like it over there, you know. They're not friendly like us. They're very reticent people – they hide their emotions. And they have no gift of language. We converse in theirs far better than they do! All they use it for is discussions about the Royal Family, and the weather, and dogs!'

129

Rosaleen laughed.

'Cathal – that's unfair!'

'And don't encourage any young men while you're there! I don't want you writing back and telling us you've set your mind on a dull English husband!'

'Good Heavens!' said Rosaleen exasperated. 'Will you stop!'

And Aoibheal said, 'Cathal, there's no guard to your tongue! I'm going to Wimborne to see Aunt Milly and Georgina and to find out what life is like over there – not to look for a man!'

At the moment Aoibheal made this statement, following it up with a sigh of exasperation, Jonathan Fielding, at home from university and having consumed a large breakfast – two fried eggs, three sausages, bacon and tomatoes – was wondering what to do with his day.

It was extraordinarily boring being deprived of his Oxford friends for these long summer breaks. Three, no, nearer *four* weeks before the commencement of Michaelmas term on 10 October. What was he going to do with himself until then? The earlier part of the holiday, when his brothers had been home from Eton, had not been quite so bad. The novelty of seeing Hugh and Tony again, hearing about their prowess in cricket and rowing, in the field game and the wall game, had sustained him for longer than he had anticipated. Their chatter, their excited report of 4 June, the speeches in Upper school which marked this, the birthday of King George III, the procession of boats and cricket matches and fireworks, was accompanied by amusing gossip about the masters who had once influenced his own life.

But after a while Hugh and Tony's teenage boisterousness had begun to get on his nerves. He had lost sympathy with their preoccupations: who, between collegers and oppidans, would win the wall game on St Andrew's Day was of little interest to him.

He began to remember just how much he had disliked Eton, its confines, traditions and uniform, which had seemed to him then uncomfortable and now merely absurd.

These were not views which Jonathan – who was by nature peace-loving – would have dreamt of expressing to either of his parents.

Particularly to his father . . .

Richard Fielding was a die-hard traditionalist for whom The King, The Empire, Eton, Oxford and The Services had spiritual connotations, although he would not have approved the use of so outspoken, so personal an adjective in connection with himself. English gentlemen might – possibly – have souls, but under no circumstances did they refer to them. The physical world, of war and risk, was preferable by far to the incorporeal, and was a subject for frequent discussion. Unfortunately for the relationship between father and son, the physical world inhabited by Richard had little attraction for Jonathan.

At twenty – twenty-one in two months' time, he reminded himself pleasurably – he looked satisfactorily physical enough to satisfy even his father. Although he was only of medium height, he was well-built with powerful shoulders and chest. His face was strong and, because his fair hair continually flopped over his wide forehead, despite his efforts to control it, seemed almost square. His nose was chunky but in proportion, his mouth wide – the lips thin – and his eyes light brown. When he was not bored the mouth curved up and the eyes twinkled. Most of the time, Jonathan hung on to his sense of humour and kept his views to himself when he felt that they would create discord. Harmony was his ideal, and he went to great lengths to avoid conflict, not because he was cowardly, but because he valued peace in a harsh world. Part of his objection to Eton had been the sheer cacophony of the place. The tranquillity of Wimborne he appreciated far more when his father was not cross.

Much of Richard Fielding's rage was directed at the red-haired Irishwoman, Milliora O'Brien, who lived in his old home. This summer Jonathan, as he had on so many previous occasions, had again heard how this opportunist had persuaded his Uncle Harry to make a will in her favour, leaving her Wimborne Manor and land.

'Where Fieldings have lived for generations!' boomed his father.

It was the anger and repetition to which Jonathan objected. The statement was fair enough. Fieldings *had* lived at Wimborne Manor for several hundred years. The local school, now attached to the Anglican parish church, had been endowed by his ancestors. Every year, Richard Fielding attended Prize Day at the school in his capacity as prize-giver. As far as he and most others in the area were concerned, Fielding status had not changed.

But they did not *live* at the manor and this, said Richard, was the Irishwoman's fault. She had taken shameless advantage of Harry during the time he had been stationed with his regiment in Ireland, and he had completely lost his head. Not to mention, later, his life . . .

Reading between the lines, Jonathan could extract some of the facts that related to Uncle Harry. Widowed and childless and transferred with the Sixth Inniskilling Dragoons to the Curragh he had accepted an invitation to the County Limericks' Hunt Ball and there met Mrs O'Brien.

She, too, was widowed and, doubtless, like Uncle Harry, lonely.

And young – twenty-eight at the time, Jonathan's mother said – and rich in her own right. A woman who had lost her husband in a drowning accident and who must have been devastated, rather than pleased, when her fiancé too had died.

However, Richard wanted no sympathy wasted on her. To hear his father tell the story, Jonathan thought, you would think that Mrs O'Brien (the fact that she had been married and widowed before seemed to exacerbate the situation) had personally been responsible for Harry's death on the hunting field instead of a killer horse. A conniving Irish gold-digger she must remain – Catholic to boot, and doubtless of peasant stock.

'I thought even in Ireland they were rather snobby about who went to hunt balls,' said Jonathan, provoked.

What a pain in the neck his father was, reaching for the weapons of class to continue hostilities in a war long since lost.

'Why don't you *mind* about losing our home?' his father said, thumping the table. 'I don't understand you, Jonathan! The place should have been *yours*.'

'It wouldn't have been if Uncle Harry and Aunt Lilian had produced children of their own,' said Jonathan mildly. 'Or if he and Mrs O'Brien had married and had a child.'

Richard emitted a trumpeting sound through his nose. 'The point is that he *had* no children. After Lilian's death your hopes for inheriting were raised and then dashed by this blasted woman!'

His father's face was purple with rage. Escape was essential.

'Ah, I think I heard the telephone ring,' said

Jonathan, aware that his father would under no circumstances respond to the summons of this disturbingly newfangled contraption.

But the threat of a repeat of this tedious discussion hung over the summer months, intensifying the boredom. His mother, whose desire for equanimity outstripped his own, lurked behind his father's prejudices, adding to the gloom.

He was tackling the third sausage and wondering whether he could manage yet another when his mother, in an afternoon dress and a straw hat decorated with mauve feathers to match her parasol, came in with handbag and every indication of being about to embark on an expedition.

'We're off to Doncaster,' she said.

'Where?'

His mother looked astonished.

'The St Leger, dear,' she said, unable apparently to accept that one of her sons could forget so important a classic.

The Fieldings, with the exception of himself, were all passionate about racing. His father, Jonathan thought, had the dates of the Derby and the Oaks engraved upon his brain, along with that of the Ascot Gold Cup race and the Two Thousand and One Thousand Guineas.

'You knew that, surely,' said his mother, laying a hand on his shoulder and giving it a pat, a signal which silently spelt out the message that she and he were the same.

They were, in a number of ways. Joan Fielding was less irascible, more sensitive than her husband, and Jonathan empathized with, loved and was irritated by her in fairly equal parts.

Responding to the pat, his gloom began to lift. So they were off, were they? The excursion to Yorkshire could be expected to last for at least a week, even longer. He could lie in bed late in the mornings without having to endure his father's dire warnings about leading a slothful life; read in peace without being exhorted to get out in the open air; sit through a blissfully solitary dinner without being asked between each course what he intended to do with the rest of his life.

As it happened, he had already mapped out his life, but, since it was patently obvious that his ambitions and those nurtured for him by his father bore little similarity to each other, this was a subject to be avoided for as long as possible.

What Richard would say when he heard that his eldest son was planning a career in publishing was only too predictable, thought Jonathan. Richard had set his mind on the army for his sons. The Colonial Service – India – alternated with Mrs O'Brien's opportunism, was a recurring topic of conversation at dinner.

Richard, who had been bitterly disappointed that his own health – he suffered severely from asthma – had put paid to an army career, had no qualms about attempting to live vicariously through his sons.

Well, he would have to continue his efforts through Hugh and Tony, decided Jonathan, since I am more likely to publish a book on India in the immediate future than to take up arms out there.

Poor Mother, when I finally announce my intentions. He will take it out on her.

'I'll miss *you*,' he said, feeling a sudden rush of affection for her. 'But I hope you back the winner and restore the family fortunes which Papa thinks we have lost!'

As he might have expected Joan, at this quip, gave

135

a quick, instinctive look over her shoulder before emitting a nervous laugh.

'I wish you were coming with us,' she said. 'It's such a wonderful event. Really, the backbone of the British turf . . .'

'Don't worry about me,' said Jonathan. 'As we both know perfectly well, I'm much happier here.'

For the first few days he indulged himself as planned. It was a superb September, warmer by far than any period earlier in the summer. The country was hazy with heat. The Fieldings' house might not have had the grandeur of Wimborne Manor but it, too, was set amongst the green fields of Dorset, overhung by trees: coppery red beech and rugged, rough fissured oaks. From his bedroom window, on one of those mornings when his parents were away, he watched a squirrel meticulously gathering nuts in preparation for winter, and was glad that Hugh and Tony, who would have been marauding around the back of the house had they still been at home, were safely back at Eton, ensuring tranquillity for both the furry rodent with the long tail and his own relaxed self.

After breakfast, seduced by the warmth and the beauty of the countryside, he decided to go for a walk. The trees grew closer together the further he went until they comprised a small wood which bordered on another field where, he recalled from his childhood, the best blackberries grew.

They would be out now, he realized, big and black and juicy; and although he had already eaten well, he felt hungry again at the thought of them.

He crossed from the edge of the wood and caught the scent of cloves, tracing it to a clump of herb bennet with its tiny, pale yellow flowers. Spiky fireweed, purple and rosy, was beginning to spread here, too.

And here was his field ahead, with the blackberry hedges overladen with fruit, just as he had expected.

What he had not anticipated was that someone else would be here before him, better equipped than he for fruit-picking.

She was a small, slim, dark-haired girl in a white dress with Magyar sleeves, bare-headed and bare-footed.

A well-dressed gypsy if ever he saw one. She was not alone. Beside her was a little girl of about five years old who was doing her best to divest the hedge of its fruits.

The latter, he noticed as he drew closer, had been wholeheartedly enjoying herself in the process, stuffing herself with blackberries and staining her face with their juice.

This did not hide its sweetness. Approaching the pair Jonathan saw there were similarities between them. They both had deep blue eyes, retroussé noses and soft, full mouths. The little girl's hair was thicker and curlier than the big one's but they were otherwise alike. Sisters, since the age difference ruled out the possibility that they were mother and child.

'Good morning,' he said to them.

They looked up, startled, but neither of them alarmed.

'Good morning,' echoed the small one.

And the big one said in the most enchanting accent, '*Dia daoibh* – good day!'

The likeness between Aoibheal and Georgina, which had struck Jonathan so forcibly, was not observed by Milly. If it had been, much of what did happen in the years to come would have taken a different course.

Milly did not notice the similarity between the girls, did not suspect that she had in essence aunt and niece under the same roof, for one very good reason: her eyesight was failing; her soft, hazel eyes were not as reliable as they had been.

What she did understand was that Aoibheal and Georgina had taken to each other from the very moment the former came into the house. She was pleased and touched and a little envious about this turn of events and, although she did not want to admit it to anyone, least of all herself, also rather relieved.

Georgina – on whom she doted; for whom, without any hesitation, she would indeed have given her life; this diminutive charmer – sometimes seemed to Milly to be suffering from a surfeit of energy.

The child was never, ever tired! She woke with the birds – on occasions, before them – and, brimming over with enthusiasm, hurtled into Milly's room to hug and kiss and wheedle her out of bed.

It was not as if Milly herself was a late riser. On the contrary, she was averse to lying in bed late, wasting the day.

But – *five* A.M.? Who but Georgina and the sparrows would want to get started then?

This past summer, Georgina, instead of sleeping later than previously, had done the converse, with the result that Milly was worn out at the end of it.

And there was, too, the fact that her body was generally letting her down. She was, she supposed, approaching That Time of Life. That, surely, was why on the one hand she wasn't sleeping well; felt, on occasions, oddly depressed; and was somewhat short of the level of patience required to rear a growing child.

Not that Georgina knew that her energy could be – well, not exactly irritating (never *that*, thought Milly, shocked at the idea) but enervating – draining. Which, of course, was the fault not of darling Georgina, but of her stupid self.

So when Aoibheal and Georgina took a liking to each other; when Georgina, instead of whirl-winding into her room at crack of dawn, pelted into Aoibheal's, Milly, waking blissfully later, had mixed reactions.

On the whole they were positive. Aoibheal was a dear, dear child. Her accent, of course, was execrable, being heavily West Clare. Something must be done about that! Really, Cathal was too bad sending the child to that island school instead of to a convent where elocution lessons could sort the problem out. Cathal had a lot to answer for, one way and the other, and why she liked a man like that she simply could not imagine.

Except that he was good to Rosaleen and the two of them were still madly in love after all these years which somehow moved your heart . . .

Stop being sentimental, Milly exhorted herself. This is a time for action. Now that Aoibheal is under my control, her accent, her decorum and her clothes can easily be straightened out. Must be if she is not to set darling Georgina a bad example over the next year.

We will start with the clothes.

'You'll need more pretty dresses, dear,' she said to Aoibheal on the third day of her stay. 'After all, Wimborne isn't East Clare.'

'But it's still the country,' said Aoibheal. 'Why do I need to dress up?'

She sounded interested, not hostile. Hers was a relevant question since Milly, it seemed to her, did not often go out to social events.

'One does,' Milly said mysteriously. 'English women do.'

'More than American women?' asked Aoibheal, and

Milliora thought – Of course, I forgot. The child was in New York.

'I expect so – yes.'

'I have my white dress,' Aoibheal said helpfully. 'The one Rosaleen made for me.'

And that's another thing, thought Milly, using her mother's first name. That must stop.

'It's very nice,' she said tactfully, 'but you will need more than that here. I will make you some more dresses. We will have to buy some pretty material. In a couple of days the three of us will go shopping in Dorchester.'

'It's hot in Dorchester,' Georgina piped up. 'Please, Mama, can't Aoibheal and I stay here and pick blackberries while you go to the shops? You can buy material for Aoibheal. She won't mind.'

'Don't say "Aoibheal won't mind",' corrected Milly. 'Let Aoibheal speak for herself.'

'But I *don't* mind,' Aoibheal said. 'I'm sure your taste is better than mine.'

Milly hesitated, contemplating a vision of Georgina trailing round the Dorchester shops with Aoibheal and herself, asking politely but determinedly what time they intended going home.

Shopping was not that enjoyable with an energetic child, however much you adored her.

On her own she could achieve very much more. Present Aoibheal with the appropriate *fait accompli* in terms of a decent wardrobe. Buy material, too, to make Georgina dresses. And two linen chemises for herself, and a crêpe-de-santé petticoat with pleated frills.

It was an age since she had been shopping on her own. She began to look forward to the prospect.

There was much to be said for the way Georgina and Aoibheal got on. She could go to Dorchester secure in the knowledge that her baby would be happy without her and that nothing untoward could possibly happen to either of the girls.

Which was how it was that the two girls went black-berrying in the field by the wood.

Aoibheal was still seeing England through bemused eyes, sliding into its strangeness. It was considerably more wooded than Ireland and the Dorset countryside was much more under the control of its inhabitants than was wild, wonderful Clare, the hedgerows trim, the fields like lawns. The animals grazing in these fields apparently stayed put and did not stray. She tried to imagine a Dorset farmer sneaking his cattle on to his neighbour's land so they could avail them-selves of its lush grass, and totally failed.

There were no ruined cottages left behind by evicted or emigrating tenants. Gardens were beautifully kept and flowerbeds neatly bordered.

The market town of Wimborne Minster with its grey and brown stone church, 'Old House', thatched cot-tages and handsome Georgian buildings, was equally delightful, almost encircled by the water-meadows of the River Stour and its tributary, the Allen.

The estate of Wimborne Manor was bordered by the Allen and situated four miles out of Wimborne Minster, near Witchampton.

On first sighting it Aoibheal wondered that warm-hearted Milly would want to live in so splendid and pompous a house. It was just too grand, upright in every sense, ivy-covered and flanked by battlemented towers, its windows mullioned.

In its great hall a beautiful painted lady with a pedi-mental headdress and a gown adorned with three roses watched her drag her luggage in.

The drawing-room was magnificent, its doorway,

which had carved and gilded friezes in the form of festoons of flowers, was flanked by Corinthian columns. Over the white marble chimney-piece was a rococo mirror from which her overawed face gazed out, and Chippendale settees and other mahogany chairs were dotted around the room.

The dining-room was equally splendid, the library full of glassed-in books and the bedrooms, although spartan by comparison, sparkled with freshly laundered, stiffly starched linen.

Taken on tour she discovered, on the top floor, the nurseries, from which a short passage led up some steps to two large attics.

There was even a shower-room where a circular tank had been raised on high supports over a pan.

'It's a beautiful house,' she said to Milly, more out of politeness than because, at that stage, she liked the manor.

Perhaps she would feel less intimidated if some of those ancestral portraits could be turned face to the wall! Or if Milly would allow the house itself to feel that real human beings lived within its walls.

'I'm glad you like it,' Milly said. 'I want you to feel completely at home in Wimborne.'

'I'm sure I will,' said Aoibheal, anxious to make Milly feel good but secretly doubting that she would ever feel at home in such a place.

How could anyone? How could little Georgina, she wondered, unaware that Georgina was over-flowing with confidence and would have been at ease even in Buckingham Palace.

Sent upstairs for a short rest, she went on thinking that each room in the manor was like a stage set with the highly polished furniture perfectly positioned, not one footstool or piece of silver or china out of place, or one picture slightly askew. She was hit by a wave of nostalgia for her own Irish home.

Was every English home so correct?

But of course Crag Liath, when Milly had been there, had been just as well maintained – she saw to that. It was only these days that things were more relaxed, that a room remained undusted for more than a day, that table-cloths and napkins were not always freshly washed.

On further investigation, Wimborne Manor was found to have its own unused chapel and a tithe barn at the back.

Intimidated at first by the manor, after a couple of days under its roof Aoibheal changed her mind. She looked again at the beautiful painted lady in the great hall and thought of her as a real person who had presumably married and come to live here as a young bride, whose children had been born and raised and grown up at the manor.

Large families would have filled the place with noise in the past. Now there was only Milly and Georgina in residence, apart from herself, and the house was a bit bereft.

Long ago there would probably have been armies of servants rushing around polishing and dusting. Even that had changed.

In spite of its size – the house had eight bedrooms – Milly employed only a cook and one housemaid to help her on a live-in basis, although two girls came in from the village twice a week to clean. The butler had recently died and not been replaced.

It was rather odd not to have a man about the place, Aoibheal thought, to hear nothing but female voices: a bit like finding oneself in a convent.

The cook was English and somewhat reserved, not at all like Mrs Markham and Mrs Cash whose friendly gossip so enlivened Crag Liath. She was not a woman who would encourage confidences below stairs or above. The housemaid was Irish with a bold, sulky face, and Aoibheal did not like her. But maybe Cook would be won over in time. And meanwhile there was Milly who, in spite of her bossy ways, radiated warmth – and darling little Georgina.

Aoibheal was not in the least put out by Georgina's effervescence. She was used to young animals and Georgina, she thought, gambolled like a young lamb and nuzzled into you for warmth just like a baby calf.

Playing with the little girl, cuddling and chasing her and making her giggle, Aoibheal realized what it was that had been missing in her life: the presence of a sister. Brothers were – in the case of Daniel, anyway – great, but having a member of your own sex around, bouncy and loving and good-natured, was marvellous in a different kind of way.

And there was the novelty of being older, of being able to dictate the terms to a small creature who looked up to you and was flatteringly impressed.

The small creature had the time of its life in the field by the wood.

'Blackberries!' whooped Georgina, and crammed them into her mouth.

'Blackberries!' Aoibheal smiled, and sat down in the field to tug off her black artificial silk stockings and cloth-topped boots before she began the serious task of actually picking fruit.

And then, out of the blue – or out of the wood – a young man materialized. Used to roaming at will in a small community in which everyone knew everyone else and stopped to chat when they met, she was not alarmed at his arrival.

She liked the look of him, she decided at once. He was handsome in a rugged kind of a way that put her in mind of an oak tree, and strong with it.

144

Returning his greeting she held out the basket she was carrying and offered him a blackberry.

'I'm Jonathan Fielding,' he said, as if he had to reveal his name before her offer could be accepted.

'My name is Aoibheal O'Mahoney and I'm staying here for a year.'

'Oh, good,' Jonathan said, somewhat taken aback.

He was not used to people supplying information for which he had not asked.

'In Wimborne?'

'Yes,' said Aoibheal, still holding out the basket. 'I come from Whitegate – that's in Clare, in Ireland, in case you didn't know. But before I was in New York.'

'New York!'

'America,' Aoibheal explained, to his mortification.

She obviously thought him a complete and absolute fool.

'That was some years ago,' Aoibheal went on. 'I haven't been back since. In fact, I haven't been anywhere very much until I went to Dublin to catch the mail boat in order to come here.'

I?

'Your sister didn't travel with you?' enquired Jonathan, helping himself from the basket.

'My sister? Oh – ' Light dawned. 'You mean – ? She's not my sister. She's not even a relation. What made you think she was?'

'Who is she then?' Jonathan asked.

It was all rather dreamlike, he was thinking – walking through a wood on a warm day, stepping into a field that was lined with wild flowers, and talking to this girl.

Who was not like any girl he had previously met. She was wonderfully uninhibited and direct and deliciously charming and fey.

And her *voice* . . .

145

'Her name is Georgina. She's Mrs Milliora O'Brien's daughter,' said Aoibheal.

Well, what about that!

'Now,' said Milly, putting her parcels down, 'tell me about today.'

She had acquired all the goods on her shopping list, including the linen chemises, and was generally pleased with herself.

'We had a great time,' Aoibheal said happily. 'We went blackberrying and we met a lovely man who stayed with us all day.'

'*A man!*'

'Yes,' said Aoibheal, blithely unaware of the impact this news was having on Milly. 'He's twenty he says, and a student at Oxford University.'

'Oxford,' said Milly, thinking – that's perfectly acceptable, but then again does one ever know with students? They're not all responsible, like Daniel and Eugene. Anything but in some cases, according to what I hear. A lot of uncalled-for drinking goes on, and noisy parties.

'*But it's all only a bit of fun!*' said a voice from the past inside her head.

Tom's voice! And suddenly she could see again the face of her young husband, bold and as handsome as a god's, and his halo of black, curly hair, tangled like a blackberry bush, and his deep, black-blue eyes.

Tom whom she had met in the grounds of Laurel Hill Convent school when she was selling roses for charity, along with Rosaleen.

They had stared at each other and she had known immediately that they would marry – had said so to Rosaleen before she sold him a rose.

But they had not stayed married for long. For Tom, too, had liked drinking and noisy parties and he had, in the brief period of their marriage, led her a merry dance, staying out late and carousing with his friends.

Even when she had become pregnant Tom had stayed out playing the fool with Jamie Keegan and the other fellows, just for a bit of fun . . .

He had been enjoying himself no end at the *meitheal*, the harvest party held annually at Crag Liath. That, too, had been a rowdy event which had gone on all night.

And after it there had been a cock-fight at the back of the house, a savage contest between two game-cocks, and Tom had still been drunk . . .

And she had lost her temper and slapped his face in front of everyone and Tom had gone off in a huff.

And, as he had done on innumerable occasions, he had dived into the Shannon to cool off. And struck his head on a rock. The shock of his death had made her miscarry.

At the memory of the tragedy Milly felt dizzy. Her face flushed. But maybe that was because of the heat . . . ?

'. . . he lives beyond the wood,' Aoibheal reported.

What was the child talking about? Milly had lost track.

And Aoibheal, in her excitement about meeting Jonathan Fielding, had failed to register the significance of his name.

She knew, of course, that Milly had inherited Wimborne Manor from the wealthy Englishman to whom she had once been engaged, but who he was she had long since forgotten.

'I asked him to tea tomorrow,' said Aoibheal, taking it for granted that Jonathan would be as welcome at Wimborne Manor as visitors always were in her parents' home.

But Milly was too hot and bothered to take this in,

being more concerned with Tom.

Between one thing and another she was unprepared for what the morrow would bring.

Until such time as her new dresses were made, Aoibheal was invited to wear Milly's. The one she wore next day was rose-coloured with a V-neckline and a bunched tunic skirt. She felt a bit uncertain about the skirt, which struck her as over-fussy, but the colour was good with her dark hair and, in the warm weather, it was a relief to get away from wearing a high collar.

She and Georgina were in the orchard picking apples when Jonathan turned up to be met by Milly.

'How do you do?' he said, unaware that she was not expecting him. 'It's very kind of you to invite me to tea.'

Milly gulped. Apart from all the other odd things that were happening to her lately she must now, she thought, be losing her mind. Who *was* this young man, and why did she not remember asking him to call?

'Do sit down,' she told him, because even if she did not recall anything about their previous encounter, she liked the look of him, approved of his manners, his voice, and his clothes, particularly his tweed Norfolk jacket with the pleats in the front and back.

A young gentleman, therefore. It was somewhat reassuring to know that her taste was intact, although her mind was not.

Afternoon tea was served.

'Where are Miss Aoibheal and Miss Georgina?' she asked Cathleen the maid, a flighty creature she had brought with her from O'Brien's Bridge earlier in the year and who was now eyeing the nice young man in a distinctly flirtatious way.

148

'Out in the orchard, Madam.'

'Then please fetch them and be quick about it,' said Milly in her most imperious voice.

To Jonathan she said, 'Milk and sugar, I presume?' groping around in her mind for a topic of mutual interest.

Where to start? The weather was safe enough.

'Such a wonderful September,' she said. 'So warm. Of course, September often is the best month of the year.'

'So my mother says,' agreed Jonathan, addressing himself to a muffin.

Then peals of laughter were heard and two figures in rose-coloured dresses hurtled across the lawn.

'You can't catch me!' shouted one of them and, 'I can, indeed!' the other called back.

Seconds later, the drawing-room door flew open.

'Mama, save me!' shrieked Georgina and, blind to the teacup in Milly's hand, hurled herself on to her lap.

'Oh, my goodness!' exclaimed Milly, for the cup was now in several pieces and her dress was soaking wet.

'Allow me,' said Jonathan, picking the pieces up.

It was a few minutes before harmony was restored, Georgina under control and the adults sedately seated.

Milly was almost her normal self when she saw Jonathan and Aoibheal glancing at each other.

Once more she was transported back in time into the garden of Laurel Hill. Her younger self was wearing a pale blue silk dress embroidered with pale pink roses which fell sheath-like to the ground, and her hair was tucked into a high chignon under a Gainsborough hat. At her side was Rosaleen in a violet-blue gown.

'How much have we made so far?' Rosaleen was

asking in terms of the roses sold.

'Five shillings and – '

But Milly had got no further, had looked across the lawn and seen an untidy young god in a clumsy suit, and had promptly fallen in love.

Rather like Aoibheal now . . .

But this cannot be happening, said Milly to herself. Aoibheal is much too young for love – and what would Cathal say?

'Have some cake, Mr Fielding,' Aoibheal said clearly.

Mr Fielding?

Milly was shocked. Harry's nephew – for that's what he must be – in her house?

Harry's nephew, or a hallucination induced by the change of life?

The latter undoubtedly. In which case she who had always prided herself on her sanity and her strength was assuredly going mad.

Tʜᴀᴛ summer Daniel – at Eugene's instigation – joined his twin in Paris.

He had been with Eugene on a previous occasion in the beautiful city, and they had stayed together as a matter of course.

But this time Eugene explained that he could not offer to put his brother up. The apartment he rented was very small – minute – and there was, he smiled, a girl . . .

'That's all right,' said Daniel, unmoved. 'I'll stay in a hotel. Do you have any suggestions?'

Eugene had.

'Hôtel de la Place du Louvre,' he said. 'I've stayed there myself. It's in rue des Prêtres-Saint-Germain l'Auxerrois. I'll take you there later. You're going to find it exciting being in Paris. You've heard of *les cubes*? Everyone here is talking of the new style of painting. In the Press the slogan is, "Our future is in the air". Artists now are interested in flying machines and science. Extraordinary work is being done . . .'

He went on in this vein for some time. He struck Daniel as tense and over-excited. Some artists, Daniel knew, experimented with drugs, particularly opium. Eugene had told him that a German painter called Wiegels, who had earlier been part of the crowd with whom he was now friendly, had been discovered hanging in his studio after an excessive dose of ether.

Telling this story, Eugene had emphasized that his death had warned other young artists off such dangerous experiments, but how could one be sure, mused

151

Daniel, listening to his twin.

He was not reassured, either, to hear Eugene declare that he intended to move from painting for the theatre into a more entrepreneurial role.

'I want to back the new theatre, Daniel,' Eugene went on. 'Art – expression is absorbing, amusing. But the real money in this world is to be made in business.'

'I would say that depends on where your talents lie,' said Daniel dubiously. 'Yours have always been so obviously artistic. This is an odd way for you to be thinking.'

'Only an idea as yet,' Eugene said airily. 'Still, there are very few artists with enough money in Paris, I can assure you of that. Oh, you can live here cheaply to be sure. I know several who manage to exist reasonably well. Juan Gris, Braque, Henri Matisse. But of that crowd only Pablo Picasso is what I would term a success. No, my thoughts are moving elsewhere. There is tremendous interest in Germany in French theatre – did you know that? I find that fascinating. Wonderful people, the Germans. With German money . . .'

But there were others in Paris that summer who had harsher and more fearful comments to make about the Germans, as Daniel soon found out. The French, said the *maître d'hôtel*, were above all civilized people; Germany and its behaviour over recent years threatened civilization.

'We must do something to countermand their brutishness. After the Treaty of Berlin, public opinion in this country is extremely suspicious of Germany. We are all on edge.'

After these conversations, it was a relief to wander round the Place du Louvre on his own, thinking not about what Eugene or the Germans might be up to, but how much the attractive old square must have changed from the days when the Roman general Labienus had his headquarters there. On the west side was the neo-classical façade of the Louvre, on the east, the church of Saint-Germain l'Auxerrois, built on the site of a sanctuary which the Norsemen had later destroyed.

Intrigued by this particular part of eastern Paris, he bought a book about it and, to his chagrin, learnt that the bell in the church tower had once pealed out a signal for a massacre to begin, plotted by Catherine de Medici.

'A three-day frenzy of killing,' he read, 'which spread to other towns . . .'

But the Seine flowed peacefully by, and in the evening he and Eugene and a girl called Henriette were going to eat and dance.

The tango was all the rage. Every smart Parisian pointed and postured in the new Argentinian import. In the night-club to which the three of them went that evening, Henriette was ordered to instruct him in its art.

Her English was not good and Daniel's French was worse, but a rapport of a kind was established between them and he got the knack of the dance.

They got back to their table to find that they had been joined by another couple, Parisians who turned out to be brother and sister. The girl was plump but extremely pretty, brown-eyed, brown-haired, with creamy translucent skin.

Her name was Monique and it was quite obvious that she had her eye on Eugene. Henriette, Daniel thought, could hold her own with the newcomer as far as looks went. She too had dark hair and eyes, but her face was more mature than Monique's, her skin more swarthy, her figure slender.

From the moment Henriette saw Monique she

153

radiated hostility. And well she might, concluded Daniel, observing Eugene's response to Monique's overt but silent invitation.

Turning in his chair, so Henriette was left with a three-quarter view of his back, Eugene concentrated on the other girl, asking her questions, listening attentively to her answers, and throwing out signals that she was the most important woman in the room.

'Shall we continue our dancing lessons?' Daniel suggested to Henriette when the tension at their table had reached an unbearable level.

Eugene took no notice, concentrating on Monique.

'Your brother is so cruel!' Henriette said as they walked on to the floor.

'You mustn't worry,'said Daniel, wishing they could communicate more satisfactorily in either of their languages, 'He doesn't mean any harm.'

'Always he hurts me. Always there are other girls.'

'He's only talking! Don't take it so seriously!'

Henriette stared at him, her eyes brimming with anger and pain.

'He likes to hurt me,' she said.

They began to dance again. Monique's brother, Daniel saw, had left the table, and was crossing the floor to talk to other friends. Eugene and Monique continued to sit, absorbed in each other.

The next time he looked that way, however, the two of them had vanished. Presumably they too were dancing, although he could not spot them on the floor.

There was still no sign of them by the time he and Henriette had tired of the tango and decided to rest their legs.

'He has gone with her!' Henriette said dramatically. 'He will not come back tonight!'

'Oh, nonsense,' said Daniel, uneasy all the same and irritated by Eugene.

What if he didn't come back? Idiot, he thought, dumping this poor girl on me without so much as a by-your-leave. I'll murder him!

But perhaps we're misjudging him . . . ?

Fifteen minutes later he knew they were not. By that time Henriette was in tears. In a mixture of English and French she was attempting to explain that Eugene was the most callous and charming man in the world, that he had persuaded her to leave her fiancé in order to live with him, that her reputation had been lost, that she had no alternative but to remain with Eugene no matter how he treated her . . .

'Where are your parents?' Daniel said eventually.

'In Lyons. But I cannot go home. They will know from my fiancé – '

She raised her hands in despair. What an ending to the evening, thought Daniel, mentally wringing Eugene's neck.

He took Henriette home and walked back to the hotel, striding along the quai de la Mégisserie, the view of the river and the Ile de la Cité diverting him from his fury.

On the Pont Neuf, to his surprise, he saw a familiar figure.

'You eejit!' he said to his brother. 'Why did you go off like that? Henriette is in a terrible state.'

Eugene laughed.

'She thinks you're with Monique!'

'Let her think!' said Eugene. 'Women are all bitches anyway.'

'She says you like hurting her.'

'She's right,' Eugene said, 'I do. It hasn't got anything to do with you and I. Why don't we forget about these damned women and enjoy Paris? It's great to have you here.'

'I should knock you into the Seine,' said Daniel.

They walked side by side back to the square where on the eve of St Bartholomew's Day the massacre had begun.

The next day Eugene came round to the hotel, acting as if nothing unusual had happened the night before, wanting to show Daniel more of *his* Paris. Questioned, he said Henriette was at home. They had made up their differences.

But although Daniel and Eugene met each day thereafter, Henriette was not included in their expeditions. Daniel left Paris without seeing her again.

Planning to visit Wimborne on his way through England, he was deflected by a letter from Milly putting him off.

'Darling Georgina has a nasty attack of measles,' she wrote. 'Aoibheal is going to travel to London to meet you there instead. I am so sorry, my dearest boy, that I cannot be with you myself.'

A second letter, this time from Aoibheal, said that she intended to stay with Kate.

How friendly would Kate be this time? wondered Daniel. As remote as she had been at Finola's wedding? He was annoyed with himself for caring so much about that. He would be better off not seeing her – not caring about her. He was twenty-six years old, after all, a qualified doctor, not a boy. It was high time he rid himself of unrequited love – found himself a girl, got married. In Dublin women had made it perfectly plain to him that he was attractive.

So what was up with him to be carrying this absurd candle for Kate?

Get her out of your system, he commanded himself, and knowing that he had done nothing of the sort, he set off for Kate's flat in Holland Walk, a pleasant lane skirting the park off Holland House.

'Is Miss Keegan in?' he asked the maid who came to the door.

She shook her head, and he who had told himself he did not want to see his loved one at all, plunged further into gloom.

Further questioning elicited the information that Kate was rehearsing at the Kingsway Theatre for the Pioneer Players, whoever they might be, and wasn't expected back.

'Even tonight?'

'I don't think so,' said the maid.

At that point Aoibheal came into the hall, hugged him tight and clarified Kate's movements.

'She's going down to Wimborne.'

'Kate is?' said Daniel surprised. 'I didn't know that she and Aunt Milly kept in touch.'

'Apparently they do. I haven't seen her yet myself – Kate, that is – there hasn't been time. But Cathleen says she goes there quite often.'

'Extraordinary!' Daniel exclaimed. 'She'll be safe enough, though. I seem to remember Kate having measles as a child – I caught them from her. Now, am I going to take you out for dinner? How grown-up you look! People will take us for lovers instead of brother and sister. Though I suppose we look a bit alike.'

'Funny thing, likeness,' said Aoibheal. 'Do you know Georgina looks quite like me – like you and Eugene as well. Isn't that odd?'

'Very odd,' Daniel said. 'I saw a nice restaurant in Kensington High Street on my way here. Shall we go there to eat?'

It was not only that she looked grown-up, he thought,

but glowing with a new radiance that made her more woman than girl.

If I didn't know how old she was, I would think she had fallen in love.

He found himself telling her about his stay in Paris, saying that Eugene was well and had acquired a pretty girlfriend by the name of Henriette.

'Did you stay with Eugene?'

'No. I found a fine little hotel in rue des Prêtres-Saint-Germain l'Auxerrois which was perfect for my needs. Get Aunt Milly to take you to Paris one day and stay there. It's called Hôtel de la Place du Louvre.'

'Hôtel de la Place du Louvre,' said Aoibheal, solemnly writing it down on a piece of paper which she produced from her bag. 'But I doubt if I'll persuade her. She says Georgina is too obstreperous to take to the shops, let alone to a foreign country! She's lovely to her, though – to me, too. I'm having the time of my life in Wimborne.'

'Is that so?' said Daniel sharply, and he looked at her again.

She *is* in love, he thought.

The little villain! What was going on? Wanting to quiz her he decided to respect her privacy – to let her confide in him in her own good time.

'Listening to Cathal, I believed that all English people were cold and unfeeling,' Aoibheal said thoughtfully. 'You knew better, having been at school here, but I – '

'Yes,' said Daniel encouragingly.

' – have other views now,' said his sister, and left it at that.

'You off?' said Richard Fielding to Jonathan before he departed for Oxford at the start of the Michaelmas term. 'Lucky fellow. Expect you can't wait to go back.'

Jonathan, who a month before would have whole-heartedly assented, grunted noncommittally.

What's the matter with the fellow? wondered his father. Damn' lucky to be at Oxford at all. Would have given twenty years of my life to have been in his position at that age. Richard, ignored as merely a younger son – it was Harry, the eldest Fielding, who had counted in the eyes of their parents – was not particularly interested in what Jonathan was reading at Oxford. Literature – which Jonathan had in fact chosen – was much the same to his father as philosophy or law: it mattered only that the boy was actually *there*.

And here he was looking off-hand about his luck. Richard snorted with indignation – snorted loudly enough to arouse one of the family cats from its slumber in an armchair. But Jonathan did not look up.

Four weeks earlier, making his escape from Wimborne, Jonathan would have been looking forward to eight weeks of simply ripping fun.

It was true that Magdalen was chock-a-block with Etonian freshmen, but it was the system, not the boys, who had got on his nerves at school.

Oxford was very different. Its treasures alone – St Mary the Virgin, the university church with its thirteenth-century tower and spire; the carved ceiling of the Divinity School; the Old Ashmolean's splendid staircase and astrolabes; Wren's Sheldonian Theatre; these and much more – had always enthralled him.

The life he led as a student could be uproarious – holding up horse-trams in the street and unharnessing the horses in the company of revelling friends; throwing bread at each other in Hall – or civilized – ordering up iced asparagus and quails in aspic, a bottle of champagne and two quarts of cold black coffee as you worked all night.

Even the idiotic 'ekker' talk, an extraordinary slang which introduced words like 'rugger' and 'bonners' and 'Wagger' and 'soccer' into the English language, did not put him off.

And he was enjoying his literature course – had prospects of taking a First.

Now, all because of a dark-haired girl he had met in a field, Oxford seemed unimportant: he did not want to go back.

Aoibheal, he thought, was better company than any he could have had at Magdalen. She was very well read, surprisingly so for a girl. He found it astonishing that someone who had been educated at an island school in the west of Ireland could have had access to Max Beerbohm's *Zuleika Dobson* and Compton Mackenzie's *Sinister Street*, responding to the gay mockery of the first and the grim seriousness of the second.

This led him to incorrectly deduce that Aoibheal must be about his own age. It was being small, he decided, that made her look so young.

When they were together there were many other things, more vital, to discuss than age. He never bothered to check. The weather had held up and he was too busy walking with Aoibheal and Georgina in the fields, gathering more blackberries, throwing ideas about and helping them feed the hens – the Plymouth Rocks and Buff Orpingtons of which Milly O'Brien was so proud – to bother about banalities.

As October approached and with it the start of the eight-week Oxford term he began to realize just how much Aoibheal meant to him. Girls were not a novelty to Jonathan, although he had no sister. But at college they turned up in droves – a few academics, to be sure, but also the less earnest girls who set their caps at undergraduates: friends' sisters, professors' and professional men's wives and widows, not to mention loose women.

None of them had Aoibheal's purity and charm – Aoibheal's intelligence. He liked, too, her independent spirit. In comparison to himself, he thought, she was free without being aggressive, capable of expressing her point of view in a few succinct words.

He did not feel light-headed or in any way foolish about her. He was not dizzy with love. He simply wanted to stay with her for the rest of his life.

And here she was staying with Mrs O'Brien, his father's *bête noire*. Even to mention her existence would be to bring coals of fire down on his head, to create the anarchy from which he invariably shrank.

Under those circumstances he could not manage to do anything else but grunt.

For her part Aoibheal responded monosyllabically to Milly's enquiry, 'Has Jonathan gone?'

'Yes . . .'

'When will we see him again?'

'December.'

'I see,' said Milly, rightly diagnosing love and concluding that work was its best antidote. 'Will you help me make sausages? And I want to preserve some eggs.'

The pigs' entrails had already been freshly washed. Aoibheal and Milly, with Georgina watching on, forced the meat into them and tied them with string at suitable sausage-length intervals.

When that was done, green earthenware crocks filled with waterglass were set on the kitchen table to hold the fresh eggs.

This kind of task Milly found relaxing – a welcome change from dealing, through Mr Grantham the estate manager, with the responsibilities of Wimborne.

There were four tenants holding between 300 and 400 acres each and twenty-nine to whom smallhold-ings of four, five, six and ten acres were rented out. On these smaller holdings the tenants kept pigs and went in for market gardening. It was astonishing how many problems could crop up, particularly in the second group. Sometimes Milly wished that she could split the estate and confine her dealings with tenants to only two, each farming 1,000 acres, along the same lines as Chilbridge, the largest farm in the area.

And on top of all the other things she had to cope with was the problem of Aoibheal in love!

He'll be on the train by now, thought Aoibheal rue-fully. And we three who have been so close to him these last few weeks could not even go and see him off.

Because of his father and all this nonsense about Milly inheriting the estate.

As if she had purloined it, forcibly removed it, inch by inch, out of the Fieldings' hands.

His father sounds terrible. How could a man like that have such a marvellous son?

And how could Cathal be so prejudiced about Eng-lishmen – maintain that they are reticent and unfriendly, that they have no gift of language?

I'll write and tell him that I have found one who has much more to talk about than the Royal Family, and the weather and dogs! Dull indeed!

But she realized that it would not only be Jonathan's wit that would be at issue if he and her father were to meet, but what Jonathan with his Eton and Oxford background represented to Cathal.

Establishment England. The Enemy.

162

Whereas Jonathan himself was all in favour of Home Rule for Ireland.

But what would he think of Cathal's methods for obtaining it?

'I'll think I'll buy some Rhode Islands,' said Milly. 'These heavy breeds are great layers. Did I tell you that Georgina and I are raising nearly 200 chicks a year at the manor? Some are for replacements, naturally, a number of our hens being twelve years old, and some for the table.'

'Our hens are *cross*!' Georgina said with satisfaction. 'They attack dogs and cats!'

'Only if they go near their broods, darling,' said Milly fondly. 'But at Crag Liath we had crossbred game hens that would stand up even to a hawk!'

Hens and hawks were of little interest to Aoibheal, lost in her thoughts.

What would Cathal say when she informed him – as she would eventually – that she and Jonathan were friends?

More than that – that they belonged together. She too was convinced, without undue excitement, that their future would be shared.

If Jonathan kept his promise to write immediately, she would hear before the weekend.

When he did she bore the letter off to her room to read and re-read it.

He presented an excellent and amusing picture of college life, using terminology that was familiar to him from Oxford. 'One had gone for a stagger – a walk – which was not the same without you, and afterwards to read the bumphs at the Ugger – which means the Oxford Union . . . played Fives . . . One man has had jugs of water poured into his bed . . . asked by a fellow I knew at Eton to tea at Balliol . . . One had just discovered Shaw . . . Now you understand how we talk and express ourselves here! It is, I suppose, all part of belonging to a club, an exclusive club which costs our respective fathers more than some of them can afford! What would *your* father make of it all, I wonder? From what you have told me of him, he would be impressed! At least the shopkeepers here give us five per cent discount for cash! I've just paid ten shillings and sixpence for new flannel-bags. Seven and a half weeks until I see you again. Write – write – write!'

Jonathan had already returned to Oxford when it struck Milly that Aoibheal's birthday must have come and gone without anyone even referring to it, let alone holding a celebration.

Her date of birth *was* a source of embarrassment. As Milly was well aware, Aoibheal had been conceived before her parents were wed. Worse than that, when Rosaleen was still married to mad Dermot O'Brien, Tom's younger brother, who had subsequently died.

After his death, Rosaleen had confessed to Milly that she was pregnant by Cathal and then they had gone off to New York where the baby was duly born. Rosaleen had written to tell Milly about this arrival, but she had not disclosed the date of the birth, being sensitive, doubtless, or possibly concerned that some-one else – the twins for instance, or Mrs Markham or Mrs Cash – might read the letter.

But it must have been in September, thought Milly. So why wouldn't Aoibheal herself, who has no knowl-edge of what went on in the past, or so we hope – why wouldn't she mention her birthday?

Unless she thinks I should be buying her more pres-ents and doesn't want to appear too greedy, the child.

Georgina would have enjoyed the excitement of it,

though – a cake and candles and gifts – and Jonathan, that splendid young man, would have been glad of the opportunity to fuss over Aoibheal.

The suspicion – perfectly correct – that Aoibheal did not want attention drawn to her birthday lest Jonathan discover her true age and think her too young to be his girlfriend, came to Milly later on.

The scamp, she thought – I'm sure that's how it is. She smiled at Aoibheal's cheek. Tough enough she is, she thought, and a good thing, too. She'll need all the resilience she has in order to cope with the Fieldings.

And I'll need mine to fob off her father's complaints when he finds out the lie of the land.

Oh, the thought of what Cathal might say! She could hear him already. She began to rehearse her defence.

'Your daughter is older by far than her sixteen years. It's the way you've brought her up. Some girls *are* mature at that age. I was ready for marriage myself when I was just eighteen.'

The age factor, she realized, was an easier fence to cross than the national one. She had no lines yet in order to cope with that.

Maybe I'm thinking too far ahead, she said to herself. Maybe it's only a passing fancy – they'll grow out of it yet.

Over the next seven weeks there was no sign of their doing that. Letters continued to arrive twice a week bearing an Oxford stamp.

''Tis another letter from Him!' Cathleen said coming in with the post. 'Is it serious they are, Mrs O'Brien, would you say, and her so young?'

'Not at all. Not at all,' said Milly, thinking that Cathleen was getting above herself, that her way of carrying on was all part of social democracy aimed at a revolution and a new world – an ugly turn of events.

Mary Markham and Mrs Cash would never have been so uppity, she said to herself. *They* know their place.

'When you see the chest and shoulders on him you'd be proud to be his mother,' Cathleen, unmoved, went on. 'But you'd be thinking a fellow like that, now, would be after an older one instead of a young banb like her, that a spoon of water might drown. You'd want to be watching her, Mrs O'Brien, I'd say. You'd never know but the tay might be wet there already!'

But this was too much for Milly.

'Cathleen,' she said in a voice dripping with ice. *'That will be enough!'*

Reunited in December, Jonathan and Aoibheal's time together was curtailed because of Christmas festivities on the Fielding side.

Superimposed on Jonathan's agenda was an apparently endless round of parties involving visits to and from uncles, aunts and cousins. He had never before realized how many relations he had, most of them dull.

And as if that wasn't bad enough Hugh and Tony were at their most exasperating, hanging on to him for all they were worth, and following him around.

On one occasion, walking through the wood – the trees dark and denuded of their leaves but their branches crispy with frost – he turned suddenly, just in time to catch sight of the pair of them hot on his heels before they shot behind a bush.

He yanked them out, delivered a stern lecture on the adult need for peace, and despatched them homewards, his equilibrium shattered.

What nonsense this whole Romeo and Juliet procedure was, he thought irritably – the secrecy about his relationship – as if Aoibheal was someone of whom he need feel ashamed.

Conspiracies were almost as bad as aggravation. On second thoughts, perhaps not quite! But disturbing, unsatisfactory elements to have injected into your life.

Seeing Aoibheal, he swung around to the view that it was worth putting up with all sorts of inconveniences in order to be with her.

But on his way home again his exasperation with their vexing situation returned, and he began to think seriously about finding a solution.

At the end of the Trinity term, on 30 June, his life at Oxford would be over. Unless something very unforeseen prevailed he would graduate, take up the offer of work already made to him by his friend Smithers' cousin, who was on the board of a good publishing house in London.

He would be earning money himself – not a great deal of money, to be sure, but an income nevertheless.

Enough for two people to live on? During Hilary term he tried to work out what it would cost to rent a house and pay for living expenses, and concluded sadly that it would be some years before he could consider marriage seriously.

Then, just before Easter, when he was again home in Wimborne, the unexpected happened. His aunt Rose – a favourite relation – died after a stroke. She had been married to an officer in the Indian army, whom Jonathan remembered from his childhood as a strict disciplinarian with no sense of humour. Aunt Rose, on the contrary, had been brimming over with life. Too vivacious by far, according to his father. A flirtatious woman who had led poor, poor Walter a very merry dance. In her drawing-room were innumerable photographs of their days in India, many depicting handsome young officers with whom Aunt

167

Rose was suspected of conducting indiscreet liaisons.

Jonathan, who as a child had been castigated by Uncle Walter for leaving an apple core on an ashtray, sympathized with Aunt Rose.

But now the house at Wimborne was buzzing with new scandal. A trunkful of papers in Aunt Rose's attics had yielded a well-kept secret. It was Uncle Walter who had been a sinner. He had fallen in love with another officer's wife and been hastily transferred from Calcutta to endure the May heat of Madras many years before.

Uncle Walter, having pre-deceased his wife, was not on hand to defend himself against what his relations had to say. Then they found something else to talk about – Aunt Rose's will.

Everything had been left to Jonathan, including a London house.

'She was quite a rich woman,' said Jonathan to Aoibheal. 'I just didn't realize she loved me that much.'

'Making up to you for the trouble you got into over the apple core!' Aoibheal teased.

But Jonathan was looking serious.

He and Aoibheal had agreed months ago that they should marry. He couldn't remember proposing to her – it was just that they had quite naturally come to that conclusion.

But that had only been agreement in principle. Now, thanks to Aunt Rose, he had money of his own.

'This changes everything,' he said. 'I'm in a position to get married. There's nothing to stop us – except for your father and mine! Even they can't prevent us doing as we like. I just can't stand the thought of the fuss! Still, I suppose I'll have to take the bull by the horns sooner or later.'

'Why?' demanded Aoibheal.

April, she thought, was the most exciting month of the year. That morning she had been woken by a chorus of birds. Looking up at the stable roof she had caught sight of a swallow building a nest out of feathers and fresh twigs. There were new lambs in the fields.

And now Jonathan and she could get married!

'If we were home in Ireland you would have brought me a sprig of mint today,' she said, 'and held it in your hand until it was moist to ensure everlasting love. Then you'd have to hold my hand for a full ten minutes without either of us speaking a word. It's just as well you didn't because I need to say something. We don't have to tell anyone about our plans, not even Milly. What we should do is elope!'

'Elope?'

'To save all the fuss. The two of us can go off and get married quietly and write later explaining what we have done. After all, we're independent now.'

'That's true,' said Jonathan. 'Present everyone with a *fait accompli* which they'll just have to accept. And, as you say, by eloping we won't involve Mrs O'Brien – cause trouble between your father and her. What a sensible girl you are, Aoibheal – I've always thought so! And now that I'm a rich man I'm going to take you on honeymoon to Paris. What do you feel about that? You did tell me that, after listening to your brother's descriptions of it, you wanted to see it for yourself.'

'I did! I do! I even know of a good hotel where we can stay. Daniel gave me the address. But I never thought when I made a note of it that I'd be staying there as your wife!'

'Not until the end of the Trinity term,' Jonathan told

169

her. 'Now, this is what we will do. You must make an excuse to Mrs O'Brien. Tell her you're going to London for the day – find a reason.'

'To meet Kate Keegan.'

Kate had been to Wimborne three times over the last few months.

'Good. Meet Kate if you like.'

'I could stay with her,' Aoibheal said thoughtfully. 'And then, while I'm there, you and I could get married and Aunt Milly will be able to feel I didn't tell her a lie.'

'Excellent,' said Jonathan. 'Remember term finishes on 30 June.'

Two days before then, on the twenty-eighth, came the news from Sarajevo that Archduke Ferdinand and his wife had been assassinated – shot.

It was a shocking and barbarous crime, but to Jonathan and Aoibheal, as to most of the world, it seemed just that, a nine days' wonder.

Their plans went ahead.

'*Married?*'

'Yes! Very quietly, before we came to France.'

It was fun, Aoibheal thought, to be shocking her brother Eugene. Jonathan, who was just getting over his own astonishment on learning, at the altar, of his wife's true age, had been surprised that she would want to look Eugene up.

'You haven't seen him for years,' he had protested. 'I thought you detested him.'

'I did,' she had said, 'but I want to see whether or not I was wrong. I was very young when we last met and maybe we've both changed.'

Now she was confronting Eugene as a married woman across a table at Maxim's, which she thought was a very attractive place done up in mauve and

green and mustard with dim mirrors and exotic droop-
ing flowers.

'*Belle époque* décor,' Eugene had already explained
in his usual off-hand way.

Musicians were playing in the background. In the
small space available Jonathan and Aoibheal would
be able to dance.

'But surely you're not of age?' Eugene went on. 'I
can never remember the age of consent. In France it's
fifteen, but in England I thought it was a year older.
In which case . . .'

'But I am sixteen,' protested Aoibheal. 'Surely you
know that. My birthday's in *September*. I'll be seventeen in another three months.'

Jonathan raised an eyebrow.

'Will you really? Well, I wouldn't say too much
about that if I were you. Do try the chartreuse of
partridge – it is quite superb. Or perhaps the Sole
Albert?'

'The sole, I think,' Aoibheal said, frowning.

Surely it didn't matter that much, her being sixteen?
Some of the elation went out of the evening, as if
Eugene had blown a candle out. I still don't feel at
ease with him, she thought.

But Jonathan was chatting away to him, answering
his questions about Milly and Wimborne Manor, and
Aoibheal, tugging her thoughts away from the possibility that, after all, Milly might be angry with her for
what she had done, turned them to Georgina.

I'm really missing her, she thought. The only unfortunate thing about my marriage to Jonathan is being
parted from that child.

'– seems to be getting along very well,' Jonathan
said, perhaps of Wimborne estate.

Aoibheal, attempting to concentrate on the conversation at the table, was distracted again by the likeness

between Eugene and Georgina.

Really amazing, she thought – much more so than exists between Georgina and myself and Georgina and Daniel, and that I thought strange enough.

'What's the matter, darling?' said Jonathan tenderly, catching sight of her face.

'I was just thinking how alike Eugene and Georgina are,' Aoibheal said innocently. 'You haven't seen her, have you, Eugene? She's so like you! Milly must have adopted her just because of that.'

Eugene jumped – actually levitated – dropping his napkin on the floor and inadvertently knocking over his glass of wine. Instantly, a waiter came, smiling unctuously, and expertly mopping up and taking away the shattered pieces of glass.

And all the while Aoibheal was thinking that Eugene himself looked shattered. Worried about making a spectacle of himself, she supposed – but, after all, it *was* only a glass that was broken and no one else was taking the slightest notice of them.

'Don't worry,' she said soothingly to her brother.

He looked at her coldly.

'I wasn't at all worried!' he said. 'I was – just considering something, thinking about the implications. Making plans.'

He dabbed at his mouth with the fresh napkin which had just been placed on his lap. The service was superb, even if you wished the waiter would be less ingratiating and more human.

'Plans for what?'

Eugene shrugged. 'Nothing. Jonathan, what do you think – '

They spoke of the recent assassination, of the burial in the rain at the castle of Arstetten of the Archduke and his wife.

It was the sixth day of July. On the previous day

172

a meeting had been held at Potsdam to discuss the situation between Austria and Serbia.

'An ultimatum to Serbia was decided upon,' Eugene insisted.

'And Russia, of course, is urging Serbia to accept Austria's demands.'

'I've been reading that the German ambassador in Vienna is also proclaiming that Austria must settle with Serbia, for once and for all,' Jonathan said.

It was all very relaxed. Aoibheal's Sole Albert was mouth-watering. She felt less tense about being with Eugene again.

It was over coffee that the conversation returned to the question of Aoibheal's age.

'You did say you'd be *seventeen* in September?' said Eugene, putting down his cup. 'I wasn't mistaken about that?'

'No, you weren't.'

Eugene said, 'I'm sorry. You see, it's a shock . . .'

'A shock? Why should it be a shock? I can't understand why you didn't know my exact age before.'

'Well, I wouldn't, would I?' Eugene said clearly. 'Daniel and I wouldn't have been told.'

'But why ever not?'

It seemed to Aoibheal that Eugene did not reply for a very long time. She stared at him, mystified, wondering what on earth could be causing such an *impasse*.

'Why not?' she eventually asked him again.

He grimaced, reluctant, apparently, to provide the answer to her question – sighed.

'You're sure you want to know?'

'Of course I want to know,' she said, agitated now.

Eugene bit his lip. 'Well, if you insist . . . You see, I've just realized that our mother was not married to Cathal when you were conceived. My father wasn't

173

dead. In other words, our mother was an adulteress, Aoibheal. You see why I was shocked! Thank you for this evening, you two. Good to talk to you. And thank you, Aoibheal, for letting me catch up on all the news.'

'DIDN'T you tell me Dermot O'Brien was insane?' said Jonathan when they were alone at the Hôtel de la Place du Louvre. 'So how can you blame your mother for what she did – or your father either?'

'I don't,' Aoibheal said. 'It's just difficult – things not being what you thought . . . And Eugene really is shocked.'

'Is he? I wonder. He's a strange fellow, that brother of yours. Clever and talented, but he has a nasty streak. I wouldn't put it past him to have known this all along. He must have had some idea of your birth month! I don't believe he's just found it out.'

Aoibheal had undressed down to her knickers and embroidered linen brassière. Jonathan looked at her approvingly. But this, unlike those that had gone, was not the night for love.

'He couldn't be that bad,' said Aoibheal, 'not even Eugene. It's terrible, the thought I have. You know Dermot O'Brien died after drinking too much laudanum. Do you think they – my parents – drove him to it? Maybe they even forced him to do it, for all I know!'

'No!'

'But how do we know that? They must have been desperate, knowing that she was pregnant with me.'

'Not that desperate,' said Jonathan soothingly. 'People in Limerick would have thought Dermot O'Brien was your father if he had lived. Even mad men make love!'

'Don't talk like that! You'll make me think that he

was my father, not Cathal at all!'

'No, I won't. Because that doesn't make sense. There would be no need for your mother to hide that fact from you, if that was the case.'

Secretly, he thought – Damn Eugene O'Brien. He's a black sheep, I know he is. I was watching his face while he was speaking this evening. He wasn't shocked. He was taking pleasure in hurting Aoibheal!

Dear Mother in Heaven but Cathal will kill me, thought Milly, on learning of Aoibheal's marriage. He and Rosaleen will have had a letter from that scamp by now, similar to the one she wrote to me spelling it all out.

He won't be disarmed by Aoibheal's revelations. He'll be hopping mad on two counts – one that his pride and joy has got married so young, and two that she has had the audacity to wed an Englishman!

The second will be the worst! He'll be over in Whitegate this minute composing an accusation addressed to me while Rosaleen tries to talk him out of it.

You were responsible for her, he'll be writing. I trusted *you* to guard her and now look what's happened!

He's a lovely young man, Cathal O'Mahoney. You'd like him yourself if you only put away your prejudices for a while. He's just the man for Aoibheal. It's his character that should be important to you, not his nationality, and you can't fault that.

Will you listen to me?

Cathal couldn't be reasoned with, even in Milly's imagination. So let him get on then with his letter while she considered another, more important point raised in Aoibheal's letter.

The children had not been married in church. A registry office wedding would not suffice for a good

176

Catholic girl, and a church officiation would have to be arranged for when the couple got back from Paris.

There was no Catholic church in Wimborne. On Sundays Milly attended Mass at the Cistercian nunnery at Stapehill three miles away.

I shall talk to Father Fleming next Sunday, Milly thought, and arrange for a nuptial Mass to be held in Wimborne Manor. That – even if it won't make much difference to Cathal – will keep God happy anyway.

Despite her apprehension about Cathal, Milly herself was happy already. Aoibheal and Jonathan were meant for each other, she thought.

Their romance put her in mind once more of herself and Tom.

And their elopement – motivated by a desire to avoid arguments on both sides of their families – was perfectly understandable.

Cathal, if he were a more reasonable man, would see that point of view.

'What do you mean, "be reasonable?" She's run off and married some eejit of an Englishman and you expect me to stand up and drink to their health! I'll do no such thing. I'm going to write to Milly O'Brien this minute and tell her what I think. Was it reasonable of her to allow this to happen? Tell me!'

'All right so – I will!' said Rosaleen hotly. 'First of all an eejit wouldn't be able to write the kind of a letter he sent to the two of us, secondly, since there's no point in crying over spilt milk, why take it out on Milly, and thirdly, won't you look on the positive side instead and consider that the marriage might work out?'

'Can you see any *reason* why it should?' Cathal replied. 'Aoibheal is only a child still. This fellow has carried her off! I've a good mind to go over to France

177

and beat the hell out of him.'

'Do that,' said his wife, 'and I'll be gone when you come back.'

This was fighting talk, and Cathal paid heed to it. He dropped going to France and contented himself with muttering about the beating Jonathan should have.

'And don't you write to Milly either,' said Rosaleen, tilting back her head to glare up at him. 'Remember how good to you she was in the past, taking you into Crag Liath and hiding you when you were on the run. *She* didn't approve of *you* then but she looked after you. Never forget that!'

'I don't!'

Cathal climbed down. To Milly's subsequent relief an accusation was not sent. But he remained hostile in his heart towards the Englishman.

Not with Rosaleen . . . Within the hour they were both ostensibly calm and walking around the lake.

'Harry Fielding's nephew,' Rosaleen said. 'The Fieldings never did take to Milly. What will they think of us?'

'Good God, look at this, Joan!' Jonathan's father bellowed on receipt of The News. 'Fellow's eloped. Married that O'Brien woman's child!'

'Richard! The child *is* a child. Let me see.'

Joan Fielding took Jonathan's letter from her husband's hand.

'It's not her child – of course,' she said, holding on to her self control with difficulty. 'It's not even a relation of Mrs O'Brien's. She's a young Irishwoman who was staying in the manor – '

'Probably a housemaid!'

I must sit down, Joan thought. A housemaid? Oh, surely not?

'Strange name, too!' said Richard. 'Anvil or something. Must have come out of a forge!'

He guffawed.

'The boys saw her.'

'Who?'

'Hugh and Tony. They told me they spotted Jonathan with a girl. They followed them into the wood. She was small and pretty, they said.'

'Made a fool of him, I suppose,' Richard said. 'Whole thing doubtless arranged by The O'Brien. Damn' woman. Still, too late to do anything about it now.'

Joan said weakly, 'I must write to them. Whatever she's like, she *is* Jonathan's wife.'

In Paris the newly-weds, like everyone else in the non-Teutonic world, were surprised by the ultimatum which the Austro-Hungarian government presented to Belgrade on 3 July. In reparation for the Sarajevo murders and as a safeguard for the future, Austria was demanding that Serbia should be degraded to the position of a vassal state.

Germany announced that she approved the Austrian note, while the outside world wondered why and what was going on.

Advised by Russia, Serbia complied, accepting most of the Austrians' demands, although not all. But whether Serbia stood firm or went to the extreme limit of complaisance hardly mattered: Austria wanted to fight.

Perhaps it was not really so serious, suggested Aoibheal, her equilibrium restored by another week in Paris. Jonathan did not agree. France was preoccupied with the trial of Madame Caillaux for the murder of the journalist Gaston Calmette. It was said that Monsieur Calmette had intended to publish incriminating

179

documents about the accused's husband, the Minister of Finance, Joseph Caillaux, in his newspaper, *Le Figaro*. The nation's attention was on the impending political scandal rather than on the demands made by Austria.

In Britain the Buckingham Palace Conference on Ulster had broken down. There was rumour that this could lead to civil war with the Ulster Volunteers, powerful and so well trained and armed, forcibly removing the nine counties should Home Rule be introduced.

In Petrograd there was a massive strike with barricades in the streets.

Jonathan thought that the Austrians and the Germans had chosen their moment cunningly. It would be pleasant to be securely back in England, he and Aoibheal, ready to move into their London house.

The honeymoon was over.

'Let's go home,' he said, and Aoibheal agreed.

'But I'd feel happier if you and I went to Wimborne first, before settling in London,' she said. 'I feel bad about Milly. I know she wrote us that nice letter wishing us happiness, but I want to *see* her, Jonathan. I want to make sure they're not blaming her back in Whitegate for allowing me to elope. And I want to see Georgina, too – I miss her very much.'

'Then we'll go to Wimborne,' said Jonathan. 'And I suppose we must visit my family as well.'

His mother too had written the newly-weds a loving letter, and so had Rosaleen.

Before they left Paris, the state of the world took a turn for the worse. Austria declared war with Serbia. In Dublin, troops of the King's Own Scottish Borderers came into conflict with gun-runners from the National Volunteers. The German Emperor, who had been in Norway, returned to Berlin amidst rumours that civil war *was* about to begin in Britain.

England did not seem chaotic. The country was warm and serene, the trees luxuriant, and calves were wandering in the fields. Roses were in bloom.

'I'd forgotten how beautiful England is,' Aoibheal said softly. 'I used to think Ireland was the loveliest land – but now I'm not sure.'

'But you're sure you can settle here? You're not going to wake up in the middle of the night and think about Whitegate and run away from me?'

'You forgot you are talking to a woman of the world! I was born in New York!'

'You've certainly lost your American accent and acquired a real brogue!'

Laughing together they arrived back at Wimborne Manor, and Milly ran out with her arms stretched wide.

'Darling children – you're back!'

She looks tired, Aoibheal thought worriedly. Under her jubilation she's upset about something. What is it? And she thought of her father with a sinking heart. They've quarrelled, he's furious with her, and it's all my fault . . .

'Aoibheal!' shrieked a shrill voice, and a small, dark-haired figure ran on to the porch. 'Aoibheal – Aoibheal, you're home!'

'Georgina!'

They hugged, kissed.

'Ah, here you are at last!' said a voice.

'You see,' said Milly delightedly. 'Eugene is here!'

She had been equally delighted two days earlier when, without any warning, Eugene had turned up at the door.

'My darling boy,' she had said then, 'what brings you back? No, don't tell me! I'm just so pleased that you're here!'

181

So that's all right then, Eugene had thought.

He put his bags down and enveloped her in his arms. 'I've *missed* you all these years!'

'You were very bad to stay away so long,' Milly said and holding him by the hand as if he was, indeed, a boy again, she led him into the drawing-room. 'Cathleen will make up your room.'

And look at you as if you were an angel dropped from Heaven, she thought, when Cathleen had been found. Perhaps not an angel so much – and there's more of the Devil in that girl's bold green eyes.

'Mr O'Brien will sleep in the Chinese room,' she said sternly, her own hazel eyes warning Cathleen to remember who she was. 'And tell Cook there will be one extra in the house.'

'Yes, Mam,' said Cathleen, but the way she left the room, with a twitch of her comely hips, said something else again.

I'll have trouble with that girl, yet, thought Milly. I wouldn't be at all surprised one day to hear that she is pregnant. If she is, I will regard it as her fault entirely – it's not like poor Kate. What possessed me to employ so blatant a hussy?

'You're looking extremely serious all of a sudden,' said Eugene teasingly. 'Does my homecoming have such a sombre effect on you?'

'My dear boy – what an appalling thought! Naturally it doesn't. Now what news have you got for me? I had a letter from Aoibheal quite recently saying that you and she and Jonathan were all together in Paris. My dear, what a shock the news of their marriage was – but quite exciting as well. They're so in love although, of course, she *is* terribly young.'

'Yes,' said Eugene thoughtfully, 'she *is* young. Still, I'm sure it will all work out well. Oh, it is splendid being with you again . . .'

Then the door flew open and a small hurricane hurled into the room.

This – is – my – daughter, said Eugene to himself, repeating the words very slowly in his mind.

He had not expected Georgina in the flesh to be quite such a shock.

It was not only the likeness, although that was so extraordinary that he could not understand why Aunt Milly did not see it too.

Georgina was wearing a white kimono hand-embroidered smock which just covered her knees, white three-quarter socks and bar fastened shoes; and he, who despised sentiment, who believed himself invulnerable, thought also of angels. Though the face is that of the child in a Michelangelo Buonarroti marble Madonna and the body (that dress!) is derived from a Japanese pillar-print, he thought wildly, hanging on for dear life to familiar references.

'Who are you?' his daughter demanded.

His stomach lurched. She was, just as Aoibheal had said, almost unbelievably sweet.

'I'm Eugene O'Brien,' he managed to say. (Not 'Your father' – oh no!)

'Daniel's twin!' said Georgina triumphantly, proud at working this out.

She continued to stare at him wrinkling her nose like a rabbit.

'Don't do that, dear,' said Milly complacently.

Aunt Milly, dictating to his child!

'Why not?' Georgina asked in a reasoning voice. 'He's got a very nice face!'

Your face – I have your face, a voice in his mind screamed out. As one day this little girl might cry out at him.

'Thank you,' said Eugene weakly.

Odd how this encounter induced a lump in the throat.

'My poor boy, you must be parched!' exclaimed Milly sympathetically. 'Georgina, dear, please ring for refreshments. And then perhaps you'd like to have a nice rest, Eugene darling. We can talk to our hearts' content when you've recovered from your long journey from France.'

Recover, he thought – after this experience? But he went upstairs after tea and began to unpack his bags.

'Could I maybe be helping you?'

Cathleen, the maid who had been contemplating him with such obvious intent downstairs. And in front of Aunt Milly too! He had to admire her nerve.

Free of an audience, they considered each other again. She was a good-looking woman, with her thick black hair and pert face and the expression in her dark eyes that said she didn't give a tinker's damn about any man Jack. She was hot-foot after him all right – not a new experience for Eugene. What intrigued him was her cheek.

For a moment he was tempted. But she was too much of a risk.

Not now. Not when he had his plan to set in motion. But maybe some day . . .

'Not this time,' he said, his eyes still on her, his tone making it perfectly plain that it wasn't unpacking they were discussing. 'But I'll keep your offer in mind.'

'Do that so,' she said to him, and the door clicked shut.

When she had gone he took out of his luggage his mother's old handbag and put it on the bed. There it was – his collection. Letters from this one and that one, all of them expressions of the same pain. The stupidity of women, each one thinking herself unique, capable of melting his stony heart.

When all he actually wanted was evidence of their pain.

Well, that he had all right.

The bag had become a necessity – something he had to have with him before he went to sleep. As Georgina, doubtless, took with her a doll or a teddy-bear.

How peculiar, he thought – I suppose Aunt Milly will ask me to see her baby tucked up in bed tonight, all angelic in a white frilly nightgown or whatever it is that little girls wear to sleep. Why does this picture move me so much? The last thing I had foreseen was my becoming sentimental about that child. What *is* this primitive link that makes me – of all people – have such an unexpected response?

He took off his clothes and folded them neatly over a chair in his usual meticulous way, and got into bed. Damn! He had forgotten to draw the curtains and the summer sun was streaming into the room. He got up again irritably and went to the window.

It overlooked the orchard. And half-way up an apple tree, perched on a branch and reaching with one plump hand for a juicy apple, was Georgina.

What if she should fall? He was about to open the window, call to her to stay where she was, not under any circumstances to move until he could come downstairs and assist her, when Milly, coming out of the house, acted on his behalf.

'Darling, do be careful! I have told you before not to climb trees!'

'It's not a tree, Mama!' he heard Georgina reply. 'It's a ship. I'm sailing to India!'

'Perhaps you are. But please stay still . . .'

Eugene put his hand to his brow. It was covered in moisture.

He pulled the curtains together and returned to bed. But he did not manage to sleep.

It was the following evening before he effected his plan. In carrying it out, his genuine feeling for Georgina came in useful.

'I must put her to bed,' Milly said. 'Say goodnight to Eugene, darling. You may kiss him if you like.'

'I do like,' replied Georgina, and came solemnly up to him to peck him on the cheek.

'You're very, very sweet,' he said to her, wishing that he could have her all to himself.

'What's the matter with you?' enquired Georgina innocently. 'You're sad! Look, Mama, Eugene's upset!'

'*Uncle* Eugene,' Milliora corrected automatically. 'It's more respectful. He *is* a grown-up.'

'Uncle Eugene. Why are you upset, Uncle Eugene?'

Before an answer could be found to this question, Georgina had been sent to bed.

'What *is* the matter, Eugene?' Milly asked then. 'You're not sick, are you, darling? Please tell me.'

'I can't.'

'Of course you can. You can tell me anything. You must, Eugene. If you don't I'll worry all night. You know I will.'

'I don't think I can tell,' Eugene said with every semblance of frankness. 'I mean – there are limits, after all. Some things we have to keep to ourselves.'

'*Why?*'

Milly, he saw, was alarmed – probably wondering if he had a terminal illness or (could she be so indelicate even in her thoughts?) contracted venereal disease through an association with a prostitute in Paris.

'It's impossible,' he said, 'it would cause you such pain. And yet I must admit it's hard not being able to

186

speak about it with someone I trust.'

It was at this point that he put to the test a piece of advice he had picked up from the stage. Tears will come into your eyes if you gaze into a light. The sitting-room curtains were drawn, more for atmosphere than because it was dark, and the lamps had been lit.

He stared intently at one of them and found himself blinking. Two tears, quite enough for the time being, ran down his cheeks.

'Eugene! Oh, this is dreadful! I insist – I *order* you to tell me what's wrong!'

He allowed himself to be coaxed. Eventually, at what he surmised to be the right moment, he said, 'I know that Georgina is Kate's child. I'm just distressed at the way Daniel let her down.'

'*Daniel*!' Milly heard herself cry out. 'Oh, my God! Eugene – how do you know?'

She was standing up. He rose from his chair and went to her, taking her hand in his.

'He told me – when he was in Paris this summer. It just came out. He would die if he thought you knew.'

'I'm sure he would,' Milly said grimly. 'And did he tell you how desperate he made Kate feel when she was pregnant – did he tell you that?'

Eugene nodded his head.

'I know . . . I suppose I always knew Daniel was capable of inflicting such pain. Was she so desperate? That's terrible – really terrible. But she never told you the truth?'

'No. She always refused to disclose Georgina's father's name. Poor child. It's all so much worse than I thought. But of course, now that I think of it, it all makes sense. Daniel was in London that Christmas. They would have been together then. Extraordinary –

187

and I thought *she* rejected him! So did everyone else. How clever of him to have given that impression – to have deceived us all. To have tricked even me . . .'

That does anger her, thought Eugene, watching her face. She was always egocentric and vain. How annoying for so self-complacent a woman to find herself bamboozled! How furious she would be if she found out the real truth!

'I'm sorry – so very sorry to bring you such horrible news!'

'My dear boy, you were right to tell me. It would have been quite wrong for you to have suppressed the facts. Apart from the fact that I'm pleased to know about both Georgina's parents. She's Rosaleen's grandchild, Eugene! But no one else must know.'

'No one else will know,' Eugene assured her, thinking – that suits me.

Certainly not Daniel! Sorry, old fellow, he thought, but it's either you or me. *I'm* not going to lose my inheritance.

'Please don't betray my confidence. Don't tell Daniel you know.'

'No,' she said vaguely, obviously deep in thought about another aspect of the affair. 'No, I won't. That wouldn't achieve anything.'

'Nothing!' said Eugene, 'And it would destroy my relationship with Daniel. That is still very important to me, Aunt Milly. After all, he's my twin.'

'You're so good,' Milly said in the same detached voice. 'But you mustn't expect *me* to feel the same about that young man. No, don't have any regrets about confiding in me. That was essential. But now justice must be done! No, don't look at me like that, Eugene. I couldn't possibly allow Daniel to go unpunished after what he has done – nobody in their sane senses would. In any case I've come to a decision.'

'What are you going to do?'

She straightened her shoulders and slightly raised her red-gold head, sticking out her chin.

'It's perfectly straightforward,' she told him. 'I cannot permit Daniel to profit from my estate. Crag Liath will be yours – yours alone. Tomorrow I'll go to London and make a new will.'

Neat, thought Eugene – a *chef-d'oeuvre*, a *tour de force* which yields an unexpected bonus, and a big one at that! What next? Wimborne Manor made over to me as well? But she didn't mention that.

Still, there's plenty of time to work on her sympathy. I've done the wise thing leaving Paris at this time. I must visit Wimborne a lot over the next year – make a fuss of Aunt Milly. This place is worth a fortune – far more than Crag Liath; especially at the present time with land in Ireland being sold to the tenants.

I can imagine living here – it's an elegant place. I'd forgotten what it was like.

Backing plays, living partly here and partly in London. The best of both worlds. And painting . . .

He yawned, stretched pleasurably out – and was arrested by a cry.

A child's cry, from next door.

But that's the nursery, he thought – that's Georgina in there.

'Mama! Come – I've had a horrible dream! An elephant is trying to get into the room!'

Footsteps in the corridor. Milly's voice. 'Never mind, dear. You see, I told you it was a mistake to go to India on that ship!'

He turned on to his left side telling himself to be sensible rather than emotional. He *had* pulled off a *coup*.

189

But he was left with a sense of treachery relating not to his twin brother but to his little girl.

'Eugene didn't stay long,' said Aoibheal when she and Jonathan were installed in the house. 'Why did he have to rush off?'

'It's something to do with a play,' Milly said. 'He had a meeting in London, I think. The more I read the papers these days the more worried I get. Have you been following the news? Germany is steering the world into dangerous waters. If she becomes involved any more in this issue, and then France, all the European interests could be implicated. So our Foreign Secretary Sir Edward Grey maintains. There's already partial mobilization in Russia, and the Germans may use it as a *casus belli*. Did you learn Latin at school, Aoibheal? I was never confident about the education you received on that island!'

And you are hiding something, Aoibheal thought – I know you are. There's something personal worrying you as well as this talk of war.

But it was the possibility of war that was troubling Jonathan.

On 31 July, news reached Berlin that Russia had ordered a general mobilization. In turn the Emperor decreed a *Kriegsgefahrzustand*, a state of danger of war. Ultimatums went out to Petrograd and to Paris – would neutrality be maintained in a Russo-Germanic war?

The King of England was to receive messages, too; from Emperor William stating that Germany regarded herself committed to such a war; and from the President of the French Republic appealing to Britain to declare herself on the side of France in hope of preserving peace.

The tranquillity of the summer was shattered. The

country quivered with a sense of impending doom. The British market was in a bad state, the bank rate rose to ten per cent and the Stock Exchange closed.

Finally, war commenced between Russia and Germany. The latter mobilized – France followed suit. An ultimatum was sent to Belgium too, Germany stating that the French intended to march.

'And now our Naval Reserves have been called out,' Milly said in an angry voice. 'Have you taken note of the way that that wretched man Mr Lloyd George has suddenly changed sides? He used to be an opponent of war. Now he's talking about poor Belgium and a threatened outrage on a little people!'

'Public feeling is with him,' said Jonathan mildly.

'Exactly! That's why he's taking this view! Politicians are all alike. You can trust none of them. Before we know where we are they'll have us involved in war! It's appalling, Jonathan. I'm surprised to hear that *you* are supporting Mr Lloyd George!'

'I didn't say that,' Jonathan protested, and caught Aoibheal's eye.

Milly O'Brien, he thought, was a bag of nerves since they had returned from Paris, and yet Aoibheal had assured him that it was nothing to do with them.

Aoibheal's parents, although startled by their marriage, had not blamed Milly in any way.

Events over the next week put Milly's troubles out of his mind. Violating Belgium's neutrality, Germany crossed its frontier. On 4 August, England declared war. The first Highland regiments of the British Expeditionary Force moved into France.

These developments formed the main topic of conversation when Jonathan took his bride to make her acquaintance with his parents.

His mother did not let him down. She greeted Aoibheal with real warmth, as he might have expected. His father scarcely seemed to absorb the fact that Jonathan had a wife.

News – just received – that his eldest son had been awarded a First was greeted with a vague, 'Good – good!'

Even to Jonathan, Oxford might have been part of another planet, so irrelevant did his time there seem to what was happening today.

'You going to join up?' his father demanded tersely. 'Country needs young men like yourself. Germans liable to serve from age of seventeen. Good thing if we had introduced such a system here. Army there very efficient.'

'So is the British navy.'

Richard ignored this comment.

'Germany's manpower for war greatest in the world.'

'What about Russia?'

'Quality of her organization, my boy – that's what counts. Best brains in Germany directed to military art these last fifty years.'

There was no arguing with this truth, even if Jonathan had felt inclined to do so.

His father was mumbling away about the French, whose army had been the object of many experiments in the past forty years.

'Our British regulars most professional in the world,' he said when the French had been dealt with. 'Problem is those fools at the Treasury! Officers at schools pressing for the use of rifle-grenades, bombs, Véry pistols and so on, but the idiots rebuffed them . . .'

The trouble is that the old man is right, Jonathan thought, for once in step with his father's thinking. People are saying that the total manpower of France, Russia and Britain, along with Belgium and Serbia, is almost double that of Germany and Austria. But the disparity is very much less if you consider the immediately mobilizable armies.

If this war is not won quickly by our side, if it lengthens out, where the hell are we then?

'Will you join up?' Aoibheal asked in a small voice when they were walking back to Wimborne Manor.

'Maybe. It depends how long the war lasts. We'll see.'

'But you are going to take up the offer of that job?'

'Aoibheal . . .' He stopped.

The world of publishing, too, seemed to have receded.

'*Sang-froid anglais!*'

'What did you say?'

'That's what you exercise!' Aoibheal said. 'Admirable self-control! But *I* know what you're thinking. You can't hide from me! You are thinking of serving, aren't you?'

'I think I must. This evening I thought that I should try for a temporary commission. You have to be recommended by two officers but that wouldn't be a problem. My father could arrange that. He'd be proud to do so. And then I suppose I would have to take an examination for Sandhurst . . .'

'In spite of having obtained a First.'

Not saying, 'What about me?'

In bed he returned to the topic of war.

'If I go you won't want to be in London on your own, will you? I imagine you would want to stay here, with Milly and Georgina. In which case – '

'We could rent the London house,' said Aoibheal. 'Although we don't know how long you would be away.'

She was trying to be brave. Even Cathal, she thought, would admire *sang-froid anglais*! Her father had not rushed into print, castigating her for marrying an Englishman, but his letters were cool and hurtful, indicative of the chasm that had opened up between them as a result of her marriage. Rage would have been preferable.

And if I went back to Whitegate, would the breach be healed? she wondered. But I can't. Surely Cathal would understand that I need to be here, near Jonathan's roots?

When he returns we will go to Ireland together.

But when will that be?

'Let's not go on thinking any more about the war,' said Jonathan after a minute.

He pulled her into his arms.

Pictures of a blue-eyed Kitchener, pointing his finger and reminding men, 'Your King and Country Need You', were going up on billboards and hoardings.

But Jonathan had already received his commission by then.

'You will have to come to London with me so I can have my uniform made,' he said to Aoibheal.

There was a queue at tailoring establishments from regular customers, all joining up.

I am married to Temporary Second-Lieutenant Fielding of the Second Brigade of the Worcestershire Regiment, Aoibheal reminded herself.

It was a famous regiment which had its origins in the *fyrd* of Saxon times – a shire or country force.

Jonathan said that in Queen Elizabeth's reign it had furnished men to beat off the Spanish threat.

'But the Spaniards never landed so they weren't required to fight.'

Aoibheal, whose own nationalistic sympathy would have been for Spain, wondered uneasily what her father would think of this.

194

But Jonathan was going on. 'Father wonders why I didn't join the Dorsets. But when I told him our old Head at Eton used some influence to get me into the Worcesters, he more or less subsided.'

Jonathan looked well in uniform. Even Cathal, she thought, would agree that he was manly.

Less attractive was his Sam Browne belt and his Webley Fosberry pistol. With this he could kill. Aoibheal stared at the gun and thought of Jonathan pointing it at another young man of his own age – taking his life.

'Look,' Jonathan said, 'it reloads itself. The cylinder recoils back over a stud. That's how it works.'

To him it was just a device, she thought. Or perhaps that's how he disciplines himself to the idea of war – by reducing weapons to mechanical objects, forgetting about death.

The regiment was billeted north of the Cotswolds. In London they were to part. Jonathan would travel alone while Aoibheal returned to Dorset.

'You'll write as soon as you can?'

'Silly girl – of course.'

Don't cry, she warned herself. He was in the train leaning out. *Sang-froid anglais* . . .

The train edged away.

'Tell me about Jonathan,' Georgina said, sitting on Aoibheal's lap. 'Read me what he says in his letters.'

'I'll tell you instead.'

The regiment had moved into camp. Jonathan made this appear quite jolly.

'Think of us as Boy Scouts.'

But Boy Scouts did not have to endure such hardship.

Aoibheal skimmed over the phrases, trying to find one that would be suitable for a small girl's ears.

'He's sleeping in a tent. They have to go on route marches with full packs on their backs. One day they marched *twenty-six miles* . . .' (And six men died from heart failure on the way.)

'Do they wear red uniforms like in paintings?'

'I'm afraid not – just khaki. That's for the officers. The men wear any old garb.'

'Do they have beards?'

'What gave you that idea? Not in the British army.'

'And will they be riding horses?'

'Not Jonathan.'

'I expect he's enjoying himself,' Georgina said. 'Don't you?'

In a way, I think he is.

'Maybe.'

But soon the regiment moved to billets at Maidenhead. Jonathan wrote to say that the regiment had a Lewis gun now and a trench mortar section.

But perhaps the war would be over before he was required to go to France . . .

'When is he going to *fight*?' demanded Georgina, in the heartless way of children.

'Maybe he won't have to,' Aoibheal said. 'After all, he still has to go to Aldershot, to finish his training in the barracks and camps.'

It wouldn't – couldn't last. What could you do but hope?

AOIBHEAL and Georgina discussed Jonathan. In Aldershot *he* discussed the war.

It was now generally accepted that for years Germany, taking British neutrality for granted, had planned to attack France and to stand on the defensive against Russia.

Jack, one of Jonathan's new friends, had lived in France as a boy and was dubious that the Germans could take the country easily.

'It's naturally strong and fortified. They're finding out now that they can't move as quickly as they'd imagined. Look here on the map and I'll show you what I mean. The French are *here*, protected by the Vosges. Dense woods. And from them this deep escarpment falling into the Rhine Valley. You've got another barrier over *here* formed by the Meurthe and the Moselle and the Meuse.'

That barrier, Jack said, ran at right angles to the German advance. And further north, on either side of Verdun, the heights of the Meuse, rising up to 1,300 feet, commanded the road from Metz.

With the exception of a thirty-mile break – the gap of Charmes, between Épinal and Toul – concrete forts stretched all the way from Verdun to Belfort.

'No modern army could squeeze through the other gap at Belfort, in the south. You'll see – the Germans will come to grief in that high wooded countryside!'

Nevertheless, the Germans, divided into seven armies, plodded resolutely on, surprise-attacked

Liège and, despite heavy casualties, succeeded in entering Brussels.

Both sides were engaged in a race to the sea, both determined to gain control of the Channel ports, repeatedly attempting to outflank each other in the open and mainly level country between the Oise and the ocean.

All too soon, Jonathan – in spite of his wife's hopes – was posted into the thick of it, while his father and brothers applauded from home.

By then the enemy had been pushed back beyond the eastern hillocks overlooking Ypres, and the French were still confident. Much of their *élan* was drawn from the fact that their field-gun, the '75', was vastly superior in rapidity and accuracy of fire to anything yet produced by the Germans.

The enemy, it was felt, was trying to play its last card, ruefully aware that the ace was in the hand held by the Allies.

The Second Worcestershires, part of the reserve of the Second Division of the British Expeditionary Force, were as cheerful and confident as the French as they went into the campaign. The Force was charged with the duty of protecting the retirement of the beleaguered and brave Belgian army which had lost thirty-five per cent of its strength: 20,000 men.

Adding to British confidence were reports of satisfactory achievement in terms of duty. The Lys had been crossed, Armentières secured, and a line held from there to Givenchy on a tiny ridge covering Lille.

The Worcestershires, in those early days, were, just as Jack had predicted, protected by frequent woods.

But soon the division was split. The other units were sent to reinforce the line in the heavy fighting going on further south, while the Worcestershires remained uncommitted. Then their situation also changed.

The village of Gheluvelt, on the high road from Menin to Ypres, was of immense tactical importance and had to be possessed by the Allies lest the Germans thrust through at that point.

Reports, from stragglers and from the wounded, were coming through of heavy fighting in that area. Overwhelming numbers of German infantry were said to be pressing the remnants of five British troops who could now only muster 1,000 troops between them.

Even Jack, who was sanguine by nature, was daunted when they learnt that the Queen's, the Royal Scots Fusiliers, the Welsh and the King's Royal Rifles had been overcome and the South Wales Borderers rolled back on the right.

Gheluvelt was lost. Rumour had it that orders had already been given for the artillery to move back in time for a general retreat.

In the midst of gloom, startling orders came through for the Second Worcestershires. General FitzClarence, Commander of the First Brigade, wished them to counter-attack with the object of re-taking Gheluvelt.

'I say – he's an optimist!' someone exclaimed.

They were a tiny force of eight officers and 360 men. Beyond the village to which they were marching, the Ypres Salient jutted out before bending back to the canal south of Ypres itself.

Unless they bridged the gap, defeated the Bavarians who were holding the village, the cohesion of the British army would be smashed.

Guided by an officer from the Grenadier Guards, the unit moved forward. Soon, through the smoke which rose up from it, they saw the church tower of

Gheluvelt and then around them the wounded and the dead.

Until then Jonathan's experience of war had been limited to periodic skirmishes with the enemy. His reaction on being ordered into Gheluvelt was one of relief. Hanging about waiting for something to happen had been getting on his nerves. The business of being a soldier, the rules, limited rations and unrelieved male company, was reminiscent of school.

But he had never peered around a playground and seen a headless man . . . He ordered himself to look only at the next man marching a yard ahead.

Orders were given to fix bayonets. The smoke emanating from the village was pretty, puffing up into the silver-grey sky. He could hear popping sounds and had to persuade himself that these were the noises of war, not of children's games.

Suddenly shells streamed out, burying themselves in the ground and afterwards exploding, sending up geysers of black dirt. Cries rang out and men fell. A shell rebounded on a stone nearby, bursting on contact, and two men were killed instantly by a lethal spray of shrapnel and shell-casing and broken stones.

He felt insulated from danger himself, exhilarated and yet controlled and self-existent. Flares and signals were going up, balls of green and red and showers that might have been golden rain. Rockets – calling for reinforcements, for retaliation – were being fired. Men screamed for help. He stepped over the body of a limbless man, his arms and legs amputated by flying steel, a transcendent being awaiting his orders from another godlike being.

By then they had reached the ridge at Polderhoek. German shells were falling fast along its crest and the ground was littered with the dead. Major Hankey was brief but incisive. They must cross this dangerous area at the double. It was their only hope.

The leading men, rushing onwards, reached the ridge at a charge.

Caught in the mêlée Jonathan saw them fall – over 100 dying or lying wounded. But the others, he amongst them, still pushed on.

Faster. And then they were on the downward slope and they could see Gheluvelt and they were charging on, wild with madness, through hedges and wire, on to the château grounds.

Gasping and gulping, some of them wiping blood from their heads and bodies, they found they were met by friends.

Believing no British soldiers left, they saw to their astonishment that the remnants of the South Wales Borderers had made a heroic stand.

Major Hankey's voice, when he found it, seemed to Jonathan to come from miles away. But even Aoibheal would have admired his *sang-froid*.

'Fancy meeting you here!' the major remarked.

And Colonel Burleigh Leach of the South Wales Borderers said fervently, 'Thank God you have come!'

The village had been saved.

In the morning Jack, on patrol, found the woman and child. She was young, not more than twenty, and she was hiding with her baby in the attic of their home, having fractured a bone in her leg and been left behind in the general evacuation. For days, Jack said, she had been terrified of what might happen to the baby and herself.

'You'd better bring her in,' Captain Clarke, the adjutant, said. 'The supply unit will take the two of them out.'

'Come and help me carry them,' said Jack to Jonathan.

'You can carry the child!'

'Thanks very much!'

Jack grinned.

'You're a married man. Pity to waste a good-looking woman on the likes of you!'

She *was* attractive, Jonathan thought, when they went to fetch her. She had the kind of slender, dark good looks that he admired, and her skin was particularly smooth, with two natural touches of pink over the cheekbones. More than ever he longed for Aoibheal. The battle of the day before had induced in both Jack and himself an intensified need for sex. They had talked about it, half-laughingly, late in the night when no one could sleep.

What can you do, he thought resignedly and, leaving Jack to carry the young mother, he picked up the child, a little boy of about six months old who, he soon discovered, was leaking like a river in flood. Lucky Jack!

The young woman, however, thought that her rescuer needed a further smile of fortune. When they reached their destination, her hands went to her ears. She was wearing heavy gold earrings inset with bloodstones. As Jonathan stood watching, noticing the unexpected grace of her movements, she undid them and thrust them into Jack's hands.

'Please take,' she said.

'I can't possibly – '

'Please.'

Jack capitulated.

'I'll keep them for luck,' he said. 'And if I survive the war I'll have them made into a ring and wear it and think of you.'

The woman smiled. As Jack said later on, she probably didn't understand much of what he said.

* * *

It made a good story to relate to Aoibheal.

'She was a pretty woman,' he wrote, 'so she made me think of you.'

Other than that he wrote about their victory over the Bavarians.

'. . . who were relaxed after their earlier triumph so we caught them somewhat dispersed. We're cited as heroes but we have paid a high price. One hundred and eighty-seven men killed or wounded.

'Yet life can be quite normal in the middle of war once a battle is over. The leaves on the trees are turning red and in spring I suppose the usual flowers will grow.'

Aoibheal received two other letters that same week. The first of these was from Rosaleen, telling her what was going on in Whitegate and Mountshannon, a newsy letter well laced with gossip and surmise.

Details emerged of a stand-up fight between two neighbours over a piece of land.

'Mr Burke points out – rightly I think – that the land belongs to him. The Burkes, as you know, own a mass of land around these parts. But the other fellow insists that a deal was done over it in their two fathers' lifetimes. The matter is going to court . . .

'Do you remember Connie Maguire – a sandy-haired girl about two years older than yourself? She's going to marry Jim Hartigan, who must be nearing sixty by now! The match is arranged, need I add, and will result in their two farms being merged. He's a lucky fellow, is Jim, there being no boys in the Maguire family to stand in the way of that . . .

'I was talking the other day to Mary Murphy of Mountshannon and she was asking most particularly for you. She couldn't believe that you're married already. Her own daughter is twenty-seven and not a sign of a suitor yet . . .'

Not a word about the war, thought Aoibheal philosophically. For all my parents have to say on the subject, it might not be going on.

Still, I suppose they're better off not fretting.

All the same she detected a note of concern, on another subject altogether, in her mother's letter.

'Your father is very occupied these days – even more than usual – with his own group of friends. They have regular meetings once a week and he's up and down to Dublin once a month as well. I used to love Dublin when I was young, shopping in town and walking over Howth Head, but I hardly ever go there these days. It's not that your father wouldn't encourage me to go, but I know perfectly well if I went with him that he'd be too busy seeing people to do the things *I* like.'

Rosaleen said no more about Cathal's group of friends. One of them, Aoibheal thought, would be Father Michael O'Flanagan, the Sinn Féin priest.

Father Michael had already made his views public about what should be done in terms of the Ulster Unionists: since England had begun to despair of compelling Ireland to love her by force, he said, Ireland was anxious at this stage to start where England had left off.

'We are going to compel Antrim and Down to love us by force . . .'

And Cathal would be amongst those using these methods.

Rosaleen, her daughter thought, must be worried sick about what might happen. And so was she and unable to talk over her fears with anyone, not even in writing to Jonathan in case she added to the stresses already besetting him.

Not Milly who would raise her eyes to Heaven about Cathal and his nationalistic views. And not her new mother-in-law whom she met every now and again for lunch in Wimborne.

She had no alternative but to keep her anxieties to herself. And read the rest of her post.

Her third letter was signed 'Daniel'.

That in itself cheered Aoibheal up. Daniel's letters were determinedly happy. Maybe he wasn't always in a good mood, but he gave that impression in words.

Daniel had never deviated from his desire to return to Clare after he was qualified. This year he had set up practice in Killaloe. He was living at Crag Liath and working long hours, up early in the morning and often called out at night.

None of this appeared to worry him. He was thriving, he said, on the hope of curing ills.

'. . . and in the process learning to distinguish between the sick man and the malingerer! You have no idea, my little sister, how many hypochondriacs we have in the County of Clare! There is a woman in Ballina who is on to me week after week with her imaginary ailments. In the last month I have "cured" her of arthritis, corns, erysipelas and ringworm, the way she can move on to complain about the onset of bronchitis and incipient mumps! In between she fell over a bucket in the back yard and ripped the skin on her knee. Oh, the bleeding! Pint after pint of blood she professed to have lost by the time I got to the place. Now I know people are nearly always frightened by the sight of blood and exaggerate the amount of it that gets spilled, but according to her ladyship four whole pints had been drained out of her and the only pity was that she didn't think of reaching for the offending bucket, in order to fill it up . . .

'You'll appreciate that there are those here who would prefer to consult an unqualified practitioner than a fellow like myself. There have been occasions when the woman of the house has called me in and the man of it has protested, saying that my being called at all was a source of contention between them. One time the man in question said that his own mother knew best and that she had been recommending his drinking the water out of a holy well. "You'll admit now," he said to me, "that St Colman and St Brigid would have more influence with The Almighty than a young runt like yourself, and you just out of that Protestant university, a fact that would only go against you with Himself."

' "Well," I said to him. "The way I see it is this: the more ways we find of contacting Him the better it will be for you, and as for the university, His Holiness in Rome allowed me to go there, so in that sense you could say I have the highest approval on earth." That calmed him, and between St Colman and St Brigid and myself I'd say he'll pull through.

'When are you coming over? We miss you here – the very countryside grieves for you and longs to have you back. A couple of weeks would make it and us feel better, and in that I include Mary Markham and Mrs Cash, both of whom are seeing to it that I am over-fed and well turned out.

'I make contact with our mother as often as I can, and every so often she comes down to Crag Liath, usually on her own. I gather your father is up in Dublin a lot.

'Now write to me. You must have time for it with Jonathan being away – at least I hope you have, thinking selfishly and dying for news. In that sense, Aunt Milly seems to have slipped up. I used to hear from her regularly, but lately not a word. Is *she* sick or what?

Mother says she's fine, that she has post all right, so it does seem strange.

'And what of Kate? I suppose she's doing great things on the stage. I know she's been here now and then these last few years, but on those occasions we haven't met up. Nor have I heard from Eugene, now I come to think of it. Have you? If this neglect goes on I'll be left to conclude that the doctor is reputed to have a contagious disease . . . Write, write, write . . .'

'A surfeit of letters!' observed Milly. 'Aren't you the lucky girl? Who's been writing to you – apart from your husband, of course?'

Aoibheal explained.

'Daniel's pining for news from us,' she said. 'He complains that you're neglecting him!'

She said this lightly, expecting Milly to declare herself guilty in the same jocular manner and promise to write at once.

But Milly did not respond lightheartedly.

'Does he indeed?' she said in an angry voice, and her lips pursed.

Bewildered, Aoibheal went on.

'You must read this letter. It'll make you laugh.'

Silence. Milly looked like one who would never laugh again.

Could she be worried about something?

About Jonathan?

'You haven't bad news for me, have you?' Aoibheal said in a panic.

But –

'My darling child, of course I haven't,' Milly said promptly.

So Aoibheal returned to Daniel's letter.

'He mentions Kate. Complains that she never looks him up when she's home.'

207

Milly glowered again.

This time she did speak.

'That's hardly surprising,' she said. 'If I were Kate I'd never see Daniel again!'

'But why ever not?'

'I can't discuss it,' said Milly. 'And I would prefer you not to raise the matter again.'

Aoibheal remained perplexed. What was Daniel supposed to have done to so upset Kate, not to mention Milly?

Whatever it was – and perhaps it was a minor matter blown up by Milly who had been so jumpy of late – *he* appeared to be as much in the dark as herself.

So there was no point in writing back to him and mentioning Milly's reaction. He would only be upset.

Trouble all over, thought Aoibheal. Even the weather is stormy.

In the next few weeks she began to realize that there were advantages in the bad climatic conditions. The defence of Ypres had resulted in the loss of 50,000 British soldiers. Many battalions, wrote Jonathan, had been completely wiped out.

This meant that the strength of the division was reduced by more than a half.

But it was – miraculously, Aoibheal thought – snowing. Temporarily, fighting ceased.

More relaxed than she had been in months, Aoibheal passed on to Jonathan the current news of those at home, adding her own surmises, silently giving thanks to God for having sent the snow.

B Y the middle of 1915 there was much to tell about Kate. Theatrically she had triumphed. Lilian Baylis, a music teacher from South Africa, was managing the Royal Victoria when she decided to launch a bold experiment, presenting all of Shakespeare's plays at popular prices.

The best producers had been enrolled to ensure her success – and the best performers on whom she could lay her hands.

It was the perfect situation for Kate. She had just been cast in the lead role in *The Taming of the Shrew* when war broke out.

The conflict made little difference to her life. She was aware of certain actors leaving the stage to join up. But the action was in France – far away from the London footlights, and once she had donned her make-up and Shakespearian costume, it was almost impossible to imagine that there was an actual war.

The Taming of the Shrew was followed by *Henry IV* Part Two, and then by *Julius Caesar*.

This programme made it difficult for her to get away to Ireland as she had done several times in recent years, visiting Jamie and her sisters but keeping out of Daniel's way.

On one of those visits she had gone to Dublin and called in at the Abbey, where she had been treated like a long-lost friend. Mr Yeats and Lady Gregory were still talking about the furore that had been stirred up by the first production of Mr Synge's *The Playboy of the Western World*. The story of a vital young girl and a stranger purporting to have killed his father had proved strong meat for Dublin in 1907. The word 'shift' had elicited a hiss from the first-night audience, and when Pegeen Mike tried to burn the stranger, Christy, with a lighted sod, there had been total uproar in the theatre.

The Playboy had gone down in theatrical history and its players had toured America.

Hearing about it, Kate had felt momentarily envious and regretful about her own failure to fit in at the Abbey. And Dublin itself was so lively – the centre of a literary renaissance which permeated not only theatre and literature but also painting. Mr Yeats's brother, Jack, was depicting the same world Synge had painted in drama and prose. William Orpen and Walter Osborne, Sarah Purser and Celia Harrison showed their skill on canvas, too.

The city's literary evenings attracted writers and artists from afar, like Augustus John and Bernard Shaw and John Singer Sargent.

But her regrets had soon faded away. Apart from the satisfaction of her success in London, there she was closer to Georgina.

In between performances, Kate had managed to get to Dorset several times for fleeting visits. Georgina was so big now – so beautiful! And yet there was little of herself in the child. When it came to looks she was Eugene's daughter all right, so that in the pleasure of contemplating her, Kate inevitably also felt pain.

This pang was not because she still loved Eugene. That emotion was gone. But the humiliation he had inflicted upon her remained – a conviction that she was somehow unclean.

She dreaded the thought of ever meeting him again. When he had been in France there had been no likelihood of the two of them running into each other.

But – according to Milly and Aoibheal – Eugene was now back in London. She had been startled to hear that he was seriously involved on some level – Milly and Aoibheal had both been rather vague about the details – in the theatrical world.

And as if that wasn't bad enough, he apparently went to Wimborne frequently.

What a nightmare it was, thought Kate. Eugene going down to see Milly and not knowing that her adoptive daughter was his little girl.

Unless he looked closely at Georgina and surmised . . .

But he had no proof – could not have. Why, anyway, would he want to prove such a thing? He would have no interest whatsoever in Georgina.

The run of *Julius Caesar* was just coming to an end. Good timing, thought Kate. I'll have the whole of Easter off. I'll go down to Wimborne. I need a quiet break. I'll just drop Milly a line. It would be quite frightful if Eugene was planning to be there. Perhaps if I emphasize my need for tranquillity, she'll let me know her plans for that weekend.

Eugene had not intended to go to Wimborne then. When Milly wrote to Kate stating that she would be their only guest for the Easter weekend, she did so in good faith.

Eugene was having difficulty coming to terms with the English theatre after the French. Why wasn't it more serious? Glossing over the fact that, under the cloud of war, audiences might need light diversion, he was exasperated by the success of such productions as John Hartley Manners' *Peg O' My Heart*, starring his wife Laurette, which had run for 710 performances at the Comedy, and *A Little Bit of Fluff*, which appeared

211

likely to play for the duration of the war at the Criterion.

This was not exactly the theatre of the *avant-garde* in which his design talents could best be exercised.

When acquaintances referred to the Shakespearian productions at the Victoria Hall, or the first licensed performance of Ibsen's *Ghosts*, which had caused a storm of protest when it had been presented at the Haymarket the previous year, he shrugged.

Anyway, he thought, I want to be in a position of real power and here I am, temporarily stumped for money with which to go ahead.

He considered asking Milly for a loan and grimaced. She was too parsimonious by nature to respond to such a suggestion, even from him. All he would get was a lecture – loving, to be sure, but a lecture nevertheless – about the necessity for everyone to live within their means.

This was a dull prospect. So he had no intention of going to Wimborne that Easter, or even setting foot out of London.

The Tuesday before the holiday weekend he went to Bond Street to buy himself a velvet smoking jacket. He was fond of clothes. The jacket he bought had silk quilted lapels and cuffs and he liked it so much that he almost gave an order for trousers to match.

But perhaps that would be too much. Such suits were fashionable but Eugene had his own, very definite, ideas about what he wanted to wear. To amuse himself further he also purchased a pullover with a low collar with points.

His hair was brushed back and slightly raised. He despised hair creams and oils but approved of the use of scented toilet water, to make himself smell sweet.

Walking back along Bond Street in the direction of Oxford Street he spotted a little girl. From a distance she bore a remarkable resemblance to Georgina, with the same dark hair.

His heart lurched. Perhaps it *was* Georgina? A woman in a tailor-made suit and a tall torque hat was holding on to her hand.

They were walking ahead of him and he quickened his step in order to catch them up.

But when he reached them he saw that the little girl did not even look that much like Georgina. She had a pale, bad-tempered face and she was dragging her footsteps and whining about being tired.

Not at all like Georgina who had all the energy in the world and was invariably cheerful!

'Come a*long*!' her companion said crossly.

To think he might have had a daughter like that!

Being reminded so forcibly of Georgina he could not get her out of his mind for the rest of the day.

I must see her, he thought. But even then he was still not thinking of the Easter weekend.

His plans for it had included a party after a show. That red-headed actress, Helen something or other, had encouraged him to accept.

But by Wednesday he had decided that Helen could wait. Georgina, not she, came first.

By then, of course, it was too late to write to Milly saying that he would come.

He tried telephoning instead.

An Irish voice – presumably that of Cathleen the maid who continued to make overtures to him when he visited the manor – informed him that Mrs O'Brien was out.

'Tell her I'll be there for Easter,' he said – a message which Cathleen only delivered on the day of his arrival.

On the train between London and Wimborne, two people had asked him why he had not yet joined up,

213

putting him in a bad mood.

'Why should I?' he had said to both of them. 'I'm Irish.'

'What difference does that make?' said the second, an elderly man with a large waxed moustache and a pocket watch with the Albert chain fastened across a fancy knitted waistcoat. He glowered at Eugene from under thick bristling eyebrows.

Eugene shrugged. 'It's none of *our* business if England wishes to embroil itself in war.'

'None of your business!' exclaimed the man with the waxed moustache, almost choking with rage. 'Of course it's your business, young man. Thousands of your fellow countrymen *are* joining up. You one of these supporters of Home Rule, are you? Bill for that has received the Royal Assent, hasn't it? What are you complaining about?'

Eugene, who had no interest in the Home Rule issue, found himself embroiled in a political debate that lasted all the way to Dorset.

He had expected Georgina to accompany Milly to the station to meet him. But Milly was there alone.

She launched into explanation.

'I have been deserted by my darling child!' she said, and although she was attempting to make light of this abandonment, she still sounded piqued.

'Why is that?'

'The lure of the footlights you might say! She stayed at the manor with Kate.'

Could she make a scene? Eugene considered as the car bore him inexorably on towards this unpremeditated meeting. Seeing me after all this time will she over-react – lose her mind – weep – scream?

Anything is possible. Damn business, Kate of all people being down at the manor this Easter.

I should have anticipated it. But somehow I thought – took it for granted – that being an actress she would have something more exciting to do this weekend than coming to Wimborne. From what Aoibheal let drop in Paris, Kate doesn't seem to have been that close to Georgina.

'. . . join up?'

'I'm sorry,' he said to Milly, 'I didn't catch . . . What did you say?'

'I wanted to know when you were going to join up, my darling boy? People have been wondering . . . I told them that an artist has a duty to inspire and entertain in times of crisis rather than to fight, but I did rather think . . . What *do* you feel, Eugene?'

Eugene's eyes narrowed. You stupid woman, he thought. Why the hell can't you leave me alone? Haven't I enough to put up with as it is this evening without you nagging me too?

What he was feeling was fully revealed on his handsome face but Milly, her eyes riveted on the road ahead, did not see it.

Careful now, he cautioned himself. Keep your temper. Tell her what she wants to hear – what she can pass on to the rest of those damn' inquisitive fools.

'You're right, I suppose,' he said quietly. 'You always are, Aunt Milly. The artist's role *is* different. War is anathema to people like us. We feel – *I* feel very strongly that most men are savage by nature and that if you train them to fight – to take life! – they respond only too well. And yet one has a duty to the women and children at home. I have been struggling with this dilemma for months.'

'Poor, poor boy!' said Milly sympathetically.

Competent as she was in most things, she was not that *au fait* with care and was steering towards the ditch.

'Careful!' ventured Eugene, out loud this time. 'You're quite sure you wouldn't like me to drive?'

'Certainly not!' Milly said with a hint of frost in her voice.

But this soon melted.

'Eventually I did attempt to sign on,' continued Eugene. 'There *is* a duty. But I'm afraid they wouldn't have me. I didn't want to alarm you at the time but – well – a small problem. With my chest. It may ease after a few months. Then again it mightn't.'

'With your chest!'

'They don't *think* it's consumption . . .'

'*Consumption!*'

'But there is that possibility. I do hate alarming you, Aunt Milly. Please don't take it too seriously.'

'How could I not?' cried Milly and drove into a hole so that the car shook violently. 'My poor boy. But you must go away immediately to where the air is clear. To Switzerland perhaps.'

'I wouldn't dream of doing so,' said Eugene virtuously. 'Not at a time like this when so many other men are suffering and dying in the war. Please, Aunt Milly, don't take what remains of my dignity away by suggesting such a thing. I'll be all right, I'm sure. As the army said to me – just a couple of months . . .'

'Tell me more about being on the stage,' said Georgina to Kate. 'Can you really make yourself look old just by using make-up? Will you show me? Did you bring your grease-paint down here with you this weekend?'

'Stop bothering poor Kate,' said Aoibheal. 'She's tired, aren't you, Kate?'

She looked it. All because of the war, thought Aoibheal, who at that stage could envisage no other reason for anyone being weary.

The country as a whole was strained. The war was

no longer contained away from England's borders. In January, strange cigar-shaped crafts had appeared in the sky over King's Lynn and Yarmouth. Zeppelins! Silver-grey death carriers, for bombs were carried inside their so-called gondolas and since then no one had felt completely safe any more.

There had been a surge of optimism in March when the British had successfully attacked the Germans at Neuve Chapelle. But artillery preparations had been patchy, grave blunders had been committed and these factors, coupled with bad weather, had added up to a high cost.

Pessimists maintained that the British army was facing an unbeatable enemy. The Germans were admirably disciplined and fought with desperate valour, assisted by many machine-guns, and it was known that they had accumulated gigantic reserves of shell.

'I think I'll turn you into a clown!' Kate was saying.

'Do – do!' said Georgina, excited at the thought. 'What will you use for that?'

'Or maybe a gypsy! That would be pretty with your dark hair. See, I can make your skin quite brown and that will make your teeth look whiter and then we'll put a scarf on your hair, and earrings, and lots of jewellery . . .'

Watching this transformation take place, Aoibheal wondered what had got into Kate today. She did not normally play like this with Georgina, although the little girl, finding her a novelty, tried to engage Kate's attention whenever she came to stay.

Kate is so lovely to look at, Aoibheal thought, peering out of the window to see if there was any sign of Milly and Eugene. Funny that she never married. You would think that she would meet lots of nice men – handsome men – in the theatre.

Some women are just like that, I suppose. They prefer to be single. Perhaps marriage doesn't go with an acting career – wives working at night and rehearsing in the day must make it awkward.

But Kate often mentions theatrical couples who seem to get along very well. Mrs Ellen Terry, on the other hand, has had *three* husbands, as far as I know, and two illegitimate children – and a lover as well! How shocked Milly would be by her carry-on!

'Rouge,' said Kate.

'You've *smudged* my cheek!' Georgina objected. 'Your hands are all shaky!'

And Aoibheal thought – maybe Kate has a man in the war. I never considered that.

All of Kate was quaking at the prospect of seeing Eugene again.

Announcing his imminent arrival on the morning he was due, Milly did so convinced that everyone at Wimborne would be thrilled to see him.

Kate's acting training saved her on hearing this news, but although she could control her facial muscles, her hands might have belonged to a different person altogether and she could not stop them shaking.

Excitement at the prospect of having her dear boy at Wimborne for the weekend blinded Milly to anything else, until Georgina said she would rather stay with Kate than go to the station with Milly.

'I see,' said Milly meaningfully.

I'm not trying to steal Georgina's affections away from you, Kate had wanted to say. Getting into Milly's bad books had made her even more nervous.

To distract herself she began in a frantic manner to put make-up on Georgina. This involved her in more physical contact with her child than she had ever

218

before experienced, and the tactile sensations underlined the duplicity of her situation. Georgina did not know the truth and Milly only knew part of it. And here was Eugene on his way to meet mother and child! Kate's whole body tingled as if it was being prodded all over with red-hot pins. She was convinced she was running a fever.

And yet when she spoke her voice was quite even.

'*Now*, look in the mirror and tell me what you think!' she said to Georgina when the offending smudge was removed.

'Mmm!' murmured Georgina approvingly, and at that moment Milly and Eugene arrived.

Georgina, anxious to impress them with her new appearance, shot out of the door. Aoibheal had already gone into the kitchens to track down Cook. Kate was alone.

She looked in the mirror, patted her hair, and swiftly examined her face. Could anyone else looking at it gauge that its owner felt sick?

And how could she be otherwise, with Eugene so near? I will *die* when I see him face to face, Kate thought. At this minute death is upon me.

'– a shock!' said Milly's voice, 'A gypsy in the hall!'

'A very *pretty* gypsy!' said an all-too-familiar voice, and the drawing-room door opened and there Eugene was.

And Kate did not die.

Her body did undergo change. The tingling went from it. Her hands ceased to shake. She stared at the handsome man she had once loved and she did not feel at all.

'*Kate!*' Eugene said suavely. 'How wonderful to see you again after all these years! How are you?'

The sound of his voice did not shorten her life.

'I'm well,' Kate said. 'Very well.'

Eugene looked taken aback.

'That's – great,' he said.

She did not even hate him.

'Look after Eugene, you two,' Milly said, and disappeared upstairs to dispense with her hat and coat.

'Kate turned me into a gypsy,' Georgina explained. 'Isn't she clever!'

She beamed at Kate and threw her arms around her thighs pressing her grease-painted cheek against Kate's hip. The shell-pink dress was later found to be stained with powder and rouge. Not that Kate cared about that, either afterwards or when Georgina demonstrated her affection.

She stroked the black curls, returning Georgina's smile, and Eugene, watching them, felt jealous and excluded. It was just as well Milly was not a witness to the scene.

'Eugene, welcome,' Aoibheal said, coming in. 'Such consternation as we have! Cook has had an argument with Cathleen and there's been a revolution in the kitchen.'

She thought that the three of them made an attractive tableau, like a painting of a family, especially as Eugene and Georgina were coincidentally so alike.

'Will we not get anything to eat then?' Georgina said, her mind on her stomach.

'You know perfectly well one of us will feed you. But I'd stay out of the kitchen for the moment if I were you!'

Georgina remained glum and Eugene serious. Of the three of them only Kate was able to manage a smile.

When Milly came downstairs, Kate and Eugene were seated next to each other on one of the sofas.

By then Georgina's attention had been diverted

away from her mother to a picture book and Milly, who had berated herself on the way to the station for being cold to Kate, had got rid of her resentment.

Seeing Eugene and Kate sitting together she thought how well they complemented each other, his dark good looks against her fair beauty.

Eugene and Kate? Why not? It would be a perfect solution for Kate, Milly thought, and rather good for him. It's time the boy settled down.

A curious state of affairs, bearing in mind the atrocity committed by Daniel.

But one perhaps ordained by the Fates.

One twin seduces and abandons the girl. The other, in marrying her, repairs the damage done. God-willed . . .

Eugene does look bemused. Perhaps he already loves Kate.

All this sudden falling in love – Tom and I long ago, then Jonathan and Aoibheal and now – who knows? – these two . . .

Aoibheal and I will have to leave them alone this weekend so the relationship can progress. And Georgina must not be allowed to get in its way either.

'I think Cook would like a private word with you later on,' Aoibheal broke into these thoughts. 'It seems that Cathleen insulted her earlier on today. Cathleen apparently said Cook has a neck like a bull!'

'Leave it to me,' said Milly grimly. '*I'll* deal with that girl!'

But Cathleen could not be found. She was not in the kitchen or in her own room at the top of the house when her employer peered in there.

About to give up and adjourn to her own bedroom for a short pre-dinner rest, Milly walked along the corridor that led past Eugene's room.

The door was ajar and through the crack Milly spied the missing housemaid. Her back was turned and she did not hear Milly coming in.

'What are you doing in there?'

Cathleen jumped and turned round, flustered.

'I was turning the sheet.'

'And what have you got in your hand?'

' 'Tis only a bit of paper, Mrs O'Brien,' said Cathleen backing away.

A piece of paper with your handwriting on it, Milly thought, glaring at Cathleen. Leaving letters for Eugene, are you? Saying precisely what?

Only to Eugene was Milly blind, and because of him, these days, Daniel. The nature of the rest of the world she saw clearly enough.

Cathleen is writing love letters to Eugene, she thought – or making him an offer of herself, to put it more succinctly. Brazen thing that she is.

This development enraged her mainly in social terms. Cathleen was a maid in the house, and staff should know their place, control themselves instead of giving way to their natural inclinations and thereby threatening to disturb the balance of the household.

Suppose Eugene had found the letter? One would only hope that he would resist Cathleen's proposition, but how could one know with men, especially bachelors who must be continually prone to temptation.

'. . . was getting out of the way of Cook,' Cathleen was mumbling. 'That one has a sharp point to her tongue, Mrs O'Brien. I was telling me mother only the other day that she has it in for me . . .'

Milly thought – *mother?* I had forgotten about Cathleen's mother. But now I remember. The woman lives in London – in Barking, I think. Maybe I should have a word with her about her daughter's behaviour. Warn her that if Cathleen does not pull herself together on all levels I may have to get rid of her.

And as for Eugene, the sooner he and Kate marry the better for everyone. The boy is simply too attractive to have in the house on his own.

Kate, released from her pain and abasement, felt like a river which has been dammed up for many years and has finally burst its banks. Glory flooded through her. And this elation showed on her face.

It got Milly thinking that Kate cared about Eugene and that there *was* a romance in the air.

'All this happiness,' she said. 'Is it because Eugene is here?'

'I suppose you could say that!' said Kate.

There was a mischievous note in her voice. Milly thought for a moment that Kate was about to dance.

Instead she grabbed Georgina by the waist and swung her round in the air. Georgina giggled and shrieked. There might have been two children in the house, thought Milly, her irritation returning, instead of only one.

'When are you coming back to see us again?' enquired Georgina. 'Please come soon. You're our favourite visitor, isn't she, Mama?'

'Yes, when *are* you coming back?' Milly said to Kate, conscious of Georgina's second question.

'Not for some time, I'm afraid. No, not *that* long, Georgina, I promise. But I definitely won't be able to get here in May. I'll be rehearsing for a new show at the Queen's. It's really my favourite theatre, I think – the red, white and gold auditorium and the domed ceiling and the Louis-Seize ornamentation – don't you love it, Milly?'

'But the stalls have been turned into a dance floor!' said Milly. 'People have tea there these days – '

'*And* dance the tango, and all for half a crown! But

223

theatre is still going strong inside that Ionic façade! What a pity you missed *Potash and Perlmutter* when it ran there last year. It would have made you laugh.'

'American-Jewish comedy – I'm not sure . . .'

'Anyway, as I was saying, I'll be busy all through May. You'll have to get Mama to take you to London to see me instead, Georgina!'

This was a provocative remark indeed. But on this Easter morning, Kate was feeling too happy and too liberated to be careful of what she said.

It was Eugene who, unable to keep away from Georgina for long, came to Wimborne in May.

He was instantly accosted.

'Have you been to see Kate in her new play?'

'It hasn't opened yet,' he countered, having no intention of seeing Kate either on stage or off as long as he could help it.

Catching the drift of this conversation Milly thought, If they're going to marry, Kate will have to give up the stage. Oh, I know Eugene too is involved with it, but there will be babies after all . . .

New babies . . . Babies which will divert Kate's attention from Georgina so I can have her to myself the way it used to be until lately.

In which case the sooner they marry the better from my point of view.

But suppose Kate, married to Eugene, tries to take Georgina back? Legally she can't do that. Legally the child is now mine.

What if Eugene and she are frank with each other about this whole business – Kate confesses to him that the child is hers, which she could very well do if she wants their marriage to be perfectly honest, and Eugene, in turn, admits that he knew all the time.

They may put pressure on me to give Georgina up,

on moral rather than on legal grounds.

Would they do that?

To *me*?

Probably not.

But there would be outings arranged for the child, requests for her to spend weekends with them. That sort of thing.

And Georgina, who is already so enamoured of Kate and who finds Eugene so irresistibly handsome, will be gradually lured away by the attraction of their youth.

And I will be left in Wimborne alone.

'*I'm* going to London to see her act,' Georgina was saying to Eugene, underlining Milly's fears. 'She asked me to go herself.'

'She asked *both* of us to go,' corrected Milly, and she thought – what am I going to do?

In bed that night, thoroughly carried away with the idea that Eugene and Kate were destined for each other, Milly considered Eugene's financial situation.

Crag Liath was his – must be handed over to him. She had dallied too long about that already. And with Crag Liath he would have, as she had always intended, a good sum of money – doubled now since Daniel was out of the picture.

But was that enough to keep Eugene and Kate and their children in comfort for the rest of their lives, especially when one considered what might happen in Ireland, with land being sold off?

She decided that it was not.

If it was not then she must once again alter her will, make the best possible provision for Eugene and Kate – and (this was not so pleasant a thought to face) also pay them off, make them feel obligated to her, so that they would not take Georgina away.

I am not a *nice* woman to think in these terms, she said to herself, at two and three A.M. gazing up at the dark ceiling. No, I am not nice, but I am realistic. I always was.

It is perfectly sensible of me to adopt these safeguards. Am I not entitled to fight for what I want, considering that, in emotional terms, I have had so little – and that was viciously snatched away?

Yes – yes, I am. Even though by altering my will in this manner I do the others out . . .

But then they never knew what I had done in the first place and therefore will not mind . . .

Where are we now in the month? The nineteenth of May, and Eugene tells me he intends to stay for three more days.

Let me think what I have in my diary for the week after then.

On the twenty-fifth that new teacher is coming here to see me to talk about teaching Georgina French.

And on the twenty-seventh, isn't there something? Yes, I have to spend that whole day with Mr Grantham, going over the accounts.

So perhaps I won't get to London to see the solicitors until the month is through.

Still, there's no rush. As long as I have made up my mind what I'm going to do, its actual implementation can wait for a couple of weeks.

More relaxed now but still unable to sleep, she lay alone in her bed. How still this night was. Second to June, when she and Tom had met, May was her favourite month, when bluebells made a rich carpet for the woods and the grass was drenched with dew.

Soon it would be light outside and tranquil no longer. Now, not then, was the time to be about, thought Milly. It's warm – hot even for this time of year.

So why not get up and get dressed and slip out for an early morning walk?

She put on the clothes she had been wearing the day before and slipped on her buttoned bar shoes, thinking that she approved of the high-fronted look. In this kind of weather one did not need boots.

She swept her hair up and pinned it loosely. She would do it again later on, puffing it out more effectively round the nape and crown. How fortunate that her hair was not going grey. That was one advantage of red – red-gold in her own particular case. Some women these days were wearing shorter hair, dressed closer to the head, but she did not fancy that.

A morning stroll, she thought, yawning – I don't know why I don't take one more often.

She opened her bedroom door and stepped into the corridor as someone else did likewise.

Cathleen the housemaid, coming out of Eugene's room.

Cathleen, not looking around, not seeing Milly, crept down the corridor in the opposite direction and vanished downstairs.

So *that's* what's been happening, thought Milly.

The girl must go. As soon as possible she must leave this house.

But first I must see her mother, talk to her about Cathleen, ensure that the creature is returned to a good moral climate.

In which case I had better go to London at the end of the month. I can see my solicitors then.

DANIEL too had been up early that morning, having a number of rounds to make. Now that he had a practice established in Killaloe, there were many demands on his time, the first of them this morning to re-set a fractured ankle.

The patient was an old woman who had fallen over a cast iron pot.

'Could we sit you up on the table so your legs hang over the edge?' said Daniel. 'I'll give you a hoist up.'

The old woman looked at him suspiciously.

'Aren't you very young to be a doctor? I've heard it said that the best way of treating a fracture is to make a plaster out of egg white and soot. You never knew that, I'd say.'

'I wouldn't have anything against it,' Daniel said, making conversation while he inspected the broken bone. 'There was a well-known bone-setter – Patrick Holmes, his name was. A Mayo man, who used flour instead of soot.'

'Is that so now?' said the woman, beginning to thaw. 'There was a fellow that was here years ago from France. He was after telling me that there they use *dragon's blood*!'

She smiled at him triumphantly, revealing the space where her four front teeth were gone.

'Resin.'

'What's that you said?'

'Hard resin – that's what he really meant. Listen, Mrs Keanneally. It's not a bad fracture at all. You must be as hardy as a mountain goat to have got over a fall like that!'

'Hardy as a snipe that wouldn't tear in the plucking,' the old woman said.

He treated the fracture and lifted her gently on to her bed.

'You'll rest now, won't you? And your daughter is coming at ten?'

She nodded.

'You'll be the picture of health by then!'

After this he went over the bridge to Ballina, passing as he did so Major Redmond, East Clare's Parliamentary MP. The two men waved.

It was good to see people you knew when you went about your rounds. He could not imagine living and working in an alien environment, as so many less fortunate young Irish men were forced into doing by lack of employment in Clare. The war was already coaxing many of them into the British army.

That made him think of Jonathan and, of course, Aoibheal. It was a pity his sister didn't come back to Clare while the war was going on.

She could live with me at Crag Liath, thought Daniel – that is, if she didn't want to be with Cathal and Mother, which, considering Cathal's antipathy to her marriage, she might well not.

Cathal, according to Rosaleen, was still caterwauling about his daughter marrying an Englishman, although these complaints were spelled out only in the confines of his own home. Aoibheal must have caught wind of them in letters, but she would only realize the full extent of her father's grieving when she set foot in his door.

So why stay at Whitegate when she could be out of the storm at Crag Liath?

That would please Mary Markham and Mrs Cash

– give them something else to gossip about in the kitchen.

He turned off left to that spot known as The Graves of the Leinster Men. Ballina, *béal an átha*, to give it its true name, meaning the mouth of the ford, was the point at which the last High King of Ireland, Brian Boru, crossed the Shannon on his way back from having extracted herds of cattle from those same Leinstermen who had braved the Munster boundaries . . .

'*Áth na borumha* – the ford of the cow tribute,' said his next patient, an even older man, when Daniel raised the subject. 'That was the original name.'

'You're looking well today.'

'Oh, nicely, thanks. No use complaining. You'd get nothing for it, I'd say.'

Nor will I for paying my last call, Daniel reckoned as he went back over the bridge and drove through Killaloe.

The tinkers were stopped two miles on, their red caravans making a splash in the grass.

Mary Markham, he thought, would go mad altogether if she knew that he was here. Like most of the country people she looked on the tinkers with a jaundiced eye, knowing full well that the minute her back was turned they would try to pinch from the house.

Only last week she had caught one of them – a skinny girl about fourteen years old stealing the goats' milk.

'For her mother's consumption, she said!'

'Well, goats do have a high resistance to consumption,' Daniel said mildly.

'I know that, Master Daniel,' said Mary. 'And I know that the Kerry cow has the best resistance yet. But is that a reason to be stealing from this house?'

230

'Maybe it is, if your mother has consumption.'

Mrs Markham had raised her eyes to Heaven at that, but Daniel only smiled. Not that there was anything amusing about the state of the people who lived on the road. Most of them *were* riddled with consumption, and most did not live over the age of forty.

So how could you blame the girl?

He could not, which was why, the following afternoon, he called at the caravans. There he had found the sick woman coughing her heart out and showing every sign of being a consumptive.

' 'Tis the weather being so hot,' said the girl by way of explanation. 'Didn't she over-exert herself in it, and sit on wet grass after.'

This was a widely held belief.

Still, I suppose pleural effusions do occur most often in warm weather, he thought. Having consumption was regarded as a social stigma, even by the tinkers, so he contented himself with examining the woman and prescribing rest, without going into details of what precisely her illness was.

The girl, too, worried him. She had the beginnings of what people termed a 'summer cold'. It might be worse, which was why he was stopping off now.

But the girl wasn't there. Probably back again at Crag Liath, he thought, driving Mary Markham wild.

At Crag Liath, however, he found, not one of the tinkers, but Cathal and Rosaleen.

For years, but particularly since he had joined up with the extremist wing of the Irish Republican Brotherhood, Rosaleen had lived in dread lest Cathal land up in prison.

Either that, or be forced to flee again to America. She wanted no more change in her life. It was bad enough having Eugene and Aoibheal away from her, but to return to New York and not have Daniel near would be more than she could bear.

She could talk about her fears – really talk – to no one. Except Cathal, of course. But he only disregarded them, quoted Patrick Pearse at her, emphasizing that there were many prepared to shed their blood for freedom, so what were a few fears?

Blood would be shed. She knew that, just as she knew that the extremists had pledged to mount a rebellion aimed at obtaining Ireland's total independence while the war was still on.

A few months ago Cathal and Pearse and Joseph Plunkett, the literary journalist and poet, and Eamonn Ceannt, who worked as a clerk for Dublin Corporation, had been amongst those at a secret meeting in the capital to plot this rising.

'That's a grandiose plan for you!' she had said, trying to neutralize her anxiety with scorn.

'We all think that,' said Cathal. 'We doubt that it will succeed.'

'Then in God's name why plan it?'

'Because to rise at all is to keep fresh in our minds the nobility of our cause.'

'And what if people are killed in the process?'

'That would be good, too. Pearce believes in the rejuvenating power of blood. You know that.'

'I don't want to know.'

But there was no avoiding that kind of knowledge, short of leaving Cathal, which she was not prepared to do, no matter how much trouble he might bring down on them.

Like turning the house into an arsenal. She had been prepared for that.

Instead aggravation came in the form of an unlikely thorn in the flesh, a man from Limerick who, it transpired, had recently enlisted.

Coming to see Cathal? That was odd . . .

Cathal and the newcomer shut themselves up in the drawing-room for several hours, talking their heads off and making no apology for excluding Rosaleen.

'What did *he* want?' she asked after the fellow went. Cathal went vague.

'A bit of a chat. You know how it is.'

'I do not! I thought it was John Redmond whose Volunteers enlisted, not your men.'

'Generally speaking,' Cathal said equivocally.

He stood no chance against Rosaleen, however. It took her most of the night but she got it out of him in the end.

The man who had come to the house was in essence a plant in the army, an extremist, one of a group who, if captured by the Germans, would spread the word amongst other Irish prisoners of war.

'What word?'

'One of our propositions is to raise a renegade brigade from within German prison camps. They would be used to fight *for* the Germans instead of against them.'

'*Why*?'

'So we can negotiate with the Germans for arms when the time comes.'

Rosaleen put her hands over her head. Jonathan, she thought. They would be fighting against Jonathan, against my own son-in-law – *our* son-in-law.

'It's war here, too,' Cathal said. 'It's not a gentleman's game. We must take our chances wherever we can. This is just one campaign.'

'How many in his group?'

But she knew that there would be nine, a circle of nine men with one leader or 'centre', the Limerickman himself. That was the way it had been with Fenians in the last century, and the IRB followed suit.

Only the centre would know the other eight. Cathal would be unaware of the identity of those men, so it was no good plaguing him for *that* information or any other at this time of night.

'We'd better get some sleep,' she said, turning her back on her husband and pretending to doze off while, in fact, she lay fretting.

A couple of mornings afterwards another fellow came in pursuit of Cathal, only this time it didn't take quite so long to find out why.

'Jesus Christ!' Cathal said disgustedly when the man had done whispering. 'Could you beat that for stupidity!'

'What is it?' asked Rosaleen.

'A couple of our men were overheard by the RUC talking about me in a bar – saying I'd had a meeting here the other day. A carful of constabulary are on their way here now. God Almighty!'

'Then we'll slip away in the boat,' Rosaleen said. 'And leave the car so they think we're still in the vicinity.'

Without much ado they did just that, knowing that when they had crossed to Mountshannon there would be friends on that side who would drive them on round the lake.

'To Crag Liath,' said Rosaleen. 'Where else would we go? We'll stay with Daniel until it's all boiled down.'

And only hope that it does. But she didn't say that.

Trouble, thought Daniel, looking at his mother's face.

'Can we come and stay for a while?' she said to him, and their eyes met.

'You're actually asking me?' he said, making light of things in order to reassure her. 'I should be offended!

234

Haven't you yet asked Mary Markham to make up your bed?'

'Ah, Daniel, thank God for you,' said Rosaleen. 'I feel better already. Crag Liath makes me feel safe even with Milly gone.'

Daniel asked no questions. They had a healthy lunch and in the afternoon he left Cathal and Rosaleen to fend for themselves and continued on his rounds. One of the patients he was scheduled to visit was Kate's youngest niece, Finola's child, who had a nasty boil on her leg.

'Don't dare squeeze it!' he warned her. 'It will spread the infection and *then* you'll be sick.'

'I'm sick now,' the child said plaintively. She started to cry. 'You'll put a poultice on!'

'I won't. I promise. Only a dressing with a solution of Epsom salts.'

This done he heard the latest news of Kate.

'Still acting her heart out!' Finola said, sounding a bit jealous. 'Some new play at the Queen's Theatre, I think. Not that *I* know where it is. I never get the chance to go to London, or anywhere else for that matter. Kate wouldn't either if she was married and had children, the same as everyone else.'

She waited for Daniel to say something revealing on this subject and when he did not she went on, 'All the same, sometimes I think she envies us – Fran and myself that is. At least we have a good strong shoulder to cry on if anything goes wrong. Isn't it an odd thing that Kate never found a man for herself?'

'Very odd,' agreed Daniel, who often thought the same. 'I suppose that's what the stage does – takes away that need and replaces it with fiction.'

'*Fiction*!' snorted Finola. 'Why is Brigid getting these boils? It's the second one in a month.'

* * *

235

Poor blood circulation possibly, he had told Finola, and made his way back home.

In one of the fields adjacent to Crag Liath land, lambs were cavorting, running up and down in a crowd as they had done each evening this week. He heard a cuckoo call.

Just as well it's not May Day, he thought, that would be bad luck. And as for hearing a cuckoo calling from trees in the churchyard on that day, that would mean a death in the family, so the country people said.

Just as they advised you not to cast a clout until May was out. But it is much too hot – unusually hot – to listen to this advice.

Drowsy with the warmth of the day, he drove up the road that led to Crag Liath's gates, swung in and was about to go round to the back when he spotted a strange car parked at the front of the house.

And climbing out of it a member of the Royal Irish Constabulary.

Cathal, he thought. Trouble for Cathal. Damn, damn, damn! It's bound to be in connection with the Volunteers. Somebody said too much, I suppose. So much for our big mouths! More Irish graves are opened any day by the mouth than by the spade!

What's the hope that Cathal's hasn't already been dug? And my mother's with it as well?

From the point of view of his nerves there was worse to come. Walking arm in arm across the fields towards the house he saw Cathal and his mother. Any minute now the constable would see them, too.

He must prevent their being surprised, hold off the confrontation until the extent of Cathal's danger was ascertained and a plan of sorts made.

As fast as he could, he drove the car between the officer and the other two, calling out at the top of his

236

voice, 'Good evening to you, Constable!' so Cathal
would be prepared.

'Good evening to *you*, Dr O'Brien!'

And Cathal – thanks be to God! – froze in his tracks,
then dodged behind some trees.

'What can I do for you?'

The predictable ensued.

'. . . trying to trace Mr Cathal O'Mahoney – not at
his house.'

'But he's here,' Daniel said affably. 'Has been for
some time. You didn't know – nobody mentioned –
his leg?'

'His leg?' said the constable looking perplexed, as
indeed he might.

'Broken,' said Daniel, as loudly as he could without
sounding odd. 'A bad break, too. Fell off my horse,
I'm afraid. Just as well it happened when I was here.
Otherwise he might – never – have – walked – again!'

The constable blinked.

'When did this happen, Dr O'Brien, may I ask?
Would it be this week?'

'Let me see – nine days ago, I think it was . . .'

(And, hopefully, as I spin out this yarn, Cathal
himself has gone inside the house. And into bed in
one of the upstairs rooms if he's keeping his head.)

The conversation went on, Daniel harping on the
details of the fall.

'A flighty mount . . .'

'Nine days ago,' repeated the constable at the end.

'Maybe ten. A Sunday, I know.'

'Is that so?' the constable said, biting his bottom lip.
'And would I be able to see Mr O'Mahoney if I went
into the house?'

'Maybe. And then again maybe not. It would
depend whether my patient is sleeping or not. In
which case you could come back tomorrow. Come in

anyway and sit down and I'll see how he is.'

Still talking, they went into the house. Daniel had hoped to encounter his mother inside who presumably could be relied upon to take her cue from his.

Instead, Mary Markham was hovering in the hall. Daniel caught her eye, willing her to play along with the charade.

'Mr O'Mahoney is asleep, is he not?'

'He is indeed, Doctor!'

The marvel of her, he thought.

'And my mother?'

'She's up in the room waiting for him to wake.'

'All right so,' said Daniel, 'that will be all. Now, constable, would you like a drink?'

WHAT he had to say to Cathal was less likely to bring a smile to his face.

'He'll be back in the morning, by which time *you're* going to be encased in plaster!'

Cathal groaned. 'You mean that?'

'I do! And you'll keep it on for a while! Should I know what's going on?'

'Two fellows were overheard talking, saying I'd been with another man a few evenings ago. They'd want to question me about that.'

'So how could you have been with this other fellow when you were here, wrapped up in plaster?'

'Good question!'

'In that case stay still and I'll start wrapping!'

So that May Cathal and Rosaleen remained at Crag Liath and Cathal stayed in plaster. Mary Markham and Mrs Cash agreed that their presence enhanced the house.

'Musha, didn't he need company, Master Daniel?' Mrs Cash said.

'Company of his own age would be better still,' Mary observed, 'and female company better again. Though I can tell you myself he never got over Miss Kate.'

'She has a power of looks all right.'

They thought about Kate for a while.

'Do you think he rubbed her up the wrong way or did she nettle him?' Mrs Cash wondered. 'One of them must have driven the other one up the walls!

But Master Daniel is terrible easy, God love him, so how could it be him?'

'Unless she treated him lightly. That would put him off.'

'Him being that sincere. I was thinking now did Herself ever make over the house to the boys?'

'She did not,' Mary said authoritatively. 'And you'd think now, with her being in England so much –'

'Not utilizing the place.'

''Tis right it should be the twins. Master Daniel's . . . What would you say Herself is doing over in England today?'

'You are quite sure you and Georgina will be all right alone?' Milly said again. 'I feel quite selfish going off to London alone!'

Aoibheal kissed her cheek. 'Please don't! We will be very happy here on our own. Although we'll miss you. You're definitely coming back on Thursday?'

'Earlier if I can. But I have a couple of rather important things to do.'

(Talking to Cathleen's mother; altering my will. In that order.)

'It's very brave of you to drive all that way.'

'It's not brave at all. Long ago I would have ridden all the way, if it had been necessary.'

'I still don't understand why you don't go by train.'

'I need the car when I'm there,' said Milly obstinately.

Barking was quite far away from the centre of London, but she did not want to explain further.

Aoibheal gave up.

'Please be careful,' was all she said in the end.

When Milly had driven away she went upstairs to write another letter to Jonathan. She was beginning to feel that she did not have a husband any more –

240

never had been married; that last summer was just a marvellous dream.

Jonathan, too, she thought, must be feeling the same, living as he did in a world of men.

His letters listed their names: Jack, Gordon, Dougie, Peter, Oswald: not all of them British, but Australian and Canadian as well.

She picked up his last letter and sighed.

'The thing about war is that in between fighting it is quite a pleasant life.'

Did someone living in that world really want to hear about hers?

'. . . all my love, my darling . . .'

But perhaps he did.

Aoibheal's looking peaky, Milly thought as she drove to London. Worrying about Jonathan. Wondering when – *if* – she'll see him again.

I don't like the way this war is going. When the Boer war ended none of us envisaged young men having to fight again so soon.

What will happen to all of us if it isn't won soon? If we lose so many boys . . . People say the Germans are committing appalling atrocities. Civilians have been shot. Woman have had their breasts cut off. Babies are said to have been bayoneted.

Or is this exaggeration? How will we ever know? Will Georgina be all right?

Her mind leapt about as the hedgerows flew past. In a way it was a relief to allow her worry to come out. In Wimborne she was frightened of appearing harassed in case Aoibheal and Georgina caught the feeling, too.

She drove steadily, stopping when she had covered what she deemed to be a suitable number of miles, journeying on again.

Eventually she reached London. Nothing had changed – well, why should it, after all? But it was a relief to look at the familiar buildings and bridges soaring over the Thames.

She was staying at Brown's Hotel in Albemarle Street, a quiet, traditional establishment which was made up of a number of discreet small Georgian and Victorian houses. The right atmosphere, she thought, for a woman on her own. Queen Victoria had visited the hotel and also approved of it, sitting in the blue velvet chair with gilded legs and arms that was proudly preserved along with a second identical one, perhaps for Prince Albert.

A fire had been lit in her room. She went to bed after a light supper thinking, In the morning I will shop, and in the afternoon I will deal with Cathleen's mother.

As Eugene had done a month earlier, she walked up Bond Street, pausing every so often to contemplate the windows. Having started off life as a town girl, Milly, returned to the urban environment, cast off her country ways.

She stopped at one establishment and bought several pairs of artificial silk stockings in pretty pale colours for Aoibheal and for herself. These were for evening wear, though why she should remain a slave to fashion and continue to put on black stockings for day she simply could not imagine. Why not have a hat to match one's stockings? Although, for that, you would need those enormous hats which were so fashionable four years ago. The toque would look quite wrong.

But at the top of Bond Street she passed a milliner's window where what was purported to be the latest style – wide-brimmed, large-crowned – held her interest.

She went inside and was shown what the milliner said was a Spanish hat, with a flat low crown.

'You note that you can wear our hats straight on the head or tilted to one side,' he said. 'Our trimmings these days consist of merely a hatband – checked or patterned, as you wish – and just one rosette. Unless the occasion requires that they be more ornate. In which case . . .'

She ended up with the Spanish hat, and a new net veil to prevent it from being blown off her head while driving in the car.

In a whoosh of frivolity she walked into Oxford Street and went to Selfridges to purchase dress material. She had always been good at sewing, and making clothes for Georgina was an ongoing joy.

The morning passed agreeably. By midday she was back at Brown's, depositing her parcels and partaking of a light lunch before leaving for Barking.

By now Cathleen's mother should have received her letter announcing her intention to call. That was all it had said. Some things, thought Milly grimly, have to be spelt out face to face.

She had never been to the East End of London before. To the smart people who lived in the more salubrious parts of London the whole area was a closed book. But she had done her homework well and had her route planned.

It took her through Whitechapel, where fine old houses had been turned into tenements. Out of fine eighteenth-century windows peered the grey-white pinched faces of small, underfed, bored children, intrigued by the sight of her car.

One of them shouted at her, 'Cor, look at that hat!'

If it had been at all practical she would have stopped the car, filled it with children and taken them all home.

Where they would be washed (and deloused, she thought – they're bound to have lice in their hair), fed, and offered the chance of a new life.

Once their accents had been corrected they would be company for Georgina.

Perhaps she would undertake such a project. Set up a home for under-privileged children in the grounds of the manor.

The feasibility of this enterprise engrossed her for most of the rest of her drive. Yellow stock brick terraced houses replaced faded Georgian façades. Disproportionate chimney pots broke the skyline. Several times she passed ramshackle stalls selling merchandise which she certainly did not want.

Cathleen's father, she recalled as she reached Barking, worked in the docks. The family had originally come from Clare, emigrating in dribs and drabs to England when the chance came up.

Their home was in Ripple Road. Hardly the redbrick, three-storey, fabled manor house (late sixteenth century) which was looming up on her left. Somebody should do something about these structures, Milly thought vaguely. This is a historic place. And Barking Abbey, which dates back hundreds of years, is somewhere round here. Before the dissolution all the land in this area used to belong to the monks. That dreadful Henry VIII. Ah, there is Number 21, that hideous old wreck.

And Cathleen's mother doubtless lived on the very top floor . . .

Enquiries about her elicited the information that Mrs O'Reilly lived on the top floor but one. Milly plodded up a staircase of uncertain vintage, taking note of the shaky banisters and crumbling plasterwork.

She stopped outside a door with a hole in it big

enough for a cat to pass through and knocked imperiously.

When it was not answered, she knocked again, more loudly this time and a woman yelled, 'Will you wait?'

But surely she knows *I'm* here, thought Milly. Then the door flew open and an older, fatter version of Cathleen confronted her and asked what did she want?

'Didn't you get my letter? I'm Mrs Milliora O'Brien – Cathleen's employer.'

'Your letter?' said the woman in a heavy Clare accent. 'No, I did not. But that wouldn't be surprising the way things are in this house.'

Do you think *you* can afford to talk, thought Milly with distaste, observing the dirt on the floor, the items of torn clothing strewn on it, the shredded curtains that had not been designed for these particular windows.

'May I come in?' she asked, reminding herself that she had seen worse in her life.

On an unmade bed in a corner three children, presumably Cathleen's brothers and sisters, were sharing a loaf of bread.

'I suppose you might as well,' Cathleen's mother said reluctantly.

No invitation was given, but Milly sat down anyway on a rickety chair that she hoped would support her weight. To collapse on to the floor at this point would be to lose dignity in front of the woman. A memory came back to her of the first time she had ever visited Crag Liath at the age of eighteen when Tom's sister Carmel had put her into a broken chair which had promptly given way. Carmel of course had sniggered, and her sister Mary had joined in, and Tom had teased her in due course about seeing her frilly white drawers.

At least they were freshly laundered, which was more than you could say about the linen in this house, thought Milly, holding on to the side of the table in case the chair fell. Cathleen's mother was looking at her with none of the kind of respect one might have expected her to show.

Milly fixed the woman with a gimlet eye and began sternly, 'I daresay you have no idea why I am here, Mrs O'Reilly, so I'll explain. I'm afraid Cathleen's morals are, to put it mildly, not what they should be. I cannot continue to employ her in my house. However, I do not want to put the girl out on the street where she might get into worse trouble. I will pay her out for the next three months and I want you to take her home and give her a good talking to about the way she's carrying on.'

Mrs O'Reilly, instead of looking concerned, wringing her hands, and nervously asking for further details of Cathleen's behaviour, the way she could put it right, sniffed loudly and rubbed her nose with the back of her grubby hand.

'Home *here*?' she said, as if she was checking an unacceptable fact.

'Where else?'

'She can't come here,' said her mother firmly.

'Why not?'

'We've got six of us here already,' Mrs O'Reilly said. 'Them three and another one as well as the pair of us. Any road, 'tisn't natural for one of her years to be sleeping alongside Him.'

'You've only got the one room?'

''Tis all we're likely to have, and Himself as thick as a stone wall with no ambition but to smoke his dudheen.'

Her fat face assumed what she evidently thought was a plaintive expression. Designed to melt Milly's heart, it had the opposite effect.

Why couldn't the woman clean up the room, she thought crossly, wash the children, demonstrate that she would be capable of keeping a second room in order if I was to rent it for her?

Which I imagine is what the lachrymose face is about. But why should I care about her in particular – this family in particular – when there are many others in need of help? The children I passed on the way here may not even have parents – at least these have her.

Still, I suppose I'll do something for the wretched woman. But not yet awhile. Not until I have persuaded her to put sense into Cathleen's head.

If she is able to talk any sense . . .

'Never mind about that for the moment,' she said sternly. 'I want you to talk to Cathleen. You're her mother, after all. It would come best from yourself.'

'Talk to her about what?' said Mrs O'Reilly sullenly. 'Are you going to inform me that she's chasing after men? Sure what's new about that with her? She's a right go-by-the-road is Cathleen. A fellow would need to be a quare eejit not to try to be great with her. She's no good to man or beast beyond being trotted!'

'That's not very polite, Mrs O'Reilly. We're talking about your child.'

'Aren't you the bostoon!' Mrs O'Reilly said, and there was scorn in her voice.

A bostoon, remembered Milly, was a soft whip made out of rushes – in other words, a fool.

'I am no fool, Mrs O'Reilly,' she said quietly. 'No fool – just a woman who wanted to be sure that the girl would be all right. I can see that there is no point in sending her here to talk to the likes of you. And I can understand now why Cathleen is as she is. I'll speak to her myself when I go home. Speak to her and make alternative arrangements for her, possibly with the nuns. It's you're the fool, Mrs O'Reilly – not me. If you had listened to me instead of being insulting, if you had shown an iota of respect, you would have got that other room.'

This was a good line on which to exit and Milly, who had a fine sense of the histrionic, did not let it pass.

Without waiting for Mrs O'Reilly to show her to the door she swept out, holding her head high, with two spots of colour rising over her cheeks.

That dreadful woman! What hope had there ever been for Cathleen, being born to a mother like that!

I shall send her back to Ireland, Milly thought – she'd be safer there and maybe Rosaleen would give her a job.

Although that would be no good either. Sooner or later Eugene will go back to Clare and the girl will tempt him again.

So, perhaps, as I said, the nuns . . .

Holding up her skirts she sailed down the stairs, passing as she did so two more children, a girl and a boy, who were on their way up. Their mouths fell open at this unusual sight, their eyes taking in her tailor-made suit and her smart Spanish hat.

One of them was Cathleen's brother. But Milly probably would not have cared about this if she knew. She had had enough of the O'Reillys for the time being. The whole expedition had been a fiasco and a waste of time and all she wanted was to get back to Brown's Hotel and have a quiet meal.

Tea would be nice first. But she could not imagine where in this part of London she could have access to a pot.

Shaking her head with exasperation she got to the front door of the horrible house, pushed it open and stalked out in the direction of her car.

Except that her car was gone.

She was undoubtedly hallucinating. The car must be there. If she closed her eyes and forced herself to stand perfectly still, regained control of herself, when she opened them again the car would be there.

It was not.

It took her another few minutes to accept that it was not her imagination that was to blame for its absence but a most reprehensible thief.

There was no point in going back to the O'Reillys. What – even if Mrs O'Reilly was friendly rather than hostile – could they do to help?

Or anyone round here for that matter . . .

Do not panic, she told herself, although she was not doing anything of the kind. There must be a railway station somewhere in Barking. You can catch a train back. I'm almost sure there is a connection between here and Liverpool Street. You can take a taxi from there.

And once back in familiar territory you can report the theft of the car.

Step one – find the station.

This did not prove as easy as she had thought. Having asked a confident enough woman the route to take she found herself lost.

Not that this was anything to worry about. Although it was getting rather late. She checked her watch and to her amazement found it was gone eight. Back in Wimborne Georgina would already be in bed. Lying on her stomach as she always did with her arms and legs splayed out. Not what you would call an elegant position, but endearing nevertheless.

And Aoibheal – darling Aoibheal – would be writing letters again, dreaming about the war ending and

Jonathan demobbed and Cathal taking a liking to him.

And Kate would be on stage. I must make an effort to see her latest play, thought Milly.

She rounded a corner and found to her fury that she was back in Ripple Road. That fool of a woman who had told her the way should be locked up!

Be calm, she cautioned herself. Go down to the end of the road and turn left instead of right. In other words, reverse the directions you were given. And after that ask the next person you meet where the station is. They can't all be fools in this part of the world!

Doubtless they were not, but most of them were at home that night instead of out on the streets. She did not like the look of the next person she saw, a weedy man with a leery face, the last kind of creature to whom she wanted to talk.

'You lost, lady?' he said to her all the same.

'Not at all,' said Milly, and stuck her head in the air.

But she was lost. And it was getting dark.

Just now I'll find the station, she told herself firmly. By process of elimination alone it's bound to turn up.

I remember this street from before. I went half-way down and turned left and that was where I went wrong.

So this time I'll continue down all the way.

And maybe when I get to the end the station will be there.

Or in the next road. Or the one after that . . .

And then it began to get dark.

Soon the stars came out and in their light she saw strange cigar-shaped things in the sky which she thought at first were birds.

But birds did not fly like that, or make that noise . . .

The fear she had contained within herself suddenly

250

burst out. Georgina! she thought – I must get home to you. Aoibheal is young. How will she manage on her own?

And, thinking that she might not, Milly began to run. It didn't matter any more where the station was. Only the planes and the noise. Only the Zeppelins and the need to escape from their threat.

But the sky was dotted with them.

'I have to reach Georgina!' she cried out loud, her voice drowned by the roar of the planes.

Then the bombs fell.

'How can Mama be dead? Who killed her? Are the Germans living in London now?'

Georgina's incessant questions were a series of unending waves swamping Aoibheal that terrible day when the news of Milly's death was conveyed to Wimborne.

Forced to tell Georgina what had happened, Aoibheal found herself well out of her emotional depths. Miserable herself, by late afternoon her concern for the little girl was tinged with a modicum of resentment that fate should have thrust her into the role of mother when she was still so young herself.

Resentment was followed by guilt. How could she harbour even a bit of rancour under the circumstances? But providing comfort and reassurance was a much more demanding and mentally exhausting business than she could have imagined.

So when Kate, responding to a phone call, turned up in Dorset and automatically assumed much of the burden, Aoibheal was vastly relieved.

Georgina turned her grief upon the older woman in a way even Aoibheal in her weary and unhappy state found hard to cope with. You would have thought the two of them were related to look at how the child hurled herself into Kate's arms before the latter even got through the doorway, and how this gesture was handled – Kate picking Georgina up and carrying her into the drawing-room and saying over and over, 'Yes, I know. I know, my darling,' as the perpetual interrogation continued.

Eventually Georgina fell asleep on Kate's lap and Kate, looking down at the tumbled dark head, said tenderly, 'I'll take her into my bed tonight in case she wakes up.'

'Milly wouldn't have approved of that one bit!' Aoibheal said, trying to smile at the thought of Milly's carefully enforced discipline being broken down so soon after her death.

That brought Milly's personality back to them and they both became weepy.

'She wouldn't, would she?' Kate said, groping for her handkerchief.

Aoibheal bit her lip in an unsuccessful attempt to bring herself under control.

They hugged each other, the tears streaming down their faces.

'It's so cold,' said Aoibheal when they had wiped their eyes. 'Shall I get you a blanket to put round Georgina?'

But, of course it wasn't really cold – it was grief that was affecting them, not the temperature in the house. If only Jonathan was there . . .

'Will they allow him leave for the funeral?'

'I shouldn't think so.'

Aoibheal was feeling very close to Kate.

'I wish she had been a relation!' she said suddenly, her emotions unleashed by grief. 'Then he might have been given leave to come home for the funeral. His letters are from another world, Kate! I read them and I think – they're full of the war. I'm ashamed of myself for thinking this way, but sometimes I hate it on such a personal level – as if it was a person, another woman, who had taken him away from me. I have no right to do that when so many people are dying out there – when Milly has been killed – but I do. Aren't you shocked?'

'Not at all,' said Kate. 'I should think most wives feel like that. And you had so short a time together. A morsel of marriage. Some women don't even have that.'

And some have chosen to turn their backs on the idea altogether, thought Aoibheal. Which category do you fall into, Kate? We have all taken it for granted that you rejected marriage in favour of the stage, but I wonder if that is true?

'Haven't you ever been in love?' she asked impulsively.

Startled, Kate looked up. Her expression was unfathomable. Her voice, when she finally spoke, was devoid of emotion. But –

'Yes. I have been in love,' she said. 'He didn't go on loving me and in the end I got over it. Yes, I think you could say I was cured.'

In her arms, Georgina stirred, fidgeted, seeking a different position.

'It's time I took her to bed,' Kate said. 'We need a good night's rest.'

Next day, Eugene too arrived.

'Where's Georgina?' he demanded of Aoibheal when Cathleen had let him in.

Cathleen was shaking at the sight of him, but Aoibheal wasn't aware of her state and the maid might have been a stray cat for all the notice Eugene took of her.

'Lying down with Kate. She stopped in her room last night but she was awake for most of it, talking and wanting to know why it was that Milly was in the place they bombed. Mind you, we're all puzzled about that. What would have taken her to Barking? She told us she was going to London to shop. Kate says Barking is miles out of town, near the docks.'

'I can't imagine,' said Eugene shortly. He looked cross rather than grief-stricken. 'When is she getting up?' he asked.

'Kate?'

'*Georgina*,' he said irritably, as if Aoibheal should have known. 'It's after six now. Will she come down again tonight, or will I have to wait till the morning to see her?'

Not a peep out of him about Milly, who had been a mother to him for all those years. Still, maybe his need to see Georgina was a sign of his grief – an indication of a concern that the child be able to cope.

And wasn't he right to put Georgina's welfare as his foremost priority? Looking on it that way his attitude could put you to shame.

Except –

There's something peculiar here, thought Aoibheal. I can feel it in my bones.

And in the meantime Cathleen was hanging around the door, listening in to the conversation as if she had every right to be present.

'You can go,' Aoibheal said to her, and to Eugene she went on: 'I'll take a peep into Kate's room in a minute and see what's going on up there. But if Georgina has gone to sleep we'll leave her be. Although the likelihood of Kate getting a good night with her in the same bed would be remote, I'd say.'

Eugene scowled. Can you beat that, thought Aoibheal, bringing his artistic temperament with him at a time like this. It's all we need.

If only Daniel was here.

'Honest to God, he massacred him, Dr O'Brien,' the tinker woman whom Daniel had encountered at the gate of Crag Liath was saying when Mary Markham came running along the avenue weeping and wailing and calling out that Mrs O'Brien was dead.

When he had partially calmed the pair of them down and told the tinker woman to come up to the house for a few minutes while he collected his wits and collected his black bag the way he could attend to her faction-fighter of a husband, he took a hold of himself.

Aunt Milly gone, he thought, and was hard put to it not to join in Mary Markham's tears. Battling against them he was assailed by the memories of the love and support he had received from Milly over the years.

In the kitchen Mrs Cash, with her hefty backside encased on a *Sugan* chair, was keening out, 'Och-Ochone! Och-Ochone!' and rocking herself backwards and forwards as if she was taking part in a wake and although she sounded more like a foxhound in full cry than a skilled exponent of the *Caoine*, his blood still chilled at the sound.

'Will you *whist*!' said Mary, hitting out at the washerwoman since she could not lay hands on the killers up in the air. 'Isn't there terror enough going on as it is without your voice adding to it. *You* wouldn't see what's right to be doing at this time, Mrs Cash, if it jumped up and ate you.'

Not surprisingly, the washerwoman looked put out at this attack and responded accordingly.

'Mrs O'Brien would turn in her grave to hear you, Mrs Markham, if she was buried yet!'

'That's enough of that!' said Daniel hastily before Mary could hit back. 'And don't either of you be attacking Mrs Nevins either. I'm going to go with her to treat her husband and take a look at that sick daughter of hers while I'm at it. You can be packing a bag for me, Mrs Markham. I'll be leaving for England tonight.'

As he went up the stairs in search of his black bag

he thought, I must let Cathal and mother know.

At Wimborne there was no indication of what was to follow in terms of Milly's will – only a rapturous reception from Aoibheal, Eugene's brotherly pat on the shoulder, and an enquiry from Georgina as to whether he would move in to the manor for good.

And from Kate a cheek proffered to kiss, a murmur along the lines that it was a relief he could be there in time for the funeral on the following day.

'My mother wanted to come,' he said, 'but Cathal was up in Dublin and wasn't expected back until next week and in the end I talked her out of it altogether. It would only upset her and it isn't as if her being here would bring Milly back. She wanted to see Aoibheal and Eugene, of course, but I said I'd do my best to persuade the two of them to come home this summer instead.'

'That would fine,' Kate said, brightening. 'I'm planning to be back myself for some of it.'

'Are you?'

'Aoibheal and I have talked about it,' said Kate. 'I'll take Georgina with me. She's heard so much about Ireland and it would give Aoibheal a break. She's a bit young to look after the child on her own and I'm happy to do it instead.'

'What about your career?'

'I daresay I can combine it,' said Kate vaguely. 'Georgina is much more important than all that, isn't she? I've cancelled all my plans for this summer. The theatre can wait.'

'But is it safe to travel?'

Only a few weeks back, the *Lusitania*, homeward-bound from New York, had been torpedoed off the Irish west coast and 1,198 people drowned.

'*You* did.'

'It's you I'm thinking of, and Georgina.'

'It happens here, too,' said Kate. 'How do we know where they're going to strike?'

'At military targets. It was the docks they were after when they bombed Barking.'

'Then they won't torpedo the mail-boat, Daniel. There wouldn't be two tragedies so close together,' said Kate.

Not in plays perhaps, thought Daniel, but in real life? He did not remind her that there had already *been* two tragedies at sea during the month of May, the American *Gulfight* having been attacked on the 1st and its Master drowned.

'Well, I hope this time you'll come and see me at Crag Liath,' he said. 'Bring Georgina. Mary Markham and Mrs Cash would make a great fuss of her.'

'She'd like that.'

'Then I'll be looking forward to seeing the two of you.'

But particularly Kate. Holding out hopes to yourself, fool that you are, he thought.

Kate nurtured no hopes about him. Still, she decided that Georgina should be taken to Crag Liath. Hadn't it been Milly's home for so long, a legendary house to the child?

'We'll visit you,' she said, both of them certain that Daniel would still be living there by then.

After the funeral Mr Ernest Spottiswoode, Milly's London solicitor, made an appointment to return to Wimborne within a few days to read the contents of her will.

Being a tactful man he did not add that she had intended to alter it the day after her death. Reinstating Mr Daniel O'Brien as co-heir with his twin to her Irish estate, he wondered? But that he would never know.

He felt sorry for Mr Daniel O'Brien under the present circumstances. *He* seemed like a decent fellow. He could not imagine what had impelled Mrs O'Brien to cut him out of her will in the first place.

Being a man who disliked waste of any kind, Mr Spottiswoode did not expend much energy asking himself questions to which no answers could be found. On his next visit to Wimborne he concerned himself merely with providing the people at the manor with the relevant facts, namely the details of the last will and testament of Mrs Milliora O'Brien. He did not mention the letter she had written to him before her death referring to need for change.

The four adults – the O'Brien twins, their half-sister Mrs Fielding (so young to be married, he thought) and that enchanting actress, Miss Kate Keegan – took up position in the drawing-room and, against his better judgement, Mr Spottiswoode agreed that the child Georgina be present.

Behind his spectacles Mr Spottiswoode had keen observer's eyes and he noticed that Mr Eugene O'Brien and Miss Keegan were in a manner of speaking fighting over the child, Mr O'Brien enticing her to sit beside him and Miss Keegan intimating that Georgina was happy with her. Miss Keegan won. The child sat on her knee, creasing the silver-grey dress which was exactly the same colour as Miss Keegan's eyes. Miss Keegan did not seem to mind about this or if she did she was actress enough to conceal it.

She was a most lovely woman, Mr Spottiswoode thought. Single, by all accounts. Curious, but then theatrical people were. Permissive, too, especially the actor-managers in the West End. Mr Herbert Beer-bohm Tree was known to have fathered a positive brood of illegitimate offspring. Miss Keegan, he devoutly hoped, kept her distance from such men.

He indulged briefly in a fantasy in which he rescued Miss Keegan, backstage, from unwanted advance. 'What can I do to express my gratitude?' whispered Kate – but Mr Spottiswoode pulled himself together before his fantasy got out of control, and he returned to the will.

'*I, Theresa Elene Milliora O'Brien hereby revoke all prior testamentary dispositions . . .*'

He plodded on through the formal legal phrases and the ears of the adults present appraised and abstracted the facts.

They found them both startling and shocking.

For not only had Daniel been cut out of Milliora's will and Crag Liath bequeathed to Eugene alone, but neither twin had been left any interest in Wimborne Manor.

That and the land that went with it was to be Jonathan and Aoibheal's on one condition – that Georgina could live there and be looked after by them for as long as she would like. Kate was not mentioned. Perhaps Milly, in looking after her during her pregnancy and acknowledging her child, felt she had done enough.

Mr Spottiswoode, peering over the top of his glasses at the O'Brien twins, noticed with interest that both looked upset.

Mr Eugene O'Brien must have been hoping for more than the Irish estate. *His* expression was sulky.

Mr Daniel O'Brien could be described as more hurt than angry.

It would be fascinating to know precisely what those two young men are thinking, Mr Spottiswoode thought, as he so often did when he looked out at those assembled to hear him read a will.

Mr Eugene O'Brien, in spite of his good looks, was far less sympathetic than his to-all-intents-and-purposes much more affable twin.

Young Mrs Fielding, having done so well out of the will, was looking thoroughly nonplussed.

'Has the man finished talking?' said the child on Miss Keegan's knee.

'Mr Spottiswoode, darling. Call him by his name,' said Miss Keegan gently.

What a delightful woman she was. Graceful. Spellbinding.

'Dear Mr Spottiswoode, what can I do for you?' said her voice in the lawyer's mind.

But what could I have *done*, thought Daniel, as the implications of Milly's will began to sink home. She always said Crag Liath was for both of us – ever since we were children I can remember her telling us that, and yet she's cut me out. He could hardly believe that she had.

It was the emotional rather than the financial side of the inheritance that he regretted losing most. Crag Liath was *home*. He had lived there since he was eight years old, drawn security from it when his mother went away, dreamed of returning to it when he was in boarding school in England.

And now he was not entitled to stay there any more. *Why the hell not?*

In what way could he have offended Milly to make her take such action against him? By being closer to Rosaleen in recent years than she – who had for so long been his surrogate mother – would have liked?

Had Milly been resentful, jealous of the relationship between mother and son?

Surely not?

And yet Eugene – who had remained distant from Rosaleen – had retained her approval.

261

In shock he muttered to Eugene, 'I'll have to move out.'

'For God's sake, man, there's no need for that!'

'But there is.'

For how *could* he stay on? He thought: If I remained at Crag Liath I would be driven out by Milly's spirit. I would feel an intruder now in the house. There's no question of my staying.

When I go back to Ireland I won't even spend a night in the place. I'll stop in Killaloe rather. I'll rent a house there or over the bridge in Ballina until I can buy one.

That was the practical side of his mind getting down to work. But emotionally he was *distant*. Crag Liath, he thought – as always when he was away from it he felt it call him back, envisaged the look and the smell of it, its colours and its furniture and its paintings.

And its people. Mary Markham and Mrs Cash and all the rest of them working on its land.

Those people to whom he had cheerfully given orders. Who, equally buoyantly, had carried them out, sometimes too slowly and sometimes downing tools a bit early in the day. But he had circumvented that, coaxed them and gently propelled them in a way they understood, and there had been harmony between all of them.

Only now he was not entitled to give orders any more, not to walk in the fields or sleep in the house.

I'll find another house, he thought. There are grand houses for sale around that area.

But none, be it grand or not, will equal Crag Liath.

Eugene thought not of Crag Liath but of Wimborne. He was devastated that Aoibheal and Jonathan should have inherited the estate instead of himself.

To think of Wimborne Manor falling into Aoibheal's

hands – Aoibheal of all people – was more than he could good-humouredly stand.

Downstairs he managed to contain his anger, but he was in a foul mood by the time he went to bed that night.

His rage was intensified rather than placated by the sight of Cathleen in his room.

'For Christ's sake be off!' he said to her.

The evocation of the Lord's name scandalized Cathleen and she quickly made the sign of the Cross.

'Do you now want me in your bed?' she said when this was done.

'I don't!'

But in fact his anger made him want sex and Cathleen sensed it.

Instead of getting out she came over to him, close enough for him to smell her sweat. A few minutes later they were in bed. She was a lusty animal, the best partner in that sense that he had ever had.

'Tell you what,' he said, 'I'll take you back to London with me tomorrow. Would you like that?'

'Do you mean it?'

'I wouldn't say it if I didn't. You can sneak out of the house tomorrow and meet me along the road and we'll drive there together.'

'But what would Miss Aoibheal say?' said Cathleen.

'You're surely not contemplating telling her, are you? My sister won't mind if you're gone. Leave her a note. Tell her you're upset by Mrs O'Brien's death, and you're going home to your mother for a while.'

'All right so.'

Eugene had gone. Daniel and Kate had taken Georgina out for a walk. Aoibheal was wondering what Jonathan's parents would say when, as she planned to do today, she told them that Wimborne Manor had reverted to the Fieldings.

She walked through the wood in the direction of the Fieldings' house, remembering the times she and Jonathan had strolled there together. She tried to envisage his face as she often did when she was alone, and found that she could not.

Panic set in, a sense that Jonathan was no longer on the same earth as herself, that they were cut off from each other for good.

Being with the Fieldings restored her faith in the fact that her husband still existed. Sometimes she thought that they felt the same about her. She was probably not the wife they would have chosen for their son, she did not fit in with what she imagined was their image of a daughter-in-law, but they were quite friendly towards her, more so this year than last.

For her part, she found their complete lack of curiosity about herself, her family in Ireland, and her admittedly small experience of life, completely baffling. In Ireland the Fieldings would have been questioned and analysed and conclusions drawn up about their characters and attitudes. But Richard and Joan only spoke to her about Jonathan and the war. Since she, too, was obsessed by both, this was all right.

Jonathan, after all, was still in the Ypres Salient and that in itself was a reason for concern, as she agreed on arrival at the Fieldings' house.

'I had such a beautiful postcard from him,' his mother said wistfully, 'embroidered in silk. Quite amazing. Apparently French women are making a steady income from such work. I'll find it for you. "To my dear mother", it says. I was surprised that it should be in English.'

Aoibheal smiled. She, too, had received an embroidered card, inside an envelope with wording

264

in English. 'A kiss from France,' it had said. Other cards had been even more romantic. Like *La Villa des Baisers*. The Villa of Kisses, depicting four open louvred windows through which lovers could be seen in various stages of passion. A British publisher would never have produced so suggestive a card, she thought – and did not show it to Joan.

'Italy doing fairly well,' Richard was saying. 'Slow to mobilize but at least had the sense to join the Allies at last. Vindicated herself in the eyes of the world. Should have done so earlier, of course, but – '

It was some time before the subject of Milly finally came up.

'Bad business,' said Richard. 'We never got on. Understandable, you might say.'

Aoibheal made her announcement.

'I think Milly felt it was right that Wimborne Manor should revert to your family,' she concluded.

For once, Richard remained silent. His mouth quivered like a child's on the brink of tears. He blinked several times, and shook his head in disbelief.

It was Joan who spoke first.

'I always thought she was a good woman,' she said, addressing the room at large. 'You never believed me, Richard, but I knew Harry was finally making a wise choice. His earlier relationships were not right for him. Even dear Lilian . . . Oh I know she was ill for much of their marriage, but she was always, always dull! And then there was all the gossip about his friendship with Sarah Masters – a ruthless woman if ever there was one, I'm told. The poor husband of hers! Harry wasn't the first man *she* led astray. Or the last, either, by all accounts. But he loved Milly O'Brien for her courage and her strength as well as for her beauty. That's what he said in his letters to us and so

I believed. It was you, Richard, who turned her into a witch.'

That his wife should speak out in this way was a second shock for Richard. He mumbled inaudibly.

Then – 'Was wrong. Made a mistake. Apologize to all concerned.'

Richard Fielding, concluded his daughter-in-law, was not without charm.

'Big place for a woman to run on her own,' he said. 'Don't know how she managed it. Remarkable. Remarkable woman. Should have got to know her. Regret that now.'

To her amazement Aoibheal watched him surreptitiously wipe away a tear. He was a real darling. Like lots of Englishmen he must have had it instilled into him since he was a baby that he would cause acute all-round embarrassment if he were to reveal a morsel of true feeling.

She thought of Cathal's cold letters and wished that he were present to witness the scene. You see, she would say to him triumphantly – the English are not dull, simply shy. All the normal emotions are flourishing in them every bit as healthily as they are in the ebullient Irish who have not been repressed.

And Jonathan was also too hard on his father, she decided. When he got back from the war she would speak severely to him about that, forbid him to run his father down.

'How are you going to cope, Aoibheal dear?' enquired Joan.

'With the estate? I can't imagine. There is Mr Grantham – but to tell the truth I'm frightened.'

'Could give you a hand if you like,' Richard offered gruffly. 'Unless I'd be in the way. Know a bit about it. Love that place. Family home, you know. Missed it all these years. Would like to help you maintain it for all our sakes.'

'Would you? I'd be thrilled – and Jonathan, too. He'll be as hopeless as I am in that respect when he comes home. Oh please help. How soon could you begin? Tomorrow? What a relief! Imagine your thinking that you could get in my way.'

Her effervescence was a bit too much for Richard. He had revealed enough of himself for one day. He retreated into inaudibility and left the women to pick up the conversational threads.

Aoibheal took her time going home, dawdling in the wood and thinking again how different the English countryside was from that of rural Ireland, for all that the two islands were so close. In Whitegate she had been very aware of the cruelty of nature – of elemental danger. In England, in spite of the war, she always felt safe. The wood sheltered rather than threatened. Sylvan serenity . . .

An illusion. As false in its own way as the vision of life – secure and comfortable – created by Milly's wealth.

Much of which was now Jonathan's and hers. What would Cathal think about that? Would he tell her that the estate should be offered to the tenants, like land in Ireland? But probably he would express no interest, taking the attitude that the English, tenants as well as landlords, could well look after themselves.

On the edge of the wood she paused to pick wild flowers to put into her room: bright yellow charlock, hairy-leaved and coarsely toothed, and bird's foot trefoil, and rosy purple bitter vetch to add contrast to the bunch. In the field beyond, the exquisite flowers of the dog rose were decorating the hedges, pink and white with yellow stamens, their red, egg-shaped hips tipping long arching stems. Further along, the hedge-row was infiltrated by flattened clusters of creamy white elderflowers. At home in Whitegate, she thought, we would use the clay from under an elder bush to soothe an aching tooth, and make the flowers themselves into a summer drink.

'Aoibheal!' a voice called out, and there were Kate and Georgina at the other end of the field.

'Hello!' she shouted back, and waved her flowers in the air at them.

'Look!' Georgina said when she came up to them. 'We have flowers, too,' and indeed they did, mauve milkweed.

'You can use it to cure warts!'

'I haven't got warts!' said Georgina, offended. 'But I'll pick some hawthorn instead.'

'Don't you dare! It's unlucky to bring hawthorn into the house.'

'Why?'

'They say the hawthorn tree was used to make the Crown of Thorns.'

In spite of this admonition they wandered amicably back to the house, where they were met by a grim-faced Cook.

She launched into speech.

'Cathleen's gone off.'

'Today?'

'Yes, Mrs Fielding.'

'You're sure she's not up in her room?'

'Yes, Ma'am – I looked.'

The indignation on Cook's face brought home to Aoibheal once again the enormity of the responsibility Milly had placed on her shoulders.

Cathleen alone was a mighty mandate!

She's a bold thing, Aoibheal thought. How am I going to keep control of her for a start, let alone the entire estate? Thank God for Richard's offer of help.

Within the hour she discovered that one liability at least was not to be hers. Cathleen's note was propped up on the sideboard in the dining-room between two silver salvers.

'My mother in Barking wants me so I'm going there now and I'm not coming back . . .'

Barking? Which presumably had something to do with why Milly had gone there.

By why hadn't she said?

MARY Markham and Mrs Cash wouldn't hear tell of Daniel leaving Crag Liath when he first broke the news to them, and when they did accept it they took the stance that he'd soon return.

'Where will you be going in the meantime?' Mary wanted to know.

'I've rented a house in Ballina along the eastern bank of the river. You can see the cathedral from there.'

'Ballina, is it? What place over there would be right for the likes of you?'

For a young prince like yourself, she might as well have said. She nodded her head as she spoke as if she was paying deference to his illustrious blood.

'What would you want to be sleeping there with Finn stabled here?'

Finn was Daniel's horse, a sturdy chestnut, seventeen hands high.

'I'd have to take him.'

'Much time you have these days for exercising a horse, Master Daniel,' observed Mrs Cash. 'You'd need Liam across with you. And *he* wouldn't be that eager to be leaving Crag Liath!'

'What kind of a place is it?' Mary said, reverting back to the new house.

'A good solid dwelling – not a byre, I can assure you of that,' said Daniel, trying to make light of things and inside feeling like death.

Sorry and raging. The more he thought about having to leave Crag Liath the angrier he got at the injustice of it. How had it been with Milly to make her treat him like that? Alone in his car he riled at her, demanding to know her reasoning, shouting disrespectfully as he had never done when Milly had been alive.

But in those days they had not been at war . . .

Rage – and Mary could feel it in him. She looked at him the way she used to when he was a boy getting up to mischief.

'And what kind of furnishings are there in that place?'

'Oh, it's all right as far as that's concerned.'

Heavy mahogany and horsehair, he thought – antimacassars on the chairs and an overmantel crowded with ornaments. But it will do for now. After a while, I'll acquire the kind of possessions I like.

'And who's going to be looking after you, may I ask?' Mary said darkly.

He was prepared for this and had planned for it.

'I was hoping you might help me find someone.'

'What else would I be doing?' said Mary, looking over at Mrs Cash for support.

'Don't be worrying at all, now, Mr Daniel,' the latter added. 'We'll find you someone.'

This turned out to be a cousin of Liam Lenihan the coachman, a big fat girl with a high complexion who was subjected to much advice from Mary before being turned loose in the new house. Her name was Edie and she was well able to cook.

'I'll expect you back at the weekend to tell me about her progress,' Mary Markham said.

That was the trouble: not being able to part from Crag Liath completely; forced out of affection for those who worked there to continually see the house which he had long thought of as home.

Each visit was at once a pleasure and an agony. Each

time he crossed the threshold Milly's ghost seemed to be standing inside it with her hand raised, ordering him to get out.

Still, the house itself seemed to want him there every bit as much as Mary Markham and Mrs Cash and the others did.

And most people behaved as if he *was* still there.

'Master Daniel, that tinker woman is here again, bothering you to do something about her child,' said Mrs Cash.

'Don't let her anywhere near the house!' Mary ordered. 'Sick or not, the tinkers are all the same!'

'I'll be with her in a minute.'

At least he had his practice – *that* he had not lost.

And in mid-July he had a visit from Kate. He came back tired to the new house to find her in the parlour, being fussed over by Edie.

As usual, his heart missed a beat at the sight of her.

'Well, now, and this is a surprise,' he said.

Dull, predictable words, he thought.

But she said, 'I've been waiting for you for ages. I hear you put in terrible long hours. It's good to see you again.'

'How long are you over for?'

'Until the beginning of September. Then I think we must go back – '

'We?'

Another beat missed at the thought that a man was with her. But – 'Georgina and I,' she said. 'Didn't I tell you she was with me? I've left her with Fran's children. They're getting on fine.'

'When did you come?'

'Yesterday – last night.'

'Aren't I lucky to see you so soon?'

'I don't know about that,' said Kate seriously, 'but I

came anyway. I hope you don't mind.'

Mind, he thought – *mind*? And aloud said banteringly, to cover his true feelings, 'The day when I'll mind you being here, Kate Keegan, cows will milk blood. Is your father well?'

'Dragging along,' she said, still muted. 'He took Milly's death poorly, as you can imagine. He loved her, you know. It's strange to think of one's parents being in love, isn't it? You tend to think that you're safe from all that, the older you grow; but love is always after you. Anyway, the grandchildren are a diversion to him. The noise they make – '

Was that why you came here, he thought – to escape the cachinnation? Anyway, you're here, and that's all that matters, and Edie will make us a meal when she's got over staring in admiration.

Eventually Edie disappeared into the kitchen and he was left in peace with Kate. She was wearing grey again, a colour that, unrelieved, turned most women into spectres but looked so good on her. What she had on was a pale grey costume with an embroidered front and large decorative buttons with a blouse the same shade. Daniel did not notice the details, only that her flared skirt was short – about eight inches from the ground which must be shocking the local people – and it gave him a pleasing look at her slender ankles. In London women were going in for high boots to go with their shorter skirts, but Kate's grey glacé kid shoes were embroidered in the same style as her jacket, another point that Daniel missed, thinking about her legs.

'You must be cutting quite a dash in this part of the world!' he said, wondering what the three old men who sat day after day on the bench on the Killaloe side of the bridge, watching the goings-on, must have thought of this exotic visitor. 'You walked over from

273

your father's house, I take it?'

'It wasn't worth cycling. Do you know my old bicycle is still there in the shed. You would think the grandchildren would have got hold of it but Pa wouldn't let them. I think he still regards bicycles with deep suspicion – although he's got a motor-car now, a Stanley Steamer no less! Very smart! Fran and Finola say it frightens the life out of him but he'll die rather than admit it.'

She chatted on about her family and Daniel listened, putting in the odd word here and there to keep the momentum going. Most people in Ireland talked a lot, affording him the opportunity to perfect the technique of encouraging them to continue on the one hand, while on the other taking heed of their expressions and gestures and body movements, all of which often said something else altogether. In Kate he could detect a nervousness that went beyond her characteristic sensitivity. She's not at ease with me, he thought. She always was in the past. Even when she was in the process of rejecting me she was relatively relaxed in terms of the two of us. Now, although her voice is under control, as you'd expect of a trained actress, her whole body is tense. What is she thinking? Is she about to confide in me or is she intent on holding back?

' – and Georgina, of course, pesters the life out of him, wanting to go for a ride.'

'She's taken a fancy to your father, has she?'

'She loves him! Fran and Finola are quite put out at the attention she's getting from him, over their lot! Odd how things work out . . .'

'Very odd,' agreed Daniel, filling the gap obligingly, although, on the face of it, there was nothing strange in Kate's father spoiling the little girl.

'Yer dinner's ready, Dr O'Brien,' announced Edie

triumphantly, and the subject of Jamie and Georgina was put aside for a while.

Kate did not think for a minute that she had romantic chances with Daniel. But, free of the full horror that Eugene had imposed upon her, she felt that she could now call upon him as a friend.

Having ordered herself to be content with friendship, she craved much more. Given any encouragement, she knew she could fall in love with Daniel.

But even then she could never allow herself to give way to her feelings. Daniel and herself were doomed to be forever separated by the lie she was forced to live.

At the very best of times she was horribly conscious of presenting a false front to her relations and to her friends. Above all she hated and despised herself as a dissembler for having to maintain such an artful masquerade in her own father's home.

This is Papa's grandchild that I have brought home, she thought, and I cannot let him know.

So how much worse would it be to involve myself in a deeper way with Daniel and not tell him the truth.

Unthinkable on two counts. Daniel and Eugene are twins – and soul-mates in a sense. I cannot speak ill of one to the other. Daniel would surely turn his back on Eugene if he knew what had happened – and hate me as the informant.

And be repelled by me, too – turn away from me in horror; see me as unclean.

So I can never confide in him; and without truth between us there can be no progression.

Not that *he'd* be interested in taking it further with me.

She became even more dejected then, lying in her old room and gazing up at the slatted ceiling, telling herself that she should never have come home. It would have been wiser to have remained in London to take up the offer of summer work, leaving Georgina in the country with Aoibheal. Working against that had been on the one hand her gradually decreasing interest in the theatre and, on the other, the flood of late love she felt for her child and the yen she had to make a home for her.

A home with Daniel . . .

Oh Kate! That's fantasy if ever there was one, bearing in mind the facts. It's an aspiration that can never be realized.

Just a bit of magic to turn over in your mind . . .

As a child she had composed many a dream before she had actually gone to sleep. Now she started visualizing the house that the three of them could live in, erecting a stage set for her play. It would be large and gracious and –

Why not Crag Liath itself? If fancy was roaming that free, Daniel could go back.

It was years since she had been anywhere near Crag Liath, but she could still see the house in her mind's eye, nestling sombrely in a cluster of trees, staring sternly at the river. In her new vision of it, Georgina was playing in the garden and she herself was standing on top of the wide, low steps and waiting for Daniel to come home. Mary Markham, who was not one year older than when Kate herself was a child, had their dinner ready and was sitting in the kitchen with Mrs Cash, the two of them as ever exchanging strong views, and Liam Lenihan the coachman was lingering at the back door and hearing more of what they were saying than he would ever let on.

And even Milly was there, delighted about the way everything had worked out, and Kate's father beside her, those two people having also decided to wed . . .

Some dream! Are you mad to be indulging yourself in such nonsense? said Kate to herself, and the idyllic image faded out of her head, and she rolled on to her right side and afterwards on to her stomach and still she could not sleep.

A wonderful sight I'll look tomorrow, she thought, with circles under my eyes.

There was no future for her fantasy. But tomorrow Daniel and Georgina and she were having a day out.

They were going in search of castles, an outing designed to amuse Georgina.

All over Ireland castles in varying stages of maintenance or decay were scattered. On the impressive side was Dromore, the Earl of Limerick's scholarly Baronial revival, Glin Castle in the same county, castellated at the beginning of the nineteenth century and with three Picturesque Gothic gate lodges added, and in Clare, stately Dromoland, home of the Protestant O'Briens since 1826.

There were medieval castles with tower-houses, castles built on rocks and islands, and Napoleonic fortifications with massively thick walls known as Martello towers.

But there were others – many others – partially ruined, overgrown with grass and moss, their owners long gone, their history forgotten, their mystery likely to appeal to a child.

Edie had packed enough food – cold chicken and ham, hard-boiled eggs, buttered bread, cake and biscuits and milk, to withstand a military siege.

She watched them drive off, Daniel and Kate in the front of the car and Georgina in the back, sitting up straight.

Well, now, so this was Mrs O'Brien's adopted daughter, was it? And who knew what *her* parentage might be and from what she might have been saved.

But the child was irrelevant. What mattered to Edie was that Dr O'Brien and Miss Keegan were casting eyes at each other.

The kettle's on the boil there, she said to herself. I wonder how long it will take Dr O'Brien to get round to proposing?

By lunch-time Daniel had discovered a talent within himself for telling stories about knights and their ladies, secret chambers entered through false garde-robes, and militant monks throwing boiling oil on Scandinavian foes. Small girls, he found out, were every bit as bloodthirsty as boys. The more gruesome the detail, the more Georgina revelled in his tales.

They had parked the car on the side of the road and walked across two fields so that they could picnic in the ruins of what had once been a high stone tower surrounded by outer stone walls. Part of the donjon was still intact, square in shape with shallow pilaster buttresses to strengthen the walls and corners.

Like a puppy released from its lead Georgina scampered off, ignoring the castle and roaming about the fields.

'There is no end to her energy,' said Kate, sounding proud, not rueful, about that, 'but she's as good as gold most of the time. Are you not worn out talking to her?'

'Not yet!'

'There are no bulls in these fields, are there?' Kate said, looking around anxiously. 'You can forget about threats like that, living in London and working on the stage. I suppose she'll be all right?'

'There are no bulls and she's well,' said Daniel reassuringly. 'If she goes too far I'll retrieve her. Why don't you relax?'

'I'm not much good at that, as you well know,' she said, but she did calm down a bit and when he spread out a rug she subsided on to it, the folds of her gauzy yellow dress billowing out around her.

Daniel, on the other hand, was feeling completely at ease. The years between had slipped away and he might have been eighteen again, enjoying the day with Kate.

Although, long ago, Eugene too would have been present . . .

'What news of my brother?' he said.

Did the enquiry make her more tense? It was hard to tell. At Wimborne she had not appeared to be in the least upset by Eugene's presence – had been, on the whole, oblivious to it.

But that could have been acting. Once again he wondered what had gone wrong between the two of them. Presumably Eugene had just been up to his usual tricks, but did you ever know for sure, even about your twin? Kate *might* have rejected him – she was beautiful enough to have her choice of men, and other suitors could have eased Eugene out.

But somehow he did not think it had happened like that. It was much more likely that Eugene had left her.

What mattered was how upset she had been – how troubled she still might be.

Unhappy enough to have turned her back on love? From all accounts these days there was no other man.

'Doesn't he write?' she said. 'I gather he's involving himself in theatre management, a risky business these days. He would have done better to have gone on painting and designing. That's his real forte, I'd say.'

All this in a detached voice, as if they were discussing a casual acquaintance, someone she did not particularly like.

'No talk of coming back to Crag Liath?'

Now he, too, was trying to keep the emotion out of his speech.

And obviously failing to do so since Kate, apparently struck by the tone of it, immediately looked up.

'No. I don't think he has any plans for that. What a waste – the house standing empty. You loved that place.'

'Yes . . .'

'And it means nothing to Eugene – nothing. Not that anything does, very much. Except for – '

She stopped in mid sentence, a hand going up to her mouth as if to block the words.

'Except what?'

'Never mind. Daniel, can you see where Georgina has gone? She was over there two minutes ago and now she's disappeared.'

He got to his feet.

'I can see her all right,' he said, still puzzled by the way she had cut herself off. 'She's coming back. What an old fusspot you're turning into, Kate – I never would have believed it!'

That got things on to a lighter footing.

'I know,' she said. 'Isn't it terrible? But it's a big responsibility, Daniel, looking after a child.'

Not 'someone else's child'. But that omission did not register with him then.

After they had eaten, Georgina wanted more stories.

'What happened in *this* castle?' she said.

He racked his brains. A good lunch undoubtedly dulled the creative vein.

'Well – '

And then he recalled a story Milly had told him as a child.

'I think Santa Claus lived here,' he said.

Georgina digested this.

'I think he did, too,' she said.

'Not on his own,' said Daniel. 'This was his *family* home. Mrs Santa Claus lived here, too, and all the little Santa Clauses – nineteen of them in all!'

'*Nineteen*!'

'And they all helped Santa make presents in time for delivery at Christmas. The castle was a kind of a factory, but only the family worked in it. They made dolls and diabolos, and tops and skipping ropes and hoops and sticks. Oh, and balls and cups. You know – the ball had a string attached to it and you threw it into the air and tried to catch it in the cup. Then there were wooden rocking-horses and floral lottos and jig-saws of the Kings and Queens of England. The china dolls were very difficult to make and Mrs Santa Claus who was a very bossy lady made sure that they had taffeta and lace gowns on before they were sent out and elegant prams to ride in.'

'Everyone got china dolls in those days – even poor children?'

'I think maybe they got rag dolls. One of the bigger Santa Clauses made marvellous picture books which unfolded as you turned the pages. But the dolls' houses were best. They had miniature furniture in them and little pots and pans and stoves and kettles and fireplaces and even tiny dinner and tea services.'

'And Happy Family cards?'

'Of course. They couldn't leave Mr Bun the Baker out. You can imagine what hard work it was getting all these toys ready to send out every year all over Ireland. No wonder the Clauses got cross sometimes – particularly Mrs Claus, as I said. She was in a terrible state by the time December came around and poor old Santa Claus and all the children wished they could get out of her way. But they couldn't, of course. They still had all the parcelling to do and then the presents had to be loaded on to Santa Claus's sleigh before Christmas Eve and – '

Georgina was sitting close to him. She put a restraining hand on his arm.

'Where did the reindeer live?' she demanded.

He looked down into her serious face and saw Eugene staring up. *Eugene*!

His stomach turned. *Eugene – she was Eugene's child.* Why had he not realized that before? Why had everyone else not seen it, since she was the spitting image of her father?

Maybe they *did* know and he was the eejit who had been left out? No, he thought, it cannot be like that. If Aoibheal knew she would have told me long ago. This secret was Eugene's and – whose?

But it was not difficult to surmise, to work out dates, to look at Georgina and Kate.

Jesus Christ! Why didn't I realize . . . ?

And Milly acted in character and took over the child.

'What about the reindeer?' persisted Georgina.

'Daniel, I'm just going for a little stroll,' said Kate. 'Do you want to come with me, Georgina?'

'I want to stay with Daniel,' said Georgina, tugging his arm.

He managed to swivel his thoughts on to the subject of reindeer.

'They grazed in these fields,' he said.

'Reindeers eat grass?'

'I'd say they do.'

Kate. Why didn't you tell me long ago? Why don't you tell me now?

This evening. When we have the opportunity to be by ourselves. Before you go.

'Did they always get all the presents ready in time?' Georgina wanted to know.

'They did. But they were dead tired by Christmas Day and what with all Mrs Santa Claus had put them through they were all vowing that they'd never do it again!'

That evening came and went, and several other evenings like it, without Kate even beginning to converse on an intimate level, let alone speak of Eugene and Georgina.

The hot, hazy summer passed, and although he saw as much of Kate and Georgina as his practice would allow, Daniel was aware that the woman he loved was keeping him at arm's length.

His suspicions he kept to himself. If they were true – and they must be; they made perfect sense – he could not confront Kate with them.

The matter was her business. He had no right to delve into it, nor did he want to. But he was convinced that if Kate could bring herself to talk about it with him, the barriers between them might break down on other levels.

Her reticence did not put him off. More of a problem was to get her on her own. He loved Georgina by then as well, while still wishing at times that Kate would leave her with her cousins again rather than – as he also suspected – using the child as a guard, a shield against himself.

Towards the end of her holiday, Georgina took matters into her own hands and announced that she wanted to play at home. Kate, unaccompanied, actually came to lunch.

And Edie, tactfully, kept out of the way.

The barriers were still up, he knew that. It's a dumb priest that never got a parish, he reminded himself – and waited his chance.

Bided his time until Kate said, 'You have been

wonderful to us this summer, Daniel. I want you to know how much I appreciate that.'

'We've made a good trio, haven't we?'

'A fine one.'

'Georgina was happy with us.'

'Yes. Yes, she was.'

This was the moment. He had his lines ready.

'If we were married,' he said deliberately, 'she could be with us as much as you would wish.'

'Married?'

'Yes –'

But she was gone from him, her face closed like a flower at night and her two hands clenched.

'No,' she said. '*No!*'

If he had been more confident with her he would have persisted, but he had been hurt by her once and he loved her too much to be sure enough of himself.

She still loves Eugene, he thought. Eugene, Kate and Georgina, that's the fine trio as far as this lady is concerned. All I'll get from her is all I ever had – her friendship.

And that I must keep.

'All right,' he forced himself to say, 'then we'll leave things the way they are. Sit down and enjoy the time we have left. I promise I won't talk about marriage again.'

Rosaleen knew without reading them that the letters Cathal wrote to Aoibheal continued to be frosty. She had once told her husband that he was jealous of Jonathan's place in his daughter's affections, that his coolness came as much from that source as from his dislike of having acquired an English son-in-law.

Cathal said that could be. He was a thoughtful, honest man, which was why she could not be cross with him for long.

Only concerned . . . In the early spring of 1916 Rosaleen sensed that the IRB's plans for a rising had taken definite shape. By questioning and observing and ruthlessly sifting through Cathal's documents when he was out of the house, his wife learned that the Volunteers intended to challenge the might of the British Empire on 24 April.

Easter Sunday. Cathal would be intending to go up to Dublin on Holy Trinity so he could fight alongside Padraig Pearse and the rest of them a few days later.

Rosaleen was also a nationalist at heart, but when she faced the all-too-likely possibility that the rising might end in martyrdom, she too was honest with herself. She loved her husband more than anything in the world, including the concept of freedom, and she was *not* going to let him barter his life against a dream.

Unpatriotic it might be. Furious it might make Cathal if he ever found out (but he *won't*, thought Rosaleen fiercely, I'll see that he doesn't), but she was going to prevent him being in Dublin on Easter Sunday, or die herself in the attempt.

She made her plans. With Cathal downstairs studying his own, she went down on her knees in the bedroom plaguing the life out of St Jude, patron of hopeless cases, to make the sun shine in the month of April.

Not so much on Easter Sunday when, according to the pious belief, the sun should be dancing with joy at the Saviour's resurrection, but in the week leading up to it.

Particularly on the Wednesday.

When St Jude obliged with a spell of exceptionally balmy weather in the last week of Lent, Rosaleen reminded him that it was the Wednesday that was all-important for sunshine. Then she got hold of Cathal.

He had already informed her that he would be leaving for Dublin on Thursday evening.

'So on Wednesday you and I could take the boat over to Inis Cealtra and have a picnic and maybe stay the night.'

'On the island?'

'Why not? The weather is beautiful and it would be a wonderful romantic thing to do.'

She looked meaningfully at her husband, reminding him with her eyes that on Inis Cealtra Cathal and she had made love long ago, when she was still married to Dermot O'Brien. Then, as now, political worries had been weighing Cathal down, but for a while she had made him forget them. After they had made love they had walked to the ruined church where other O'Briens had been buried, and Cathal had shocked her by suggesting that she should commit her mad husband to a mental home.

That had been before she found the truth about Dermot – learned that he was not, as she had believed,

286

as gentle as a lamb, but a ruthless killer who, before madness overtook him, had seen to it that a killer horse had thrown and trampled Harry Fielding.

In spite of that one jarring note, their day on the island had been one to remember and cherish forever. So small wonder that Cathal would look at her now and smile.

'But would I have time to stay the night?' he said, more to himself than to her.

'We can be off at crack of dawn. You'll have plenty of time. Oh, go on. You're going to be away from me all over Easter.'

The smile went off his face.

'I know I am. But staying over the night – '

The island, one of the most famous monastic sites in the country, was uninhabited. Cattle were grazed there, having been swum across from the mainland. Where St Colm and St Caimin and other Christian hermits had once lived was now left to birds and rabbits and rodents.

'We'll bring masses of blankets!' said Rosaleen. 'And we can take shelter in the church!'

'If our daughter could hear you she'd laugh!' Cathal said, beguiled by his wife's enthusiasm. 'You could be sixteen the way you're talking.'

'I'll have you know that when I was sixteen I didn't ask gentlemen to stay the night with me on uninhabited islands!'

She would never have believed herself capable of such play-acting. The dishonesty of it was killing to live with, as was her guilt in one way in relation to the Volunteers.

But it was Cathal that mattered – looking after his welfare, keeping him alive – and no cost was too great to ensure that.

Including the amount of money she was paying out

to young Willy Danaher. He was the greediest fellow in Whitegate but mercifully discreet and, just as importantly, because he earned his living fishing, he had access to a boat.

Rosaleen and Willy had a final meeting on Tuesday afternoon to run over his instructions.

'You're sure now you know?'

'I do,' he said, his eyes wild with curiosity.

'Then here's the first payment. I'll see you on Sunday morning. Don't be late.'

His father, an IRB supporter, would lynch him if he knew. But he would never know. No one would ever have the truth of it, only herself.

On Wednesday morning she loaded the boat with food and blankets and they set off across the lake and the water lapped against the side of the boat in the insistent and caressing way it had done on that long-ago day.

('I want you,' he had said, and 'I you,' she had answered, and white plumed mute swans had flown over their heads.)

Apart from their own memories, the island had erotic as well as pious associations. The Lady's Well, final station of pilgrims, reflected the faces of those whose sins were promptly forgiven but, in pre-Christian times, many a pretty girl drawing water out of it had been carried off by the local squireens.

The phallic quality of the round tower, the *Cloigtithe* or bellhouse, was the subject of many a joke composed by men in the absence of women likely to remind them that the island was once a centre of learning and commerce; that Brian Boru, the last High King of Ireland, had rebuilt its monastery and that his brother Marcan had resided there as abbot.

Having moored their boat, the O'Mahoneys walked hand-in-hand towards the ruins of this revered past, carrying their blankets and food in their free hands. This way, they had to make several trips from the boat to the church of which Rosaleen had spoken, one of five ancient churches which had stood in this place; but neither of them cared.

Since Cathal's arms were tired from rowing, and his back aching, they rested before eating and exploring.

There was much to see. The Graves of the Ten Unknown Warriors who had died in defence of Ireland. The five Bullaun Stones, used by pagans for mixing ritual herbs and spices. And the Bargaining Stone through which monks shook hands.

In the evening they lit a fire and wrapped their blankets around their shoulders and huddled in front of its flames.

'Remember – ' began Cathal, thinking back.

'Yes.'

But she was not recalling the past. She was thinking – Willy. For God's sake let me depend on you.

'Jesus Christ!' Cathal swore. 'The boat has gone!'

'It can't be. You secured it so well.'

'It has.'

He stopped, ran his hand through his hair, cried out to the birds and the wild creatures, 'What am I going to do?'

Willy. Willy. Thank God for you.

'What could have happened?' she asked, marvelling at her new-found histrionic talent and hating herself at the same time.

Only loving him.

'Someone untied it. They must have done. It was a calm night. It hasn't been torn loose from its moorings by wind because there wasn't any. Someone stole it.'

Or was paid to tow it away in that clear, starry night. Thank You God for listening to St Jude and making Willy Danaher greedy and – hopefully – discreet.

'Then there's nothing we can do but wait for another boat to go by.'

Which may not happen by the grace of God this day. And the next day there will definitely be no boat, being Good Friday with no work being done, no fishing, and most people in church. And on Easter Saturday they will be in church again for the blessing of Holy Water.

Please dear God don't let anyone come until Willy does, as planned, on Saturday night. Please, please, God.

'There was an uprising in Dublin,' wrote Aoibheal to Jonathan. 'Thirteen hundred Volunteers and 200 troops of the Citizen Army were involved in it and Patrick Pearse and his men took up positions in the Post Office but they were bombarded out of it. Hundreds of people are dead. Rosaleen says the rebels hadn't a hope, being outnumbered by twenty soldiers to their every one. Cathal is very depressed. He is, as I have told you, a friend of Patrick Pearse. I suppose he feels he should have been there himself. It's a miracle he kept out of it.'

And a miracle that *you* are safe, she thought. She was beginning to think that Heaven was on her side, keeping him alive.

To have survived so much without even a wound, that was luck for you.

At Whit even Kate, miles from the front, sustained a slight injury when a bomb fell a few yards from the St James's Theatre.

'Kate was rehearsing there at the time,' reported Aoibheal. 'Broken glass hit her.'

But Heaven was watching Jonathan and he was unscathed.

The postcards still arrived. Aoibheal could follow the history of the war by looking at her collection.

It was March 1917, and Mr Lloyd George, who had become Prime Minister of Britain, had new theories for bringing the conflict to an end.

And surely, surely that must happen soon. For weren't the British troops advancing upon the enemy lines in France? And the Germans were falling back.

Soon, soon, soon, the war would be done.

Jonathan knew other, more disturbing truths, which he kept hidden from Aoibheal – like the strength of the enemy's infantry and cavalry detachments, still occupying points of advantage along the line of defence.

Yes, the Germans had fallen back, but in their wake were ruined buildings, looted houses, desecrated graves; and the partial remains of men, whose limbs had been amputated by flying steel, or horrendously blown to bits. Men had been buried alive in the fighting. Machine guns spat out streams of nickel-coated lead. He was familiar with the faint garlic-onion smell of gas, with the sound of shells bursting over his head, with the necessity to simultaneously fire his revolver and jump into a trench as bombs went off.

But these were not the truths he told to Aoibheal when he wrote home.

Focusing on routine matters he attempted humour:

'We have foot inspections after every march. The men wash their feet and wait for the platoon officers and NCOs to examine them for blisters. The variation in toes is quite staggering – long, pudgy, thin, crooked. You would laugh to see such a solemn, bare-footed line!

'Once in a while there is a chance for a bath, a platoon at a time in a wooden laundry tub, while uniforms are fumigated and deloused.

'In the line or resting we are fed on stew of a kind. Otherwise it's tinned bully beef and biscuits and black tea. I dream of chocolate cake and roast beef and Yorkshire pudding and jam.'

No need to add that empty jam tins were used for making bombs. Nor that the enemy had fouled the wells.

'Still, sometimes, I sit in a comfortable armchair while the company barber attends to my hair!'

The chair, installed in his dug-out, was removed, along with other furniture, from an abandoned house. Why tell her that?

Instead, report that friend Jack, too, has survived. That poppies and cornflowers and yellow daisies bloom in the fields.

That cats continue their own war against rats and mice and, incredibly, in the blue sky, larks still sing.

Young Hugh Fielding was called up. There was only Tony at school now and, unless the war ended within the next few months, he too would be in the army.

Joan Fielding was sick with worry over her boys. So said Richard to Aoibheal.

Richard was proving a marvel in helping her run the estate. More than that – he had virtually taken it over.

'Until Jonathan comes back,' he specified every now and then, but Aoibheal suspected that, even then, Richard would turn up on a regular basis to bend Mr Grantham's ear and promote the cause of dairy farming over the keeping of pigs.

Richard was noticeably more at ease walking the fields with Mr Grantham than he was in the house with Kate, of whom he was rather endearingly shy. Kate was living permanently at the manor. Her last performance on stage had been in January in a play called *The Aristocrat*, a story of the French revolution, a popular subject.

In spite of this success, the theatre was in the doldrums. There had been a series of recent air raids and most people were scared to go out at night.

'Do you know, the one thing that did pack in audiences was the Whit bombing last year!' said Kate. 'Next day King Street was jam-packed with sightseers and the theatres did good business that night! But the excitement soon wore off. Still, I enjoyed acting with George Alexander. Although I would have preferred playing the part of the Duchess of Anteville to that of darling George's daughter. That marvellous scene when she is being led to the guillotine and her courage breaks. Lots of whimpering and wilting! Wouldn't I do it well?'

'But it's an old woman's part,' protested Aoibheal. 'You're much too young.'

'Age has nothing to do with it. There she is, faced with the prospect of a dreadful death. The mob is roaring and she pulls herself together and goes nobly to face them. I think I could do that! I never thought Geneviève Ward was quite right for the part.'

'Only the other day you told me you were thinking of giving the theatre up for good.'

'I was – I am! No, Aoibheal, I'm quite sincere about it. When I'm here with you and Georgina I don't crave for the stage. If you told me now that I would never go on the boards again I would be perfectly content. But when you see an actress putting on a performance that isn't quite right and you know you can do better,

293

it's natural to have a few regrets. And darling George looked so handsome in that glittering costume with his lace and his silks and that gleaming star on his breast! I wish you'd been able to come.'

'So do I,' Aoibheal said.

She was restless, like a young horse in need of being exercised. Spring did that to you, so you longed for excitement – for love.

'Come on, let's walk into Wimborne and have lunch at the King's Head,' she said to Kate. 'Where's Georgina? We'll dress her up and take her out for a treat.'

The King's Head, once one of Wimborne's four coaching inns, was the best hotel in town. Georgina was located, her face and hands scrubbed and a fresh dress put on her.

'We'll be back later this afternoon,' Aoibheal said to Cook.

In spite of the grey sky – a dead, dull grey, not like the silvery shade that Kate often wore, but one which was drained of vitality – Aoibheal felt full of life. And anyway the leaden look of the sky was countered by brilliant flashes of yellow springing out of the ground – daffodils and dandelions and gorse. Amongst the brown trees were some showing pale green signs of spring. There was white blossom on apple trees and black crows were flying overhead and making their usual racket.

'I like crows, don't you?' she said to Georgina.

'They're *ugly*!' Georgina said, wrinkling up her nose.

'You're imitating Kate!'

'I am not!' said Georgina indignantly.

'You are, too. She makes a face just like that. Don't you, Kate?'

'Do I?' said Kate, sounding odd.

Aoibheal looked at her, but Kate's face was turned

away. Funny, thought Aoibheal, and they went along the High Street and into The Square in search of their good lunch.

There was Spotted Dick for pudding, and when it arrived Georgina, who hated raisins and sultanas, wrinkled her nose again.

They do say you can grow to look like animals if you spend enough time with them, Aoibheal thought. Like Helen Wells who hunts so well and really does resemble her horse. And that woman who has a Pekinese . . . But I suppose the same principle can also apply to people.

Georgina and Kate are almost inseparable most of the time, which must be why I think the child is getting a look of her.

'Do I have to eat it?'

'I think you do. What would happen if it was served to you in a private house?'

Georgina looked agonized.

'But we're in a hotel now. *Please* . . .'

'Oh, very well,' said Kate, weakening.

'I wonder what The Last Generation would say if she could hear you giving in?' Aoibheal said to her.

The Last Generation was their code name for Milly. They edged away from direct reference to her in case Georgina was upset.

'Not much! She didn't believe in giving in. I shouldn't, I know, but I always remember the way Fran and Finola used to make me eat up, stuffing me with all sorts of horrible things. I don't know how I survived the pair of them. At least Georgina is spared that.'

In spite of the pudding, the lunch was pronounced A Good Idea.

After coffee they strolled along West Borough, Wimborne's finest street.

'A smuggler used to live here,' said Aoibheal, stopping outside Number 45. 'Jonathan told me. His name was Isaac Gulliver and when he had done with smuggling he became respectable. In fact, he even ended up as churchwarden of the Minster and was buried in the church. There's a tombstone with his name on it in the Baptistry wall. Shall we go and look?'

'Why not?' agreed Kate, and off they trooped to investigate.

Eventually, they ended up in the Chained Library.

'Twenty-six steps,' said Georgina when they had finally descended the spiral. 'Why so many?'

'It was so no one would be able to make his way down with a drawn sword in his right hand and make an attack on the Dean who used to be down here all the time in the old days.'

'But someone might be left-handed.'

'Oh, no – they wouldn't! In those times children who didn't want to use their right hands for most things had their left ones bound behind them and they were beaten until they were the same as everyone else. Now come and see what other children from the local orphanage made long ago.'

Aoibheal pointed to the chains. They were fixed to the front of the library books with a metal hasp which went right through the leather bindings and into the oak bookshelves so no one could take them away.

'They are copies of the ones designed by Michelangelo for the Laurentian Library in Florence,' she said.

'I think these books are too heavy for anyone to take away,' said Georgina. 'Are they very, very old?'

'Most of them were written before the eighteenth century. But that doesn't mean that they're dull – even for someone as young as you. Come and see this. It was printed in 1614, imagine that, and written by Sir Walter Raleigh for Prince Henry when Raleigh was locked up in the Tower.'

'*Historie of the World*. You don't spell History like that.'

'They did then. Now, look here at the bust of this man. His name was Matthew Prior. He became a famous writer himself, a poet and a diplomat. He was Ambassador to France. Some of his books are in the library, too. Anyway, one time he was in here studying *Historie of the World* by candlelight, and he fell asleep and knocked over the candle. It burned a hole through 104 pages of the book. Mr Prior nearly died of fright when he woke up. Do you know what he did?'

'What did he do?' asked Georgina wide-eyed. 'Was he burning by then?'

Aoibheal groaned, shaking her head.

'He repaired every single page. He cut out 104 thin circles of paper and he gummed one on the top and one underneath each page, and wrote the text in very neatly on each side. It must have taken him ages.'

This evidently was not a task which appealed to Georgina. Too reminiscent of school work, Aoibheal thought. It had done the child a lot of good going to school every day, instead of staying at home, away from other children. She had friends of her own age now who – this being the first week of the Easter holidays – often came round to play.

'What else is there to look at?'

'Burton's *Anatomy of Melancholy*.'

'Really, Aoibheal!' said Kate.

'Burton was great fun! He's always talking about the melancholy of "having too much religion" or "being too much in love".'

'What's fun in that?'

297

'Well – you have to read him to know. He goes on about "windy melancholy" and "the melancholy of having piles"! His remedy for melancholy in general is blood-letting followed by strong purging with rhubarb!'

But Kate had obviously had enough of Burton's dry sense of gloom.

'Let's go home,' she said. 'You'll be recommending purges for ourselves yet! You've really fallen in love with Wimborne, haven't you – the way you go on about it?'

'Only about the books!' said Aoibheal mildly.

But that wasn't strictly true. She had grown more than fond of the pretty market town. She felt part of it in a way Milly never truly had done, and that was causing her more than a little hidden conflict.

What would Cathal say if he knew that his daughter was having a love affair with Dorset? Because it wasn't only Wimborne she had grown to like but the beauty and variety of the whole county.

That doesn't mean I have grown away from County Clare, from Ireland, she said silently to her father as they walked home that day. For that matter I still have an affiliation to New York.

But surely love for places needn't be like love for a man. You don't have to stick to one country, one county.

Who said you did? Cathal answered back. Spread out your love all over the world as far as I'm concerned. Just don't waste one iota of it on an English town.

There is no need for you to be so prejudiced against English towns, his daughter told him crossly. The people of Wimborne are every bit as decent as the people of Whitegate. If you came you'd see that for yourself. I wish you'd do that and stop writing me those horrible cold letters – lying letters. There should be complete honesty between us as there is between you and Rosaleen.

And you and I used to be so close.

'You've gone very quiet all of a sudden,' said Kate.

'Sorry. I was miles away.'

'In Ireland?'

'In a way.'

'I wish I was there,' said Kate. 'I'd love to go home.'

They were on the outskirts of the town, passing The Almshouses, a group of thatched single-storeyed cottages with cob walls. In medieval days there had been a leper hospital on this site, and the Chapel of St Margaret and St Anthony which had served it then now served the almshouses.

'I miss Ireland too,' Aoibheal said. 'But I feel content in Wimborne. It's so pretty, Kate – so serene.'

'I'd rather be in Clare,' said Kate obstinately.

Georgina chipped in. 'Because of Daniel,' she said knowingly. 'She wants to be in Clare because of Daniel, don't you, Kate?'

'Georgina! What nonsense you talk.'

'No, I don't. Anyway, I also want to be with Daniel.'

Kate was soon in control of the conversation once more but she was still pink in the face.

Interesting, interesting, thought Aoibheal, elated. What's developing between those two again?

'You should go back, the two of you. I'll be all right here on my own if you want to go.'

Kate muttered something inaudible, shaking her head. Georgina broke with them and ran ahead, chortling.

'I'll catch you!' Aoibheal called, and ran in pursuit, and Kate, affected by their high spirits, sprinted after them.

Breathless and laughing they reached the manor.

299

But Cook was waiting for them on the doorstep, an envelope in her hand.

An official envelope . . .

'Mrs Fielding, this has come for you,' she said, and Aoibheal, taking it from her, went into the house.

By 12 April the British had achieved their goal of breaching the German wall and had taken the two villages of Wancourt and Héninel which faced each other across the Cojeul River, adding to their gains another 1,000 yards of the Siegfried Line.

But this news was not as good as it sounded to those who waited at home. It would have been mass suicide to make full use of the breach with a quick cavalry dash, for this would be countered by machine-gun outposts.

The only alternative was to progress slowly as an army, hoping this would wear down the foe. The men were jaded and disheartened, the weather alone enough to vex them sorely. In England conditions were pleasant – in France snow fell; later a south wind brought squalls of rain.

Through this they pressed on. By the end of the second day only their loaded rifles were clean. The men who carried them were filthy, unshaven, and in some cases lice-ridden. They were every bit as disreputable as the German prisoners Jonathan encountered, some marching, some imprisoned in cages.

Many of his own men were strangers to Jonathan, either replacements for those who had fallen or soldiers isolated from their own regiments who had joined up with the Second Worcestershires. Most of those he had once counted as friends were dead, except for Jack.

He could no longer write to Aoibheal of flowers in the fields. The earth was broken by shell-holes and they waded knee-deep in mud ten hours at a time, figures in a trance with their bayonets fixed.

On the third day he realized that the enemy threatened from the side as well as from ahead.

'Some of the men are sleep-walking, I swear!' he said to Jack. 'I daresay the only thought they have is of bed.'

'And empty beds at that!' Jack said wryly.

They were his last words, spoken as a German sniper was already taking all-too-accurate aim.

One minute he was there beside Jonathan as he had been for so much of the war, and the next gone, his body slumped on the oozy ground. Beside it, fallen from a pocket, was one heavy gold earring inset with bloodstones, a gift from a long-distant past.

Death was beginning to be more natural to him than life. There were bodies, thousands of bodies, decomposing in the fields. His stomach no longer wrenched – it was accustomed to the smell.

Days merged. They reached a village transformed by war into a looted shell. It was difficult to believe that families had lived there, ordinary people making love, quarrelling over small issues, children playing. To the worn-out men who came there that night it was just a place to sleep.

Jonathan woke to what he thought was the cry of a cat nearby. There had been cats in the vicinity when the army arrived, eight or nine of them, their dubious lineage detracting not one whit from their natural insolence. He had always been amused by cats, by their hauteur and unpredictability, but the merry days were gone.

Now that he was properly awake he realized that it was not, after all, a cat that cried but a man – a man calling for help. He stood up and reached out for the petrol can which contained his drinking water. The fellow would be thirsty, grateful even for water which tasted of the chloride of lime with which the cans were cleansed.

The cry had come from one of the ruined houses beside which they were encamped. He walked towards it, pushed open the broken door and peered cautiously round it.

Lying on the ground was a German soldier with half his left leg blown off. His face was ashen. It was no novelty to perceive that he was pitifully young.

Jonathan supported his head and he drank from the can before sinking back exhausted.

How he had managed to get into the house was a mystery – crawled perhaps. He might have been there for days. The mutilated leg-stump was both pathetic and disgusting.

Nevertheless, his predicament was not – in the present situation – in any way unique. He was one more war casualty, and an enemy. He would either die or be taken prisoner, most likely the former.

But Jonathan's emotions, numbed by recent horrors, had been re-sensitized by Jack's death. The injured German encapsulated for him all young men caught up in the war, including his own brother. He was about Hugh's age. Had there ever been a time when Hugh had got on his nerves?

'I'll fetch help,' he said to the boy, who probably didn't understand.

His eyes reflected alarm at a second abandonment. The fact that he had fallen into British hands apparently did not worry him. He was beyond that. Their eyes met and Jonathan, who had marvelled at the bravery and forbearance of his fellow men, felt his own control slip away to be replaced by a raw red anger that this boy and he and the thousands of others

302

should have this suffering imposed upon them – this distortion of life.

In rage he yanked at the door which had fallen half-shut, tugged it towards him and strode out.

He saw no one, only heard the shot, and then almost immediately was assailed by pain.

Falling, he had one thought: his attacker – surely – knew there was an injured countryman in the ruined house. Why hadn't he helped?

Aoibheal, having taken the envelope to her room, stood perfectly still with her back to the closed door staring at its contents.

Killed in action.

But her mind refused point-blank to accept the meaning of these words. Instead it focused on the inconsequential.

I must remember to check the hen-run to see if there are eggs, she thought. Eggs are good for you but Georgina simply won't eat them. I suppose she's copying Kate. *She* never liked eggs, either.

'*Aoibheal*?'

Kate's voice, calling from below.

And then footsteps on the stairs. Someone stopping outside the door, knocking – 'Aoibheal? May I come in?'

The door being gently opened.

'What's happened? Are you all right?' A hint of panic in the voice.

'Yes, I'm all right,' Aoibheal said, not turning round. 'Of course, I'm all right. Why shouldn't I be?'

'Cook said it was a telegram you had.'

'Did she? I must check the hens.'

'Aoibheal?'

'Kate,' she said, 'you should eat an egg now and then. If you did Georgina would do the same. She's always imitating you. Do you think she'd be good on the stage when she grows up? Milly always thought it wasn't ladylike to be an actress. I'm sure she told you. She was wonderfully bossy! Did you mind being thought suspect? I wonder if a time will come when actresses will be really acceptable in society. Not that *I* care about society one way or the other.'

'Come and sit down,' said Kate.

'I haven't time to sit down. There's always so much to do. We shouldn't have taken the morning off, you know, and now most of the afternoon is gone, too.'

Words seemed to be pouring out of her at an accelerated rate. She wondered if she was not perhaps speaking too fast for Kate.

'Do you understand?' she asked.

'Yes,' Kate said, her eye on the telegram. 'Yes, I do.'

Grief had the effect of turning Joan Fielding in on herself. Kind-hearted as she was, she could not reach out to Aoibheal. Richard had never been good at showing his emotions. His show of compassion for his daughter-in-law was limited to a pat on the shoulder and a few mumbled words. Alone, he wept.

Kate, able to express her feelings, was her empathetic self as Aoibheal made the transition from refusing to acknowledge the reality of Jonathan's death to sad acceptance.

With recognition came an anger similar to that Jonathan himself had felt towards the end. She did her best to suppress this emotion, not understanding that it was natural under the circumstances.

Despite her efforts, this anger seeped out of her every now and then, so that to others – Kate, Cook, even Georgina – she was quick-tempered and irascible. The spurts of irritability surprised her as much as them. In years to come they would refer to this as Aoibheal's cranky time. To her it was as if a devil composed of wrath and resentment and grief was bursting to break out of her soul.

Kate's sympathy and affection soon proved too much for her and she started to shrug them off. Never one to handle rejection well, Kate was peeved.

Inevitably this led to a tiff. Like most rows when people are operating under stress, this one was triggered off by only a tiny spark.

There was no porridge for breakfast.

'We've run out of Quaker Oats,' said Cook. 'Miss Kate was going to get me some yesterday in Wimborne but she forgot so I made scrambled eggs instead.'

'I don't like eggs,' complained Georgina.

And this, of course, reminded Aoibheal of the day when the telegram had arrived telling of Jonathan's death. Her head started to pound.

'All this nonsense about eggs is your fault,' she said to Kate. 'You set the child a bad example with your pernickety ways.'

And why shouldn't I set my own daughter any example I want, thought Kate, indignant. But this she could not say.

'What does it matter?' she said instead.

'She's got to eat something. If you hadn't forgotten the Quaker Oats – '

This sniping would have been much better ignored, but Kate, wanting to be loved on every level and made miserable by non-approval, was incapable of doing that.

'You're so difficult lately,' she said. 'I try so hard to be nice to you, Aoibheal, and you snap my head off in return. If you're going to continue to be like that then Georgina and I will go out and have breakfast in the hotel!'

'Just as you like!' said Aoibheal.

So Kate and Georgina went and after they had eaten the two of them drove to Poole to inspect the shops.

They had scarcely got into the car when Eugene, with superb timing, came to Wimborne for reasons of his own, but ostensibly to offer his condolence.

'You poor little girl!' he said gently, putting his arms around Aoibheal. 'This is truly terrible news.'

Aoibheal was going down the hill of her anger on the other side, and was near to tears, a fact that Eugene observed.

'Oh, Eugene!' she whispered.

'My little pet. I can just imagine what you're feeling. I'm pretty distraught myself. One of my friends was killed this very week in France. God, there's no end to the misery. If only I could help.'

'Oh, but you are,' she said. 'Just by being here, hugging me, you are.'

And he was. Somehow he was releasing her devil. Within a few minutes she found herself telling him of the existence of her anger, and when she was done with the telling her fury was dead.

And Eugene was killing her guilt about having harboured it.

'It's normal – *not* wicked! – to have those thoughts. Don't you know that it's natural to seek a victim amongst your nearest and dearest when someone you love dies?'

'Is it?'

'Completely natural.'

'And I'm not silly – or weak? I must be – attacking Kate like that. What must she be thinking of me? We'll never be friends again.'

'Never mind what Kate thinks!' said Eugene with utter sincerity. 'It's you I'm worried about. Now listen to me, my pet. We all do things that we think other people might find silly or weak – and they never do. Shall I tell you why?'

Aoibheal nodded. She felt like a small child huddled in Eugene's arms. But he was being so lovely to her that she didn't mind revealing her vulnerability to him now.

'Because they're too busy thinking about themselves! Kate will be contemplating her own troubles and concerns just now – not brooding on yours! Anyway, Kate herself can be weak and silly on occasions – we all can be, as I said.'

'You too?'

'Of course! More than anybody! Not to mention sentimental. I'll tell you a secret about me. I kept one of Mother's gloves with me all the years she was in America and I have it still. And I a grown man!'

'You must have missed her much more than anyone realized,' Aoibheal said, hugging him tight. 'Why have you never told me about that time? And there was I in America, having Rosaleen all to myself.'

'Indeed you were!' Eugene said, keeping the grimness he felt out of his tone with effort. 'Anyway, we won't talk about that period of my life. It's over – that's all that matters. It doesn't do to brood on the past!'

'No . . .'

'And don't you be telling anyone else about that glove! I don't want to be thought silly, either! Especially by Mother. After all, I want her respect. So don't tell her. She might laugh! See, *you're* smiling!'

And she was, although she still felt desperately sad. But it was something to find benevolence in a brother you had never much liked.

A talented brother, too. He stayed on to prove it, to paint a portrait of Georgina which they all agreed caught the very essence of the girl.

Aoibheal wanted to hang it in the dining-room before the paint was even dry.

'Isn't Eugene brilliant?' she said to Kate, their row having long since passed. 'I wish he'd concentrate on portraiture instead of involving himself in the theatre, don't you? It seems obvious that's where his talent lies.'

'That's true, I'd say.'

'We'll have to persuade him to paint *your* portrait next.'

'I think you'd have a job doing that!' Kate said drily. 'But as you say, Eugene has bags of talent.'

E UGENE'S genuine talent was being smothered by an ambition to go to New York after the war and back the productions of Jacques Copeau who had founded the French Théâtre du Vieux-Colombier.

Copeau was an admirer of Edward Gordon Craig's and much influenced by his work, and Eugene was fascinated by his concern with a practical stage, on which sets made up from cubes could be arranged in a variety of ways.

Encountering Copeau in Paris, Eugene, already comparing his own work to that of Picasso and *les cubes* and finding it wanting, was almost ready to give it up and embark on another career altogether.

Copeau had talked then of his plans to set up an experimental acting school which would contribute to the art of the theatre. Since then he had taken his revolutionary productions to New York, where they were currently creating sensations.

This is the kind of theatre people will flock to after the war, Eugene had been thinking before he came to Wimborne.

And the war *must* end soon. Already there have been attempts to negotiate for peace. Germany will have to give in – the Americans will force it upon them.

And when it's all over people will crave stimulation, escapism, gaiety – art. The creative thinker will run the world instead of politicians and soldiers.

And in this new climate I can make money –

provided I have the necessary capital in order to start me off.

Crag Liath, he acknowledged, could not generate the amount he needed to have at his disposal by the time the war ended, not unless it was sold.

But he did not want to sell Crag Liath. It was years since he had been back there but he liked to think of it as a secure home, waiting in the background of his life.

No, he wouldn't sell Crag Liath. He had another possible source of income which had to be explored.

Mulling over the possibility, he was heartened by the manner in which Aoibheal had responded to him of late.

'You're every bit as nice as Daniel,' she said once. 'Only I never knew.'

'I think it was my fault that you didn't,' he said seriously. 'I used to be jealous of you – did you know that? After all, you had Mother to yourself all those years and I felt left out in the cold.'

There was enough truth in this statement to make it convincing.

'I should have thought of that,' Aoibheal said, looking conscience-striken.

Good man yourself! said Eugene to Eugene. His plans were going well.

It was 6 April 1917, the eve of his birthday. In a sense he had already received one important present: American intervention in the war four days earlier, President Wilson having been provoked too far by the sinking of five American vessels; Germany's offer of alliance to Mexico; and her engagement to remove Texas, New Mexico and Arizona from the United States.

'To such a task we can dedicate our lives and our

fortunes, everything that we are and everything that we have, with the pride of those who know that the day has come when America is privileged to spend her blood and her might for the principles that gave her birth and happiness and the peace which she has treasured.'

It could have been an inscription on a card addressed to himself.

The other presents would surely follow. The cessation of the war paving the way for his own ambitions. And certain funds siphoned off from Wimborne Manor estate.

If only Richard Fielding wasn't always around, poking his nose into Aoibheal's affairs, examining the books, telling Grantham what to do as if he controlled the estate.

And having too much influence with Aoibheal.

Damned fool of a man, who had never heard of Picasso or Matisse, let alone Copeau and Edward Gordon Craig. The kind of a fellow who automatically distrusted artists and who had made it plain from the outset that he could not stand Eugene.

Since his own purpose was to insinuate himself with Aoibheal to the extent that she would permit him to handle her affairs, Richard Fielding was a bloody nuisance to have hanging about at the manor.

It was awkward enough for him with Kate around all the time when he came down for weekends. He was always on tenterhooks lest her control break down. Occasionally in nightmares Kate raged in front of Aoibheal and the past emerged.

To compensate for all this there was Georgina, a continual joy to see, to hug and to instruct. He found to his delight that she was beginning to draw, to respond to his lessons in painting. What unmitigated

Heaven she was, compensating for and diverting him from the other exasperations of his life.

Any diversion was welcome that year with the war dragging on. At Passchendaele 300,000 British soldiers lost their lives. Mustard gas, introduced by the Germans, inflicted painful burns and blisters on those who dared to oppose them.

The French army was deteriorating. The nerves of their allies were badly frayed. And the Germans planned a great attack in the west.

Between one thing and another, Eugene was relieved to go to Wimborne one weekend and learn that Kate would be in New York for the best part of a year.

'She didn't really want to go at all,' Aoibheal explained. 'And I was sick with worry about her travelling by sea, as you can imagine. But the offer of work was so good she couldn't turn it down. The London theatre isn't offering enough scope any more – and Kate thinks she's old!'

'She *is* thirty.'

'That's not old. But she worries about not being secure – being short of money. She's a terrible worrier – did you know that? Half the night she doesn't sleep, and if I wake myself I hear her getting up and going downstairs. I don't know why she's concerned. Her father will leave her something. After all, Fran and Finola are married, so Kate would get his house, I imagine. And she's welcome to live here with me. I like having her.'

The period when Aoibheal and Kate had fought was gone and they were as friendly as ever.

A bit too friendly for Eugene's liking. I hope to God Kate never gets it into her head to confess – to open her heart to Aoibheal, he thought. At least she's out of the way for now.

'What work has she got?' he asked to keep in with Aoibheal.

'A French play. *Pelléas et Mélisande*. Have you heard of it? I hadn't, I'm afraid.'

'Yes, I have,' said Eugene, hiding his irritation.

Pelléas et Mélisande was a Copeau production. He did not like the idea of Kate getting a foot in that world.

Still, it gave him an opening for what he wanted to discuss with Aoibheal.

'Copeau is brilliant,' he said. 'Kate's involved herself with the right people there. Actually I have been in close contact myself with one of Copeau's friends. He's formed a company which plans to take West End shows across to the United States once the war ends.'

This was all wishful thinking, and Copeau's so-called friend was only Eugene himself.

'Does he?' said Aoibheal innocently. 'I hope it will mean more work for Kate over there.'

'I'm sure it will. Lucrative contacts are already being fixed up with producers in New York. There's big money to be made there once peace has been won.'

Aoibheal only nodded. Of course, thought Eugene bitterly, *she* doesn't have to worry about making money – she's got enough, or will have when the estate is wound up.

'You should consider investing yourself,' he said. 'If you're interested, I can find out a bit more for you.'

'Would it benefit Kate if I invested?' asked Aoibheal.

The naïvety of her! Sometimes he forgot that she was only twenty – what else could he expect?

What else would he want!

'Indeed it would,' he said gravely. 'But there's nothing wrong with your benefiting either. Now that you're an heiress you will have to make careful

313

investments, Aoibheal. Women in your position can't be too careful.'

'I suppose not,' said Aoibheal looking solemn.

'Don't look so serious!' he said, giving her a hug. 'You've got a brother to help you.'

'I've got two brothers,' she said. 'Don't forget Daniel.'

To hell with Daniel, he thought.

'He's far away, isn't he? The two of us will have to go over and see him together one of these days. It doesn't do to lose contact with your family – especially twins. The two of us have always been so close.'

She liked that.

'It must be lovely being a twin,' she said wistfully. 'I realize now what I missed being apart from you and Daniel when I was a child. And to think I used to relish being the only one – getting all the parental attention at home.'

To which *I* was entitled, Eugene thought. The memory of his mother's desertion still had the power to disturb him, to turn him silently into the anxious and angry child he had been then.

When he had first learnt of her absence he had been traumatized by the fear that she had not just – as Milly said – gone to New York, but was dead, buried somewhere in the clammy earth near Crag Liath, and that Milly was lying to himself and Daniel. With trepidation he had searched the fields for a freshly-dug grave in which his mother might be interred. When he had not found one he had not been reassured.

For surely his mother would not go away and leave him? She loved him too much.

If she was not dead (and he was not convinced that her body had not been taken away to a graveyard),

314

she must be on the verge of death, incarcerated in a hospital, perhaps in Dublin, too ill to be treated at home.

And then he and Daniel had received a letter from her post-marked New York. Instead of being encouraged by her declarations of love and assertions that she would return 'within a couple of years', he had been terribly shocked.

Why had she gone away? That question, too, was soon afterwards answered. She had remarried. Her new husband was Cathal O'Mahoney, the man Eugene had once seen embracing her. Kissing passionately, glued together as if they were incapable of ever becoming unstuck. What they were doing was wrong, his mother being a married woman and Cathal only her friend.

But not *his* friend. Tim-Pat, the groom with whom he had discussed the incident, had assured him that Cathal was not a bad man, merely one bewitched, that what had happened was his mother's fault, that she was a woman with power over men, fundamentally wicked.

And yet he had missed her, even though at the back of his mind was the conviction that she should be punished for what she had done; that *women* should be unempowered, and he should hold sway over these sadist-witches who cast spells over men.

Including Aoibheal.

'Talking about missing people,' said she innocently, 'Georgina is pining for Kate. I never would have believed such a bond could have grown up between the two of them. And as for Kate, she was distraught at parting with Georgina.'

'Was she?' said Eugene, seething.

He hated Kate's influence over their child. Every

315

day he grew more besotted with Georgina. At nine she was more enchanting than ever. She must be by far the prettiest girl in her school.

In the entire county . . . And Kate was closer to her than he.

But he wouldn't think about that. After all, Kate was out of the way in America, and he had important plans to make.

Wimborne Manor estate was not yet wound up, but when it was he wanted to ensure that a substantial sum would be available for himself. In preparation for this he concentrated his efforts on maintaining his new image as a caring, responsible, and above all indispensable older brother – and wished that Richard Fielding would stay where he rightfully belonged, away from Wimborne Manor.

But instead of absenting himself, Richard continued to, in Eugene's terms, trespass on the estate. By October, he was accompanied on these excursions by Hugh, who was convalescing at home after being wounded in France. The sight of father and son – the former striding along with the confidence of a man who imagines himself taking stock of his own land, the latter limping beside him – infuriated Eugene.

How to effectively deal with the Fielding threat? The question was in the forefront of his mind as he and Georgina returned hand-in-hand from a visit to the wood.

'We have to paint those trees,' Georgina stipulated.

One day she would paint superbly, make a name for herself as an artist. His pride in her, already enormous, would become gargantuan.

He told her as much, describing the degree of his pride: 'Elephantine! Fat and getting fatter!'

Georgina giggled. She had a most delicious laugh,

he thought, throaty and rather wicked.

'Amplitudinous!' she said.

She loved finding new words.

'Megalithic,' Eugene said.

At this magic moment between father and daughter, two figures loomed up ahead. Richard and Hugh.

A meeting was inevitable. When they had gone through the necessary ritual of greeting each other, Georgina asked Hugh if he was also going to assist Aoibheal with the running of the estate.

'Oh, I shouldn't think so,' said Hugh surprised. 'After all, it's none of my business.'

Richard started. He hasn't registered the fact that once more the Fieldings are cut out, thought Eugene, watching the older man. Because he's still shocked about Jonathan's death? But it isn't just that. He doesn't want to face the fact that the estate was left jointly to Jonathan and Aoibheal – that Hugh isn't the next in line. Perhaps I should just emphasize that point – bring it home to him who is in control.

'Must be hard for you knowing that your family has no further right to the place,' he said. 'Aoibheal is looking forward to running it herself, of course, can't wait for that day; but she does appreciate your interim help.'

'Can't wait . . .' Richard seemed stunned.

'Good God,' said Eugene, glancing at his watch, 'is that the time? We must be off. Come along, Georgina.'

'Goodbye, Mr Fielding,' said Georgina. 'Goodbye, Hugh. Come and see us soon.'

She was most satisfactorily polite. Eugene hoped that she would not report this conversation verbatim to Aoibheal. You couldn't trust even the very best of children not to repeat what you said.

'I'm going to paint my trees yellow, down to their roots!'

Her mind was on her forthcoming project, not on the Fieldings. Thank God for that!

'Richard hasn't been here all week,' Aoibheal said. 'Do you think he's sick?'

'I shouldn't think so,' said Eugene. 'I should imagine he's too occupied with having young Hugh home at the moment to think about the estate.'

'He must be. At least *Hugh* is safe . . . Eugene, I need Richard. How can I manage this place entirely on my own?'

'You're not on your own,' he said. 'I'm here. I'll help you run it. For Heaven's sake, I grew up at Crag Liath. And even an artist is able to come to terms with accounts.'

He moved the majority of his possessions to the manor and took up residence there. By the New Year he was beginning to feel that he was establishing adequate control over Aoibheal's affairs.

Richard kept his distance. Every so often Aoibheal commented on the oddness of that, and Eugene countered, putting it into her head that Richard Fielding was a testy fellow who fundamentally resented the estate having once again passed out of Fielding hands.

'But he was so helpful just after Jonathan died,' Aoibheal would say, bewildered.

'Yes – then. It took him a little while to work things out, face facts. Then he reverted to his original position vis-à-vis Milly. The green-eyed monster took possession of him again!'

That had the desired effect of making Aoibheal wary of Richard, widening the gap between them.

Slow but steady work. At the same time he began to oversee the accounts, looking to the day when he could take them over from Mr Grantham.

And waiting, waiting, waiting for the war to end.

There was one relatively bad day. Aoibheal had gone to Bournemouth in search of curtain material for what was now regarded as Eugene's permanent room, a Heavenly mission, as he thought of it later on.

Georgina was with her. And, by a stroke of good fortune, it was Cook's day off.

He was wondering when Georgina would return when the door bell went.

'Coming!' he called.

On the doorstep was a bloated, dirty-looking woman whom he thought was a contender for an odd job on the estate.

'You want the manager – ' he began – and recognized Cathleen.

He was seized with rage. What was this slut doing coming back here? In London, having had enough of her, he had almost forcibly ejected her from his rooms. She had screamed, howled like a dog, he recalled, returning on a number of occasions to plead to be let in.

At long last she had given up and gone in search of work. He had never expected to lay eyes on her again.

'What brought you here?' he asked. 'Are you mad, trying to find me now?'

''Twasn't you I was after,' Cathleen said boldly. ''Tis money I want. I'm out of a job and down on my luck.'

'Look,' said Eugene, 'you're not getting any money from anyone in this house so you might as well be off. If you have any thoughts of blackmailing me you can forget them. No one here will believe you if you tell them stories. Do you think anyone in their right minds would look at a fat, dirty thing like you and connect us two?'

'Miss Aoibheal would help me,' she said. 'You can't stop me seeing Miss Aoibheal.'

'She's not here. There's nobody here. You'd better get out.'

Eventually she went, her girth ballooning under her filthy skirts. But at least he had got rid of her before the others came back.

That Cathleen of all people – socially the lowest of any of the women he had been involved with, though admittedly the best of them all in bed – should turn up in Wimborne now!

The others – Kate, Henriette, Monique, a couple of others whose names he could not for the life of him remember – had all rushed into print, pouring out their feelings for him on page after page, begging him to come back. But none had given him quite so much trouble as lowly Cathleen! He peered out of the window again. It *was* all right. She had well and truly gone.

It was autumn again before the German people – realizing that they faced not secure expectation of victory but imminent defeat – finally rebelled. Resistance to prolonging the war began on 29 October with a naval mutiny. An application for armistice was declared. By November it was over.

And Kate, who had stayed on in America longer than she had originally planned, was at last coming home.

Georgina was ecstatic. 'Will she take me to Ireland again, Aoibheal?'

'If that's what you want I'm sure she will.'

'Will you come too?'

'Probably – or I'll follow you later on.'

'We'll see Daniel!'

'Yes!' said Aoibheal. 'We definitely will!'

* * *

Kate was laden with presents for Georgina. And Georgina's enthusiasm for her was not diminished by the months she had been away. Eugene scowled.

'Are you living here permanently, Eugene?'

That was another irritating thing – Kate was not one whit in awe of him any more. It was disagreeable, distressing, to feel that his power had ebbed away.

'Aoibheal needs me.'

He poured himself a stiff whiskey. He was not a heavy drinker but he was edgy. He swallowed quickly, refilling his glass.

'Hmm!' said Kate.

'What are your immediate plans?' he said to her, twisting the glass in his hands.

'Mine? Oh, I'll stay here for the time being, with Aoibheal's permission, and in a couple of weeks' time I'll go to Ireland.'

'And I'll come with you,' interceded Georgina.

'Good! That's a pact.'

What about me? Eugene thought, looking at his daughter. You're my child, mine. Forget about your mother. She's of no consequence. I'm the one who will turn you into a fine artist – introduce you to the right people in the art world. Be *my* little girl!

Smart Kate. In England women were still wearing utility clothes.

'Dressing like servants!' in Eugene's disparaging terms.

But Kate was as glamorous as ever in her pretty pale dresses.

'Don't look at me!' said Aoibheal. 'I'm so unfashionable by comparison to you! You're going to create a sensation in County Clare!'

Fashion was picking up again after the long war. The tubular look was in. Skirts looked like barrels, waists had disappeared and women were wearing 'flatteners' round their busts to give them a boyish air. Hems were going down again towards the ankles and hair was flat on the top of the head and curling over the ears.

Kate laughed.

'I don't think so. Anyway, I'm not interested in creating sensations. I just want to be quiet. It's so good being in the country after all that time in New York.'

'But you're so lucky to have been there. I wish I could go back.'

'But you can – any time you want.'

'I suppose I can. But it would be different if I had someone to go with – if Jonathan was with me.'

They were sitting companionably by the fire. Georgina had long since gone to bed, worn out with the excitement of welcoming Kate back.

'I know,' Kate said. 'I'm lonely, too.'

She paused, lost in thought. Then – 'Daniel has written to me a lot. His letters have been the best thing that has happened to me this year.'

'Not acting in New York?'

Kate shook her head.

'It's hard to explain what I feel about the stage. It's becoming more and more difficult for me to fantasize – does that make sense? And yet it's all I've got in a way. I haven't married like Fran and Finola – or you. I wish – '

She stopped.

'Wish what?'

'Ah – let's not talk about me!'

'Daniel will think you're the smartest woman he has ever laid eyes on!' said Aoibheal to Kate before she and Georgina left.

'I hope he does.'

There was something of a challenge in Kate's voice as she spoke – a challenge in her eyes as she stared at Eugene.

He glowered, furious about the excursion to Ireland. Georgina taken away – and by Kate. No one had consulted him and he could not protest.

Kate had never succeeded in winning his love, but he was beginning to feel another polarized emotion for her – hate.

To think that she could exercise power over Georgina like that – power over himself in the sense that she could remove his daughter from England at the drop of a hat.

'When are they coming back?' he asked Aoibheal.

'I don't know.'

'But what about Georgina's schooling? She can't just be moved from one country to the other without considering that. You're her guardian. You shouldn't allow Kate to take her away.'

'She's only young,' Aoibheal said, surprised at Eugene's fierce reaction. 'I don't think it will make that much difference to her schooling. Irish teachers are wonderful. You know that. And they're all learning the same thing – you don't count any differently there than you do here, or read differently, either!'

Eugene slumped into a chair and put his hand over his forehead, the very picture of misery.

'What is up with you? I know you're mad about Georgina, but so is Kate, and Georgina is mad about her. So what's wrong with their going to Clare?'

Take a hold of yourself, said Eugene to Eugene. You don't want Aoibheal asking you what's up all the time. Aoibheal's attention should be on other matters altogether.

At long last the estate had been wound up. He could never have imagined that the process could be so long.

But finally Aoibheal had her own money in the bank and the time was ripe to urge her to invest it at his discretion.

She was ready to do so. She had said that to him on his last visit.

He got a grip on his emotions and instead of allowing Georgina to distract him he thought how pleasant it would be to lay hands on Aoibheal's funds.

Particularly on *Aoibheal's* . . . Nothing, he thought, would make him happier than to siphon off his half-sister's money.

What an actor he had been these last couple of years! Aoibheal had no idea that, underneath, he loathed her every bit as much as when she had first set foot in Ireland as a child.

Even before then he had hated her. And now he was going to pay her back.

By making her pay him!

'Never mind the way I go on about Georgina,' he said in a lighter voice. 'It's just that I love children. Always have. I should have married, of course, but – '

'But what?' said Aoibheal.

He was becoming as enigmatic as Kate, leaving half-finished sentences dangling in mid-air.

Eugene, however, went on. 'There was a girl in Paris I wanted to marry,' he said. 'Her name was Henriette and I was deeply in love with her. She didn't feel the same about me, I'm afraid. There's never been anyone else. Every time I lay eyes on Georgina I think – if I could have married Henriette, had children. Been the same as everyone else.'

'You *are* the same as all of us,' said Aoibheal prosaically. 'Daniel's not married. Kate's single. And I'm a childless widow.'

'Well, you know what I mean,' said Eugene, holding on to his patience. 'Anyway, enough of my troubles. They're nothing in comparison to what *you* have been through. I've spoken this last week to Jacques Copeau's friend, Monsieur Rouché, and he assures me that you still have time to invest in his company.'

Monsieur Rouché did not exist, but Eugene had mentioned him so often to Aoibheal in their discussions that he sometimes found it hard to believe that the man was only a figment of his imagination.

'What a relief,' said Aoibheal, just as he would have wished. 'I thought we were going to be too late.'

'So did I at one point,' Eugene said, 'but Monsieur Rouché tells me if we let him have the money urgently all will be well.'

'We'll go to the bank together in the morning and arrange everything,' said Aoibheal.

He might have scripted her lines himself.

'And you feel quite happy about making the payment direct to myself?'

'Aren't you my brother?' she said.

Someone in Heaven had written this particular play, he thought, especially for Eugene O'Brien.

'And next month you and I will go to Ireland to see Daniel and Mother.'

And Georgina. How could he stay away?

These arrangements having been made, Eugene got out of the house.

Playing the role of the responsible brother was a strain. It helped to take a walk.

It was a surprisingly warm day for that time of year.

He left his jacket behind draped over a chair.

Good cut, expensive material, thought Aoibheal, tidying it up. Eugene always has nice clothes.

She took the jacket up to his room to hang it in his cupboard. As she opened the cupboard door she was thinking that the curtains she had made for him were not bad at all, considering that they had been sewn from war-time fabric.

And then she saw the bag. Her mother's handbag! She recognized it at once, even after all those years.

Astonished, she looked up at it. Was she dreaming? Apparently not.

So could this be another bag, exactly like the one Cathal had bought for Rosaleen in New York?

How could it be?

That bag had been made in America. Eugene, or one of his friends, would have had to go there in order to purchase it, and the likelihood of a pre-war design having been repeated in recent years was more than remote.

No, it was definitely Rosaleen's long-lost bag.

What on earth was it doing in Eugene's room? It had been placed on the shelf above the hanging rail just over her head, and she reached up on tiptoe to pull it down.

The bag slipped out of her grip. Falling, it opened, spitting its contents on to the floor.

Letters – lots of letters. And one photograph, lying face up.

A picture of Eugene and Kate, with their arms around each other.

Aoibheal picked it up and examined it more closely. As photographs went it was not a particularly good one. Eugene and Kate were too much to the right of the picture, so the image was unbalanced, and their feet were cut off.

But there was a fair amount of background showing. She thought: I know that street, that hotel. Why would I not? The street is rue des Prêtres-Saint-Germain l'Auxerrois and, as for the hotel, I spent my honeymoon there.

AOIBHEAL turned the photograph over and read what Kate had written on the back twelve years before.

'Eugene and Kate – two people in love.'

And there too was the date of that holiday in Paris.

Eugene and Kate in love, she thought – and to think that none of us knew. What could have gone wrong? To see them together these days you would certainly never know. They don't seem to like each other very much.

Who could have broken it off? Eugene maybe. He told me himself that Henriette was the big love of his life, so he can't have cared that much for Kate.

And Kate, who I am sure is keen on Daniel, was once in love with his twin!

What a mystery! What excitement! thought Aoibheal, crouched on the floor in front of the scattered letters.

She started to gather them up. And as she did so saw that they had been signed by several different females.

Wicked old Eugene, she thought, amused. All these letters from women. What has he been up to? Here are some in French from – yes, Henriette!

She shouldn't snoop. Of course not. She should tidy all the letters up and put them back in the bag and forget them since they were none of her business.

And Eugene would quite rightly be wild if he found her spying on his love life.

To read the letters would be a disgusting intrusion. Only –

It *is* all rather mysterious, said Aoibheal to herself. I mean – why does he have this bag?

And why did Kate never mention him to me? She talks of Daniel often.

One of these letters is from her. Would it matter all that much if I read it? She'd never know, and Eugene wouldn't, and if I found out what went on between them it might help Daniel's case.

Oh, go on, Aoibheal – it's less Daniel you're concerned about than satisfying your own curiosity. Admit it!

Well . . .

Not the other letters. I won't read them.

Just this one.

Killaloe in the month of March and rain falling mercilessly. Wild west winds blowing ruthlessly in from the Atlantic. Temperature low. Spirits lower.

'Why did we come?'

It did not suit Georgina's personality to be trapped inside, and Kate had committed a cardinal sin by forgetting to pack her paints.

'You wanted to be here just as much as I did.'

'I know.' Georgina wrinkled her nose. 'When are the other children coming?'

'After they finish school. I should have sent you but there was only one week of term left. Next term though . . .'

'I'm all right. It's only – '

'I know. The rain.'

They surveyed each other glumly.

'Why does Daniel have to be away in Dublin all this week?' moaned Georgina. 'I want to see him. When is he coming back?'

What to do with her?

'Take her to Crag Liath,' suggested Jamie. 'Mary Markham and Mrs Cash would love to see her. They've been surmising for years about what she could be like. Satisfy their curiosity. Anyway, it's time she saw the house where Milly lived for so long.'

Georgina's face lit up. 'Will you come, too?'

Jamie's face clouded. 'I don't think so,' he said. 'Too many memories . . . Off you go, and don't forget to show her the cupboard off the stairs.'

'What's there?'

'A secret passage all the way to the river – but it's blocked off now. Away with you. I guarantee you'll like it at Crag Liath.'

An hour later Kate was sitting at the kitchen table with Mary and Mrs Cash while Georgina explored upstairs.

Mary's sight was not good, but Mrs Cash's black beady eyes were as yet unimpaired by age and now these eyes – having stared hard at Georgina – were focused on Kate.

'Isn't that the grand girl you're after bringing home to us, Miss Kate? And a wonder it is that anyone would want to part with such a child. Where did you say Mrs O'Brien took her out of?'

Kate swallowed. 'I didn't say.'

'And you don't know? I was just wondering, like.'

Kate's cheeks might have been burnt so hot did they feel. I shouldn't have come, she thought. The sooner we leave for home the better. I'd forgotten what Mrs Cash is like.

'Will you stop bothering Miss Kate,' said Mary, appalled. 'What would she know about that?'

'She might,' Mrs Cash said, unmoved by Mary's attack. 'Hasn't she been living over there in Wimborne most of the time?'

330

'Don't you know that this year gone she's been acting in New York?'

Kate might not have been present in the room the way they were going on.

Ignoring Mary's admonitions, Mrs Cash returned to the inquisition. 'You'd be thinking that you could place an order on a child, say to them that does be in charge, I'll have that one over there, that would match up with one of the two boys I've reared already.'

God help us, thought Kate.

'What do you mean by that?' demanded Mary.

'Only that Miss Georgina is the spitting image of Master Eugene as a child.'

That was bad, but Mrs Cash wasn't finished yet. She took a noisy sup of her tea and put down the cup.

'She's close to yourself, Miss Kate.'

'She is,' said Kate the trained actress.

'. . . copies your ways.'

'Children do that.'

'Indeed they do,' said Mary. 'I remember now with the boys and Mrs O'Brien – '

She started to reminisce. A long story followed and Kate began to relax.

She had rounded up Georgina and was ready to leave when Mrs Cash got hold of her and began to stir the pot again.

'You'll be seeing Master Daniel,' she said.

'We will.'

'The finest man in the land! And carrying a torch for yourself!'

'I'm not sure about that,' said Kate, trying to laugh it off.

'Ah, well sure I am. That man hasn't changed in his thinking all these years.' Mrs Cash paused and looked meaningfully at Kate. 'A forgiving man. A good confessor he'd make if 'twas a priest he'd been instead of

a doctor. You could tell Master Daniel you'd committed the Seven Deadly Sins and he'd be giving you
absolution.'

She didn't know. She couldn't know. But didn't she
have the blood of gypsies in her veins?

Jamie wanted to chat when Kate and Georgina got
home, asking about Crag Liath.

And all the while Kate was longing to be alone, to
gather scattered thoughts.

You could tell Master Daniel you'd committed the
Seven Deadly Sins and he'd forgive you them all, Mrs
Cash had said; but how would he react to the one sin
of Kate having made love with his twin, not to mention the resultant consequences of Georgina's birth
and the necessity for deception?

The finest man in the land he had been called, and
she could second that.

So maybe Mrs Cash was right and he was also
forgiving; but what if she were to give way to the
temptation to confess to him, to unburden herself of
the secret she had concealed for so long, wouldn't
that make mischief, terrible mischief, between Eugene
and himself, and wouldn't he hate her for that?

'So Mrs Cash is her old loquacious self, is she?'
Jamie said, shaking his head. 'You never could beat
her for that!'

'That's true!'

And Georgina said, 'What I want to know is when
is Daniel coming?'

The schools had broken up. Georgina had been
scooped up to be part of a gang of children undeterred
by the weather from playing in the fields.

Daniel and Kate walked close, under one umbrella.

'Seventy-five seats went to Sinn Féin,' said Daniel,

speaking of the election which had secured Lloyd George and his government in office. 'And only twenty-five to the Unionists. Ireland's declared against Parliamentary action with no uncertain voice, and in favour of abstention. It won't be Home Rule we'll demand any more but absolute independence.'

'And Cathal I suppose will be in the thick of it.'

'Oh, no doubt.'

Walking so close to each other and yet with a wall between them. I wish to God, thought Kate, that I could heed Mrs Cash.

'Aoibheal is going to come home,' she said. 'Just for a holiday.'

'Eugene's still staying with her?'

'Yes.'

'Is that a good idea?'

'Why shouldn't it be?'

'Because Eugene hates Aoibheal,' Daniel said. 'He always has done, she having had Mother's attention at what was a vulnerable time for him. He's not the best person for her to be with. It would be an uneasy alliance for him. Why is he there all the time, do you think?'

'I don't know,' said Kate. 'I've never thought about that very much. He's – just there. But what harm could he do Aoibheal?'

'Enough, given the chance. I know my brother like the back of my hand, Kate, what motivates him and, up to a point, what he's capable of doing as a result.'

She considered this, slowing down her pace.

'And it doesn't bother you?'

'Naturally it bothers me. Isn't he my brother? But you have to deal with what there is, not with what you would want.'

They had gone across the bridge that links Ballina to Killaloe and walked up Main Street to the top of the hill where Kincora, royal residence of King Brian Boru, had once stood. Through the sleety rain it was still possible to see far up into the lake, to catch a glimpse of the dark blue mountains.

'And if you heard bad of him,' she said, 'wouldn't that put you off him? Or off me, if you heard bad of me?'

'I told you,' said Daniel, 'I *know* Eugene. I accept him for what he is, whatever he does. Forget about Eugene for a minute. And you – nothing would put me off you. Don't you know that yet?'

The temptation was very strong. Give way to it, said the voice of Mrs Cash. What did I tell you – this is a fine man?

The man for you.

I know that, Kate thought. The pity is that I didn't know it long, long ago.

Oh, be off with you, said the voice of Mrs Cash. Them that looks back at the past deserves the past. You have the future in front of you, Miss Kate, and if I were you I'd reach out one of them white hands and grab it, so I would!

And still she vacillated.

I'm not good enough for him, she thought, and Mrs Cash put her hands to her head and muttered, Indeed you're not! But doesn't he love you? Doesn't that matter to you?

'Nothing? Truly nothing?'

He said, 'I told you to forget Eugene. I should have said – except in relation to you. That's what we're talking about, isn't it – you and Eugene? It won't make any difference to me, you know. I'll love you anyway. I always have done.'

'It must do. It must make a difference.'

'*No.*'

'Then I'll tell you about it,' she said.

* * *

334

'Hmm – foulard silk!' said Eugene in the evening. 'You're beginning to dress up, Aoibheal! I must say it's heartening to see women looking like women again. Green's a good colour for you. You should wear it more often.'

'I think so, too.'

'Marvellous dinner, too. And Cook's gone off, I hear. I didn't realize you were so talented in the kitchen!'

'I thought we might need fortifying, you and I,' she said. 'Still, roast beef and Yorkshire pudding can't compensate a father for the absence of his child!'

Eugene's fork, on which a piece of rare beef was impaled, was mid-way between plate and lips. His left hand froze. He played for time, not speaking. Her anger sparked – flamed. But her tone was still cool.

'Oh, go on, Eugene – eat! Don't let the fact that I know Georgina is your daughter put you off your food!'

He put his fork down.

'What leads you to that conclusion?'

'What does that matter? I know – that's the important thing. I know that Kate was desperately in love with you and that she became pregnant and that you let her down. Just as you let down – *hurt* – all those other women over the years.'

'You've been reading my letters,' he said.

He still did not show any anger himself. But he had lost colour and she knew that he was shaken.

'So?'

'So first of all you have no right to do such a thing, even if you are my sister. And secondly, reading letters which I have received only gives you half the picture. You did not read the letters I wrote to the women concerned – obviously.'

But it was a weak line. Even as he was speaking she could see he knew that.

He placed his knife next to his fork and stared down at his half-full plate.

'It's a pity to waste my cooking,' she said.

'And it's even more of a pity for you to involve yourself in my emotional affairs,' he said. 'I find it – horrendous. However, I don't see why my admittedly turbulent past has to cause problems between you and me.'

The flames of her anger spread.

'But it does,' Aoibheal said. 'Believe me, it does. However, I'm still curious. Tell me, why did you take the bag?'

'The bag?'

'Our mother's bag. A big leather handbag with a handle to match. She was mad about it. Cathal gave it to her for a present long ago in New York.'

He contemplated her, thoughtfully stroking his chin with the side of his index finger.

'That was the point,' he said. 'That it was Mother's bag. And that *he* gave it to her. Surely you can understand that? You seem to understand everything else only too well. I wanted to punish her.'

'And all the others as well.'

'Naturally. I would have thought it makes perfect sense. But not you, Aoibheal. You're my *sister*. I want to protect you. I couldn't bear it if you were injured. You know that, don't you?'

She said, 'I don't think I do.'

'You should. I've been here enough these last couple of years, keeping you company, trying to cheer you up, being supportive – '

'And persuading me to invest in Monsieur Rouché's company. All the time I believed in you – and I believed in that, as well. Now I've lost faith in both!'

'That's absurd,' Eugene said. 'Just because you find out that, where women are concerned, I'm not as pure as the driven snow, you're allowing your prejudices to extend. Grow up, little sister! Men are like that.'

'They're not. Jonathan was not like that. Neither is Daniel. Eugene, I'm going to tell Daniel what has gone on.'

'For what reason?'

'So Kate will feel free to marry him – to make a home for Georgina.'

'In *Ireland*? You're suggesting she stays in Ireland for good? I won't allow that.'

'I don't think you'll have any option. It will be up to Daniel and Kate to decide where she lives.'

'Daniel! Daniel's a fool!' he said. 'What is he but a country doctor? He has no experience of life. I've always been too clever for Daniel by far.'

He pushed his plate away violently – slammed the palm of his hand on the table.

'How do you think I managed to do him out of Crag Liath?'

'No, I'm not shocked and no, you're not wicked,' said Daniel again. 'How many more times do I have to tell you? Doctors aren't easy to shock and to me you're just Kate, the woman I've always loved.'

'I don't deserve you to love me,' Kate said in a small voice.

She wiped away a tear and gulped, swallowing.

'No histrionics! I'm no actor – I can't match you! And you're getting soaking wet, out here in the rain. You'll be one of my patients if we don't go home soon.'

'Not yet.'

The grey eyes were misty. There was a drop on the

end of her nose. She was not Kate at her best, but he had never loved her more.

Wet as she was he pulled her into his arms and kissed her cold lips. She shivered and clung to him, oblivious to the rain and wind.

The doctor in him gave him a nudge: For God's sake, man, she'll get her death of cold, and where will you be then?

Reluctantly he pulled out of the embrace, caught her by the hand, grimaced at the sight of their umbrella blowing down the hill.

'Come on, this is madness. You're coming home with me and Edie will draw the water and you can have a hot bath. And afterwards – when your hair is dry and I'm more confident that you have a long life ahead of you – we'll talk.'

'Not about Eugene . . .'

'I've had enough talk of Eugene to last me a lifetime,' Daniel said. 'I want to talk about us.'

Going back down the hill and across the bridge he had thought that she would later resist him – her guilt would see to that.

And sure enough when she joined him in front of the fire, her head wrapped in a towel and Edie's alternative blouse and skirt on her, she had retreated into herself.

In the past this would have inhibited him and he would have been bound by his own fear of inadequacy and the likelihood of rejection.

But he was no longer afraid. Before she could go too far from him he kissed her again, taking her by surprise, so she did not have time to consider.

He had wasted too much time when he could have been with her – both of them had. He kissed her thoroughly, thinking: Enough nonsense. I want this

338

woman and I'm going to have her and that's all there is to it.

The towel fell from her head. He had an idea that the wind blowing through from the hall window had partially opened the drawing-room door, that Edie in the kitchen could see straight in.

She should have the decency to look the other way under these circumstances. Improbable, this being likely to be all Edie would ever see of love.

The consciousness of her presence helped him stay in control. Kate's warm response, now that her guilt was temporarily silenced, assisted not one whit.

For the second time it was he who drew apart, holding her by the shoulders and forcing her to look up at him.

'You know I love you. I think you love me. Say it if you do.'

'I love you, Daniel.'

'Oh, Kate,' he said. 'Only you could introduce tragedy into those words! It's high time you gave off playing sad roles! Time we were married, made a home for Georgina. And don't mention Eugene now – please. And don't say "but"!'

'You don't think I was serious, do you?'

Eugene, his rush of anger abated, leant back in his chair. On the wall behind him was the portrait of Georgina. The child, vivacious, happy, insouciant, seemed, as she so often was, on the brink of laughter.

'Of course I didn't do Daniel out of Crag Liath! I was teasing you, Aoibheal.'

'I don't think you were.'

'Of course I was. Nobody's that mean. Daniel's my twin.'

'That wouldn't worry you. Look what you did to Kate.'

339

'I told you – the way I behaved was typical of a man when love goes sour. Would you have wanted us to marry and be unhappy for the rest of our lives to suit convention? I'm an artist, Aoibheal. Artists do not have to conform. They need to be free. That is their nature. You can't fence them in. Kate is a beautiful woman but I was never that deeply in love with her. Is that my fault?'

'You didn't feel for her as you did for Henriette?'

'Exactly.'

'But you left her, too.'

Eugene sighed.

'It's really very difficult to explain. How can anyone explain about love? It's not something you understand yourself, why passion wears off. You've only been in love once, you're very young – how can you judge?'

'Indeed. And I didn't feel qualified to make a judgement on my own. I was too upset anyway to think clearly. So I enlisted some help.'

Sitting on Eugene's bed with Kate's letter in her hand Aoibheal had been sick at heart, her stomach turning with the shock of what she had read, and her thoughts – as she tried to come to terms with Eugene's cruelty, Kate's suffering, Georgina's position in the family and disgust with her own curiosity – milling around too quickly.

Cathal, she thought, too – I wish that you were here. Anyone in the family . . .

Anyone but Eugene.

At least, for the time being, *he* was out of the house. If only she had someone to talk to.

Richard and Joan?

Except that they had been so odd lately, or Richard had, keeping away from the manor, being cool and unfriendly.

But trustworthy – they were always honourable people, reliable, which Eugene patently was not. And they were Jonathan's parents, her own in-laws, and if she couldn't confide in someone of their calibre she would surely go mad.

Afterwards she was cross with herself for getting into such a state, for arriving, weeping by now, at the Fieldings', clutching the bag of letters.

Joan Fielding opened the door herself.

'Aoibheal!' she exclaimed, and then taking note of the tear-streaked face, 'my dear child – come in! Whatever is the matter? Come into the drawing-room and tell me.'

In the drawing-room already was Richard, reading *The Times*.

'Good – ' he began, rising to his feet, then taking note of Aoibheal's condition, 'Good Lord! What's wrong, my girl?'

And promptly melted.

'My dear!' Joan said when Aoibheal had finished her story, 'what an extraordinary thing. I must confess we had our suspicions about your brother. That strange conversation the girl Cathleen had with Cook.'

'Cathleen?'

'She used to work at the manor, I believe. She came here some time ago looking for a job. There was no situation, but I told Cook to give her something to eat and she insisted that your brother had taken her off to London with him at one stage and then abandoned her. Not what one would call the action of a gentleman. Still, never mind, he *is* your brother.'

'I've been a fool about Eugene,' Aoibheal said. 'I should have known better. I was more accurate in my assessment of him when I was a child. It's just, I suppose, without Jonathan . . . And Cathal – if my

341

father had been here . . . And then *you* were too busy, Richard, to come to the manor any more and help me out.'

Richard looked surprised. Embarrassed, he coughed.

'Didn't *want* me around,' he muttered. 'Made that clear.'

'Didn't want you?' repeated Aoibheal. 'Who said that?'

'So, you see, Eugene,' she said to her brother, 'we compared notes about you and what you have done, and we came to the conclusion that you may have had reasons of your own for keeping Richard away. Perhaps above all away from the accounts? That's what Richard thinks and I'm afraid I agree. However, we don't have to worry about that. Richard will be here in the morning to help me the way he used to do. In fact, I didn't think there was anything to worry about any more until just now.'

The food on his plate was congealing. Aoibheal, noticing it, thought – I'll never eat roast beef again without thinking of this day!

Eugene was showing every sign of having had enough. He put his hand on the back of his chair and, getting to his feet, pushed it back.

'Don't go yet.'

Eugene had taken up a dignified stance, head slightly back.

'I've something else to say to you.'

'I'm certainly not going to remain here to have insults thrown at my head.'

'It involves Georgina.'

He hesitated – sat down with a show of reluctance.

'What about Georgina?'

'I'll explain. Before I do I want to extract a promise from you.'

He laughed sardonically. 'So now you think I'm capable of keeping promises. We do change!'

'This is one you might be persuaded to make.'

'What the hell do you want?'

'You to tell Daniel – not me, not anyone else, only Daniel – how you managed to do him out of Crag Liath.'

'Don't be ridiculous!' Eugene said. 'I've already explained – that was only a joke.'

'No. And I don't want to talk about it any more. Talk to Daniel – tell him. And then see to it that his half-share in Crag Liath is restored, the way he can go back!'

'Are you mad?' Eugene sounded derisive. 'You want me to revoke Aunt Milly's will, reinstate Daniel? Even if I had done him out, why should I reinstate him – lose out on a half-share?'

'Because if you don't,' Aoibheal said clearly, 'one day I will destroy you in Georgina's eyes. I'll show her the letters I found in Rosaleen's bag. What do you think she'll feel when she knows how you hurt Kate? Do you imagine she'll ever want to see you again – let alone care about you? And I don't think you'll be able to explain yourself to her as you tried to do to me because there'll be the other letters for her to see, too – like the one Henriette sent. And she'll despise you, hate you, turn her back on you. You'll probably never see her again.'

The laughter was gone out of his face. He said, '*You* wouldn't do that.'

'Aren't I *your* sister?'

'You couldn't be so cruel to a child, to Georgina. Nobody could.'

'I'd only be telling the truth.'

343

'Where are the letters? I suppose you've taken them out of my room, hidden them in the house. I'll find them. I'll – '

'I took them to the Fieldings, Eugene. They're locked in a safe. Talk to Daniel. See that he can go back to Crag Liath. I want evidence that he can legally do that. Then I'll give them back.'

'I can't afford to do that. I may need to sell Crag Liath. I'll need money now that – '

'You won't get it from me? Why don't you paint, Eugene? Use your talent to make money. Anyway, that's your problem. While you're working it out you can be considering what I said. Remember – Daniel knows the facts, Daniel is reinstated – or one day I'll tell Georgina the kind of man you are.'

A muscle twitched in his cheek. He stood up slowly, turned, surveyed the painting he had made of his child.

'You mustn't let any harm come to *her*,' Eugene said.

Then she knew she had won.